MANHUNT FOR THE TRUTH

By

Boyd Wilcox

AUTHOR NOTES

From the first days of man's existence on this earth there has been an ongoing struggle of good and evil. A struggle that all mankind has been challenged with. It has always been the choice to do good or evil. It is my belief that all men are basically good but are persuaded by the evil adversary to follow the path of least resistance, a path of much glitter and colored lights that says come follow me. Look here, look there at all I have to offer you. You can choose whatever your heart desires, with no strings attached, no penalty to pay, just sensual pleasures beyond your wildest dreams. The teller of all this is known as the author of all lies. There is a price to pay and none there be that can escape the consequences of their behavior.

This story tells of the efforts of Matt Savage, Niki Blinski and Baxter (Aleksandar Blinski to bring to justice three rouge F.B.I. agents who crossed over to the dark side of the road years ago. These three men had planned and carried out elaborate schemes to have banks robbed that were having difficulties and then covering up the bank's mistakes with the robberies.

This book can stand on its own as a great story, but reading the first novel, "If The Truth be Known" would add to the enjoyment of the reader. That would complete the story.

The Federal Bureau of Investigation is an organization made up of some of the finest men and women collected into one bureau to protect our country's freedoms. These agents should always be given our highest praises.

****

Published 11/7/2013

TABLE OF CONTENTS

****

Thanks to Marie, my eternal companion, editor
and to our children,
Bryan, Bryce, Nancy & Roger

****

Grateful appreciation is expressed to all the people
who have contributed to this book.

****

Thanks to Jordan & Kelly Taylor for the book, cover and picture.

****

Truth will abide when error passes away

Names of Characters in this Book

Matt Savage

Penny Savage

Baxter (Aleksandar Blinski)

Niki Blinski

Viktor – Brother and Son of the Blinski

Tim Headley – F.B.I. Agent

Nancy Burgess – Hitchhiker

Brook Staggs – Baxter's F.B.I. Associate

Jim Fletcher – Rouge F.B.I. Agent – Assumed Alias Jimmy Dubois

Jimmy Dubois – Alias for Fletcher

Tom McGee – Bean Counter for the F.B.I. – Bad Agent

Bobby Blackstone – Most Dangerous of the Three Agents

Warren Tidwell – A New Alias for Blackstone

Sergey Felipovich – Final Alias for Blackstone

Bryan – S.L.C. Director

Jim Webb – Retired Agent

Wilford Duke – Box Elder County Sheriff

Derek Svindal – Behavioral Scientist

Zevinsky – Ships Captain

Petrov   Russian Sailor

Gregory Ivan'ch – Spy and Snitch

Toby Marquez – Caracas Merchant

Paulo Barrios – Hired Hit Man

Ned & Boomer – Hired Muscle

Jeff Burrow & Bob Sanders – Once friends of Fletcher

MANHUNT for the Truth

Sequel to – If The Truth Be Known

Chapter 1

A vicious killer shot Matt in the back, and had left him to die alone under an old cottonwood tree. Now that he had been laid to rest, Penny just didn't care about much of anything.

The phone rang at the Savage residence once, twice, three times and on the forth ring, Penny answered it before it went to message.

"Hello."

"Hi, I hope you remember me. This is Agent Headley."

"Oh yes, I do remember you. To what do I credit this call?"

"I can't tell you over the phone, but I would very much like to stop by and talk with you. Would you mind? It's very important."

Penny had a tremendous amount of respect for F.B.I. Agent Headley. She liked the man for the kindness he had shown her during a very troubling time in her life.

"Sure, that would be fine."

"Good, I'll be there in a few minutes."

Within five minutes, a knock sounded on the front door. Penny opened it with some caution.

"It's my good fortune to see you again, Mrs. Savage."

Penny looked at him with questioning eyes, wondering what this visit was all about. "I bet you would like to know why I'm here."

"Of course, I'm more than a little curious."

" I'm in a bit of an awkward position. I would like to be up front with you and tell the whole story right off, but I've been advised by my superiors to handle this situation slowly. I'm asking you, Mrs. Savage, to come with me and my partner for a drive to Salt Lake City. There is something we would like to show you and then offer you the complete explanation to the story as we know it. Would you mind coming with us?"

"But why, at this time of night? Couldn't it wait until tomorrow? I don't know. So many things have happened lately that I'm not quite sure how much more I can take. I only want to put this horrible nightmare behind me."

"I assure you that our hearts go out to you. I can only surmise the heartache you've felt. Would you please go with us? It's imperative you see what we have. I guarantee you will understand when we get there, I promise. 'No,' is not an acceptable answer. We have already waited too long and we can't wait any longer. Can we go now?"

"Okay, I'll go, but why can't you tell me now what we are going to do?"

 Penny first met Tim Headley years ago, He had shown her genuine care and concern when Matt was arrested. If he hadn't been so kind, she most likely wouldn't have trusted him enough to go with him.

Penny and Matt's children were all grown and had their own families. There was no one left at home for her to tell she would be leaving with these men tonight.

"Please, Mrs. Savage, sit here in the front seat. I think you would be more comfortable. My partner can ride in the back."

The last two days since she had buried Matt were the most difficult days of her life. If it hadn't been for her faith in life after death, she was afraid that she might have lost her mind.

Agent Headley backed his black Mercury Marauder onto the street and headed east towards Interstate 15. Penny's mind was racing. Thoughts were flashing through her head like exploding flash bulbs, wondering and fearing what this trip was all about. Meanwhile, Tim rambled on about nothing important.

Penny hadn't noticed that a car exactly like the one they were driving had pulled out from a side street and was now following them. As they entered the southbound on-ramp a third black Marauder sped around them and now they were following it. Matt had always teased Penny about not paying attention to the make and style of cars. She would say, "As long as it runs it doesn't matter if it is a Ford or a Lincoln. I only care that it gets me from point A to point B." Yet, this night, she did notice the last car and curiously watched as it sped past them toward Salt Lake City.

They had only driven another mile or so when Agent Headley pulled out and shot past the lead car and then quickly pulled back into his lane and returned to the speed limit. Then again, one of the following Mercury's passed them in the same manner. Their actions reminded her of a game of leap frog.

When they reached the Kaysville exit, Agent Headley sped down the long off-ramp and screeched the tires as they came to a jolting stop. Then, with the tires smoking from the power of the agent's supercharged car, they sped up the on-ramp and were soon back in the group of three.

With a puzzled look on her face, Penny asked, "What's going on with all this jockeying around, anyway?" She didn't particularly like or understand what was happening.

"Oh, it's nothing to worry about. It's a little freeway shell game that we like to play now and then."

For the remainder of the trip the three continued with their shell game until they reached North Salt Lake where Headley took the Sixth North off-ramp. He headed east into an older part of the city called the Avenues. Penny wondered where the other two cars had gone. She never saw them again.

"Where are you taking me? This ride is rattling my nerves, Mr. Headley."

"I'm sorry for upsetting you. We will be there soon."

Tim drove around the State Capitol building and up and down the Avenues as if they were lost. They weren't lost of course; they only hoped that all this effort would throw anyone off who might be following them. Penny instantly recognized the University of Utah Medical Center, nestled in the foothills.

"I know this place."

But before she could say more, they were driving through a large open door which quickly closed behind them.

"Was someone chasing us?" Penny asked.

"I certainly hope not, Mrs. Savage."

Without the slightest hesitation, Agent Headley's partner was at Penny's door and had it open for her. Walking along with the two handsome F.B.I. agents made her feel secure. They soon arrived at the elevator door, which she noticed was the only door in the large empty room. The elevator door puzzled her because it had only one button, which said "up."

Tim began to experience some apprehension as the door finally opened and the three entered. He hoped the plan he had carefully orchestrated in his mind would work, as he had never experienced anything like this in his career as an agent for the government. What would he do and say? How would Penny react to the shock she was about to experience? He had no idea because he had never been trained for this sort of contingency. He offered a silent prayer that he would be able to handle the situation gracefully.

When the elevator door finally opened, there stood a very serious looking police officer. He looked at the agents' shield's hanging from their jacket pockets and, acting as if he knew they were coming, turned, pointing them to the right hallway.

Penny couldn't ever remember feeling such overpowering stress and she wasn't sure why. It was as if she was a clock spring, wound-tight, and on the verge of flying apart.

The three walked hurriedly down the hall to a pair of large glass doors. There was a desk and another equally serious looking officer sitting there, watching them intently.

He spoke, "Is this Mrs. Savage?"

Penny answered, "Yes, I'm Mrs. Savage."

The agents handed the officer their I.D., which he examined and handed back to them.

"Go ahead," the desk officer spoke as they entered the second hallway. Once inside, Tim placed his hand gently on Penny's shoulder and said, "Please wait here for a moment, I've got something to say. In the next few minutes you will experience something beyond belief. Remember, we are here for you and let me assure you that all will be fine."

Penny seemed to sense in her heart that this secretive thing had something to do with Matt, but she could not comprehend what it might be. Nothing that had happened this night seemed to make any sense.

Tim slowly opened the door to a large hospital room containing one bed with many pieces of medical equipment around it. The room lights were dimmed somewhat. Penny's eyes took a few anxious moments to adjust to her surroundings. She stood motionless in the doorway with her eyes affixed on the person lying in the bed.

Suddenly, she blurted out, "It just can't be!" Her knees started to give way as the two agents caught hold of her arms to steady her. "Oh it can't be! I just buried Matt two days ago and now there he is." Carefully, she made her way around his bed and looked down on the man she had loved for so many years and had lost. She slowly reached down taking hold of his motionless hand, which was warm to her touch. She knew he lived. The tears began to flow from her gentle blue eyes.

After a few minutes Penny heard a voice call her name.

"Mrs. Savage."

Penny turned and saw a kindly looking woman standing next to her.

"Yes," she answered.

"I'm nurse Kay Vance, I've been assigned to care for your husband since the day he was brought to us. He is a very lucky man. His condition is serious, but he is stable. The reason your husband is so quiet is because his doctor has put him in a medically induced coma so he can heal quickly without all the external stress."

"How long will he be in this coma?"

"I don't know. It will be up to the doctors to answer that question. Maybe we will know in a few more days."

"Is there anything I can do for him?" Penny asked.

"No, not really, but maybe he will sense your presence and that could help."

Tim slid a chair up to Matt's bedside for Penny to sit on. She slowly relaxed into the chair never taking her eyes off Matt, while clenching his hand in hers. The tears were rolling down her cheeks in a steady flow, but these were tears of gratitude and thanksgiving, not like the tears she shed at his funeral.

No one spoke for a few minutes, then Penny asked, "How could all this happen? Why did you let us bury him believing that he was dead?"

"Mrs. Savage, we deeply apologize for what has happened to you and your family. We have plans to rectify all of this if we can. Of course we've witnessed a small miracle in not losing Matt."

"Can you tell me more about what happened to Matt when he was shot? I never was told a complete story about the shooting. It seemed to me the

Sheriff's Department really didn't know very much or maybe they were just being tight-lipped about the whole matter."

"We will be happy to tell you all we know, however, there is a whole lot of this story that we don't know. We were given instructions, that came from somewhere up the chain of command to assist you and your family. We were to keep you safe and out of harm's way."

"What do you mean? Are we in danger?"

"We saw what someone tried to do to Matt, so yes, you might be the object of the next hit. If we can continue to make it look as though Matt is out of the picture, then we will have some of the equation taken care of."

"But Agent Headley, I don't know anything about why anyone in this world would want to kill Matt or harm me or my family."

"That's part of the puzzle we don't know either. It appears that your husband was working inside one of our government agencies and someone wants him silenced. That's all we know at this time and maybe that's all we will ever know."

"What's next?" she wondered, but she wasn't that concerned. She was so happy that her love was alive.

Chapter 2

Box Elder Sheriff

"Would you like me to read the written report the Box Elder paramedics wrote about the call and how they found Matt? We were given this report, which we can share with you, but it has to remain a secret between us for the time being. It can't be repeated."

"I would very much like to hear what's in the report. Please read it."

"Alright."

"Ma'am, could you please give me your name and phone number?"

 "Sorry, I can't do that." She sobbed while attempting to give the dispatcher the best information she could to locate Matt. When she did, she hung up her cell phone. The dispatcher, an employee of the Sheriffs Department, didn't know who the caller was and had no way of calling her back or getting more information from her.

On August 9th at 9:30 am, Deputy Sheriff Ritchie and his partner, Deputy Talon, were enroute to a training session at the Brigham City Regional Medical Center when they received a call, "Man shot. Caller didn't know the address, but she said there was a dirt runway on the farm, and the farm belonged to Matt Savage and a friend, Jim. The victim was lying next to a large, old cottonwood tree, along a ditch bank."

 Baxter and Niki pulled over and parked their borrowed F.B.I. car under a large oak tree. With intense interest, they listened carefully to their police scanner broadcast the activities of the Sheriff's Department, all the while wondering if they could be of any assistance but knew that wouldn't be a wise thing to do.

Deputy Talon knew where the farm was located for he had recently spoken with Mr. Savage, who had shown him around the farm. The deputy knew they were only a couple of minutes away from the location.

When the deputies found Matt, their first impression of his condition wasn't good. They felt as if they were looking at a dead man, but regardless of their suspicions, they went to work checking for vital signs. When Ritchie failed to find any signs, Deputy Talon then carefully checked but to no avail. The two used C.P.R. for the next ten minutes with no visible change in Matt's condition. The only honorable thing to do now was to cover his body and wait for the homicide detectives to arrive.

As they started to place a blanket over his still body, Deputy Talon hollered out, "Wait just a minute! I think this man is alive. His eyes just opened and closed."

Matt was alive but teetering on the edge.

"Rescue One, send us an ambulance and preferably an air- med. We have one lucky man here and we hope his luck holds out a little longer."

"Oh Dad," Niki screamed, "Can you believe what we just heard?" She jumped across the seat grabbed her old dad around his big Russian neck and squeezed him with all her might. Niki hadn't seen her dad smile this way in a very long time. She felt a wonderful hope and a joy in her heart that couldn't be described.

Without wasting any time, Baxter was on his phone. "Hello, this is Agent Aleksandar Blinski. I need to speak with your boss immediately. This is urgent!"

Within moments Baxter heard, "Hello, this is Director Bryan speaking."

"Director, we have had one of our operatives shot by someone we believe ordered it from within the department. Our man is in extremely critical condition and will be transported shortly by life-flight to Salt Lake City. We don't know which hospital he might be sent to. We hope and pray his life can be saved. No one can know he is alive, for his safety and the safety of his family are crucial. Can you please help us?"

"I'll have the flight routed to the University of Utah hospital. They have a facility for this sort of thing."

"Thank your people for their help. Could you have your agents advised that all those concerned with this incident are to keep their mouths shut about Mr. Savage. For the time being, we want everyone to think he is dead."

"Will do. You are welcome, but we must talk soon. Do you understand?"

"Yes sir, I do."

Within a couple of hours after speaking with the director of the Salt Lake Regional Office of the F.B.I., Agent Blinski (Baxter) walked into his office for their little chat.

"Come on in and have a seat. Shall I call you Baxter? I remember that you always liked that new American name you chose so long ago."

"Sure, that's been the name I've used since coming to the United States. I hope everyone always remembers how grateful my daughter and I are, now we are U.S. citizens."

"That's good to hear."

It's been many years since I talked with you last. By the way Baxter, what's the department got you doing these days?"

" I thought you knew. I've been working as a trainer of operatives that we've recruited through a program called 'Back Door.' Have you heard of it?"

"Yes, matter of fact I have. Is the fellow that was shot one of your students?"

"He was once a student, but that was many years ago. Matt was as good as they come. He handled a number of operations for us along with my daughter, who was his partner. He was an altruistic young man that I thought of as a son. I can't tell you a lot more because the 'ops' were highly classified and I'm not even sure where those orders originated from. What we were involved in was questionable and left me wondering some of the time if they were legitimate. But, every time I received an assignment, all was in order, so we handled them the best we could."

"Why would someone in the department order a hit on this man who was loyal to us and did all that great work, as you say?"

"Matt was highly thought of for the work he had done for the agency. As confident as we were in Matt's abilities there came a time when he fell out of grace with someone higher up. At the time we didn't know for sure who they were. Now I believe these people are the mother of these operations, and they had became very nervous about Matt's silence."

"Are you telling me there was something illegal about what you were doing?"

"No, I'm not saying that at all or will I ever. It was one of those cloak and dagger sort of operations that no one ever talks about, do you get my drift?"

"Actually...Yes, I understand what you're saying, but to my way of thinking there is too much of that sort of crap going on throughout our agency as well as many other government agencies."

"You're probably right. Bryan will you continue to help us with Matt's concealment until we can move him and his wife to a safe place, and hopefully, find out who the antagonist is?"

Bryan agreed reluctantly. "I just hope I don't get questioned about what I'm doing for you. Frankly, I'm not sure about this whole affair. I suppose we can sort it all out later." Bryan frowned at the thought.

Chapter 3

Agent Headley

Agent Headley entered Matt's hospital room around five a.m. "Excuse me, Mrs. Savage. May I speak with you?"

"Of course."

"I need you to remain here for the time being until we get things sorted out. Everything will be provided for you here at the hospital and there is a comfortable bed in the adjoining room. In just a few minutes I will be calling your daughter to arrange a meeting with her and your sons. They need to know about their dad. I'll explain that you're with Matt and as soon as we can arrange it we will bring them to see him. Please don't worry about anything at home because I'll see that everything is taken care of. One other thing, I can't permit you to call out, for security reasons, and don't talk to anyone about what has happened to Matt. Okay?"

"Sure, Tim. All of this stuff doesn't seem to matter right now. I'm overwhelmed with joy that Matt is alive and nothing else could bother me. God bless you, Tim, and thank you so very, very much for all that you've done."

"You're welcome. I'll see you later today." He slipped out of the room feeling more at ease than he had since receiving this assignment.

Chapter 4

Brook Staggs

Baxter didn't waste any time making a call to a good friend in D.C. who he knew could help him scrutinize certain people in the agency that might be suspect.

"Hello, is this Agent Staggs?"

"Yes, it is, and with whom do I have the privilege of speaking?"

"Hey, butt-brain, don't you recognize the voice of an old Ruskie friend?"

"Is this Baxter, my old friend? I thought you had died and gone to hell with all those other old Russian comrades of yours."

"Maybe all us old communist's will go to hell as you say, but you better be nice to me, Brook, or when I do die, I'll make darn sure I come back to haunt you." They both laughed.

"Well, Baxter what can I do for you?"

Agent Brook Staggs was one of the most intelligent agents Baxter had ever known. He had the ability to uncover almost anything that was happening in the department. He did it mostly for his own satisfaction, even when it wasn't any of his business to know. It was a game for him to discover what others were up to. Some did criticize him for putting his nose where it didn't belong. No matter how hard they tried to cover their operations, he would find out about them nearly as soon as they would.

Staggs, a formidable intellect, graduated from Harvard Law School in 1975 and placed top in his class. After graduation, he went on with his schooling and received his doctorate degree in foreign relations.

"Can I talk freely on this phone line, Brook?"

"No."

"Okay, why don't you give me a number that I can call you on later this evening so we can talk shop. I hope that would be alright with you because I do need your help."

" I have no reservation about giving you my private number, but let me call you back with a phone number you can use without feeling afraid of being compromised."

"Sounds good. I'll be waiting to hear from you." The line went silent.

Niki and her good old dad weren't ready to return home just yet. There was a great deal to do before this would be resolved. They were determined to find conclusive evidence about the man who ordered the hit on Matt and do whatever necessary to put the mutt away.

"Niki, I'm going to take a drive north to Box Elder County and see if I can speak to their sheriff. Yesterday I called him to see if I could meet with him for a conversation about the shooting. He told me he would be in his office all day and welcomed the visit. Don't feel bad if I don't take you along. I'm not giving those boys any chance to figure out you were the one who called about the shooting. It could complicate things."

"Sure, Dad, I understand. Dad, you make sure you drive safely." Niki always worried about her dad's driving habits.

The drive north on I-15 took Baxter about an hour to reach the office of the county sheriff in Brigham City. The city was named and founded by Brigham Young, an early Mormon colonizer of Utah and a prophet of the L.D.S. Church. The city's main street was lined with beautiful, old sycamore trees that added to the charm and beauty of this small city.

A young, quite pretty female deputy accompanied Baxter to the sheriff's office and knocked softly on his door.

"Come on in."

"I spoke to you yesterday on the phone, Sheriff. My name is Baxter and

I'm an agent for the F.B.I."

"I'm glad to make your acquaintance. My name is Wilford Duke. Please have a seat. By the way, is there anything I can get you, a soft drink or coffee?"

"No thanks, I'm just fine."

"What can I help you with? I have a pretty good idea what this visit is about, but I should hear it from you." The barest wisp of a smile animated his lips.

"Sheriff, what can you tell me about the shooting of a Mr. Matt Savage?"

"With a lot of care I meticulously read over the many reports my deputy's generated during their investigation of this double shooting. I came up with many more questions than answers. We found a shell casing near the outlaw, Paulo Barrios, that is possibly the one that shot Mr. Savage. No matter how hard we looked, we never found a gun or shell casing around where Mr. Savage fell. We first believed that Savage may have shot Barrios, but the pieces of the puzzle don't fit. Then there is the matter of the young lady who called in the shooting to our dispatcher and refused to I.D. herself. We would love to talk to this woman, if we could locate her."

Baxter did not respond, he only watched the sheriff with cold, calculating eyes.

"By the way, Agent Baxter, there were some questions about Mr. Savage's condition when he was put on the life flight helicopter. Our paramedics first thought that he was deceased, but discovered he was in fact alive. What can you tell me about him?"

"I'm sorry Sheriff, he didn't make it. His family buried him last week."

"That's too bad. He could have cleared up a lot of questions we have."

The sheriff's lack of sensitivity angered Baxter, but he held his tongue.

"I'm curious. Why is the F.B.I. so interested in this case of ours? It's a homicide in our county, completely within the jurisdiction of my department. We didn't invite, or need any help from your agency."

"I'm quite certain, Sheriff, my answer to your question won't be to your satisfaction. For the time being, I can't give you much information. I can't, and won't, tell you why we are interested in this crime, but let me assure you that it is of great importance to us. I would be happy to tell you the complete story, as we know it up to this point, but if I did that, another innocent person might die. I can't have that on my conscience."

"Well, it sounds very intriguing, but not very helpful."

"Sheriff Duke, I can tell you one thing that might be of some help to you. We believe, and eventually we will prove it, that Paulo Barrios is the murderer and we feel that someone else is behind it. So, I ask that you just let this case ride for the time being. I promise you when we solve this crime, I'll tell you the complete story. Agreed?"

"I suppose I don't have any choice in the matter. I'll be anxiously awaiting to hear from you."

Baxter stood up from his chair. "Thanks for your time, Sheriff." He shook Duke's hand and left the room.

Chapter 5

Visit From Old Friends

"Dad, how long can we stay here in Utah? I would like to stay around until Matt is well enough to be moved to a safe location and away from the threats of those vipers.

Are you," she asked, "considering getting us in to see Matt? I would be so grateful if you could. Dad, you were the one from the very beginning who trained Matt and lead him down this path. I would think that if anyone should have the right to see him it would be the two of us." Niki knew her dad would get them in to see Matt, yet, she felt the loving daughter approach would be better.

"I'm certain we can see him. It will be no problem, my daughter. You know, Niki, I can still see that love in your eyes for Matt. You have never been able to hide it from me."

She blushed, and said, "Thanks, Dad, for noticing. I do love Matt and always will."

"Niki, I'm going to call agent Headley right now and tell him we are going to see Matt tonight. If he refuses, which he won't, we will go anyway. Niki, I would like to see him again as much as you, he is much like the son I lost so many years ago." A tear rolled down his weathered face.

Apprehensively, Agent Headley agreed to the visit. He knew that this man they call Baxter was behind his orders to keep Mr. Savage safe. He didn't know the full story and was extremely worried about this man's safety. He had no idea where a threat might arise.

The three agents, Baxter, Niki and Headley met in a predetermined location at the University Hospital, with all arriving at different times and coming from different locations. Agent Headley escorted Niki and her father through several corridors with locked doors until they arrived at

Matt's hospital room. Penny was asleep in a chair next to Matt's hospital bed when they looked in.

Niki spoke first. "I hate to wake her but this might be the only time we will get to see Matt."

Tim Headley walked over to where Penny was sleeping and touched her gently on the shoulder. She looked up. "Oh, it's you. I'm sorry you caught me asleep."

"Penny, we have some visitors who would like to see Matt and this might be a good time to introduce you."

"Who might they be?" Penny looked across the room and saw Niki standing in the doorway with her father. "Oh, I know that lady. She was at the cemetery. Please come in."

Niki spoke first. "Mrs. Savage, this is my father. Everyone calls him Baxter."

Each warmly shook Penny's hand and sat down next to her wondering what they were going to say next.

With a sadness that nearly betrayed her, Niki kept glancing at Matt, lying there so still, wondering if he would pull through.

Penny was good at remembering names. "I do remember your name. Isn't it Niki? You introduced yourself when we first met at the gravesite."

"Yes, that's right."

Penny loved people and had a wonderful way of making all feel at ease. She looked at them and smiled with sincere feelings for them."

After a moment, she spoke. " I'm at a loss. Things have gone on in Matt's life that I'm not aware of. I have a feeling that maybe you can fill in a few of the blanks for me. It would certainly make me feel a whole lot better."

Niki looked at her dad as if to say, "The ball is in your court."

A deep sadness came over Baxter as he considered all that had happened to Matt over the many years they had known each other. All Matt had ever wanted was an opportunity to work for the Secret Service, which he had promised him, in an off-handed way. He knew it wouldn't happen, but he let him believe it.

Baxter reached over, taking hold of Penny's dainty hand with his old and tired hands and said, "My dear, I'm so very sorry for all that you have been put through. I can't help but feel that I'm responsible for all your troubles. You see, years ago while Matt was working for L.A.P.D., he was recruited by a government agency, I can't say which one, to do some special assignments for us. I was assigned to be his training officer and my daughter, Niki, eventually became his partner. I shouldn't even be telling you any of this, but if anyone deserves to know, you do. I would like to relate to you all that happened over those years, but that's not possible. I'm afraid the party or parties responsible for Matt getting shot are within our department. They must have been the ones who originally planned the assignments we handled for them years ago. I'm afraid for Matt because, for some unknown reason, these people want him out of the way. Mrs. Savage I personally promise you that I will find out who is responsible for hurting Matt and I will make them pay."

Penny eyed Baxter speculatively. She simply didn't know what to think. He had just unloaded a truck full of enlightenment that she didn't see coming and was dumbfounded by it.

Changing the subject, Niki spoke up and said, "Penny is there anything we can do for you or Matt?"

"I don't think so. I'm fine. But poor Matt just lies there so very still and it worries me more than anyone can know. The doctors tell me everything is progressing well and they will bring him out of the coma in a few days. Yet, I'm not at all certain the coma he is in wasn't caused by the trauma he experienced from the gunshot. As I see it, if that is the case, those doctors might not be able to revive him."

"Can I call you Penny?" Asked Baxter

"Why sure, I like first names best."

"Penny, you shouldn't worry. These doctors are among the best and I'm certain that when the time comes all will work out fine."

"Mr. Baxter, I do hope you are right."

What Penny had said about the gunshot causing the coma started Niki wondering and worrying too.

While the three talked, Agent Headley sat quietly in the darkened corner of the room, listening and contemplating what he was involved in. He recalled from years ago, when he had taken Matt into federal custody, Matt had told him that people from the government were involved.

Penny looked haggard and exhausted and the stress was showing.

Niki walked over to Penny and spoke to her in a kind, gentle voice. "Penny, we should be going now. Please get some rest. We will be calling on you again soon. Everything is going to be fine."

Agent Headley found the nurse as they were leaving and asked her if she could give Mrs. Savage something to help her rest. He worried about her standing up to unyielding stress.

Throughout Matt's long stay in the hospital Penny remained next to her husband, sleeping very little and thinking about what might be in their future. This predicament they were in was something she had never dreamed of and she worried about what was going to happen when Matt was well enough to be moved.

The following morning Baxter came to his daughter. "Niki, I need to make a quick trip back home. There is a man I need to talk with but, I hate leaving you here all alone. Why don't you fly back with me, it would be good for you to take a break from all of this. It will only take two or three days to complete the business I have and I'm sure Agent Headley will be able to manage the security for Matt and his family. It's not likely the doctors will bring him out of the coma before we return. What do you say?"

"Okay, I'll tag along. By the way, Dad, what is so all-fired important that we need to go at this time?"

"My dear Niki, did you hear me promise Mrs. Savage that I would take care of whoever was responsible for Matt's shooting?"

"Yes, of course I did."

"With ever fiber of my being I meant what I said. I have already made a phone call to a man in D.C. who seems to know everything that goes on in the agency. He is a good friend of mine and I believe he can point us in the right direction. I failed once on a promise I made to your mother that I would find Viktor. I believe I would have found him if the K.G.B. hadn't set me up to be conveniently arrested to get me out of the way. As only time would prove, it turned out to be a good thing, I'm sure, because now the two of us are Americans. It was a heart-breaker that we never found Viktor and knowing how your dear mother died from a broken heart. You can see why I must not fail this time."

The old memories of her lost family brought an air of sadness to her mind that hurt so deeply she didn't want to dwell on them. She did not respond to her dad's promise, but continued watching the city lights from their hotel room. After a few moments, she finally spoke.

With determination in her voice, Niki said, "Dad I'm with you in your quest to catch those pukes. I know one thing for certain, there are few secrets that remain secrets. These men will be found out. They will pay the price for what they did to Matt. We will find them Dad, I know we will."

With the wisp of a smile, he said, "Thanks, Niki, but where in the world did you pick up that word, pukes?"

Niki laughed at her father's question. "That's one of Matt's favorite words he uses to describe the bad guys. He says that it's a better word than calling them a-h. I thought you would have heard him use that word. Of course, I did spend a lot more time with him than you did."

Chapter 6

Back to Virginia

The following morning was a perfect day for the flight home. Salt Lake International, a Delta hub, had numerous flights to the east coast and they had no trouble finding the right one.

Shortly after landing in Virginia, Niki and her dad rented separate cars and headed in different directions. Niki drove to their new home in Madison Hills, to make some preparations for plans they had discussed during the flight. Baxter drove straight for D.C. to see his old friend, Brook Staggs.

Baxter had been considering pulling the plug and retiring from the agency where he had been working for longer than he liked to remember.

All these years he had been training young cops, like Matt once was, to do jobs for different government agencies that were a contradiction of what he believed in.

These operations were, for the most part, on the outer fringe of being illegal. Now, he had one more job that would require all his years of experience to complete. Then it would be time to slow down and take a shot at the easier life.

It wasn't a long trip to the nation's capital, but it was a drive that filled his senses with the beauty of the Virginia countryside. He passed the Arlington National Cemetery and crossed the Potomac. Seeing the splendor of the Capitol of this great country gave him pause. What a remarkable place Washington D.C. is. It's a place with a history that astounds the mind, when taken into account all that's happened in this vibrant city. Everywhere one looks, there are reminders of the nation's history, which was thrilling for Aleksandar Blinski.

[He loved the United States, possibly more than the average American, because he knew the vast difference between a communist government, which dictates everything to its citizens and a true democracy, where men are free to make their own choices.]

Washington D.C. is comparable to most big cities. It has its dirty underside with crime running wild and the homicide rate is the highest in the country.

You probably would not want to examine it with a magnifying glass because there is a possibility you may not like what you may see. There are fools who profess their beliefs on every street corner coupled by the fools found in every branch of the government. Hopefully rational men and women will prevail, Baxter thought, as he pulled into a parking garage near Pennsylvania Ave. and 10th, not far from the office of his friend.

"Good afternoon, Brook Staggs, you old dead beat. It's good to see you again."

"You had better be nice to me you dim-wit old fart, or I won't help you." They both laughed and gave each other a real old fashioned Russian bear hug.

"You, being known as the great wizard of the agency, who knows all and sees all, could point me in the right direction. Have you come up with anything?"

"After receiving your phone call a few days ago, I started milling over in my mind all I had heard over the years. One name keeps coming up. In fact I believe you were friends with the guy at one time in your career. Mind you, Baxter, in whatever you do, use a lot of discretion. At this time I don't have anything that's concrete on the guy.

"Spit it out, Brook. What is his name?"

"It's Fletcher. He works over in the anti-crime division."

"No way man, it couldn't be Fletcher. He and I have been friends for many years and he isn't the sort of man to order a hit on one of my own men, or anyone else for that matter."

"Like I said, be discreet and take your time ferreting out the culprits. They are not going to make it easy for you, but just the same, start with Fletcher and see where it takes you. Let prudence guide your actions, my friend."

The following morning, after a long night of deliberating, Baxter placed a phone call to Fletcher's office with the phone number his friend, Brook, had provided him.

"Hello, Fletcher, this is an old friend from the past, Baxter. How are you doing anyway?"

"What a surprise it is to hear from you. I'm doing fine. What do I owe the honor of such a welcomed call?

"If you recall, I've always been quite a history buff and I just thought I would drive up here and visit the Smithsonian and spend a couple of days doing something I've wanted to do for a long time. I'm going to absorb some of the great history found there."

 "Are you in the D.C. area?"

"Matter of fact, I am," replied Baxter.

"Well then, maybe we could get together for dinner, and it's on me. What do you say?"

"I would like that and thank you."

" I'll send a car by to pick you up at seven. By the way, where are you staying?"

" I'm at the Marriott. I will be out front waiting. See you then."

The car arrived promptly at seven. Baxter jumped in and with a big grin greeted Fletcher. "Hi, my friend. Good to see you again after all these years. You haven't changed all that much. So anything new shaking?"

Fletcher commented dryly, "I've been thinking since you called, I find it hard to believe you came all this way just to visit some old museums. You're not the sort Baxter. There must be something on your mind that you're searching for an answer to. Isn't there?"

"That is the truth. I'm here for a little R&R, that's all."

"Well, if you say so!"

Fletcher and Baxter were like two sparring partners throughout dinner. Each searching for answers and saying very little that would give away their true intentions. Fletcher had all the answers that Baxter wanted, yet he wasn't sure if his old friend, Fletcher, was the man he wanted.

At the end of their dinner, Fletcher asked Baxter if he could catch a cab back to his hotel because he had something important he needed to take care of. The two shook hands warmly and as they departed, Fletcher turned and said, "Whoever you are looking for, old man, remember just one thing, be careful whose ox you gore."

Pondering over all that had been said, Baxter was feeling he had validated some of his suspicions, especially with that parting comment of Fletcher's, referring to the ox.

Chapter 7

At Odds

"Hello, this is Fletcher. I want you to listen and listen good." He snarled with rage. You two boneheads have really screwed the pooch this time! Meet me tomorrow at 'the place,' twelve noon, be there!"

At noon the following day the three men met in Fletcher's cabin, not many miles from D.C., in the Virginia countryside. Only these two friends knew about his hideaway. Fletcher wasn't married and was somewhat of a loner, keeping his private life quite secret.

His two associates, Tom McGee & Bobby Blackstone had worked with him for many years and helped him create the program with the code word, "Starlight." It was the same plan Niki and Matt had been deeply involved in and had now brought them to this crossroad in their lives.

"Come on in, Bobby and Tom. We have some very serious business to take care of."

"By the way Fletcher, what gives you the right to get pissed off at us and start with the name calling?"

"You two don't know, do you?" retorted Fletcher.

"No, I suppose not. We don't have the slightest idea what you're getting at." Tom responded.

"Certainly you two remember, not that long ago, the heated discussion we had about Matt Savage and the potential threat he might pose to the three of us if he were to spill his guts."

"Sure we remember, and we took care of the problem."

"Oh really. Against my advice you two hired that slime-ball of a hit-man,

Paulo Barrios, to kill Savage, and this I bet you didn't know, someone killed Barrios out there in Utah. The newspaper reported it and the F.B.I. identified him as a wanted man who they were happy to have off the streets. To top it off, I'm not so sure that Savage is dead."

"Why would you say that?" Tom blurted out.

"It's a gut feeling I have. Yesterday, an old friend named Baxter, an agent with our beloved F.B.I., unexpectedly called me out of the clear blue and pretended to be visiting the D.C. area, but he was nosing around. If you two remember, Baxter was a trainer for the agency with that program called, "Back Door." He had a genuine love for Matt Savage, which gives him tremendous motive to find us."

Bobby spoke, "What do you suggest we do, Fletcher? Are we going to sit around here waiting until he puts all the pieces of the puzzle together and makes us disappear?"

I know the story about Baxter and his membership with the K.G. B., but I don't know how he became a member of the F.B.I. and with such a distinguished record. However, I have no doubt that this man wouldn't falter for a minute, putting us away for good," replied Fletcher.

"Do you think that he would rat us out?"

"No I don't think so, Tom. He never knew the complete story about Starlight. I'm sure he had skepticism about the operation but, unless he went out of his way to discover what we were up to, he never knew."

"So, you are saying that he will most likely kill us."

"Yes, Tom, you dumb fool. It very well could be. If it is, then what are we going to do about it?"

"Tom and Bobby, I'll tell you right here and now what I'm going to do. I'm too old and tired to fight with Baxter so I did something this morning before I drove out here. It is something I've wanted to do for a long time. I pulled the plug. Yes, I retired and now I can enjoy some of that ill-gotten money we so cleverly stole. I couldn't give a care what you two do. I'm tired of baby sitting you two. So I strongly suggest you both disappear and don't let Baxter get his big Russian hands on you."

"Where are you going Fletcher?"

With a trace of rancor in his voice, Fletcher said, "It's truly amazing that you two ever lasted in the agency, let alone were accepted as F.B.I. agents. I'll always remember you both as nothing more than simple abstractions. Now get out of my house."

The mood of the room changed abruptly. His once old friends stood up and started for the door. Tom turned towards Fletcher and said. "I hope that big Russian gets his hands on you and rips your ugly face off, you good for nothing S.O.B."

Bobby flipped Fletcher the finger and turned with the tiniest smirk to see a 357 S&W pointed at his head. "It won't look good you simpleminded fool," sneered Fletcher.

Bobby quickly slipped out the door "Did you see that gun he was pointing at me? It scared the hell out of me."

On the drive back to the big city, Bobby and Tom seriously discussed the predicament they were in. To their way of thinking, this Baxter fellow was one scary old Russian, a person they didn't want to deal with. These two uncommon criminals never had the guts to do any of their own dirty work; they always pawned it off on someone else.

Tom McGee was a mousy little guy with thick, horn- rimmed glasses who worked in the accounting department. He came out of college with a degree in accounting, which at the time, gave him a job with the agency. He loved the title. F.B.I. Agent but wasn't a tough guy. In fact, he had never made an arrest in his entire career. Not to overstate it, he was one scared little man thinking about what Baxter would do to him.

"What are we going to do, Bobby?" He said with a quiver in his voice.

"I don't know what you are going to do, but for me, I'm going to do the same thing that Fletcher did. I'm quitting this afternoon, taking my retirement and my share of that filthy lucre we stole, that's stashed away, and I'm getting out of Dodge. You won't see me again, my friend."

"What can I do? I still have a wife and a home. I can't pick-up and leave."

"Why don't you tell your understanding wife about our lives as thieves? Maybe she might understand and forgive you and the two of you can hit the road together. Possibly, you might find a cute little adobe hut somewhere in South America to live in for the remainder of your lives," Jim then sneered at them in a threatening sort of way.

" I thought we were friends and that we would always look out for one another."

"You're right Tom, we are friends, but this is where our friendship ends. By tomorrow I'll be done and I'll pray that Baxter doesn't catch you and feed your scrawny body to the wolves."

That was the last time those two ever saw each other. Blackstone did what he said he was going to do and signed off with the department and with haste departed the city.

Tom took the remainder of the day off and drove to his home in Alexandria where he went to his study, locked the door and cried like a baby. Every vision of his past activities with those two friends in crime flashed through his mind. The thoughts brought him no pleasure. "With all the money I have, I should be able to do whatever in this world pleases me," he considered, but fear gripped his soul and he didn't know what he was going to do. The only thing he could hope for was that Baxter wouldn't discover he was part of the conspiracy to kill Matt.

Throughout the entire night Tom paced back and forth in his den like a jailed inmate waiting for the firing squad to come and take him away. The one thought that kept popping up in his simple mind was this, "Why didn't we listen to Fletcher and just leave that Matt Savage alone. All those past illegal activities we were involved in so many years ago have run their course and the statute of limitation had removed us from prosecution. But no, like the dumb fools we were, we now have new charges that will put us away for good.

"The more time I take to consider this awful mess I'm in, the additional realization comes back to hit me smack in the face, we didn't have to put a hit on him. That Savage guy went to jail and never spilled his guts to anyone that we know of. Now, I believe that he never would have told his story."

After a troubled-filled night, Tom left for work under a dark cloud of fear and worry. He felt the wise thing to do, since his partners in crime had skipped out, would be to remain at his job and hopefully, attention would be directed elsewhere.

Chapter 8

Induced Coma

Four days later, the doctors informed Penny that they felt it was time to make an attempt to bring Matt out of the induced coma. He was healing well and all his vital signs were good and there were no problems with his blood work.

Penny knew very little about the risk her husband was facing.

Medically induced comas are considered dangerous and very risky by many doctor's standards. Complications such as pneumonia can arise because of the patient's immobility. It's also difficult to tell the severity of a patient's brain damage as traditional neurological tests are not as accurate when a patient is in a coma. Some doctors prefer the idea of using sedatives to put the brain to sleep to lessen the chance of further injury to the brain and possibly other organs. In Matt's case, the specialist thought he might have suffered a stroke because of the severe trauma he experienced or he may have suffered oxygen deprivation, which put his brain at risk.

Agent Headley had spent a lot of time with Matt's children the last few days and wanted them to be present when their dad, hopefully, came out of the coma. He made very careful arrangements to bring his four children to the hospital so no one might be the wiser. He hoped that Baxter wouldn't mind, but since he wasn't around, Headley felt he could do what he thought best.

At the appointed time, Matt's family stood in silence around the room, watching the doctors carefully monitor his condition. They had discontinued all the sedatives, which were used to induce the coma and now, only time would tell. The doctors were touching Matt, speaking to him and shining a small light into his eyes, watching for a response. After several minutes, Matt's arm moved upward a few degrees He faintly said, "No." The doctors smiled as his family hugged each other with a great deal of hope in their hearts.

After a few more minutes, with the doctor's talking to Matt, his eyes slowly opened. He gazed, around the room, looking at one person then another with lonely bewilderment written all over his tired face, which spoke so clearly to his family, "Who are you people?" and his eyes closed again.

One of the doctors put his arm around Penny's shoulder and quietly said, as their children moved in closer so that they might hear, "Mrs. Savage, this sort of thing happens quite frequently when a patient comes out of a coma. Just give him time and I'm sure he will be just fine. All in all he has progressed very well we can all be very thankful for that."

Penny grasped the doctor's hand and squeezed it tightly in hers as if to say, "I do hope you are right."

Standing very quietly, back in the shadows of the hallway, Niki and her father watched with great concern as the doctors worked with Matt. They remained there, not wanting to disturb the family.

Penny stayed with her husband day and night watching the medical staff with great concern as they tended to Matt. Matt's first attempts to speak proved difficult. His speech was slurred and labored. It wasn't a pretty sight to see as he drooled and stammered much like a victim of a stroke. There is not much human dignity found in a hospital.

This morning had to be one of the happiest Penny had experienced since that night she learned her husband was alive and not six feet under. He sat up in his bed and, with a slight smile on his lips, spoke a complete and very intelligent sentence. She let out a squeal that brought the nurses running.

"Oh Matt, you don't know how happy I am. It's as if you have returned from the dead a whole and complete man."

Penny couldn't tell her dad or anyone that Matt was alive and doing better each new day. She wanted to speak to her father for he was the only one she felt comfortable talking with. She couldn't tell her dad the whole story for now, but maybe some day it might be possible.

Chapter 9

Safe House

"Dad, I just can't stand to live here anymore. Since Matt's death everything in my life has been turned upside down. I have decided to move away from here to a place where I might get a fresh start at life."

"Now wait just a minute, Penny! You can't do that, it's not fair to your family."

"I know it's not fair, but if I'm going to keep my sanity, I must do this for myself. There are just too many old memories floating around to deal with. Everywhere I go something reminds me of Matt and my heart nearly breaks."

Penny was grateful for her husband's life and her children whom she could turn to for encouragement and support in this difficult time. They had faith and hope that Matt would recover, but everything seemed to move at a snail's pace.

"My precious children, I have called you together for an important family meeting. There are certain things I need to talk to you about. The most important bit of information is that Agent Headley informed me yesterday that as soon as your dad is well enough, the government is going to relocate us to a safe house until his life is no longer in danger."

"But Mom, what are we going to do? How can we reach you?" Nancy Marie asked with a quiver in her voice.

"I'm sorry my children. There can't be any contact with us for the time being. We are not permitted to tell you where they are moving us and at this time we don't even know. Until the danger passes, it will be as if I picked up and moved. Hopefully, the bad guys believe your dad is dead. Not too many people know your dad survived the shooting, but on the other hand, there could be plenty of leaks out there."

"What are we supposed to tell people when they ask about you?" asked Bryan.

"Just tell them I've gone on an ocean cruise and won't be back for a couple of months. That should hold them for a while. Whatever you do, promise me you will tell no one your dad is alive."

"Mom, we will take care of your home and make sure everything is taken care of."

"Thanks, Bryce. You'll need to check with Agent Tim Headley because he told me he would take care of the bills and other important items. Make sure, when you call him, that you call from some phone other than your own."

Penny's children were afraid, worried and confused about all the cloak and dagger stuff, yet they would do their part. Roger took his mother in his arms and with a tear running down his cheek said, "Please, Mom, be careful."

Matt's recovery was slow and not without complications. His back wound healed well and he was regaining his physical strength but his memory was woefully suffering.

As each day passed, he became more and more distant from his wife. If the truth had been known, Matt didn't know who Penny really was. Everyone around Matt continually told him she was his wife and they had been married for over thirty years and he had children and young grandchildren. As hard as he tried, Matt couldn't remember any of them. He felt that in order not to hurt any of their feelings he would pretend he knew them. His family quickly recognized that something was dreadfully wrong. He was withdrawn and whenever anyone would ask a question of him he just stared off into space and never answered.

Matt and Penny were relocated to a safe house in central Oregon, in a small town named Bend, south of Redmond. It was a place where they could rest in peace until all was safe for them to return home.

The home that had been provided for them was a modest white frame house with a lovely picket fence and a beautiful yard landscaped much like their yard back home. This pleased Penny.

The fed's had Penny and Matt settled into their home, along with new identities, and invented stories of their past, Penny was hopeful Matt's memory would come back. Twice a week she would take him to the medical specialist the government had arranged for, to get treatments.

Ever day Penny would plan something new for the two of them to do. One day she would take him shopping, another day they would look at new cars. She even located a radio control airplane club who invited her to bring Matt to watch them fly their planes at an old abandoned airstrip outside of town.

Matt loved muscle cars and Penny felt that an up-coming car show in Eugene, might be the ticket to shake his mind loose and return him to his old self. She had read about the show in the newspaper.

"There is a car show in Eugene next Saturday. It's going to feature a lot of old muscle cars, the kind you like and was always talking about. Would you like to go, Matt?"

"Sure, that would be fine," he said without showing any emotion.

"I'm wondering, Matt. Do you remember that special muscle car you built? The one you spent years restoring?"

"No. I have never owned a muscle car."

She had a difficult time believing that Matt couldn't remember his beautiful car. She wasn't sure what was going on inside that mind of his. "Darnit Matt, It was a 1970 AMX. Can't you remember anything?" She stormed out of the room in disgust and frustration.

The following Saturday morning, the day of the car show, they arose early, and enjoyed a country style breakfast in town before leaving for the ninety-mile trip to Eugene. Penny drove, as always, not trusting Matt behind the wheel. Penny was always quite a talker, which helped with the one-sided conversation. No matter the topic, she couldn't entice Matt to say more than a few words at a time.

She enjoyed the trip and being out of the house. Penny sometimes wondered where all those beautiful cars came from because they are not normally seen on the road. Of course silly, she said to herself, "The owners protect those cars like their girlfriends, which some of those guys love more than their wives."

The two walked up and down row after row of spectacular cars, all of which glistened in the afternoon sun seemingly pointing out the hours their owners spent preparing them for this show.

All Matt said about the car show was, "How can these people afford those expensive cars? I know I could never afford one."

"Wake up, Matt. It's a beautiful Sunday morning and I think it would be nice if the two of us went to church. What do you say?"

He frowned at the thought and finally said, "What church will we go to?"

Penny struggled, keeping her emotions in check. Matt had always been an active and devoted member of the Mormon Church and took his church assignments seriously.

"What am I to do? He can't even remember what church he belongs to, who his wife is or who his children are. She ran from the room and collapsed into a chair and sobbed quietly.

Penny had taken from home all of her family photo albums because they were priceless to her. She spent hours looking through them and showing Matt those precious family pictures. "Matt, don't you see that you are in these pictures with me and our children?"

"Yes, I can see that it's me but I can't remember having those pictures taken. I'm so sorry, I can't recall any of those pictures."

He tried so hard to recall memories. The harder he tried the more frustrated he became with himself. It came to the point he wanted to run away and hide from it all. He just didn't know what to do.

There wasn't the slightest degree of predictability in Matt's actions, Penny never imagined that he would do this. At the end of three long months, Matt just gave up trying to make sense of it all and, in the middle of the night, he drove away, leaving Penny all alone. He wasn't sure about anything that had happened to him since that dreadful day when he was shot. The only people in the world that he remembered were his old friends, Baxter and Niki, who lived somewhere in Virginia. Hopefully, they could help him, but how would he find them?

That morning Penny awoke to a silent and lonely house with Matt nowhere to be found. After searching for a few minutes she found the note Matt had left for her. It was a simple note written on a crumpled piece of brown wrapping paper. All it said was, "I'll be okay and when I get this mess figured out I will let you know. I'm so sorry for all the hurt I've put you through."

Without a moment's hesitation, Penny was on the phone placing a call to Agent Headley. She wasn't certain Matt knew of the peril he was in by leaving this safe house. The F.B.I. agents had briefed Penny about the danger they might be in and that information had disturbed her greatly. She doubted Matt had understood any of it.

"Hello, Baxter, this is Agent Headley. I'm afraid I have some troubling news. Our man has disappeared. Mrs. Savage called me only a few minutes ago, stating that when she awoke this morning, Matt was gone. He left a note saying that when he had this mess figured out he would call her and let her know."

"Do you or Penny have any idea where he might have gone?" asked Baxter.

"No, not even the slightest."

"Did he take the government car we gave them?"

"Penny says it's still parked in the driveway."

"What disturbs me the most is Matt's mental condition. Penny says he doesn't know her, their kids, or anything about their past lives together."

"Oh boy, that means he most likely doesn't remember working for the agency or the people that felt threatened by what he knew. He is in greater danger than he was before that time they tried to kill him."

"Tim, get to Penny as soon as you can. Convince her she needs to stay put for her own good and tell her we will find her husband. Look for any leads that might point us in the right direction and report back to me P.D.Q. Good luck, Agent."

"I'll need some luck." The phone was silent.

In the early hours of the morning, Matt had borrowed (stolen) the neighbor's car and drove to Portland where he left the vehicle in an airport parking lot. He purchased a one-way ticket to Richmond, Virginia, using his real name, not worrying or considering how easy it would be for them to follow him.

Throughout the duration of the flight he sat quietly with his eyes closed, pondering all he had heard and seen these past few weeks. Some of the time he slept. He didn't want to talk with anyone, but worried and wondered how he was ever going to find his friends. He was a man without any help or recourses and these thoughts frightened him. His sub-conscious was trying to tell him that something was missing in his life.

With one small bag in tow, Matt made his way through the airport where he found a bank of phones. There he located a phone book for the Richmond area and began looking up every name he thought his friends might use, with no luck. How silly, he thought to himself. Niki told me how they loved the country. Remembering that bit of information was a big help in eliminating the big cities. Now he could look elsewhere, but where? This is a big state with thousands of small towns and cities and his friends might not live in an incorporated city.

"Operator, I'm looking for an Aleksandar Blinski or a Niki Blinski."

"What area do they live in, sir?"

"All I know for sure is they live in the state of Virginia."

"I don't know how I can help you unless you can give me a place to look."

"Ma'am, I really do need to find these old friends of mine. I'm here in your state and quickly running out of resources. Could you please help me?"

"If it was me, I would get your hands on a computer and Google White Pages and start searching. That should be your best bet. Good luck, and have a nice day, sir."

After some serious searching, Matt found a Blinski in a place called Madison Hills, northwest of Richmond. It's about one hundred miles or so, the rental agent told him as he filled out the rental agreement for his car.

The drive took him a couple of hours before he found the little place called Madison Hills. With the address in hand, he stopped at a convenience store to ask for directions. Oh how he hoped this was their home, for his head ached so much that he was having difficulty seeing and he felt he couldn't travel another mile.

Shuffling up to the front door, Matt reached over and reluctantly pressed the doorbell. It seemed the longest time before the door opened and there stood Baxter. Showing up unexpectedly was a shock to the old man. Even though he knew Matt was missing, he never thought he would show up on his porch, but then he should have known.

"Oh no, what have you done, Matt? You are not supposed to be here. You should be with your wife in that little town where we put you to keep you out of harms way until we solve this case."

"Please don't be angry with me. I just didn't know who I could turn to and I'm so very tired."

"Don't just stand there with your face hanging out for the whole world to see, get yourself inside, right now!"

Baxter shook his head. "This is one grievous mistake you've made, Matt. If those people are watching us they will know you are alive and well, and not a ghost on the prowl."

Once inside their home, Matt simply fell into the nearest chair, not having the strength to move another inch. He was spent and had no idea how sick he was. Those people that he left behind had to have some significance in his past, but for the life of him he couldn't figure it all out. It was as if he was existing inside a large sphere with faint streaks of light occasionally shining through.

"What am I to do with you?" Baxter murmured quietly to himself as he appraised the man slumped in his front room chair. He loved Matt as his own son, and was fearful he might also lose him as he had lost Viktor.

He spun around and headed for the kitchen to get Matt a cold glass of water. While filling the glass he hollered out at the top of his lungs. "Niki, come down here this very minute!"

Within seconds Niki appeared. "What is it, Dad?"

"Come and see what the cat dragged in." He smiled at her knowing how pleased she would be to have Matt around.

"Oh my Heavens! I can't believe it is really you. What are you doing here? You are supposed to be in Oregon waiting for the day when you and Penny could return home safely."

Niki's dad hadn't told her Matt had flown the coop, leaving Penny behind, because he didn't want to worry her just yet, at least not until he had some plan in mind. Now he could skip plan A and move on to plan B but he didn't have a plan B.

Niki watched this old love of hers, pathetically slumped over in the chair, not responding to her questions and looking more dead than alive. The love she had suppressed in her heart for so long simply gushed forth and she moved quickly to comfort him. She sat down and softly pulled his head to her shoulder. "You poor man. What more can they do to you than they have already done?"

His eyes closed and he was asleep. Father and daughter helped Matt to a nearby couch where they laid him and covered him with one of Niki's comforters.

Just before midnight the phone rang. Baxter answered it. "Yes."

"This is Agent Headley. One thing is certain, Matt didn't try to make his escape a secret. It didn't take us long to find out he had purchased a plane ticket to Virginia. We have agents in the Richmond area looking for him as we speak."

"I want to thank you for your good work Agent Headley, but you can call the search off for Mr. Savage."

"But why?"

"You won't believe this. Matt showed up on our front porch this evening. Apparently he remembers Niki and I and was somehow able to find us."

"You are kidding me, aren't you?

"No, I'm dead serious."

"What is it you would like me to do?"

"Please do everything in your power to keep Mrs. Savage comfortable and let her know Matt is okay and we will do our best to keep him safe. She needs to stay put and not leave the safe house. Don't tell her where Matt is, I don't want her showing up here, understand?"

"Positively, I'll do just as you ask."

"Thanks again, Agent Headley. We are going to need all the help we can muster if we are going to have any hope finding the person or persons responsible for his condition. I'll talk to you soon as I know anything of relevance."

Chapter 10

Looking for the Man

"Niki, after mulling this over in my mind, I have a strong feeling I should go back and visit once more with Fletcher. Brook Staggs suggested I should start looking at Fletcher as a suspect, but I disregarded his suggestion, due to our old friendship. Will you take a short trip with me to D.C. tomorrow? I could use your help sniffing around. You could pick up on something that I might miss. How about it, Niki?"

"Like I told you once before, Dad, I'm with you for the long haul and I will do whatever is necessary to catch those boys."

The next morning, around ten o'clock, they arrived at Fletcher's office and were told by the receptionist he was no longer working there and that he had retired the day before. Baxter was outraged at the thought, not wanting to believe that he had retired. The receptionist walked them back to his vacant office to let them see with their own eyes.

With one of Niki's beautiful smiles, she asked the receptionist, "Could you please give us his address? It is imperative that we talk with him."

"I'm sorry, Ma'am. He didn't leave us a forwarding address or phone number. Perhaps you might check with the administration office. Maybe he left them the information you are seeking."

The administration office told them the same song and dance. They didn't seem to care one way or another.

"Where are you sending his retirement check to?" Baxter questioned.

"A bank."

"Which one?"

42

"You know as well as I do that I can't reveal that information."

"If we had someone with a little more clout maybe they would be willing to help us, Niki. On the other hand they might be telling us the truth."

"What rotten luck, I'm afraid we have spooked Fletcher and now he is going to be that much harder to locate."

At least the girls in the administration office gave them Fletcher's home address in the D.C. area only a few blocks from his office. A little badge flashing does wonders when you are trying to get into a residence without a warrant.

The apartment manager said, "I don't like it, but what else can I do? Lock up when you leave."

"No problem, and thanks. By the way, I don't think your renter will be coming back any time soon."

"What makes you say that?"

"Oh, it's just a gut feeling."

Carefully they searched Fletcher's apartment for any clue he might have overlooked. He was careful about leaving any sort of evidence that would point an accusing finger at him. It was a practice he religiously sought after, but with his quick departure it was possible he may have overlooked something. With little concern about him returning and finding them rummaging through his things, they spent all the time they needed in searching his apartment.

Like a couple of home-grown burglars, Niki and her dad put everything of interest from his apartment in two pillowcases, for a later examination.

A few hours later they met with Brook Staggs, who was their "ace in the hole." If anyone in the department would be able to help them find Fletcher, Brook was their man. He seemed to have an inside track on everything that went on in the D.C. office.

Everything they had gathered from Fletcher's apartment was now on Brook's kitchen table waiting for their examination.

"Hey, Dad. Look at this utility bill I found in an old shoebox. This bill isn't for his residence here in Washington, it's for a place somewhere in Virginia."

"Good, that's something worth looking into."

Chapter 11

Hideout

Fletcher had chosen to hide out in his Virginia cabin for a few days, giving him time to decide on his next move. He knew it would take valuable time for Baxter to pick up his trail, if he was convinced Fletcher was the man he wanted. For now, he would kick back and see how things would shake out. But just in case Baxter found the clue Fletcher had left and showed up sooner, he would have a little surprise for him.

Tom and Bobby were the only people who knew about Fletcher's place and for the immediate time they would be more worried about covering their hienies.

The next morning, before the sun had risen over the Atlantic Ocean, they were in Stagg's office. "Listen up folks. My staff has developed a nice list of people to start looking at. I've highlighted those names you should be most interested in."

"By the way, Niki, we found an address for the utility bill of Fletchers, the one that had only a P.O. box."

"Thank you, this will be a great help. Maybe Dad and I could drive to his place and see what we can scare up out there in those woods."

"By the way, how is Matt doing?"

With great concern and a troubled heart, she said. "How do you know about Matt?"

"You see my dear, there isn't much around here that I don't know about, I promise you I will do my best to help you every way that's in my power to find those culprits. I'm truly sorry I've troubled you."

"Mr. Staggs, we have been trying our best to keep him out of the picture, hoping that those people still believe he is dead. If they believe they did kill him, then we will have a better chance of keeping him alive."

"Let's see that address of Fletcher's, Niki, would you grab me a map?"

"Here is the address and I'll get a map."

"Fletcher's place is somewhere near the border of West Virginia close to Millboro Springs, I think. His address is on a route, which can make it a little more difficult to locate and according to the map his cabin is in the Appalachian Mountains."

"Do you think he might be holed up there waiting to see what we are going to do?"

"It could well be, Niki, I just don't know what that man is thinking. There was a time, years ago, I believed that I knew him well. I was wrong, I didn't know him at all."

"If we can leave soon we should be able to drive to Millboro Spring by early this afternoon and check his place out."

"Let's hit the trail. Time is a wasting."

"Dad, I can tell you've been reading those Louis L'Amour westerns again."

"Why not, there is nothing wrong with that. Maybe you should read one of his novels. They are great stories."

"You might be right, but I've never been that interested in cowboys and Indians and the shoot-em-up Old West. By-the-way Dad, I would like you to stop by the house, it's on our way, and lets pick up Matt and take him with us. I think it would do him good to get out of the house and see some new country."

"Are you out of your mind? We have been trying to keep him hidden away, with the hope that these people believe he is dead and buried, and now you want to take him out for the whole world to see?" The old man, lost in his thoughts, shook his head in disbelief.

"Dad, I haven't lost my touch with reality, just hear me out. Did you know that your friend, Brook Staggs, knew all about Matt?"

"Well! I didn't know that, but it doesn't surprise me one bit."

"So, don't you think the cat's out of the bag and we should pursue a different course of action?"

Obviously worried about what she had told him, he stared at her without responding to her question. Nonetheless, he was thinking about how he could protect his friend. If Matt wasn't such a close friend he could be more objective about the whole matter. But it wasn't the case, for he had promised Matt's family he would find the scumbags and protect him from them.

"Dad, I must persist. Matt was a good agent and able to take care of himself. I believe he would like to help find those men and bring them to some sort of justice."

There was no fat in Baxter's conversation. "What about his health and his mental state of mind? He can't remember his own family, which worries me continually. I don't want to take that kind of a chance, Niki."

Niki's mindset was confirmed. She wanted her way and no one, not even her dad, was going to change her mind. She truly believed it was time for Matt to come to bat and give them the help they most desperately needed.

"Dad, remember this Russian cliche'?" Live in the past and you will lose an eye, ignore the past and you'll lose them both. It's time that we adopt a new change of plan."

"My innermost feelings tell me no, and that's how I cast my vote on this matter, but I know you, Niki, better than anyone else in this world does and I trust your wisdom. I also know how you loved him once and I know that you would do nothing to harm him, so I'll go along with your wishes."

"What brings you two home this time of day? I've had a wonderful morning so far, just sitting around and wasting my time watching the boob tube."

Niki spoke up first. "Matt, I think you'll enjoy the rest of the day and I can promise you there will be no more T.V."

"That part sounds good so what do you two have on the agenda?"

"I'll tell you all about it when we're on the road. Get yourself put together and we'll leave in ten minutes."

"Now that we are on the road do you mind telling me about our outing on this beautiful day?"

Baxter remained silent about the day's activity. He was extremely worried about Matt's safety because he had no plan, being that Niki had caught him completely off-guard with her request.

"We've a great deal to talk about, Matt, and we can discuss everything on our way to the Appalachian Mountains, but first things first. We are hopefully on the trail of a Mr. Fletcher, a recently retired agent from the F.B.I. We have reason to believe he's behind operation Starlight and you being shot."

"How is it that you suspect this guy?"

"When Dad started nosing around, Fletcher retired the next day and disappeared. He also made some silly threats directed at Dad, which at the moment, he didn't take seriously."

"Absolutely, it was to our good fortune that I found a utility bill of his and obtained an address from it, now that's where we are heading."

"Is this Fletcher guy the one who shot me?"

"No, he didn't do the shooting. Dad and I were there trying to stop the shooter, but we were a little late, I'm so sorry to say. Dad made sure he will never take another life."

"Niki, it seems like a recurring dream I keep having. I see your face close to mine with tears running down your cheeks, saying, "Oh, look what they have done to you.' "

"Matt, that is no dream. It was the worst day of my life."

"Where did this shooting take place?"

"On a farm you and another guy own out in Utah."

"I don't own a farm in Utah or any other state." Matt spoke with determination in his voice, which boggled their minds and saddened their hearts.

The phone rang. "Is this Fletcher?"

"Yes, it is."

"They are on their way. You have a couple of good hours before you need to act. Take care."

Fletcher had prepared for this eventuality years ago. He knew one day his luck might run out and he wanted to be ready so that he would have a decent advantage in making his escape.

He had deliberately left an old utility bill where they would find it. He wanted them to pursue him to this spot where a clever trap was waiting for them. That act should ward off any further trouble from them. If Baxter and Niki were erased from the picture there wouldn't be anyone left to tell the story or point the accusing finger at him. He wasn't that worried about Matt because he was always below Baxter in the chain of command, but if he should get caught in the trap, then all the better.

Beneath his well-kept cabin was an elaborate workshop, specifically built years ago for any of his special needs. There was a 400 ft tunnel that ended in his garage on the far side of the hill, behind his cabin. The road from his garage went down a completely different way than the road to the entrance.

"Matt, I want to know if you remember all those years that you and I worked together on some pretty iffy operations, for the agency?"

"Sure I do, Niki. It seems that all of my life was associated with you and your dad and nothing else. We did some pretty dastardly things back then, didn't we?"

"That we did."

If Matt was truthful with his friends he would tell them that much of his past was foggy and unclear. But how could he tell them the truth.

Baxter finally spoke. "We'll have time to discuss those matters later Matt, but for now we need to focus on catching up with Fletcher and asking him some pertinent questions."

As the miles rapidly passed by, Matt watched out the window enjoying the countryside, completely taken by its unique beauty. One phrase he had heard somewhere in his past came to mind. "It's a glorious world to behold." Oh how true that statement is, Matt thought.

"Take a look at the mail box next to the driveway. I believe we have found his place, Dad." The drive was lined with wild azaleas that looked as if they had been planted by hand.

Baxter said, "We'll leave the car parked here and walk to his place."

"Hey, you guys! Wait just a blasted minute. If I'm going to help out, I'll need a piece."

Baxter reached into the glove box of the car and removed a new blue steel Colt, model 1911. It had an extended barrel and some beautiful custom work done to it.

"Can you handle that beauty?"

"There is no question I can. It's not a gun you could carry concealed, but I bet I could place a tight group with this baby."

With circumspect, they made their way through the trees and under-growth towards the cabin.

Inside the cabin, Fletcher was sitting in his favorite chair reading a mystery novel as he waited. His property was equipped with the best sensors money could buy and he had no fear of them sneaking up on him.

"Good." He spoke out loud as the alarm went off, making only enough sound to be heard inside the room. Quietly he stood up, closed his book and placed it on the table next to his chair. He had carefully orchestrated his plan. The booby trap only took a minute to activate because he had prepared it well in advance of their arrival. It was simple but very effective.

He picked up his pace, making his way to the basement, via a secret door in the back of the pantry. Within a couple of minutes he had made his way through the tunnel and arrived at his garage. He climbed to the top of the garage, which was constructed with nothing more than walls of limestone and shale rocks with bushes for cover. There he could sit tight and watch, for he had a good view of his cabin. It would now be a waiting game.

Down below Fletcher's cabin and well hidden from view, the three stood in the thick undergrowth watching his place, wondering if he was there. Baxter and Niki observed the cabin with keen interest, hoping they might discover what they wanted to know.

Matt found it hard to concentrate. He thought to himself, "This cabin looks like it belongs to a woman, not an old cop." It was nicely painted with white shutters on the windows. Small, but pretty spots of flowers were growing around the perimeter of the cabin. There was asphalt laid around the front and part way down the drive, but no sign of a vehicle.

To the far side of cabin grew a magnificent oak tree. There were many other varieties of trees that Matt wasn't familiar with. He supposed that they might be ash and beech.

After an hour of waiting and not seeing the slightest movement inside, Baxter spoke in a coaxing tone. "Let's go. Be careful and keep spread out until we reach the cabin. Matt, you go around the back and check it out."

Cold and detached from any decent emotion, Fletcher sat waiting and watching with an insatiable curiosity to see what would happen. He was loving every moment.

Niki and Baxter each positioned themselves next to a window and carefully peered inside. Not seeing anyone, they moved toward the front door. It was unlocked. Baxter pushed it open and waited for the unexpected.

Around the back of the cabin Matt caught a whiff of gas that, for a moment, stopped him where he stood. Then he remembered something all too well. "Oh, no!" he thought. He ran around the cabin to warn his friends. Just as Baxter was feeling around the wall for the light switch, Matt shouted at the top of his lungs, "Run like hell!" If he had flipped the light switch to the lamp, the exposed filament would have sparked the fuel and made a monstrous explosion. Fletcher had carefully removed the glass from the light bulb, setting the trap.

"What rotten luck!" he blared out. He wanted them inside when the explosion occurred. They had escaped the first booby-trap but they wouldn't the second. Fletcher grabbed a radio-controlled transmitter and pushed the button. The roof of the cabin blew straight up as if it was being launched and came down on the house as the backside of the cabin collapsed. The front windows and doors blew out, sending glass and debris over the bodies that were lying in the dirt driveway. The blast had hurled the three to the ground, knocking them unconscious.

With naked hate in his eyes, Fletcher watched from his vantage point but could see absolutely nothing because of the dust and rubble falling through the trees.

"Considering the force of the explosion, those three pursuers have to be dead. I don't have time to wait around for the authorities to show up. It's time I go, and only hope for the best." He laughed like a mad man.

Chapter 12

Snakebite

Carefully, Fletcher stepped through the shale and limestone, making his way to where his car was parked in the garage. He didn't see it, but he heard it, all too late. The big eastern diamond back rattler struck with lighting speed and sunk its fangs deep into the calf of his right leg.

Fletcher yelled out in pain as he fell to the ground, grabbing his leg and spewing out of his mouth all the expletives he had ever used. He saw the snake slither off.

He grumbled loudly, "That's the biggest rattler I've ever seen. Damn, that does hurt but I need to leave now before the authorities show up and I get questioned. I don't need that sort of trouble."

He pulled himself up, using a tree, and stood for a moment to gather his senses. In his front yard he saw three bodies lying motionless and thought to himself, "Good job old boy, they can't follow me now."

Now, he needed to attend to his snakebite as quickly as possible. A few miles down Highway 39 was a doctor's office he knew about. He hoped he could make it there before the snake's venom took control. In the back of his mind he was recalling the stories he had heard about people who died each year from snakebites. He wondered how long he could keep up and would he become the next victim?"

Trying to negotiate the winding mountain road concerned him. Suddenly, he saw a small voluntary fire station at the side of the road and pulled in as the lone fire truck was pulling out with its red lights flashing and siren sounding. Fletcher hollered at the firemen for help, but they must not have heard him. His head seemed to be spinning and nausea gripped at his guts. He opened the door to his car and vomited violently. His hope was quickly disappearing and he laid his head back on the seat to wait for the end. Fletcher was more of a quitter than a fighter.

"Mister, can I help you?"

"I would greatly appreciate it. I was bitten by a rattler a few miles back and need a doctor, pronto."

"You stay put, you hear. I'll get my car and take you to Doctor Hennesy, down the road a piece."

The old gentleman helped Fletcher into his car and they were off, leaving his car parked next to the fire station.

"Why didn't the firemen stop and help me?" Fletcher asked the old man.

"I don't know that answer, but I heard them say there a cabin fire burning out of control."

Fletcher perceived the cabin fire was his place going up in smoke and of course he knew how it started. He would never again be spending time in his get-away. The thought caused him to feel a little melancholy about the loss. He would miss his cabin in the hills, and if he made it through this episode in his life, he most likely would build another hideaway, somewhere in the west.

A few miles down the road, the old man slid his pickup to a stop in front of an attractive, white frame house with a sign over the front gate that read, "Dr. Hennesy."

"This is the place, mister. Please just sit tight and I'll get the doctor to help you."

The man hobbled off as fast as his old legs would carry him. A minute later Dr. Hennesy and his nurse were at the car door helping Fletcher out and into the treatment room.

The doctor had no reservation about cutting away his pant leg, to expose the snake bite.

"Mister, do you know what kind of snake bit you?"

"Certainly, I do. I've seen those around on several occasions. It was an eastern diamond back and it was one big sucker."

It seemed like only seconds and the nurse was at the doctor's side with the anti-venom serum in hand. The doctor prepared the shot while his nurse wrapped a sterile bandage around the wound. The area around the bite was swelling fast.

"By the way, mister, what's your name?"

"Jimmy Dubois," he answered."

He would never use his birth name, Fletcher, again. From now on he would be known as Jimmy Dubois and he had all the I.D. to prove who he was.

Jimmy was feeling mighty sick and the doctor could see it in his eyes. He kept checking his pulse and respiration every few minutes.

The old doctor was one of a dying breed. He was a true-blue country doctor who loved people, especially the ones who lived in these hills. He would never get rich, like so many doctors, but his reward was in the service he provided to his fellow man. Being of assistance always warmed his soul.

His favorite pastime was talking with anyone who had the time to listen. Once engaged in a conversation, there were few people that could out-talk the old gentleman.

"Well, Mr. Dubois, how are you feeling?"

"I feel like the ragged wheels of hell, if you don't mind."

"My friend, I get several snake bites every year and some of them get pretty sick, just as you are experiencing, but I haven't lost one in ten years. So, you shouldn't worry none. Just do as I tell you and everything will be fine in a day or two."

"Nurse, would you please fetch me a tetanus shot? It's better to be safe than sorry, I always say."

"That eastern diamond back that bit you is the largest venomous snake the United States. Did you know that?"

"No, I didn't"

"That snake can reach up to 72 inches in length and carries enough venom to kill six men. If you're interested, his scientific name is 'crotalus adamanteus."

"Fantastic, doctor, but that's not the sort of information I wanted to hear at this time."

" I can see the area around the bite is swelling and I know you are hurting. Have you experienced any other symptoms, my friend, like a headache, nausea, vomiting and abdominal pain?"

"Yes, exquisite pain, and some nausea and vomiting. Right now my gut seems to be on fire."

"Mr. Dubois, it's my opinion you're going to be just fine, but we need to monitor your condition for the next day or two. We don't have a hospital here but, if you don't mind, you can sleep in this adjoining room and my nurse and I will keep an eye on you. I'll give you something to help with the pain and a sedative to help you rest."

Dubois was greatly relieved with the doctor's assessment. In his mind he could see himself dying and never getting the opportunity to spend any of the money he had acquired from his elaborate scheme.

The nurse helped him get comfortable. As he drifted off, he thought, "Are these people inconsequential fools, or are they the genuinely good people, the kind that I know little about."

Chapter 13

Ambush

Lying in the driveway, with the taste of dirt in his mouth and heat so intense it was starting to hurt his back, Matt lifted himself up and looked over his shoulder to see the cabin totally engulfed in flames. He knew he must move, but where were his friends? Then, he saw Niki close by and struggling to get up. Baxter was face down, several feet ahead of him and not moving.

With a loud shout that would please any Marine Corps Drill Sergeant, Matt hollered, "Niki, get up, and help me with your dad!"

With all haste, Matt and Niki, dragged Baxter by his arms down the drive and into a patch of flowering dogwood. Niki checked his vital signs. "Dad, wake up!" she kept repeating this frantically as she brushed away the dirt from his face.

His eyes finally opened and with a silly grin, he said, "Boy, that was one hell of a blast."

Even at their distance from the cabin, the heat was extremely intense so they scrambled farther away.

Matt shouted out, "This fire could cause the whole forest to go up in flames!"

Just then they heard sirens approaching. "I hope they can keep the fire from running wild."

Baxter said, with a definitive scowl on his face, "Come on guys. We need to get away from this devastation before it's swarming with cops with too many unfriendly questions,"

They scrambled to the cover of the woods. When the fire truck had passed them, they moved to the main road where they had left their car. All three were shaken from the blast. Matt seemed to be the least affected from the explosion, so he drove. Two miles down the road a county sheriff's vehicle flew by them, heading in the direction of the fire.

"How lucky can three people be, to escape such a sinister booby trap?"

"You're right, Dad, but maybe there was some divine intervention that saved our lives today."

Matt had a warm feeling in his heart as he listened to their conversation, for he knew Niki was right. "We should have been blown into fodder, making it difficult for the coroner to identify our remains."

Years ago as a L.A.P.D. officer, Matt had been taught about such a booby trap, much like the one Fletcher had attempted to kill them with. When he smelled the gas it revived his memory in full, vivid color. He knew what was about to happen. How grateful Matt was when he reached Baxter in the nick of time, before he flipped the light switch.

"Hey you two sad sacks, why don't we stop here and get something to eat? It looks like a nice place. I'm hungry and it would do us all good to rest and shake the cobwebs from our heads. What do you say?"

"That's a good suggestion, Matt. We both vote yes."

It felt good to be sitting in a cool, quiet, comfortable place, away from death's doorstep and that evil man, named Fletcher. I wonder where he is right now, Niki thought.

Not much was said as the three waited for their meals to be served. They had much to consider.

"We should have no doubt in our minds that Fletcher is our man, the one who is gunning for us. He has laid all his cards on the table. But, the sad matter of fact is, we have no idea where he is, or if he was ever there at the cabin to set off the trap."

"You're right, Matt. What I wouldn't give to have a few hours to search through the remains of his place. I bet we could find some sort of clues."

Niki's voice was tight, "Like the one I found that led us here? I'm sure he intentionally left the utility bill for us to find, hoping he could snare us into his trap."

Matt reached over and softly touched her hand. "Please don't blame yourself. It wasn't an inadvertent mistake, it was a clue that anyone would have followed."

"Thanks for your reassurance. Never-the-less, I feel terrible that we nearly bought the farm, but grateful, we are all alive."

"All right you two. We need to have a plan of action before we do another thing. Do you have any suggestions?"

 Niki spoke first. "I suggest we stay around here until tomorrow and go back to where his cabin was and carefully start poking around. We might get lucky and find something of importance."

"I respectfully disagree, Niki. I feel it would be best to let this area cool down before we get too nosey. Maybe we should go back to the starting point and take a fresh look at it all. I'm sure will find something there." Matt said.

"Matt, if you're not willing to take a little risk in this search we might not ever find Fletcher and in a year or two down the road we will discover that we are no better off than we are at this very moment."

Baxter interrupted, "All right kids. I cast the deciding vote in this matter. We will get a hotel room at the next friendly place we see and go hunting tomorrow. Don't feel too bad Matt, Niki and I have been in this business for a long time and have a feeling of what needs to be done. Okay?"

"Sure, I understand."

"Can I help you, sir?" The desk clerk asked.

"Yes, I would like two adjoining rooms for the night. Do you have them?"

"One moment sir, while I check. We can accommodate you. How would you like to pay?"

"Credit card."

"Doesn't this look sort of suspicious, the three of us with not a single suit case between us?" Matt asked.

"Maybe it does, but you always seem to worry about the silliest things, Matt. It doesn't matter, so drop it."

"Women sure can be bitchy at times. I wonder what's bothering her? I suppose being we were nearly all blown to hell could be a just reason for her ill-temper."

When they arrived at the rooms, Baxter held the two sets of keys in his hands and said with an impish smile, "Okay, who sleeps with whom?"

"Dang it, Dad, sometimes you try my patience. You're not at all funny." She hit him with a sharp blow to his arm.

"Sorry, little lady. I was trying to be funny in my own sort of way."

Baxter handed Matt a key and said. "Oh well, I tried."

Matt couldn't, and wouldn't answer that comment.

The following morning Niki and her dad had to knock loud and hard on Matt's door before he opened it. They found him looking like a man with a bad hangover, but he didn't drink.

"What's wrong with you? You're not looking all that good."

"It's an extremely bad headache that kept me up for hours. I even stood in the shower for the longest time hoping the hot water would relieve the pain, but it didn't."

Baxter and Niki looked at each other wondering if his past injury or the amnesia was causing the problem. They were very worried about Matt's health, and his appearance this morning didn't help their concerns.

"Why don't the three of us walk over to the restaurant across the street for a little breakfast. Getting something to eat may help you feel better."

Matt spoke, "Do either of you have a couple of aspirin? Sometimes they can help."

"You only had to ask." Niki pulled a small bottle of the pain pills from her purse and handed them to Matt.

He gave her a warm smile and said, "Thanks, you're my guardian angel."

"Why did you say that?"

"Just because you are so special, that is why."

She appreciated those endearing remarks. "Thank you Matt, that was kind of you to say."

Then she recalled something she had once heard. "The saddest words there ever were are the words it might have been."

She thought to herself, "How would my life have been different if I could have only enticed Matt to marry me?"

After finishing a quiet breakfast, the three started back toward the place where Fletcher's cabin once stood. Matt was in the back seat with his eyes closed and his head reclining on the back of the seat.

Niki kept looking back at Matt, knowing he was suffering from his headache, and wondering what she might do to help.

All of a sudden, to her dad's surprise, she climbed over the seat.

"What are you doing, Niki?"

"Don't you see that Matt isn't feeling any better? I'm going to see if I can help. That's all."

"Matt, lay your head on my lap and let me rub the back of you neck. Maybe that will help."

Niki didn't want to see him hurting but she also wanted to be close to him and this was a good excuse. With much tenderness, she massaged his neck and shoulder and before long he was asleep. She loved the touch of his skin and feel of his masculine shoulders. It was impossible for her not to rub her fingers over his sleeping body and enjoy these precious moments of being close to the man she had always loved.

Matt awoke, but remained very still, not wanting Niki to know. The softness of her legs against the side of his face felt wonderful. He could never remember anything in his life that felt so good and he never wanted her to stop. His headache was much better but he wasn't about to let her know, at least not yet. Then he remembered a time, years ago, when he and Niki were involved in an operation for the agency and they were confined in the back of a semi-truck trailer. One thing lead to another and Niki kissed him with a very passionate kiss, a kiss that he never forgot. Matt became uncomfortable with his thoughts and sat up.

"Why was it that I never married this girl and who was that pretty lady that claimed to be my wife?" His mind was a jumble with questions and very few answers. All of these thoughts disturbed him.

"Matt, we are getting close to Fletcher's place. Keep a look out. Maybe we might find someone we can strike up a conversation with and ask a few questions."

Baxter stopped directly in front of Fletcher's driveway and noticed the police ribbon cordoning off the area. "Trespassing today wouldn't be a smart thing to do. Maybe another time, Let's cruise the area for a while and see what we might find out. It's unlikely he made many friends around here since he lived in D.C. most of the time, but you never know what we might shake out of the trees."

After driving the back roads around the area of Fletcher's property, they came upon a road directly above his place.

"Stop Dad! You can see where his cabin once was. The surrounding area is blackened and all burned down. Maybe we can find out something from this side of his property. There are no 'keep out ribbons' on this side. Look at that. The only thing remaining of his cabin is the stone chimney. It looks like a monolith or a statue for some unknown thing. It should be a lone marker to that evil man. Fletcher is the only man who probably ever used this place."

Niki explored the area, wondering what she might find, when she saw a wooden door ajar; it led into a room that appeared to be a garage.

"I can't imagine finding a garage in this rocky hillside. Dad, do we have a flashlight in the car? It is dark in there and I would like to take a look around. This garage might belong to Fletcher, considering the proximity to his property."

"Come here you two. See what I've discovered in the back of this garage. There is a stairway leading down into a tunnel. Follow me guys and be careful where you step. We don't know where this goes or what we might find in this place. Oh, Niki, there might be a snake down here. Do you still want to look around in this place?" Matt teased.

Matt knew she was deathly afraid of snakes and wanted to see the reaction he would get. She responded the way he knew she would.

"Darn you, Matt! Why did you have to say snakes? Here, you take the flashlight and lead the way and if there is a snake down here I hope you're the one who gets bitten."

With the tiniest smile, he stepped forward, took the light from her and started to chuckle. But, if the truth be known, Matt hated snakes nearly as much as Niki did.

They slowly and with an abundance of care, made their way through the long tunnel. Matt kept saying, to irritate her, "So far, so good," until they were stopped by a wall of debris.

"Well, what do you two think?"

"I'll tell you what I think. Let's get the heck out of here. This place doesn't look at all safe, and what I'm thinking is the rubble standing in front of us is the remains of Fletcher's cabin."

Back in light of day they discussed at some length what this Fletcher guy was all about. This cabin of his seemed a little much for a recreation hideaway.

With a quizzical glance, Baxter said, "We will probably never know what he had hidden away in the basement or what he was using it for. Maybe when we catch him and beat the living hell out of him, then he will tell us the complete truth."

Not knowing they were following the same road down the mountain that Fletcher used after getting snake bit, they came upon the small volunteer fire department. Baxter said, "Let's stop and show Fletcher's picture around. Hopefully someone might have seen him."

The two gentlemen inside the fire station had never seen the guy.

Standing next to their car, the trio was discussing what the plan of action might be. They had no plan at that moment.

The same elderly gentleman who had helped Fletcher get to the doctor approached them and said, "It looks like you folks could use some help."

"No thanks," Matt said. "On second thought, I take that back. Have you seen this man around here lately?" Niki handed him the picture of Fletcher.

He studied the picture for a moment. "Why yes, I certainly have seen this man and it was only yesterday. The poor fellow had been bitten by a rattler and was feeling mighty punk, so I took him to Doctor Hennensy's home a few miles down the road."

"Thank you, mister. This is great news. By-the-way, how do we find this doctors place?"

"I'll take you if you like."

"No, that isn't necessary. Tell us where he lives and we'll find it."

"It's no more than five miles down the road and on the left side. It's an attractive white framed house with a large sign over the gate which says, 'Dr. Hennensy.' You can't miss it."

"We had better get going. Thanks again for all your help."

"You're very welcome folks. There is another thing I just remembered. This man you're looking for left his car parked right over there." The old man turned to point where it was and exclaimed, "I don't believe it! The car was there a few hours ago and now it's gone."

Baxter abruptly asked, "Mister what make and color was his car?"

"It was a silver four-door Buick. It had Virginia plates, but I don't know the license plate number, sorry."

As they sped down the highway, Baxter gave the other two instructions. "When we locate this doctor's place, I'll go to the front door and you two go around back and be careful. If luck is on our side we might catch this old mutt."

Niki approached the rear of the house with extreme caution. The gun in her hand felt reassuring. Matt followed and was determined that no one would get the drop on them.

It seemed the longest time before Baxter hollered, "Come on you two. The chicken has flown the coop." Dr. Hennesey, without any reservation, did I.D. Fletcher's picture. He said this guy we called Fletcher was using another name, Jimmy Dubois. He was suffering from the snakebite and should have rested for at least another day before leaving. He couldn't say for sure when he sneaked out, but he was now gone and he had no idea where he was headed.

"Dr. Hennesey," his nurse said. "Would you look here? Mr. Dubois left us five hundred dollars on his bed. Five brand new crisp ones."

"How thoughtful of that man. I haven't seen new bills like these in quite some time."

Chapter 14

The Whole Truth

"Well, you two, what do we do next? He has disappeared like a fart in a wind storm."

"Dad, do you have to be so crude?"

"No, I suppose not. On occasion I love to see you get upset with me. It reminds me of your mother and all the times she would scold me for saying such things."

Niki grinned at her dad and shook her head as if to say, "I remember."

With a quick grasp of the matter, Matt spoke up. "I have a proposal. I feel that it's time we get some additional help catching Fletcher or whatever name he is using."

"How do you suggest we do that, Matt?"

"I've been considering this idea for some time. I believe we need to come clean and tell someone in the department what happened so many years ago. At the time we were following legitimate orders and they can't fault us for that. I'm certain they will be very anxious to question Fletcher and whoever might have worked with him. If the agency considered our actions not to be criminal and a part of our job, carrying out our orders, then I believe they would likely do nothing to us. There is no way they would want such a story to rise to the surface and become public."

Matt looked over at Baxter, expecting something more than what he saw. He was a man alone with his thoughts and he said nothing.

"Okay folks, consider this. Fletcher is guilty of conspiracy to commit murder. With nothing else on the table, this crime should cause the agency to foam at the mouth."

Niki spoke up first. "Your suggestion makes a lot of sense, Matt. Dad and I have committed ourselves to the effort of catching Fletcher and bringing him to some sort of justice. We will always hold true to this promise. This is however a possibility, if we spill our guts and divulge the whole truth about operation Starlight, then Dad and I risk getting fired and losing our pensions. That's not a happy thought."

"Someone within the agency must have the understanding and compassion to deal with this problem," Matt answered. If they were brought to the understanding that they were crimes planned with the most devious intentions in mind, and they used young operatives to accomplish the task of robbing banks under the pretense that it was for 'God and Country,' so these culprits could pocket the money, surely someone would listen. What is disgraceful is Fletcher and his associates were F.B.I. agents, sworn to up-hold the laws of this land. I'm sure the agency would do the right thing."

"Don't be too sure of that, Matt," Baxter said. "I've known so many fine and honorable men over the years, yet at times some cowboy comes along with some crazy agenda and upsets the cart. I'll consider what you've suggested, but for the time being, my consideration is all I can promise."

"Whatever grand endeavor we three have gotten ourselves into, I want you to know I would never allow or want to see my dear friends lose anything, especially their jobs or retirement, because of this punk. As far as I'm concerned, Fletcher will get his just punishment the moment he dies and steps over to the other side. This I truly believe. Let's drop that idea for the time being."

"Fletcher will get his punishment in this life if I have anything to say about it. What you say, Matt, about the next life is a fine thing to consider, but I'm a here and now sort of guy. I want a pound of his flesh and I promise you I will get it."

"Baxter, can we catch Fletcher with our limited resources?"

"Yes, Matt, I believe we can. I can get us a lot of help without exposing ourselves. Let's give this a try first before we get all moralistic and cave in."

"Dad, will Brook Staggs continue to help us?"

"Yes, Niki, he will. I know Brook very well and I'm sure he would love to see us catch Fletcher. As soon as we return home I will get in contact with him. He will be intrigued with our story thus far."

Chapter 15

Sick and Tired

Jimmy Dubois (Fletcher) believed there were no pursuers, because he figured they were all dead. Yet, if for some strange reason they were still alive and close behind him, he would never for a moment let down his guard. Unknowingly, he had escaped capture just in time and had caught himself a break.

When he thought of his clever booby trap, blowing them all to hell, he felt a morbid sort of pride swell in his chest. Over the years he had become a zealous advocate of evil, progressively becoming a self-centered evil man with no redeeming values left in his heartless soul.

Jimmy Dubois, (Fletcher) was driving west, with each mile putting distance between him and personal danger. He was still a sick man who was in need of sleep and rest and determined that as soon as he spotted a decent looking hotel he would stop and rent a room until he was feeling stronger.

Fletcher's original plan was designed to have himself at least three states away from the scene of the crime by this time. Due to the unforeseen snakebite, he was still only miles away, which made him uncomfortable.

He drove southbound, knowing he would run into a town or city sooner or later. With no map in the car, he could only guess what he would find. Not having a map was a stupid oversight and he vowed he would buy one the next time he filled up with gas.

The highway wound through miles of beautiful forestland, but he didn't take time to appreciate its beauty. Never in his life had he taken time to slow down and see the exquisiteness of nature, whose beauty is a gift from God, that's free for all to enjoy.

Fletcher snarled, "When will this cursed road ever end? I've driven forty miles and all I want to do is stop and sleep. I feel like road kill and sleep is the only thing I need.

"Is that plausible? After all this time driving there's a sign. Ten miles to White Sulphur Springs! I'm going to stop there, even if I'm forced to sleep under a tree."

As he drove into town he noticed a clean looking, most likely privately owned motel. He stopped, not wanting to drive another foot. Fourteen hours later Fletcher awoke, feeling somewhat better, but hungry, dirty, and his leg throbbing with pain.

Fortunately, he had been able to retrieve his car back there in the hills. The car contained all his worldly belongings. His suitcase had several changes of clothes. A hot shower and fresh clothes made a new man out of him, for the time being.

He had always known the day would come when he would be forced to hit the road to parts of this country he had never visited. The day had arrived, sooner than he had planned, when he would have to decide where he would go. California, with its warm climate and sun appealed to him. Living on the east coast had worn thin for him and he was excited about this new adventure and California being his destination.

"This three thousand mile trip wasn't going to be made in a day or two, so why not take time to visit as many places and cities as I wish, along the way. It could be an interesting experience, something that I've always wanted to do." Fletcher mulled the thoughts over in his mind.

He was feeling somewhat insecure about the condition of the wound from the snakebite because it looked as if the flesh was deteriorating around the area. He drove to the nearest drug store and asked the pharmacist how he should care for it. After receiving some good advice, he purchased disinfectant and bandages, hoping that would help.

"Why not head for Nashville? I would love to see the Grand Ole Opry. I never admitted to my friends in D.C. that I enjoyed listening to country music. I suppose I'm a redneck at heart."

His concealed gun permit from Virginia might cause him trouble in some of the states he would be passing through, so he stowed his Glock 9 mm in a hidden compartment inside his suitcase.

At one time he had memorized his fake I.D., but now he didn't completely trust his memory. He repeatedly rehearsed the credentials over and over, until he felt comfortable using them again.

Somewhere in the recesses of Fletcher's mind were thoughts that worried him. He didn't have all the answers he had hoped for before leaving town. Were his old "comrades in crime" free from the law or were they flapping their gums, trying to save their own lives.

Nashville was an easy day's trip and as long as he felt well he should make it in less than eight hours. He knew that breaking the traffic laws would attract unwanted attention, so he would be an exemplary driver, obeying all the rules.

Later that afternoon he arrived in Nashville, coming from the east on highway 40. Every mile was new to him.

Having been given good directions, Fletcher found the Gaylord Hotel without making a wrong turn, which pleased him.

The Gaylord is a grand hotel and convention center like no other. The new theater features the Grand Ole Opry stars just a block away. This theater replaced the original Rymer, which is still downtown.

"Thank you sir," the bellhop said, as Fletcher handed him a five spot.

"If there is anything I can get for you, please let me know. I'll be happy to serve you."

He started to say no thanks, then stopped. "Young man, there is something I would like. Get me a fifth of your best southern sipping whisky."

"Be glad to. Give me five minutes and I'll be back."

For the moment all he wanted to do was rest and take another look at the swollen leg that was hurting more than he thought it should.

"Hell man," he said quietly. "All around the bite area it's looking worse than it did yesterday. Some of the tissue is turning black and flaking away. Man, it's ugly."

The whisky was smooth and its taste pleased his palate. He hoped it would mask some of the miserable pain in his leg. Sliding his body back into a comfortable chair, while slowly sipping the liquor, helped him relax and he soon fell asleep.

Two hours later he awoke. It was still light outside. Feeling some hunger pangs, he made his way down to the lobby. The desk personnel directed Fletcher to possibly the world's largest atrium, directly in the middle of the hotel. Water surrounded an island with restaurants and stores, while boats glided on the river surrounding the island. Thousands of tropical plants and trees grew everywhere. It was all open, right to the skylights, several stories above where he stood.

After enjoying a tasty sandwich and a cold beer he made his way outside where there was a line of waiting taxicabs.

"Sir, where would you like to go?"

"I'm new to your city, but I've heard a guy can have a good time downtown at this place, I believe its called Printer Row or Printers Alley or something like that."

"You're right about having a good time, but the correct name, which hangs over the street, is Printers Alley. It's quite a tourist spot, with more bars and honkey tonks than you could possibly visit in one night."

"Good, it sounds like the place for a lonely man to find some entertainment for an evening."

"By-the-way, sir, what's your name?"

Fletcher stammered and then answered. "Dubois." He thought. "I've got to be careful, I nearly said, 'Fletcher.'"

The cabbie went on to explain, "About 1940 the clubs starting springing up on the alley, and over the years the alley's nightclubs fathered many country and western greats, such as Hank Williams, Chet Atkins, Boots Randolph, Waylon Jennings and Dottie West."

"That sounds interesting, but how did it get the name, 'Printers'?"

"Rightly, I don't know when Nashville first started in the printing and publishing business, but it goes way back to the early 1800's. As late as 1960 Nashville was home for over 36 Printing Companies and numerous businesses to support the printers."

"How in the world did all those printing companies in Nashville ever find enough customers to support them?"

"Mr. Dubois, I'm sure that you've heard of the Bible Belt?"

"Yes, matter of fact I have heard that term."

"Well, you are smack dab in the middle of it, with more Southern Baptists around here than you could count. Being I'm a good Roman Catholic boy makes me a real minority," he said, laughing.

"What church do you attend?"

"I don't go to church. It's a waste of my time, you see, I don't believe in God."

"Oh really!" The cabbie responded. "I don't hear that statement very often around here. I suppose many of these good old folks are somewhat hypocrites. You ought to see them party when they're not in church. Printers Alley, where I'm taking you, was once called Nashville's dirty little secret. It didn't matter what you were looking for, you could find it there, and it was all protected by the politicians and police."

"Here we are, Mr. Dubois. What do you think?"

"My first impression? It looks like Bourbon Street in New Orleans."

"I've heard others say that. See the neon sign half way down the street with the word Fiddle on top. If you want to have some fun, start your night out there."

"Why not, and thanks for your history lesson. I enjoyed listening to it."

For the first hour or so he sat at a small table with a cold brew and thoroughly enjoyed listening to fiddlers and steel guitar players render some great tunes. These artists were true professionals and as good as he had ever heard.

Dubois had determined to walk the streets and see the sights. The streets were crowded with people looking for a good time; some were obviously drunk, while others were swiftly on their way. Most of them were loud and rowdy.

"My cabbie was right," he thought, "There are more bars than I could ever visit in one night."

He moseyed into a lively-looking western bar where lovely ladies and handsome men kicked up sawdust as they danced. Each dancer was dressed in western attire and proved an entertaining sight. After finding a comfortable place to sit, he ordered a whiskey on the rocks and leaned back in his chair to enjoy the atmosphere of the night.

A serious thought crossed his mind as he sat drinking his whiskey. "I better keep a check on the number of drinks I consume or I might not be able to find my way back to the hotel, or even worse, I might get myself arrested for public intoxication. I don't think they wouldn't arrest a tourist for being drunk in public."

Dubois remembered how nasty he became when he drank too much. He wasn't sure how many drinks he had downed. Using some discretion, he determined it was time to head for home.

The following morning he purchased a ticket for the Grand Ole Opry. He took a local tour of Nashville City and the country and western star's homes. It was times like this when he wished he had someone to share these new experiences with. Even his ex-wife would have been better than being alone.

Before leaving Nashville, he concluded, if he were smart he should visit the hospital. His leg wasn't improving and only the liquor helped dull the pain. The doctor in the emergency room insisted he stay overnight and let them treat him. The medical personnel treated him with IV's and antibiotics that night. The following morning he headed west, against the better judgment of the doctor.

Dubois's mindset was to find a quiet little town somewhere in California, settle down and hopefully, live out his years in peace, that is, if Baxter and his gang never found him. He was afraid of Baxter and his bulldog tenacity. "If he ever finds me, I would not hesitate killing that patronizing dog. I will never go to jail."

Chapter 16

Heading West

"I do hope that Baxter and my everlastingly stupid, jackass partners go to hell! Those people have underscored my life with a red pencil that I can't erase."

Nonetheless, Dubois had made no concrete plans for his future. He would drive until he was tired or the mood struck him to go and do whatever he wanted.

The flatlands of the mid-western states, void of mountains, weren't to his liking. He was born and raised in Colorado and, until he joined the F.B.I., mountains were an important part of his life. He drove doggedly on, wanting to get this flat, monotonous country behind him.

To help pass the boredom of mile after mile of the same unchanging scenery, Dubois kept changing the radio stations, trying to find something of interest, without much luck.

For some strange reason he couldn't account for, he left the station on a religious channel. It was something he had never done before. A Bible thumping minister, as he called them, was talking about happiness, a virtue he hadn't experienced much in his life.

This minister Puzey went on to say. "The Savior, Jesus Christ, showed us the way to happiness and told us everything we need to do to be happy. As we study the teachings of the Savior and thereby understand the purpose of our existence, we feel and express our happiness. The Lord said that we should worship Him with a glad heart and a cheerful countenance. We can experience a speedier and surer course to our 'ever-after happiness' by developing certain habits and attitudes that encourage happiness.

"This great man wrote in one of his many books the following words,

"I am an optimist!" My plea is that we stop seeking out the storms and enjoy more fully the sunlight. I am suggesting that as we go through life, we 'accentuate the positive' every day."

Dubois reached down to change the station, but hesitated as the sermon continued.

A statement was made and a retort spoken, which pointed out the basic difference between optimism and pessimism. The first character stated that he had found true happiness. The second character replied, "There is no such thing as true happiness - - at best we have a few happy moments."

As Fletcher pondered this exchange he believed the second character did not understand the difference between fun and happiness. What he called "happy moments" were in fact the moments when he had fun.

 What he did not know then was that happiness is much more than just fun. Fun is a fleeting moment, but happiness is a lasting matter.

Dubois was not a nice man. He was uncaring. Now the man delivering the message via the radio was teaching him an important lesson.

"The founding fathers of our nation considered happiness to be of such importance that it was ranked with life and liberty. In The Declaration of Independence it states: 'We hold these truths to be self-evident, that all men are created equal, that they are endowed by their Creator with certain unalienable rights, that among these are, life, liberty and the pursuit of happiness.'

To quote James E. Talmage, "The present is an age of pleasure-seeking and men are losing their sanity in the mad rush for sensations that do but excite and disappoint. In this day of counterfeits, adulterations and base imitations, the devil is busier than he has ever been in the course of human history in the manufacture of pleasures, both old and new; and these he offers for sale in most attractive fashion, falsely labeled, 'happiness.' In this soul-destroying craft he is without peer; he has had centuries of experience and practice, and by his skill he controls the market. He has learned the tricks of the trade, and knows well how to catch the eye and arouse the desire of his customers. He puts up the stuff in bright-colored packages, tied with tinsel, string and tassel; and crowds flock to his bargain counters, hustling and crushing one another in their frenzy to buy. Follow one of the purchasers as he goes off gloatingly with his gaudy packet, and watch him as he opens it. What finds he inside the gilded wrapping? He had expected fragrant happiness, but uncovers only an inferior brand of pleasure, the stench of which is nauseating."

"Why am I listening to this dribble? I don't believe in a God or any of the things this man is talking about." But, Fletcher sensed there was an air of truth in his words, which held his interest.

He continued listening to his words while pondering their meaning.

"The other night, while bar-hopping on Printers Alley, was I having fun or was I experiencing happiness?" That notion gave him something to think about and raised more questions for him as he kept on the straight and lonely highway.

A few miles west of Oklahoma City he noticed a sign. 'El Reno.' He knew all too well about the Federal Correction Facility located there. A slight chill crawled up his spine. He wasn't naive enough to believe he couldn't end up in a place like that, but he would exercise all his powers to prevent it.

The tediously long interstate miles can give a man time to think and contemplate many things about his misspent life. He didn't consider his life a waste. He had acquired a great deal of cash that would keep him comfortable in his retirement and that achievement made him happy.

His mind was far from his driving chore, when out of nowhere, an Oklahoma State Highway Patrolman, with his lights flashing and siren blaring, shot by Dubois, startling him so that he nearly lost control of his car. Murmered, a few swear words. "I nearly messed my drawers." He grumbled, "If the law were after me, my butt would have been theirs. I didn't see that cop until he was next to me. When I get to Amarillo I'm going to trade this Buick in for something new and different. Those folks back there in D.C. might know my car and I don't want anything leading them to me." He felt confident, but not safe.

"Thank you, Mr. Dubois, it's been a pleasure doing business with you and I know you'll enjoy the truck, it's a beauty. By-the-way, where can we send your plates?"

"I'll just pick them up here at your dealership. When will you have them?"

"It's Thursday, I'm sure we will have them for you Monday morning. Will Monday be okay?"

"Yes, Monday will be fine. I'll see you then."

His new Texas plates were displayed proudly on his gorgeous new Ford F250. It had leather interior and every option offered by Ford. This old boy had never before owned a pickup, even though secretly he had always wanted one. Now he was as excited as a kid on Christmas morning with a new toy.

Before living Amarillo he decided to find a western clothing store and buy himself some authentic western duds. It just wouldn't do for a man driving a pick-up in Texas to be seen wearing a city-slicker outfit. Everything in his suitcase was purchased on the east coast. He needed some new clothes that would help him fit in and hoped his new attire didn't make him look like a dude. He would watch and listen to the folks around him and to learn how to dress, act and talk with a western vernacular.

Chapter 17

New Mexico

Santa Fe, New Mexico, would be Dubois next stop on his trek west. He recalled some of the things he had read about Santa Fe and considered this might be an interesting place to explore for a while.

Santa Fe has a rich history of native Pueblo Indians occupying this area between 1050 & 1150. The Spaniards took the land and claimed it for Spain. Eventually, the Pueblo Indians drove the Spaniards out of their homeland.

A greenhorn he was, but after spending a week in Santa Fe it didn't seem to matter all that much. It was a real tourist town and people dressed the way they liked.

The one bedroom apartment he rented suited him but was more expensive than he had anticipated. Santa Fe is a Mecca for tourists and artists looking for a start, so prices are set accordingly.

On the outskirts of town, Jim Dubois found a raunchy saloon, which suited his taste. During the past week, he spent several evenings there drinking beer and listening to honky-tonk music.

On this particular evening he was sipping a cold one, feeling melancholy and regretting many of his life decisions, and wondering why he was such a lonely man. All of a sudden a large Navajo jumped up from his chair, hollered something undistinguishable, and smashed the guy sitting next to him. The haymaker hit him on the side of his head, knocking him out cold.

Taking a classic karate stance the big Navajo shouted, "I know karate and I will kill you all. Now you people stand up next to the wall and don't move!"

Dubois didn't respond to the Indian's directions at first. He kept drinking his beer and watching this crazy man's actions. When the Indian started toward him he decided to humor him and take his place along the wall with the other patrons.

"All right, you pale faces, don't you move."

Two county deputies, who had been summoned by the bar tender, walked in.

"All right mister, what are you doing to these poor people? Can't you see they are scared and would like to go back to their seats?"

The second deputy spoke, "Come on, Indian, lets go outside and talk this over."

" I'm no Indian!"

"Then what are you?"

Standing erect, he proudly announced, "I'm an Eskimo!"

"Oh really, then where are you from?"

"I'm from Albuquerque."

The bar patrons broke into uncontrolled laughter and the incident with the drunk, rowdy Indian was over.

Chapter 18

Madison Hills Virginia

Back in Madison Hills, Virginia, at the home of the Blinski's the three sat in the front room staring at each other and wondering what course of action they should take next. For the life of them they had no idea where to begin and were tired and discouraged with the events of the past two days.

"Let's wait until tomorrow and take a fresh look at this puzzle," Baxter said, with a weary look on his face.

Matt settled in front of the T.V. wanting to relax and get his mind off all the things that were disturbing him. As the local news played on, he thought, "It's no different here than other places in the world, just trouble compounded by more trouble."

Niki spoke, with a captivating smile that melted his toughness, "Matt, would you like a little company?"

"Yes, you know I always enjoy your company. Have a seat right here next to me and we can talk. What should we talk about?"

"I would like to talk about you, Matt."

"Why me? There are far more interesting subjects. Let's pick something else to discuss."

"I don't think so, Matt. I've prayed for you many times, wishing I had the powers to heal you and return you to the man you once were. Although, if I could have my heart's desires, I would keep you just the way you are, having complete oblivion to all your past, so you and I could start with a clean slate and could live together in a new life."

Matt's eyes met hers with a quizzical glance. He didn't understand what she was talking about. He knew he had been shot but had recovered from it. The matter about the two of them living happily ever after didn't seem to be a problem, or was it?

Niki endeavored the best ways she knew to help him remember. She considered, what if he never remembers all those special people in his life? Would she be out of line in keeping him for herself? He had always been the only man she ever wanted, but she was a real lady and hoped not to let her deep-seated emotions override her good judgment.

The two friends talked at length about things long past. Niki was amazed how Matt could remember, with such clarity, some things and not others.

"It's time for me to go to bed, Matt." But, that's not exactly what was on her mind. She wanted to say..... Oh never mind.

She slid across the couch, up close to Matt, took his face in her gentle hands and kissed him softly on his forehead.

"Goodnight, my dear, Matt."

Even a simple kiss on the forehead had a way of recharging his batteries. For a few minutes he sat there thinking about this lovely lady and the emotions he felt.

The following morning, after a simple breakfast of cereal and toast, the three sat around the kitchen table and discussed how they were going to catch their man.

While at the table, Baxter placed a phone call to Staggs in the D.C. office.

"Hi Brook, I sure could use your help."

"What's up, my friend?"

"If you're free this afternoon, I'll drive up to D.C. and we can talk. You need to hear what happened to us. Is that okay with you?"

"That will work for me. Meet me in my office at 14:00 hours, Baxter, and we can chat."

The two longtime friends sat across the desk making small talk for a few minutes before Staggs spoke up.

"Baxter, I'm more than just curious about what happened with Fletcher. Did you catch him?"

"No, I'm afraid not, but Fletcher nearly caught us in one clever booby trap he rigged up at his cabin. He blew his cabin all to hell, Brook, and I'm sure he thought we were inside. The three of us only escaped because of the quick thinking of Matt."

"You're pulling my leg, aren't you?"

"No, not for a minute. All that's left of his summer home is a tall rock chimney and a basement, which seems unusual. There is also a long tunnel leading to a garage about 400 ft behind his cabin."

"Now, without question, we both know Fletcher is our man, so where is he now, Baxter?"

" I only wish I knew. It was with some good fortune, we found a country doctor who had treated Fletcher for a rattlesnake bite, but after his doctor visit, his trail goes cold. Fortunately we found out from the doctor he is already using a fictitious name."

"What's the name?"

"Its Jimmy Dubois. This bit of information should be helpful."

"If I were in a your position, Brook, I would send a clean-up party out to Fletcher's place and take a long, careful look through all the basement rubble. What if our boy is a double agent? Wouldn't that be something? He has given us plenty of reason for suspicion."

"You're probably right. I'll see what can be done."

Brook Staggs offered them hope. "Okay, listen up, this is what I'm going to do. First, I've started a search for anyone who could have been associated with him. There is bound to be someone we are not aware of. Second, people always leave a money trail. Sometimes these trails are harder to follow, but not at all impossible. Third, we will follow that new name of his. We might even get lucky and have the snakebite lead us to him.

"I'm sure the F.B.I. has its faults. Our agency seems to float on rumor and unsubstantiated gossip. There are those who have loose lips, which at times makes it difficult to sift out the truth but, if I'm given the time, I will always find out what I need to know."

Staggs smiled in a grim sort of way and said, "The agency could turn you three into sacrificial goats unless we are very careful in our actions. I want you, Baxter, and the other two, not to do anything unless I give you the order. Don't worry about catching Fletcher, I'm sure we will be able to shake him out of his hiding place sooner or later.

With a concise list of ten names given to Baxter (Aleksandar Blinski), by Brook Staggs, he went to work considering each name carefully to see if by chance any of the names had connections with Fletcher.

After several days of cross-checking the list, Tom McGee and Bobby Blackstone's names appeared with Fletcher at a greater frequency than anyone else named on the list. These two were definitely associated with Fletcher and Baxter could see a pattern emerging, however, this interesting information, didn't rise to the level of proof they needed. It only pointed them in a certain direction and gave them confidence they would discover something important.

Brook Staggs informed Baxter that Bobby Blackstone retired the day after Fletcher had pulled the plug, and hadn't been seen or heard from since. The good news was Tom McGee was still around working in the same department as an accountant.

Baxter discovered, after hours of searching through Tom's files, that he had a gambling weakness. He was referred to around the office as, "the man with no balls," afraid of his own shadow, and one who only felt comfortable when his head was buried in someone's accounting ledgers.

Finding a man's weakness was a good thing to know for a clever agent like Baxter. It gave him an opening and he knew exactly what course of action to take with this man. He would exploit McGee's fears to the point where his subject would lose control of rational thinking. If Tom were involved with Fletcher, he would do something stupid and reveal his guilt.

"So, where does Tom McGee factor in?"

"I don't know for sure, but I will soon find out."

Baxter wanted to see how McGee would react to a surprise. From his years of experience all he had to do was watch a man's face, when questioned, and he could tell if he was guilty or innocent.

Baxter walked directly to McGee's desk with an air of bulldog persuasiveness he displayed so well. Baxter spoke in a low, guttural voice, "Tom McGee, I'm Baxter. How do you do?"

Tom looked up from his accounting ledgers, directly into the cold, calculating eyes of Baxter. His eyes didn't blink and there was no smile on his face.

In his life, Tom never remembered meeting or seeing Baxter, but he definitely knew his name. Fear choked his words as he attempted to speak.

"Yes...sir, what can I do for you?"

Baxter reached over and snatched a chair, pulled it up to Tom's desk, where he could look him directly in his face, and said, "I'm looking for Agent Fletcher. Do you know him?"

Tom answered quietly, continually looking at the floor. "Yes, I met him once, but I don't know where he is."

 Agent Baxter reached into his coat pocket, pulled out a business card with his name and phone number and tossed it on McGee's desk.

"You call me if you see or hear from him. Understand?"

"Yes, sir."

Baxter left McGee's office the same way he entered. He chuckled to himself because he had gotten the precise reaction he was hoping for. He said to himself, "That mousy little rat is guilty. I'm going to have some fun with him before this story ends."

After work, Tom scurried off to his car, which was parked in its usual spot. Nervously, he checked his surroundings for any suspicious looking persons. He particularly didn't want to see that Baxter guy hanging around.

The first thing Tom noticed after leaving the parking garage was a shiny, black, government Suburban following him. "It can't be." He was troubled. "That vehicle looks identical to the ones we use in the department." Now he was very nervous. His mind was running wild with fearful thoughts. "Are they going to arrest me, or are they tailing me to get information? Why are they so obvious? Even I can spot this tail. How would it look, me on the six o'clock news in handcuffs. Oh my, I can't go to jail. Maybe I should make a run for it like my partners. What should I do?" He didn't have the slightest clue, for he had neglected to make a plan for a situation such as this and now it was too late.

Niki and Matt were having great fun following Tom and playing with his fears. They were going to tail him for a few days to see where it might lead them; hopefully, to some answers.

When Tom arrived home he literally ran into his house, leaving his car parked crooked on the street and unlocked. His actions caused Matt and Niki to laugh out loud.

During the following few days, Tom was confronted at every turn he made, by one of the three agents. They didn't speak to him, just watched. These actions were designed to make him talk when the time was right.

Staggs and Baxter wanted Tom to worry, so they monkied with his bank account, letting him know someone was trying to acquire information.

"Hello, Mr. McGee, this is Tammy at the First National Bank. I wanted to inform you that your account has been compromised, but not accessed. Your money is safe with us and we will keep monitoring it. Thanks for your business."

Chapter 19

Gambler

Tom had an insatiable appetite for gambling. It was most likely the only excitement in his miserable life. His wife treated him with contempt. The love they had once shared, had long ago been lost. He had often wondered why he was still married to the old bag, but divorce could be expensive and being the tight-fisted old Scrooge he was, he would never stand by and let her take a penny of his money. If he had stepped outside the box he and his wife had created, he would have realized that it was he who had changed, not his wife.

On Saturday evenings, Tom, along with several of his gambling acquaintances, not friends, would get together and play poker, sometimes until the sun came up the following morning. He would win a little and lose a lot but it didn't seem to matter as it was his way of relaxing.

Learning of McGee's inherent gambling weakness, Staggs helped Baxter devise a plan to catch him alone. They would pull off the capture in the dingy old hotel room where he gambled. It would be a perfect place to question him without drawing any attention to their activities.

The following Saturday night Baxter and Staggs went to the hotel where the weekly card game was played. They placed a note on the door stating, "See you at the alternate." Niki and Matt conveniently parked a car in front of Tom's driveway, making sure he would be late for the game. The only way he could leave was to call the police and have the car towed, which would give them plenty of time to set the trap.

When they were certain the other card players had come and gone, Baxter and Staggs removed the note from the door, went inside and waited for their pigeon to arrive.

Staggs and Baxter were master interrogators and couldn't wait to question this worm. The two agents spoke quietly while waiting for the phone call. The cell phone rang. "Dad, he's on his way up, be careful."

Staggs rose from his chair, walked over to the door and stood so he would be behind it when it opened. He didn't want Tom to see him until he had stepped inside.

Tom knocked twice.

"Come on in." Baxter answered.

Tom opened the door and walked in, but froze where he stood when seeing Baxter sitting alone at the card table. Tom spun around as Staggs slammed the door. To his shock, he discovered a gun pointed directly at his face.

"Put your hands up nice and high where we can see them, don't do anything stupid and turn around slowly." Tom did as he was instructed only to face a second gun, held in Baxter's big hand, pointing directly at his gut.

Staggs searched Tom carefully. He didn't think he would carry a gun but one never knows what someone else might do.

"All right, Tom, set your scrawny little ass in this chair, right now!" Tom didn't waste any time doing what he was told.

Staggs walked over to the door and secured the deadbolt. The sound of the locking bolt caused Tom to flinch. It was very evident the man was genuinely scared. Several minutes passed while Staggs intentionally stood behind Tom, not making a sound, which caused Tom's fear of the unknown to grow.

"What have you got to say for yourself, agent McGee? And I use the title agent loosely," Baxter added.

With all the spunk Tom could muster, he said. "What in the world are you talking about!"

Baxter raised his arms above his head and slammed his big fists down on the tabletop with such force that the impact broke two fist-size holes in it. Tom jumped back and fell to the floor.

"You little piss ant. Don't you talk to me with such contempt, or I'll bust you, just like I busted this table."

Staggs reached down and grabbed McGee by the shirt collar, lifting him to his feet, and said sharply, "Pick up your chair and sit down!"

Staggs walked around McGee and took a chair next to him.

"Now, what do you think we should talk about? We are here in your favorite gambling den, very much alone. As I see it, it's a perfect time for you to spill your guts, rat your associates off, come clean, or do something new for a change, tell the truth."

"What is it you want to know?"

"You spineless man, McGee, you know precisely what we want. But since you asked, I'll spell it out. We want to know where Fletcher is. We want to know who else was involved with you two in that covert operation called Starlight and who ordered the hit on one of my men?"

He didn't answer the questions. Beads of sweat formed on his shiny forehead. Tom was considering what to say but had no idea how to answer their questions.

"What's wrong, are you deaf and dumb? We will get the answers we want if we have to stay here all night and in the process beat the living guts out of you. Do you understand? Now start talking!"

McGee buried his face in his hands. "Alright, I'll tell you what I know. Years ago Fletcher told me something about his plan to make some easy money on the side. His plan wasn't exactly legal. I told him I didn't want any part of it and that's where it ended. As far as I know Fletcher just retired and I have no idea were he's at."

Tom knew from the looks on their faces they didn't buy a word of his lies.

"How dare you insult our intelligence with such a bunch of damnable lies? Are you just a simple fool, or are you a sadist who wants a good old fashion beating?"

Staggs and Baxter slowly arose from their chairs. The hard stern expressions on their faces would have put real fear in the devil.

"Come on guys, wait just a minute, will you?"

With measured steps, the two agents walked around the table where Tom was seated, glaring his way and saying nothing. They continued circling him for a time, letting him wonder what they were going to do. Then, like a bolt of lightning, Baxter kicked Tom's chair out from under him, causing him to crash to the floor. He lay there, afraid to move while Baxter and Staggs stood over him. As they watched this pitiful man, they saw a wet spot appear on the crotch of his pants. Now they knew they had gotten the desired effect they wanted.

"Get up and sit down!" Quickly McGee was back on his feet and seated in his chair.

"Tom, you listen carefully to what I'm going to tell you. At the present time, the agency doesn't know all that you and your associates did. We are sure Fletcher and Blackstone were your partners. Are we not correct in our assumptions?"

Tom slowly shook he head in the affirmative.

Baxter spoke again. "If there is to be any hope for you, now is the time to make an important decision. That decision must be to help us find Fletcher and Blackstone."

"We will give you a little time to consider what we have talked about. Now, before we let you walk out of here, I want you to understand that we will be watching your every move. You won't even be able to pass gas without us knowing. I hope you realize your predicament. Now get out of here and if I were you I would change my pants before someone see you," Staggs mockingly suggested.

Chapter 20

A Safe House for Penny

Alone, in her government provided home in Bend, Oregon, Penny Savage felt as if she had been abandoned by the whole world. Her husband, who had no memory of her or his children, was gone and she couldn't call her family or friends for fear of compromising their safety.

She spent many long hours praying for the lives of her family to change for the better. These hopeful thoughts were always with her as she carefully appraised them daily.

Penny was a strong and determined woman who would do her best handling this challenging situation. She made friends easily and had involved herself with a group of ladies at the church. The organization, called the Relief Society, gave her new acquaintances, something to occupy her time, and some much needed help to cope with the loneliness.

Surrounding a quilting frame at the local church one day, a group of ladies and Penny were stitching a quilt, creating beautiful patterns that would soon please the new owner.

"Penny, we are happy you have joined our group, because it's always nice to have new faces in our community. I don't want to put you on the spot but, would you like to tell us a little about yourself? We would all enjoy hearing your story."

"I don't have anything interesting to tell. I'm just a country girl, raised on a Midwest farm. My husband and I had a dairy farm, which I sold. I thought a change of scenery would be a good idea. My husband had lived in Oregon as a child and always talked about how beautiful it was here. I don't know much about this part of the country and thought it would be an adventure to try new surroundings. When my husband died, not long ago, I decided to move away and leave all those memories behind."

As she spoke her eyes were fixed on the floor and it was obvious she was uncomfortable with the question. The ladies dropped the query. Penny found it extremely difficult to lie about anything, even in this case of such great importance.

What she loved was gone, what she lived for had vanished. Penny felt alone, detached from it all, but hope was still with her.

Chapter 21

Santa Fe

Dubois (Fletcher) had remained in Santa Fe for several weeks, much longer than he had planned. He enjoyed the city with all its charm and history. Every day he would visit something new. On Canyon Road, east of the Plaza, he discovered many art galleries with a wide array of artistic works, from contemporary to Russian art. He had to suppress his desire to buy some of the art pieces, which he coveted. He knew one day soon he would be on the road again and it would be a burden to take them along.

"If only I had a crystal ball so I could see what's going on back home, then I would feel more at ease." Dubois had considered trying to find out if the agency was on to him. He didn't think so, but the unknown bothered his sense of well-being.

These concerns were still bothering Dubois as he drove out of town, heading for somewhere new. He spoke out loud, "You dummy! The agency wouldn't be looking for you unless Baxter had spilled the beans and you don't believe he would have done that, and remember, you saw him and his friends lying dead in your yard." These morbid thoughts pleased him.

Yet, as he continued on toward Albuquerque, those worries kept surfacing, causing him to wonder if he had really erased those three or were they alive and searching for him.

He was now speaking out loud as if someone was riding with him. "I must know for sure what their status is if I'm ever going to have any peace of mind." The only person he could call was his old partner, Tom McGee. He didn't trust him, and never did consider him much of a man.

Dubois remembered strongly advising Tom to get out of town and vanish. But, knowing Tom as he did, he didn't feel he would ever take his advice and leave. He was too much of a homebody.

Approaching the city, he pulled into the first convenience store he saw and determined to make a phone call to settle his concerns.

"Hello, is this Tom?

"Yes it is, Fletcher. I thought you were long gone. What gives?"

"Listen, Tom, you need to answer me one question. Is Baxter still around?"

"You fool, of course he is and he and his posse are looking for you."

Fletcher slammed the phone down and cursed under his breath. "I want to kill Baxter, that dirty back stabber, and one day I will."

Fletcher (Dubois) was on the move, traveling farther west to put more miles between him and the Baxter gang, as he thought of them. When he found out his booby trap hadn't taken them out of the picture, he was naturally upset. Yet, taking into consideration the big picture, he didn't believe Baxter would expose him and his illegal operation to the F.B.I. Without the assistance of the agency, he didn't think Baxter could ever find him on his own. With this belief, he decided not to change his plans.

After leaving Albuquerque, New Mexico he decided to head for Salt Lake City, Utah.

Chapter 22

Another Attempt on Matt

"Dad, agent Staggs is on the phone and wants to talk to you."

"Okay, Niki, I'll be right there."

"Hi, what's up?"

"I've got some good news. Fletcher, or Dubois as he's now known, made a big mistake. He called McGee today and asked him if you were still around." McGee said, 'You fool of course he is and he and his posse are looking for you.' Then the phone went silent. You have him genuinely spooked or he would have never called and given away his location."

"Where is he, Staggs?"

"The call came from Albuquerque, New Mexico. We both know he is long gone from there by now, but it does give us a starting place and a probable direction of travel. Listen to this, McGee called me not an hour after the phone call to tell me Fletcher had called. Our scare attics worked very well on him."

"I bet he believes this peace offering will cause us to leave him alone. If he only knew the truth. We won't leave him alone until he has told us everything we want and need to know." Baxter replied.

"My friend, be patient. We will find him, I have no doubt of that. Remember, perseverance."

"All right, I'll take your advice, but it won't be easy, waiting to get my hands on him. Fletcher made it a personal quest when he went after Matt."

"I do understand. Why don't you just take a few days to relax and clear you mind? You just might come up with some new ideas."

"Where are you two going?"

"Just for a short walk, Dad. It's a beautiful evening to get out and enjoy some fresh air. Would you like to come along? We would like your company."

"Not this time, Niki. You two be careful."

"Will do."

They were secretly anticipating a pleasant walk together as their thoughts were entertaining some time alone to be with each other. Years ago, when they first met, they enjoyed being together. Those feeling hadn't changed. They strolled casually down the two-lane country road watching the late afternoon sky change colors and enjoying the silence for the moment.

Niki reached out and took Matt's hand in hers. He looked at her and she gave him a smile, which warmed his heart.

"Do you mind, Matt?"

"No, of course not." Her hand in his felt wonderful and had an air of comfort to it.

In the past, Matt had always tried to suppress his feelings with respect to his partner and friend, Niki, because he was married and loved his wife. Now he was lost to his past life and Niki wondered how he would respond to her. She had always wanted Matt for her very own, and no one else; yet, knowing about Penny kept her from turning on her charm, at least for the time being.

Hand in hand they walked quietly along, watching the sun setting in the west with the brilliant reds and oranges slowly transforming to cooler colors.

"Isn't this sunset beautiful, Matt?"

"Yes, it is."

The sight of a splendidly spectacular sunset was something they both loved. Niki put her arm around Matt's arm and squeezed it softly.

Matt's voice broke the magic of the moment. "What shall we do now?"

"Let's just keep walking for a while. You know I love being with you."

Matt found it hard to express his feelings so he just smiled and said, "I feel the same way."

It was an hour before they returned home from having a pleasant time talking about many things not related to work. Matt enjoyed hearing Niki's stories about her childhood in Russia, which made him appreciate growing up in America even more.

During the next two days Matt and Niki walked around the little community of Madison Hills, enjoying each other's company, and talking more than Matt ever remembers talking in his life. He seemed to like all the conversation.

Unexpectedly, Baxter told Niki he had to fly to Spokane, Washington to put out a small fire. One of his men was having some difficulties and it shouldn't take more than a couple of days to resolve it and he would be back home.

Baxter had a genuine concern for Niki and Matt's safety, so before he left, he arranged for one of his men to keep a close eye on the two. He hadn't told them they would be tailed and watched because he was afraid they would be upset with him.

A short time after Baxter left for the airport, Niki approached Matt and said, "Listen up. How would you like to do a little sight-seeing today and have a picnic?"

"It sounds like a great idea. It would give me a chance to see some of your beautiful state. What did you have in mind?"

"I have two different locations in mind. The first one is not far from here. It's called Lake Anna, and is a very pretty place to have a picnic but there is not a lot to see. The second spot is further, but well worth the drive. We could visit the birthplace of George Washington, and Robert E. Lee plus there is a lovely state park right on the Potomac River. Which one would you like to visit?"

"That's an easy choice. Let's head for the Potomac."

Matt went out the front door and waited in the yard for Niki to back her car out of the garage. He had no idea what kind of car Niki owned. He was surprised to see her in a stunning, new, chrome yellow, Cobra Mustang.

The big grin on Niki's face told him she was one very proud lady. It was a car that would make any woman smile. It had style, dual overhead cams and a muscle car sound that would cause everyone to turn and look. Matt didn't ever bother to ask her if he could drive. He remembered very well, as partners, how they fought over who was going to drive.

After making a quick stop for food for their picnic lunch, they were off, heading east, anticipating new sights.

It was such a pleasant day. Neither of the two thought or worried about those men who were a constant threat. It felt great not to worry about every little thing.

"Do you realize, Niki, we are not young anymore?"

"Speak for yourself, Matt. You're as young as you think you are."

"Now listen, Niki, I'm in my fifties and you must be somewhere in your forties, given you would never tell me your age, I have to guess. You know, Niki, you have never lost any of your stunning beauty." She smiled.

Matt said, "I can't do the things I used to and I'm starting to feel more aches and pains. My mind tells me I'm still young and tough, but I know it's all a lie. They both wondered where all those years had gone. Matt's mind had a large void, which made him sad, and he hesitated talking about it to anyone.

Visiting the historical sights was a thrill for Matt. He never had the opportunity to visit these places before and was happy he could do it, before he grew too old.

They walked hand in hand through the Westmoreland State Park until they found a spot under an old oak tree. The vista from this location offered a perfect view for watching the boats moving up and down the river. It was a special place to have a picnic with a beautiful lady. The day was slipping away as sun was low in the west.

A gentle breeze blew softy from the Potomac River rustling Niki's lovely hair. She closed her eyes and drifted off in relaxed slumber. Matt instantly reached over to catch her before she fell. Just as he did, he heard the loud, cracking sound of a rifle shot and the whistling of a bullet passing close by his ear, hitting the tree behind them. "Oh no, not again," he thought.

"Niki!" Matt shouted at the top of his voice. Someone just took a shot at us. He jumped on her to cover her body with his, hoping to protect her.

"Don't move. Lay very still. Hopefully he thinks he hit me with that shot."

After a few seconds, Matt instructed Niki to quickly crawl behind the tree. There they sat, glued to the tree, trying to determine where the shot came from.

Hoping the shooter had gone. Matt and Niki moved away, in the opposite direction. from where they thought the shot came. Once in the cover of a grove of trees they stopped and tried to assess what action they should take next.

With their guns in hand, they cautiously made their way from one group of trees to the next, every second, watching for the shooter. When they were close enough to Niki's vehicle, they ran for it, jumped in and were on the road.

"Well, Niki, I suppose we will leave our picnic lunch for the squirrels. Maybe they will enjoy it."

"We just got shot at and here you are, saying something stupid!"

"Oh well, my dear little Niki, what should I say? I'm most likely as scared as you are and as every moment passes, my suppressed temper is getting closer to the surface. To be real blunt, I'm as mad as I have ever been and I wish I knew the person to whom I could direct my anger."

"Do you think Fletcher (Dubois) has returned?" asked Niki.

"Actually.... no, I don't. I have a feeling he is heading to a place where he thinks he can live in safety and doesn't want any part of this mess. We both know what a lily-livered little snake Tom McGee is. It's not likely he would take a shot at us. Then there is a third guy, what was his name?"

Niki answered, "Bobby Blackstone."

" We don't know anything about this player. He could be the shooter."

"Matt, what are your feelings about this guy? Do you think he will give up on us, or do you think he will come after us again?"

"I wish I knew for sure, but my gut feeling tells me, he won't give up just yet. He will be coming after us and we need to be extremely alert if we are to survive."

"We out-gun him Matt, and our years of experience should help if it turns into a real gun fight."

"You're right, but this has me spooked. We know he wants us dead, so if it comes down to a shoot-out with him, he is going to die. I'm not letting him win."

" Why don't you let me drive home tonight? I would feel a lot better if I were driving under these circumstances." In the recesses of his mind came the vivid memory of Rock Springs and the bullet Niki took. He didn't think he could live through another one of those nightmares.

"No, Matt. No one is driving my Mustang. I know this baby better than anyone else. I've even taken it out to the local race track on several occasions and have registered quite a few hot laps."

"Well, I'll be. I was wondering why you had roll bars installed. Now I know."

The quibbling went on as to who was the better driver. Neither of them ceased watching for suspicious vehicles and after a short time they both quit talking, each thinking of the eventualities this night might bring.

Once through Fredericksburg, a small amount of the pressure they felt, lifted. They were hoping this devil had not followed them. For the past forty miles they hadn't seen any suspicious vehicles behind them

Just after Niki turned southwest on highway 20, he struck again.

The highway was considerably quieter tonight. For no special reason, Niki watched her rear view mirror as much as the road ahead. She noticed a vehicle approaching from the rear faster than normal.

"Matt! We have a vehicle coming up on us pretty fast and it concerns me." With a quick grasp of the matter, she said, "If this car slows up when he pulls next to us, watch out, because I'm going to lock up these brakes and make a four-wheel skid to a stop. With these custom disk brakes there aren't many cars that will stop as quickly as mine, then we will be behind this cowboy and have a big advantage."

"What if it is just someone checking out your wheels?"

"Oh well. We will be a little embarrassed, but they won't know who we are."

Matt was turned in his seat as far as the seat belt restraints would allow, watching the vehicle approach. It started to slow down. He grasped his Colt tightly in his hand while every fiber of his body went on full alert.

"It's a truck, Niki, and it's really slowing up."

"Hang on!"

She did just as she said she would do. The front of the Mustang pitched down just as a brilliant flash came from the passenger side window of the truck, accompanied by the sound of a bullet slamming into the car.

Her Mustang made a perfect straight-line stop with all four tires smoking, in just 120 ft. The Chevy pickup slid on down the road for another 70 ft. before it stopped, giving Matt and Niki time to bail out and take cover behind the car.

Their nemesis was now out of his truck and firing at them with something larger than their handguns. Matt was on the ground, shooting under the truck, attempting to hit him in the legs. Niki and Matt laid down numerous rounds into his truck before he jumped back in and sped away. This scum-bag wasn't going to get away from them without a real fight.

Matt had never seen his Russian partner so ticked off.

"Look at my beautiful car!" She shouted in rage. "The front windshield is gone and what else am I going to find damaged tomorrow?" She screamed, shaking her fist in defiance. "You filthy puke! We are going make you pay, and you are going to pay dearly. I promise, by all that is in heaven & hell, we will get you! "

The chase was on. With an enraged woman at the wheel it was absolutely no problem for the Cobra to keep up with the truck. Now with the windshield missing, Matt took careful aim and fired three rounds into the cab of the truck.

Matt shouted, "I hope I hit him!"

The truck swerved a couple of times but continued on until an off ramp appeared for Locust Grove. Down the off ramp, through the small town and into the hills they chased him. He fired a couple of times with Matt returning fire, hitting the truck with each burst.

As they chased him through the winding roads it was becoming more and more evident the shooter was getting desperate.

"He has to know he can't outrun us, Matt. So what are we going to do with him if we capture him?"

"My dear, the only thing we can do is turn this bad boy over to the local authorities, and hope for the best."

Just then the truck careened off the road, traveling straight down the hill and splashed into a small stream. It was a moon-lit night, but very hard to see anything at the bottom of the ravine. They stood at the side of the road and watched for a short time wondering what to do.

"Looks like he got the bad end of this gun fight, Niki."

"Do you think we should go down there and find out what happened to him?"

"I want to know who he is, but no, I don't think it would be a good idea. It could be like going into the den of a wounded bear. Let's make some tracks for home and hide this car of yours. Niki do you have one of those untraceable cell phones on you?"

"I do."

"Call 911 and report a traffic accident at this location. Tell them to be careful, the driver is armed."

Matt slid in behind the wheel. This time Niki didn't offer a protest. Her prized car was a mess and this realization was starting to set in. She was past the angry state and all she wanted to do was sit quietly and think.
.

For the next few miles Matt kept watch on the temperature gauge as it slowly rose.

It was now a short trip to the Blinski's home and Matt was relieved that no lawmen had seen them. If they were ever questioned this would be a difficult story to sort out.

The engine was overheated. Niki opened the garage door and Matt pulled the Cobra inside and shut it down. He made a cursory check of her car, and then covered it.

"Niki, we were lucky to get your car home. Did you know it was having a heating problem? I don't think we would have made another mile before it would have quit running."

"That's just dandy. What else could be wrong with my beautiful car."

"In the morning I'll check your car over and assess the damage."

Within a few short minutes Niki was on the phone with her dad.

"Your presence is needed now! Things are happening fast! Can't talk, but will fill you in when you return. We are all okay. Love ya, Dad."

Shortly after receiving Niki's call, Baxter was making a phone call to Staggs.

"This is Baxter. I'm in Spokane and can't get home for at least a day. Niki called me a few minutes ago saying things were happening but didn't want to tell me over the phone, which concerns me. Could you check on them? It would be greatly appreciated. They're at home. Thanks!"

Niki's home phone rang. "Hello."

"Niki, do you know who this is?"

"Yes, I do."

"Listen. I'll be there in couple of hours, so we can talk. You're dad called me and I'll be staying with you tonight. All right?"

"Sure, that's fine with me. See you soon. Good-bye."

I'll call you tomorrow, dear. I'm driving down to Baxter's home in Virginia." Staggs kissed his wife good-by and hurried out the door.

"Come on in Mr. Staggs. It's nice to see you and thanks for coming. I feel terrible you had to drive down here tonight."

"You've definitely aroused my curiosity. What has happened?"

Niki spoke up, "I know I should start this story from the beginning but there is something I want to show you. Follow me."

All three walked out to the garage. Matt pulled the cover off Niki's once sexy mustang.

"Look at my car! That puke tried to shoot us and in the process he destroyed my beautiful new car. I don't know if it can ever be repaired." Tears welled up in her eyes.

Matt tried to assure her that her car could be fixed, but he was doubtful she believed him. Under the lights of the garage, it looked even worse than what they thought it would. There were numerous bullet holes in the car causing Matt to wonder how they ever got it home.

"Let's go back inside. I need to hear this story from the very beginning."

Niki wanted to tell the story, and did it well, except for a few comments Matt interjected.

Brook Staggs asked many questions as she told him about the harrowing event.

"I'll be staying here, at least until Baxter returns home. It doesn't hurt to have an extra set of eyes and body around, especially not knowing who the shooter is, or where he might be."
The following day Baxter returned home on a hurried trip from western Washington. He was worried about Niki's phone call. Knowing her all too well and her reluctance to tell him the complete story, concerned him.

Staggs was outside the Blinski's home surveying the area when Baxter drove up and parked in the driveway.

"Good to see you my friend, and thanks so much for filling in for me. What's the skinny?"

"Before Niki and Matt come out I need to tell you something they don't need to hear. The agent you assigned to watch out for your daughter and Matt is in the hospital suffering from a serious concussion. I think he will be okay in time but we will have wait and see."

"What happened?"

"I'll tell you more later. Here they come."

Niki, seeing her dad in front of their home, came running to him. "Oh, Dad, I'm so happy you are home. You will not believe what has happened."

"Come on inside and let's talk. I need to hear the whole story from beginning to end."

For the remainder of the afternoon the four friends sat around the kitchen table and discussed all that had happened. They asked far more questions of each other than they had answers for.

"Do we have any more information on this Blackstone guy?" Baxter asked Staggs.

"We have nothing on him since he pulled up stakes and retired. Maybe it was wrong for us to assume he had left the country, and now it looks as though he is up to his old tricks again."

"What about Fletcher (Dubois)? Do we know with any certainty where he is?"

"No, we don't." Staggs answered.

Matt spoke up, "I have a feeling about him. I personally feel he is trying to get as far away from this place as possible. I just don't believe he is around, I could be wrong, but I don't think so."

"We know more about McGee than the other two because he's under our microscope and I don't think he could pull off anything like that without us knowing," Staggs commented. "Besides, he doesn't have the guts for it."

Baxter tossed the question out to be answered. "Did either of you get a look at the driver of the truck?"

"No, we didn't. The only thing we could tell for certain was the driver was a man and he was alone. Dad, we did want to go after him but the situation wasn't right. Hopefully, the scumbag is dead and that will be the end of him. Yet, we all know from years of experience, the bad guys don't die so easily."

"With little reassurance, we feel Blackstone is the shooter. We're not even sure he is still alive but we need to be on alert. It could also be the suspect is a contract shooter like the one who shot Matt."

"I want you three to pack some bags and take a trip to my summer home in North Carolina. No one in the department knows the location of this home and I feel it would be a wise move for the time being."

Baxter started to protest.

"Listen to me, it's not up for discussion."

Before they left for North Carolina, Staggs and Baxter talked quietly, away from the others.

"Tell me about my man in the hospital. Do you know what happened to him?"

"He was found next to his car, by a jogger. Of course we haven't been able to talk to him. I promise as soon as he comes around and we get the opportunity to find out what happened, I will fill you in on the details."

"I'll be anxious to know the details, and tell him we are thinking of him. Again, I thank you Staggs, for all of your help."

"You're welcome. Here are the keys and address to my home. Be careful and keep alert. I'll call you on your cell phone whenever I get anything new."

The following day, at Staggs comfortable summer home, Matt was sitting on the porch relaxing as a gentle breeze freshened the air. The view, which overlooked a wooded area and picturesque trout stream, was an enchanting place to see. In his hands was a great novel and he was thoroughly enjoying the story. Niki was in the kitchen preparing one of her special meals, while Baxter was on the phone.

Baxter called out, "Hey you two! Meet me in the front room, I have something new to tell you."

"The shooter that tried to take you two out hasn't been identified by the police yet, but we do know he is not Blackstone. Staggs checked it out. The authorities don't know the cause of death. It could have been a gunshot or possibly the accident. They are actively looking for the suspect or suspects who shot this guy. For the time being we will have to keep this story quiet."

Matt lowered his head and said, "Is it worth all we've gone through? Niki and I could have been killed, and now we are wanted by the police. Do you really think we can talk our way out of this predicament and everything else that's happened over the years?"

The culmination of events had brought Matt to wonder about the future.

Baxter could tell Matt was losing some of his resolve and he hadn't seen his daughter so upset, in years. He knew it was time to do some fence mending before those two quit on him and then the job would never get finished.

"Listen you two. We never said this would be an easy job to complete, so quit acting like a couple of sick cows, and toughen up."

"Okay, Niki, this is what I'm going to do. Tomorrow I'll call some very special friends of mine to pick up your Mustang at our home. They will transport it in an enclosed trailer to their shop and repair it so you could never tell it was ever damaged. No one will know, because these people do this sort of work for the agency, all the time. How does that agree with you?"

"Thanks, Dad."
Matt went back to reading his novel with less interest than before and Niki returned to preparing their meal.

The evening was spent thinking, with little conversation, for there was much to consider. Before retiring for the night Baxter took Matt aside and absolved him of any wrongdoing.

"None of this was your fault, Matt, do you understand?"

Chapter 23

Blackstone in D.C.

Waiting in a roach-infested hotel on the outskirts of Washington D.C., Blackstone sat on his lousy bed, considering his options. Twice he had paid to have Savage killed and each time the assassins had failed, and now both shooters were dead. The thought of their deaths didn't bother him in the slightest degree, but the money he had spent on those two failures put a knot in his colon.

Blackstone never considered the enormity of his crimes and he never would. He was a borderline psychotic.

"What should I do? Try for the third time, which might be pushing my luck or should I take my new identity and leave the good old U.S. of A. I have plenty of money to keep me in fine shape for years to come. My plans are sound and I don't think the agency is looking for me, or even cares about me. Yet, if any of them ever get in my way, I will kill them without the slightest hesitation."

Blackstone wasn't sure Baxter and the others knew it was he who had been trying to kill Matt, but, if they did realize it was him, then all the better, he thought. Knowing he was still lurking around would eliminate any peace of mind in their lives.

Bobby Blackstone was a decisive person who never sat around trying to make up his mind. While on the phone making reservations, he gathered his essentials, packing them in two suitcases.

The 26-mile taxi ride to the Dulles International Airport in Chantilly County, Virginia got him to the Air France terminal in plenty of time. He used his correct passport with his real given name. In fact, he hoped they would discover he had left the country.

Bobby had been around the block a few times in his life and had an eye for trouble. As he sat waiting, he never quit watching the crowds for anything suspicious. He felt good about his assumption they hadn't had time to put together anything incriminating on him.

The boarding call came and he took his first class seat with an air of conceit. He said to himself, "I'll never again fly with those inconsequential people."

Bobby never had any trouble with his self-esteem, in fact if you knew this guy you would say he was one arrogant punk.

Once the plane was in the air, Blackstone started to relax. The flight to Paris was a long one, but he didn't care. The service was good and the trip would give him plenty of time to read and sleep as much as he wanted.

DeGualle Airport was an impressive place. He had been there once, on assignment, years ago and felt he would enjoy seeing the city again. Of course, what he wanted most from this place was to hook up with some of his old culprits in crime. These were the people Blackstone had once known, and they possessed all the wonderful talents for forgery and disguises. He needed some new documents, different than any he had used in the past.

In due time Paris, France would be the last place where Blackstone would exist; he would simply disappear, hopefully for all time. There was no doubt, whatsoever in his mind, that the F.B.I. would one day track him to Paris, for he hadn't tried to hide the fact. If all went well they would never discover his new identity.

Two days later Blackstone contacted his connection to the people who would do the work for him. It wasn't going to be cheap but that was expected and all a part of the plan.

"On that we are agreed, are we not?"

"Yes of course, your price is what I anticipated and the work looks exceptional." Blackstone laughed and said, "My friend, I hope I never see you again."

"You're welcome here anytime old man, as long as you have plenty of cash in your pocket."

He was no longer Bobby Blackstone the American who once worked as a trusted agent for the F.B.I. From now on he would be known as Warren Tidwell from Birmingham, England, a retired businessman. He was now the elusive enemy he had always wanted to be.

Blackstone had been transformed into a distinguished looking English gentleman, in his late sixties, with graying hair, small neatly trimmed mustache, steel rimmed glasses and a walking cane. The expensive tailored suit and bowler hat stated he was a man of means. His new image was one that pleased him. He had always considered himself a cut above everyone else and now he could act the part.

Briefly, Warren Tidwell (Blackstone) studied the train schedule that would haul him to Calais in northern France. The Euro Tunnel would take him 31 miles under the English Channel to the White Cliffs of Dover. Traveling on the high-speed Eurostar sounded exciting. It was something he had always wanted to do, from the time he had first read about the completion of the tunnel. The Channel Tunnel is also used by the worlds largest roll-on / roll off vehicle transport train, and international rail freight trains. A prestigious engineering magazine, American Society of Civil Engineers identified the tunnel as one of the Seven Wonders of the World.

Warren could only imagine what his train trip would be like, as he waited to board. In today's world, this train is considered to be "state of the art." Having an English passport, driver's license, and all the other important paperwork in hand, verifying his existence, made him feel confident about his future success.

Now that he was inside England's borders, all he wanted to do was melt away into the populous and disappear from those who would want to destroy him.

Some distance up the Thames River, from London, Warren Tidwell found the perfect place to settle down until he was ready to make his last move. Oxford was the place where he rented an authentic, true-to-life,

English cottage. It was just as he had pictured in his mind, with a white picket fence, cobblestone sidewalk, and beautiful rose bushes encircling this ideal cottage. The perfection of his new residence was to enhance his image as an English gentleman. The new person he had become was far removed from what he once was as an American government agent. He found it challenging, acting as good guy. He had always believed "good guys finish last."

Without the slightest doubt in his mind he knew Baxter would eventually come after him with the intent and purpose to put an end to his "evil ways." Yet Blackstone, now Warren Tidwell, believed he was superior intellectually, physically and in every other way to Baxter and, if by simple luck, this stupid Russian did find him, well he would just have to kill him.

From some inner source of malice, (Blackstone) remembered the hatred he had for his old comrade, Fletcher. Who did he think he was, lecturing him about contracting a hit on that Matt Savage? It was a needful thing to do and he was the only one with the resolve to do it. When Fletcher told him Savage was still alive and his hired hit man was dead, he became extremely angered, so he hired another killer. Somewhere in his dark, depraved soul, he found an enjoyment in ordering someone killed.

Chapter 24

Confession

"Hello, Baxter, How does my home suit the three of you?" Staggs said.

"It's absolutely a special place. I'm sure you and your lovely wife can't wait for your retirement."

"Listen up, I called to tell you Blackstone has left the country. A couple of days ago he flew out of Dulles for Paris and that mutt didn't even try to hide his tracks."

"What do you think he is up to Brook? Do you think he has given up on us?"

"Maybe he has, but I truly don't know."

"Have a safe trip home tomorrow. Lock the place up and I'll talk to you when you return."

The following morning they left early so that they might have a casual drive home, and arrive before dark. The conversation, as usual, was pleasant and stimulating. The passing countryside was a beautiful sight to behold. All in all it was a great morning.

Two hours into the drive home Baxter's cell phone rang.

"Good morning, my friend."

"It is a good morning, Staggs. What's up?"

"I want you folks to be cool when I tell you what has happened. I'm sure deep inside you knew this day would come and well, it's arrived. This morning I was called into my boss's office for a little sit-down conversation. Some pretty difficult questions were asked of me that I wasn't equipped to answer."

"Are you on the level? I hope not."

"There is no bull in this conversation, everything is true. Tomorrow morning at 9 am the four of us will be in the director's office or there will be hell to pay, he said. Promise me you guys will do as he says!"

"What choices do we have?" Baxter answered.

"I'm sorry for spoiling your day. Baxter, I will meet all of you at your home when you return. I think it would be a good idea to compare notes. We don't want to lie to the man or confuse our story."

There was an air of deathly silence as Baxter explained the predicament to Niki and Matt. Deep in each of their worried souls they wondered if this meeting tomorrow would bring and end to their freedom and careers.

At the Directors Office:

"Good morning, folks. Please come in and take a seat." He pointed to the four chairs sitting directly across from his desk.

Apprehension hung heavy over this group and Matt felt he was carrying the whole load.

For a few moments he shuffled a stack of papers on his desk, not making eye contact with any of them. It seemed the longest time before he spoke.

He glared at them with his fiery blue-eyes, that were dangerously narrowed, and finally berated them, impatiently. "For the present time I want all of you to sit there like good children and listen to what I have to say. No questions, no comments, no excuses. Just listen! When the time is right I promise you, I will have enough questions to go around.

"A few days ago I observed an ugly scab in my command, you might say. It's curious, the more I scratched at it the more it bled. The more it bled the more questions arose, with no answers."

"Brook Staggs, Aleksandar Blinski / Baxter, Niki Blinski, each of you have served the agency well and I can confirm this. The agency is proud of your service. Now, Mr. Matt Savage, I'm not quite sure how you fit into the picture. The only thing I do know about you is you're an ex-con. Matt lowered his head in shame and didn't look up. For the moment he felt alone, detached from it all. Niki reached over and took hold of Matt's quivering hand and held it tightly in hers. The director stopped talking and focused his attention on Matt and his hand in hers.

He continued, "It was brought to my attention, quite unexpectedly, that a team of my F.B.I. investigators spent a considerable amount of time out at Fletcher's destroyed cabin, at your direction, Brook."

Brook started to speak, but his boss held up his hand as if to say, not now.

"I know you three were snooping around Fletcher's place," pointing at Niki, Matt, and Baxter.

"As I looked into this situation I found something very interesting. Agent Fletcher retired quite unexpectedly, a few days before his cabin blew up and then another agent, who was a friend of Fletcher's, also retired. His name is Blackstone. It's strange; we don't even know where either of these men are. It's as if those two agents completely vanished from the face of God's green Earth."

"Lady and gentlemen, I'm in a quagmire. Something stinks to high heaven and one way or the other I'm going to get to the bottom of this. I've picked up one end of the stick, so now I'm required to take a look at the other end. What I find on the other end of this better not be dog shit. Do you people understand me?"

All four shook their heads in the affirmative.

"No matter how long this session takes, we are going to come to an understanding. It will be an understanding, which I'm completely happy with, where I know the whole truth. I truly hope and pray no one leaves my office this day in handcuffs."

Matt felt dreadful and could only guess how his friends were feeling. He felt like the odd man out. His thoughts sickened him. "If any one of us goes down, I'm sure I will be the one they make the example of. I have no juice with this man. I have served time in a federal prison and I well know how cops feel about ex-con's." Never before had Matt ever wondered if his friends would stand up for him, but now he wasn't all too sure.

For the next half hour the Director never stopped talking, barraging them with one concern after another. With an unrevealing smirk he asked, "Mr. Savage, how is it that you're a part of this situation? Go ahead, you can speak now. I would like some answers."

"Sir, in 1972 I was recruited by a Secret Service agent named Webb. At the time I was working for the Los Angeles Police Department. He told me about a program called, 'Back Door'. I was told it would give me an opportunity to work for their agency. A short time later I was introduced to Baxter, who became my mentor and trainer. Much has happened over those years and I call Niki and Baxter my dear friends."

"Very interesting, Matt. I'll get back to you."

"Does his story agree with you, Baxter?"

"It does."

Baxter didn't like being on the receiving end of questions, but the time had come for their story to be told, no matter what the consequences might be.

"It seems obvious you three want Fletcher for something more than a tea party. Baxter, you answer me this question. Why do you want Fletcher?"

"Sir, we have good reason to believe Fletcher hired a hit man to kill Matt."

"Well, did Matt get shot?"

"Yes, he did. We tried to prevent the shooter from taking that dreadful shot but we were a little too late. Niki got to Matt first, where he lay. She spoke to him and he faintly answered as he slipped away, or so we thought. From a distance we called the paramedic to the location and watched and listened on the police radio. Through their careful examination they found he was barely alive and transported him by life-flight to the University of Utah Medical Center. Then, with the help of the field agent in Salt Lake City, we kept him under wraps. The news believed he was dead and his family put him to rest, believing he was dead."

"Baxter, what happened to the shooter?"

"I'm proud to say, he will never again shoot anyone in the back, and yes, I shot him just before he took the second shot aimed at my daughter, Niki."

"I don't understand this story. What would have ever motivated Fletcher to hire a professional killer?"

"Well, it's like this, Fletcher was afraid of what Matt might say some day," answered Baxter. Now comes the part of the story I wonder if I can sell you on. However, the story is entirely true."

"Well, give it a shot. I can't wait to hear what you have to say."

" In 1976 I received an assignment from the bureau labeled Top Secret. The assignment was professional, spelled out in detail. Precise directions were given for me to follow, which at the time I found hard to believe, but being the obedient agent that I was, I went ahead and carried it out as ordered."

"Alright, Baxter, spit it out. I'm all ears!"

"This first operation was to take a bank down in Ely, Nevada."

"You've got to be kidding me!"

"No sir, I'm not."

"Who did the robbery?"

"Matt and another agent. I only met the other agent on one occasion and have never seen him since. Everything these men needed was provided, even an aircraft for the get-away. This operation was given a code name, 'Starlight,' by whoever was the author of it."

"In all my years working for the F.B.I., I have never been so completely surprised by such an inconceivable story. You are right, Baxter, this is one story that will be hard to sell and who in their right mind would ever believe it?"

"Sir, you will, when all the story and facts are known."

"How many robberies were you three involved in?"

"Four in all. The last three my daughter and Matt handled. One was in Grand Junction, Colorado, another in Rock Springs, Wyoming and the last one in Henderson, Nevada. This last bank robbery had several others helping with a distraction ploy and the get-away."

The director leaned back in his chair, shaking his head in apparent amazement. He stared out the window and said nothing, which kept his audience wondering and worrying about what his next move would be.

"Do any of you have proof that this story is nothing more than a pipe dream?"

Matt and Niki both spoke up in unison and said, "No sir, we don't."

After a short pause, Baxter replied, "You know sir, I've been around for many years and have seen just about everything anyone could dream up. So, when I received those orders I was suspicious, but I had no one to verify their authenticity. I knew I needed to protect the three of us against the unknown. Against protocol, I copied two of the three orders. I hid them away and up until now I've told no one about them."

"Baxter, you never cease to amaze me. You realize I will need to see those copies."
"It can be arranged, but it will take me a couple of days to retrieve them."

Then the slightest smile appeared on his lips. "All of this information is putting an overload on my circuits. I'm giving each of you a direct order, which you will obey to the letter, or I promise you I will hang all of your hides out for the whole world to see. Do you people understand me?"

They all quickly answered, "Yes!"

"For the present time, each of you will cease to pursue these men, and above all keep your mouths tightly shut. I will be calling all of you in for another meeting. I think we are finished here for the day. You can leave now."

Three men and one lady walked out of the director's office feeling humble, full of fear and trepidation. What the future held in store for them was something to be seen. At least they had all cleared the first hurdle.

The next move was up to Baxter to bring the director some proof to substantiate their story, and it needed to be irrefutable. If for some terrible reason he wasn't able to find the records, Matt was afraid all hope would be lost.

"I'm truly sorry, Brook, for exposing you to this mess, but I needed help and didn't know who to turn to."

"It's alright Baxter, I've weathered a great deal around here over the years and this too will pass. But, to be blunt, nothing quite as dramatic as this has ever happened to me."

Matt wandered off, found a chair, and slumped his weary body into it. He was undoubtedly worried about the possibility of being made an example, by being sent off to jail with his friends abandoning him, and then walking away from it all. He had the frightful feeling of spending the remainder of his life locked up, which in his mind would be the same as a death sentence.

There is no accuser more dreadful than the one, which resides inside our mind. Matt's accuser was working overtime and he felt the guilt.
"Oh, there you are, Matt. I was wondering where you were. What do you say we get out of this place and head for home before the man changes his mind about something he hadn't thought of."

"Most certainly, I would like to leave and the sooner the better."

Chapter 25

Walked Away

He felt even more depressed as he gathered together his few possessions and in the quiet hours of the night, walked away from the only anchor in his life.

Leaving his friends behind made him feel completely worthless. He wanted to die and bring an end to all of his problems. Matt's emotions were completely out of character for him, but he hardly remembered how he once was so he had little to compare his feelings with.

Matt's depression was a combination of several factors. One, which wasn't so evident, was his physical condition. He struggled with the lack of strength and energy. Mentally he felt like a lost soul. He couldn't see anything positive about his life except for his two friends and he felt the only thing he did for them was put their lives at risk. Leaching off the goodness of his friends wasn't helping with the realization he didn't have any money, a job or a career.

He hiked in the foothills for a time until he found a large pine tree with low hanging boughs for cover. He climbed under the tree and wearily leaned his body against the trunk. For the remainder of the night he stared into the cool darkness until the sun arose, shaking him loose from the shadows of his feelings.

Solitude is a wonderful thing when one is at peace with oneself, yet peace wasn't something Matt enjoyed at the present time. The beauty and solitude of the moment didn't quite make everything right for Matt.

The next morning Niki went to Matt's room to see if he would join them for breakfast.

When he didn't answer her call, she hollered out again, but louder," Hey Matt!" After a few seconds she slowly opened the bedroom door and quietly crept inside. His bed hadn't been slept in. Lying on the pillow was piece of paper. "I'm so sorry I've become such a burden to you and your father. Good-bye, my dear Niki."

Niki screamed out, "Dad, Matt is gone!"

Baxter came to Matt's room and quickly walked through it, checking for anything unusual. "Niki, I don't understand what's going on in that man's mind. Why would he just get up and leave like that?"

"Dad, take a look at this note he left on his pillow."

Baxter said nothing after reading the note. He crumpled it in his hand while glaring at Niki. What had happened between the two of them?

"Come on, Niki, let's see if we can find the knot-head before something else awful happens to him. Doesn't he realize there are people who would kill him in a moment if they found him wandering alone in these hills?"

All day Baxter and Niki drove around the county searching every conceivable place they could think of, without any success.

On two different occasions Matt saw his friends searching, but he wasn't ready to be found.

Niki was worried sick about Matt. She loved this guy and knew how vulnerable he was. He wasn't his old self and maybe never would return to the man he once was, and now they couldn't even protect him.

It was a long and miserable night with no sleep for Matt. He was considering all of his options, which were few. He felt like a loser knowing what he was putting his friends through, and still not knowing what he should do.

In the wee hours of the morning, Matt made up his mind. He knew he was made of better stuff than what he had exemplified lately. With new resolve, he hiked back to the Blinski's home, found a seat on the front porch steps and waited as he watched the sunrise ushering in a new day, with new hope for a better day.

Niki shouted out when she saw Matt sitting on the steps.

"Should I kick your butt now or later? What were you thinking of, running off like that and worrying us to death? I want you to know we have been looking for you all over this county. Don't you know we love you and couldn't stand it if something else happened to you?"

She sat down next to Matt and gave him a loving hug, holding him tight in her arms.

Baxter stood quietly in the background and watched. Niki had said it all and there was no need for him to say anything more.

"Alright, you two we have a meeting with Staggs and the director in a couple of hours. Hurry and get yourselves ready."

Chapter 26

The Director's Office

The director invited them into his office. "Welcome to this meeting folks. I'm hoping the decision I've made with this plan will ultimately bring this situation to closure. "I'm happy to see you back with us, Matt. You need to be tough and hang in there. One day this will all be over.

"Baxter, I appreciate those documents you sent as they helped a great deal. I've looked them over and my first impression is, they seem to be legitimate. Do you have copies?"

"Yes sir, I do."

"I've spent many hours investigating your stories and carefully looking over the documents you were so wise to hang on to, Baxter. Those papers might be the only proof we have.

"I don't know how you came to your conclusion, but you have seriously suggested you believe these three men, all at one time, were working for the F.B.I. and are the ones behind 'Starlight.' Now, I too have to consider them persons of interest. We don't have a solid piece of evidence on those three, but given enough time, I'm sure we will dig up something on them.

"Those crimes you folks committed under the directions and umbrella of the agency have no bite to them anymore. I'm sure you understand the statute of limitations.

"One of my biggest fears is that this story gets out to the news media and the sky-rockets go off. The damage it would do to the agency would be irreparable. So, I'm warning each of you to use great caution in everything you do and say. For the immediate future, I've decided to let you continue on with your search, unofficially that is.

"Baxter and Niki Blinski, both of you have had stellar careers and more than enough years of service in the department for a good retirement."

Niki looked over at her dad with a troubled frown on her face.

"I want both of you to fill out your retirement papers and date them with today's date. I will hold them in abeyance in case something happens. You can each continue working for the department as if nothing has changed. Your only assignment is to catch these scoundrels. Agent Staggs will continue helping you with whatever you need, but you will keep your association with him quiet. For the time being, all of you let agent Tom McGee alone. I personally want to keep an eye on him.

"Matt, I can only say one thing, the agency really screwed up when it came to taking care of you in that program called 'Back Door.' It looks as though promises were made that were never kept. We only used and abused you in taking care of certain unpleasant things we weren't willing to do ourselves. I'm sorry to say this; you don't exist in the eyes of the department. Although you have my permission to keep working with your friends, just be careful, and get well.

"I will keep in touch with each of you through agent Staggs. Good hunting."

Chapter 27

Force a Confession

On the drive home, Matt wondered what they would do to force Fletcher to come clean, once they had captured him.

"Baxter, how are we going to compel Fletcher to talk? He is venal and a corrupt man who won't give up his secrets without a fight. Maybe we could bribe or trick him into talking."

Baxter had all the virtues of age and knew what to do. He was determined to make Fletcher tell it all, and he had the device that would accomplish the task. "The Russian water grave."

"Folks, I have the perfect solution, guaranteed to make him spill his guts."

"Please tell me, Baxter. I'm listening. Whatever you're talking about, sounds intriguing."

"If those liberal half-wits in our country believe water boarding is a form of torture, well, if they saw this device it would fracture their minds.

"I'll tell you all about it, Matt, when the time is right, but for now it would be best if I don't explain the device in detail, but there is one thing I will tell you. Many years ago I saw this contrivance demonstrated in Russia, during the time I was a K.G.B. agent, and it is something I've never forgotten."

Niki remained silent, carefully listening to her dad. She knew exactly what he was talking about and didn't like that thought. It caused cold chills to run up her back. One of two things would happen to a person who was subjected to this device. They would eventually talk or simply lose their mind.

On numerous occasions, Baxter acted as an advisor to the C.I.A. and had met with their agents to discuss techniques on gathering information, particularly ones he was familiar with. As a Russian agent, he had seen many methods of extracting information from unwilling parties. These particular methods were not known in this country. He often wondered how it was that one human could be so cruel to another human being. The techniques used fear, physical pain, mental torture, and were all fused together to cause the most abundant and exquisite pain.

The intelligence community encompasses more organizations than anyone can begin to name, but all have one function in common, and that is to gather information. Every world government and military survives or dies on knowledge, or the lack of it. Even big businesses need to know what their competitors are up to. Without that valuable information they too would simply die where they stand. Baxter understood completely the importance of gathering information, because his whole life had evolved around this type of work.

Chapter 28

Niki's Cobra Returned

With some careful conniving and a few little white lies, Baxter had been able to get Niki's Cobra returned to their home and parked in the driveway without her becoming any the wiser. You wouldn't believe the amount of damage a few nasty bullet holes could do to the body of a beautiful, prized car. Considering the abuse it had suffered, it was amazing how good the car looked. Every speck of damage was repaired to a condition better than new.

The bill from the auto repair shop told the story. He was so grateful none of those shots had hit Niki or Matt. Any one of those bullets could have been disastrous. The thought sent a cold chill up his back.

"Oh, Niki!" Baxter shouted. "Come here! I've got something to show you." She walked into the study with a warm, loving smile on her face.

"Yes, Dad, what is it?"

"Come with me."

Father and daughter walked to the front porch where he covered her eyes with his hand before letting her step outside.

"Take a look, will you?"

Parked there, looking exactly as it did on the day she bought it was her beautiful chrome-yellow Cobra.

She let out with a squeal of a little girl on Christmas morning, jumping up and down with glee.

"Dad, I love you!" Tears rolled down her cheeks.

"Go on and take a look at it, you silly girl."

Baxter stood tall and straight with his arms folded watching Niki examining her car. This sight of his daughter brought him much joy and happiness. He knew how much she loved her Cobra.

"Dad, no matter how hard I look, I can't find anything wrong with my car. It looks perfect, certainly not anything like the last time I saw it. Did the repair shop give you an invoice? I would like to see the total bill."

"They did and I paid for it, so don't you worry yourself about it."

"I appreciate your kindness Dad, but just the same, it would be interesting to know everything that was fixed on the car."

"Alright, Niki. There is quite a list, are you ready for me to read it?"

"Oh yes, when it comes to my car you have my undivided attention."

"First on the invoice, both front and rear windshields had to be replaced. It looks as if one bullet took them both out. Another bullet ripped open the roof like it was a can of soup. Three other shots hit the grill, completely destroying it along with the radiator. The water pump was cracked. Your battery had a hole completely through it. I'm surprised you got the car home before it quit on you, altogether. The dash pad had to be replaced and one side of the rear seat was ruined. Many more small items had to be restored so they looked like new.

As Baxter read through the long list of repairs, he realized all to vividly the danger Niki had been exposed to. He was a loving father and was sickened at the thought of the possibility of losing his daughter. Twice before in her life he had lost her for a time but she had survived, somehow. He felt it was more than good luck that he still had his daughter around.

"Come here, Niki." He pulled her close to him and hugged her tightly as he offered a silent prayer of gratitude, in his heart, to his Heavenly Father for saving her life.

"Well Dad, what did it cost? I need to know."

"After deducting the shop discounts and some of the minor things they did for free, the total bill came to $12,793.00.

"That's a lot of money, Dad, and I want to pay you back."

"If it hadn't been for the friends I have in our own departments repair shop we never would have been able to get your Cobra repaired without involving the Sheriff's Department and that is something we do not want to have happen in this matter."

 Matt stood back and became a silent observer to their conversation. Often he felt as though he was a member of the Blinski family, but not today. He was quite aware he wasn't part of this family, at this moment in time.

Chapter 29

Albuquerque

When Fletcher realized he had stepped in it, he left Albuquerque with piston-like speed, in fear of being tracked down and caught. It was a stupid thing to call McGee, but he had to know if Baxter was alive and still snooping around for him. Hopefully, the agency didn't know about the phone call. If they knew, well, he would be long gone from there before they acted on the information and if they didn't know, he had nothing to worry about.

He had no concrete plans from one day to the next, related to his destination. Traveling this way was more exciting and fun for him than making a set of regimented plans he had to stick to.

After driving several hundred miles, he arrived in Salt Lake City. It was late in the afternoon, so he decided to stop, rent a room and have himself a good meal at an upscale restaurant.

From the hotel lobby, Fletcher picked up a few travel brochures of interesting places to visit in the area. The brochure that caught his fancy had a picture of a fly fisherman on a beautiful stream. That was something he had always wanted to try.

The next morning he spent some time on the phone trying to locate a fishing lodge outside of Jackson Hole, Wyoming. A few years back he had inquired of these people about a fishing trip. Fletcher remembered how excited he was when thinking about the prospects of spending a few days fishing on the Green River for those beautiful rainbow and brown trout.

With thoughts of fly-fishing foremost in his mind, the concerns about his past problems seemed to fade away. What fun it would be to hook a five-pound rainbow or maybe even a larger one.

While trying to find his way to the interstate he drove past something that caught his attention. He wondered, what is this place? He knew Salt Lake City was Mormon country and this must have something to do with them. To satisfy his curiosity he found a parking space and walked back to the entrance. The sign read, "Welcome to Temple Square."

Religion had always confused Fletcher and he hadn't found much use for it in his life. Yet, as he stood at the entrance, looking in at the beauty of the grounds he saw, it pleased him, so he walked in.

"Good morning, sir. May we help you?" a young lady asked.

"No thank you, I just want to look around."

"If you have any questions, we would be happy to try and answer them for you."

He nodded his head as if to say, "I understand," and walked away.

For more than two hours he wandered through the beautiful gardens. He read the plaques on the statues, walked through the museum, sat in the Tabernacle and listened to the demonstration of the unique acoustics of the building that was built so many years ago by pioneers.

When he saw the statue of the Savior after his resurrection, he took a seat and gazed at its beauty and pondered many things. In his thoughts he felt surprised at what he was feeling. It was certainly an emotion he had never experienced before, but what he found most strange was he liked the peace that surrounded him.

Before he left Temple Square he turned around and took one last look at the marvelous building they called a temple. The words written on the temple said, "The House of the Lord."

What does that mean? he thought "I know the Lord doesn't live there."

When he walked back to his truck he remembered something he had long forgotten. Matt Savage was a Mormon. He never knew the young man or much about him. How he wished his partners hadn't put a hit out on him, for it had changed his life situation for the worst.

The first thing he saw was a parking ticket under his wiper blade. He snatched it up and threw it on the seat. "This is one ticket I'm not paying," he said out loud, in disgust.

The next leg of his trip was around 200 miles. Fletcher [Dubois] pulled into Jackson Hole, Wyoming. Because of the late hour he decided to wait until morning before driving to the lodge. The last thing he wanted was to get lost out there in the boon-docks. They had no street addresses and he wasn't sure if his cell phone would work.

At the first light of day he was up, and excited as any young boy would be, going on his first fishing trip. He called the lodge for directions, and had no trouble finding the place. The lodge was at the end of a dirt road, and was much farther from town than he had thought.

For the next three days he floated the Green River with his own personal guide, catching more beautiful trout than he could count.

He was sad when the fishing trip come to an end. "Thank you so much, Marvin, for these special days of fishing and an unforgettable experience."

"Mr. Dubois, you are more than welcome. We hope you will visit us again someday."

"You know Marvin, I don't believe in a heaven, but if there is one, this must be what it's like."

"Well, my friend, there is a heaven and you just got to sample a small portion of it."

Fletcher, smiled warmly at his new friend. He threw his suitcase in the back of the truck bed and drove off down the dusty dirt road. He thought to himself, "There wasn't anything like this back home. What have I been missing in my life?"

Fletcher's wanderings over the following two weeks took him to places he had only read about.

Yellowstone Park, with all its natural wonders, thrilled him. Seeing this place in all its inherent beauty was really something to enjoy. There was Old Faithful, the geysers, hot pots, wildlife and of course the fishing streams and lakes with all the excitement and possibility of great fishing. His only regret was that he didn't have someone to enjoy all these splendid adventures with.

On the outskirts of the West Gate of Yellowstone was a small town called West Thumb. Not knowing where he wanted to go really didn't concern him. He stopped, bought some groceries and studied his Idaho state map for possibilities of places he might like to see. To the southwest was a national monument called Craters of the Moon and northwest from there was the Sawtooth Wilderness Area, which tickled his fancy.

"Well, lets see old man, what we might venture to this day. Time is wasting and I'm not getting any younger." Fletcher didn't like talking to himself but found he was doing it more often these days.

The lodge pole pines grew up to the edge of the road, towering high above it. He was feeling like a mouse passing through the bottom of a deep canyon. This scene continued on for the next twenty miles. For him it was quite a pleasurable sight to see.

Chapter 30

Hitchhiker

A young woman was hitchhiking on the outskirts of Rexburg. As he passed her, he said to himself, "Why not?" He pulled over and carefully backed up to where she stood. She walked over to his truck as he rolled down the window.

"Good morning. Where are you heading?"

"California."

"You have a long trip ahead of you and you're welcome to ride as far as I go. Put your gear in the back of the truck and hop in."

"Thank you for the ride. I've been standing out here for a long time and was beginning to think no one was going to stop."

"My name is Jimmy Dubois." He held out his hand and she cautiously shook it. Fletcher felt comfortable announcing his new identity.

"By-the-way, what's your name?"

"Nancy Burgess."

"Nice name. When I was in high school I was head-over heels in love with a girl named Nancy. Oh, that was many years ago."

"What happened? Did you marry her?"

"No, I'm sad to say. We just grew up and went our own separate ways after graduation. I never did see her again."

"That's sad. Are you married?"

"Not any more. My wife passed away a couple of years ago, and I finally got up the gumption to get out and see the rest of the country. I just visited Yellowstone Park. What a place that is!"

He could lie with the best of them. Certainly, he wasn't going to tell her he hated his "old lady" and they had been divorced for years.

Jimmy Dubois, thought to himself, "This is nice having someone to talk to and especially someone as pretty as she is."

"Nancy, what part of California are you headed for, if you don't mind me asking?"

"San Jose." She had a troubled look on her pretty face when she said, San Jose.

Both were silent for the next few minutes.

Dubois smiled. "I've an idea." He could be quite charming when he wanted to. "I'm also headed for California but not in the most direct route. You see, I've been sort of sight-seeing at different places of interest. I'm not in a great hurry to get there and no one is waiting for me nor do I know anyone there."

"What are you suggesting, Mr. Dubois?"

"I feel a little awkward even saying this, but Idaho Falls is coming up soon and I had planned on turning west for a place called Craters of the Moon. I had better say what's on my mind. If you would like to take a different route to California, which of course would take a little longer getting there, you're more than welcome to tag along. I would enjoy the company. You see, I get tired of talking to myself," and then he laughed out loud.

"That's nice of you to offer, but no, I don't think I should."

"I understand. You don't know me. We just met a few miles back and it was quite brazen of me to suggest such a thing."

Dubois asked, "Nancy would you watch for highway 20 going west? We are entering Idaho Falls and I've never been in the town before. I can let you off there, if you like."

After a few city blocks she said, "There is the highway marker, Mr."

Dubois took a left and pulled over to the curb and said, "It's been nice having you for company and I wish you a safe journey."

Nancy slowly opened the door and stepped out of his truck. She looked back at him wondering what she should do. He could see that she was struggling with indecision, trying to decide if she should change her mind.

Dubois recognized the look, and said. "Nancy the offer still stands. I have lots of food and more money than I can spend. This trip will cost you nothing and when we get to San Jose I will drive you to your front door-step."

Poor Nancy had very little money and hadn't eaten a bite since early yesterday. She was starved and worried where she might get something to eat. This was an offer too good to refuse.

A big grin appeared on her face. "Mister, you've got a deal, and thank you."

"I'm glad you changed your mind. Seeing all these beautiful sights alone isn't nearly as fun as when you have someone to share them with.

"Come on, get back in the truck and I'll take you out for a good meal. Would you like that?"

"Sure, I would like that a lot. I haven't eaten since yesterday, and boy do I have hunger pangs."

Jimmy Dubois enjoyed watching Nancy woof it down. He couldn't ever remember seeing a girl eat so much food. It was as if she was afraid of not getting another meal.

When they finished eating he asked Nancy if she would like to go shopping for some camping gear. He hadn't needed any gear before now, but this might be the best time to buy some.

"Sure, it's been quite a spell since I've had the opportunity to go shopping for anything. I have been stuck on my uncle's ranch, way out in eastern Montana and we didn't get to town very often."

"Okay then, we'll have fun spending some of my money."

The truth of the matter was, he was having more fun spending a chunk of change at the sporting goods store than he had in a very long time. Maybe it was because he found it gratifying to spend money on someone else, other than himself.

"You spent a lot of money in town. Can you afford that?"

Dubois nodded with real pleasure. "I sure can. That gear is all yours," and he made sure she understood they each had their own tents.

With his truck loaded, the two new friends headed west, to see what they might see.

"Sure, it's only money and what good is it if you can't spend it? Furthermore, I've worked many years for this so that one day I could enjoy it."

He had "worked many years for his money," was a true statement, but he certainly hadn't earned all of it.

Naturally Nancy had some concerns about heading into the unknown with a strange man. So far, he had been a gentleman and made her feel at ease. She hoped nothing would change her feeling about him.

Nancy Burgess was a young woman with fine features that were accented by her blonde hair, which was gathered into a ponytail. Her blue-green eyes sparkled with animation. She was a tall girl with a superb figure and Dubois could only imagine how she would look in an evening gown.

Fatigue took over Miss Nancy. She laid her head back on the seat and closed her eyes. As she was dozing off, a thought crossed her mind, "I have a real live sugar daddy here. Don't spoil it girl."

Dubois wondered what she was running from. Whatever it is, it couldn't have been good or she wouldn't have risked hitchhiking. These days are not safe for anyone, especially a young woman as pretty as she.

A number of miles down the road Dubois noticed his passenger had awakened. "How did you rest, Nancy?"

"Just fine, thank you. I didn't realize how tired I was."

"Would you have ever believed the first nuclear-powered submarine reactor and simulator were built just a few miles north of here, by the famous naval officer, Hyman Rickover. Admiral Rickover was called the 'father of the first nuclear submarine,' named the Nautilus. Pretty intriguing stuff."

"If you say so. I've never given that subject any thought."

"I would suggest if you ever get time to read, you might find it very interesting to read about Admiral Rickover. He was an amazing engineer and quite a character!"

"Mr. Dubois, I apologize if I seem disinterested, I'm not. I enjoy listening to you talk, so please don't stop on my account. Maybe I'll learn something new." She smiled warmly at him as if to positively punctuate her statement.

The remainder of the day was leisurely spent stopping wherever he had the notion to. Whenever there was a picture to be taken he was out of the truck snapping pictures. The Craters of the Moon National Monument stirred their interest, causing both of them to wonder what had happened there so long ago. It was weird and impressive with miles and miles of lava fields that closely resembled the surface of the moon.

"I've an idea, Nancy. How would you like to see the world famous Sun Valley Ski Resort. It's not far from here!"

"That would be fine with me, but remember I'm just along for the ride,"

Nancy answered. "You don't need my permission."

"I know, but it would please me if you were able to enjoy yourself."

There was still daylight left as they drove into Ketchum, Idaho. The ski resort was a couple of miles up the road from town. Of course, it was off-season for skiing, but that hadn't stopped the tourists from enjoying its beauty.

With a questioning look, he said. "Nancy, do you feel comfortable walking around this resort with an old man?"

"Don't be silly, there's nothing wrong with you."

"Alright, let's go."

Dubois stopped at the first clothing store he saw. He walked Nancy inside and said, "I insist you buy some new clothes, and get yourself a coat and some boots while you're at it."

"No, Jim, I shouldn't."

"I won't take no for an answer. A young lady as pretty as you, should have something nice to wear. When you're finished shopping, I'll meet you by the cashier to pay for it. Alright?"

Somewhat embarrassed, she said, "Thank you," and walked off.

Dubois hurried across the street to a ski lodge and reserved two separate rooms for the night.

"That will be $200.00 Mr. Dubois."

He handed the clerk two one hundred dollar bills.

"Sir, it's our policy that we see some sort of credit card, if you don't mind. Your credit card will only be used if there is a balance left on your account."

Even though this sort of policy angered him, he was no fool. No comment would be made about his feelings, as he didn't want this spud farmer remembering him. He took a Visa card with his new name Jimmy Dubois out of his wallet, which satisfied the clerk.

Dubois returned to the clothing store just as Nancy approached the clerk with several articles of clothing in her arms. He smiled warmly at Nancy as she beamed with excitement.

" Did you get every thing you need?"

"Yes, I believe so."

He paid the clerk $273 dollars and was grateful for his credit card. Once outside the store Dubois suggested, "Lets sit here on this bench and talk for a few minutes, if you don't mind.

"I can only imagine how uncomfortable and possibly afraid you might be about this whole situation. You might believe I'm trying to buy some special favors from you, because I bought you these clothes. Please let me assure you, I have no such designs. I only wanted some company on the remainder of my trip, that's all." He grew a small smile and continued. "Well, maybe I bought you these clothes and camping gear because I've never had a daughter of my own to buy things for." Both sat in silence as they considered his statement.

Finally, he said, "If, at any time you want to go, just tell me and I'll buy you a bus ticket home. Is that alright with you?"

"Of course. I've had a lot of questions cross my mind today. I suppose I would be a downright fool not to worry. I'm a desperate person who needs to get away from her uncle, and I do appreciate your help. I guess we will have to work on gaining each others trust. Time will tell."

"Okay, Miss Nancy, how does this sound for starters in gaining each others trust?" He reached in his pocket and handed her a room key. "This is to your own personal room at the lodge across the street. I believe you should be comfortable there."

"That's nice of you, Jim, and thanks."

"If you would like room service they could bring you something for dinner or I could take you out, whatever you prefer."

"If you don't mind, I would like something brought to my room. It's been a long day."

"That's fine with me. The truck is unlocked so you can get your things. If everything else is okay I'll see you in the morning in the lodge dining hall."

"Goodnight, Jim, and thanks again."

"See you at 8 am."

He had been wondering if she would show up this morning or if he had scared her off. When he saw Nancy walking through the dining hall he folded his newspaper neatly and placed it on the seat next to him.

"Sit down, Nancy," he said cheerfully. "Did you sleep well?"

"Yes, I slept fine. I haven't slept that well in a long time, and to top it off, the hot shower did wonders to wash away my anxieties."

He was curiously quiet for a spell. "Nancy, please forgive me if I've unintentionally caused you to fear me."

"Mr. Dubois, it's only a natural concern for a young woman, who is headed for the unknown with a man she just met, to be a little nervous. To be honest with you, I'm far more worried about my uncle showing up. He's a brute!"

He wondered what this man had done to cause such fear in the young lady. Jim was curious and wanted to know the whole story, but for the time being he would wait until she was ready to tell him.

"Don't worry about your uncle. If he does show his face, I'm quite sure I can put him in his place," he chuckled.

"That makes me feel better."

"By-the-way, Nancy, I can see that you have good taste in clothes. The outfit you bought looks very nice on you."

"You don't know how long it's been since I have had anything new to wear, and it feels simply wonderful."

They finished their tasty breakfast while he continued looking over the Idaho State Map. "North of here, Nancy, we have the Sawtooth Wilderness area and the Sawtooth recreation area. From what I know about these places they should be splendid areas to visit. I hope you like to fish!"

"I've never had the opportunity to fish. I suppose that's my loss, but I think someday I would like to learn."

"I'll be happy to teach you and if you enjoy it, it will be something you can do the rest of your life. It seems when most people are exposed to fishing it gets in their blood and they can't leave it alone."

They stopped on the top of Calena Pass to stretch their legs. A cool breeze rustled their hair as they stood quietly and absorbed the serenity of the moment.

"Will you look at that vista, Nancy? It's absolutely breath-taking. There's one mountain after another, as far as the eye can see. You can easily understand how these mountains got their name, Sawtooths. For us flatlanders, speaking of myself of course, these high mountain roads can make a person mighty nervous. Look ahead to where the road leads down the other side of this pass. I can only imagine what it might be like if we were caught up here in a snowstorm."

"Jim, I'm sure this road is closed during the winter months. With all the snow they must get here, it would be impossible to keep it open."

It was equally obvious, Jimmy Dubois enjoyed talking, or maybe it was he liked listening to himself. Being alone, all those years and not having anyone to talk to, or listen to his ramblings, had to be the reason he talked so much. Now he had Nancy, who was a willing and polite listener.

Nancy seemed to enjoy listening to his stories. She was more reserved and didn't say a great deal. She knew her reserved demeanor would change as she became better acquainted with her new friend.

"That's a beautiful river down there, do you know the name of it, Jim?"

" From the way I read the map it looks like it's the east fork of the Salmon River, possibly it's only the Salmon river. I'm not quite sure. The map is not quite that clear."

"Well anyway, Jim, it's a splendid river to behold."

"Here is a tidbit of information, which just popped into my mind, while studying this map. Did you ever see a movie called 'The River of No Return,' starring Marilyn Monroe and Robert Mitchum? See, here on the map, there's a river named The River of no Return, north of here. I'll bet that's where the movie was filmed."

"Boy, aren't you full of a lot of trivial information today," she said with a jocular air to her comment. "Sorry, Jim, I didn't see the movie. Yet, I do remember Marilyn Monroe. She was quite a beauty queen but I understand, not such a great actress."

"Well, Nancy, let's try our luck and see if we can catch us some fish for dinner."

They drove to what seemed to be a good spot for casting their lines.

Standing in the current of the river, only a few feet from shore, Dubois attempted one cast after another, hoping he might impress this young lady with his fishing abilities. Nancy was curious, watching his moves with a great deal of interest from a large rock she was perched on.

"Oh look, Jim, what are those cute little animals over there?" He thought they looked like weasels, yet he didn't believe they were.

On the far bank, three river otters played their games together, sliding down a mudslide into the river, one after another. They would chase each other back up the bank to repeat the game. These little critters are beautiful, and curious but never a danger to anyone.

Jim must have caught their attention. The trio swam out to where he was fishing and circled him, curiously checking him out. He wasn't sure what they were, so he stood still, watching them, not knowing what they might do. After their curiosity was satisfied they returned to their animated games.

With one cast after another, Jim Dubois placed his streamer carefully on the water's surface, in various locations of the river, without a single strike. Fishing can be a pleasant, relaxing sport, but it can also lead you into a state of complete frustration. Maybe he had somewhere lost the touch. Of course he remembered all the variables that come into play if you want to be successful at this sport, but that knowledge didn't help his mood.

After another unsuccessful cast, he mumbled quietly, not wanting her to hear, "damn," and worked his way back to the shore where she waited.

"Would you like to give it a try, Nancy?"

"Yes, I would, it looks like a lot of fun."

Jim, not wanting to pass up this opportunity, moved behind Nancy, putting his arms around her to demonstrate how to hold the fishing pole and use the spinning reel. The fishing gear was all new to her, but she was a quick learner. After a few attempts at casting and a few blunders, she made her first unassisted cast. Nancy placed the fly near the far side of the river.

"Let it drift, Nancy."

Instantaneously, at the very moment she started to reel in, her line snapped tight. In a flash, a fish broke the surface, tumbling through the air and splashing back into the cool, blue-green water.

She squealed with glee as if she were a schoolgirl again.

"Keep the tip of the pole up and don't let the line get slack in it. Okay, slowly reel the fish in. If the fish pulls too hard stop reeling!" Jim shouted.

With great care she slowly maneuvered the fish to shore where Jim grabbed her line and lifted the fish from the water.

"Look at this, will you. You have caught a magnificent rainbow trout. It's a good 15 inches long and must weigh at least a couple of pounds.

Nancy was justifiably proud of her accomplishment, and merriment sparkled in her eyes as she examined her prize.

"Did you know, Jim, this is the first fish I've ever caught?"

"I'm happy for you, it's a fish to be proud of. Let me get my camera. We need a picture of this moment."

"What are we going to do with my fish, Jim?"

"Would you mind if we release it? Many of these streams and rivers are catch and release only."

"I hate to give it up, it's so pretty, but I think it would be a good thing to do."

With tender care, she placed her first catch into the water, gently holding it in the current until it was able to swim away.

When Nancy finally stood up, she turned and threw her arms around Jim's neck and gave him a bear hug that caught him completely off-guard.

"Thanks so very much for that special experience. It was great fun."

"You're most certainly welcome, my dear." As he considered his new friend, and this moment, he thought, "I've never known such a special person." And he too was happier than he had been in a very long time.

"What do you say if we look for a campsite before it gets too late in the day? Tomorrow you can give fishing another try. With your beginner's luck you should do just fine."

"Jim, do you have any ideas where we might find a camping site for to-night?"

"Actually.....yes. Here on the Idaho map it shows camping at Redfish Lake, just a few miles down this highway we're on. This will give us an opportunity to try out our new camping gear. I only hope it's as good as the salesman stated it would be. I can only see one problem."

"And what might that be?"

"It's my cooking. I hope you can stand it. I'll have to honestly admit, I'm not the best of cooks."

Nancy responded with a wistful smile. "Maybe I can help in that regards. I don't want to brag, but you need to know, I'm a very accomplished cook."

"That's a relief to know. Thank you."

Chapter 31

Redfish Lake

The drive to Redfish Lake didn't take long. There were plenty of nice camping sites around the scenic lake that was encircled by majestic mountains. Jim hurried to build a fire and set up their tents. The tent openings were facing the fire with the lake in the background. Nancy went about preparing a tasty meal on their newly purchased propane camp stove.

After the meal was over and the gear stowed away, Nancy and Jim sat down on logs, with the pleasant bonfire between them, to talk and enjoy the beautiful evening.

Her gentle features were bathed in the moonlight of the night. The wind stirred, causing the flames to dance a curious little jig. How pleasing it was having her to talk with. It was as if he had known her all his life. For the longest time they spoke about one thing or another, completely enjoying the ease of the conversation.

This evening, Jim Dubois, (Fletcher) shared more of his past with this young lady, whom he hardly knew, than he had with anyone in his entire life. Would this be his undoing? Deep down inside he realized that revealing his life could be dangerous. His past training as a F.B.I. agent had taught him to always cautiously guard information and only use it to his own advantage.

"Willingly or not, Jim, I need to get some sleep. It's been great fun sharing stories with you, but I'm tired. I hope those new sleeping bags are warm and comfortable. Good night." She slipped into her tent.

"And a good night to you, Nancy."

Dubois walked to his truck and rummaged through his belongings until he found the bottle of smooth sipping whiskey he had bought in Tennessee. This would be a fine time to toast the end of a good day. For the next hour he sat next to the fire, sipping from the bottle and trying to make sense of his life. The drink started to take effect. He stood up, stretched and ambled off to his tent.

Comfortable in his sleeping bag, he thought of Nancy and wondered about her life. And yet, of this he was sure, there was something troubling his friend. He hoped that he might help her if she would only open up and let him in.

An owl hooted,... inquiringly, as he drifted into tranquil sleep.

The following day was entirely spent fishing the shoreline of Redfish Lake. It was a pleasant and completely relaxing day for the two friends. This day would be one they would not soon forget.

"I've been wondering, Nancy, what should we do today. What would you think about taking a hike? Just south of here there is an interesting sounding trailhead. Did you happen to see it yesterday while we were fishing?"

"No, I didn't see it."

"I suppose, you were more interested in catching fish, right?"

"We did catch quite a few beautiful trout and that made for a great fish fry last night. As for the hike, I would like to go as long as we don't get ourselves lost."

"Don't worry, that won't happen. I picked up a map at the Ranger Station yesterday and I also have my trusty Boy Scout compass."

"What would you say if we head out right after we clean up the camp?"

"Okay, Jim, but you will have to do some serious hiking, old man, if you are to keep up with me," she giggled.

"On your part, Nancy, it would be wise if you showed a little respect for your elders. I just might surprise you, kid."

Before they departed, Nancy put together some sandwiches and energy bars in her daypack. In Jim's pack he put water, a tarp, matches and a few other essentials. When she was distracted, he quickly stowed his Smith and Wesson 44 magnum revolver in his pack. It is the worlds most powerful hand gun. He didn't want her to see the gun; he wasn't sure how she might react to it. Some people are afraid of guns and feel they are tools of the devil. As far as Jim was concerned, he would feel far safer having some firepower along. He considered to himself, "You never know what might happen. My father always said, better be safe than sorry."

"Look here, Nancy. I've got us some nice hiking sticks. Choose which one you like best and we'll be off. There is the trailhead just up ahead of us."

"I'm getting excited about our hike, it should be a lot of fun."

"This trail is one of the shorter ones, it's only five miles long. We should have plenty of time to enjoy the hike and be back before dark."

Some distance up the trail Jim stopped, turned around and looked at Nancy with disgust. "Darn!" he said, not wanting to swear in front of her. "I forgot to register at the Ranger's Station before we left. All back-woods hikers are required to register before leaving. The rangers want to know where to start their search if the hikers don't return. I'm not going to hike all the way back down there. I suppose we will be okay."

Nancy spoke up, "It's not like we're camping out here in the wilderness for days. We will be coming back today. I'm sure we will be fine, so please don't worry."

"Whatever you say."

The trail they had chosen was longer and much steeper than they had bargained for. Each of their steps had to be taken with care. Rocks and tree roots covered their path. Every few minutes they stopped to catch their breath.

"Never had I imagined that air could smell so refreshing, Nancy. The air I'm accustomed to on the east coast stinks in comparison."
"You're right, Jim, it does smell wonderful, but my favorite air is just after

a summer rain storm. There is something about it that's indescribable."

"Well, young lady, or should I say kid, do you think you can make it all the way?"

"Heck yes, I've only begun. I'll have you crawling on your hands and knees by the time we get there." she said with a girlish giggle.

A little further up, the trail leveled off onto a grand knoll with several hundred acres of alpine meadows, pines and quaking aspen groves. The vista was splendid with beautiful beds of wild flower carpeting the area.

"Would you like to stop here and eat our lunch? It looks like a good place, Jim."

"Sure, this sure beats the ambiance of any fine restaurant I've ever dined in."

Under a small grove of aspens they found a fallen tree that provided them with good seats and cool shade, where they could enjoy their simple lunch.

After eating a few bites of their sandwiches they were soon engaged in small talk.

If they were courageous enough to admit it, they had both had enough hiking for one day. It had been a long, mostly uphill hike and they weren't even sure if they had reached the end of the trail.

Unbeknownst to Nancy or Jim, the western sky was noticeably darkening. If these two had been accustomed to recognizing the changes in the weather, they most certainly would have been alerted to the fact that it was due time to get themselves off this mountain, post-haste.

Nancy arose from her seat, stepped away from the log and laid down in bed of tall, soft, cool grass and gazed up at the billowing clouds. She thought, "There has to always be times like this when you just sit still and listen, feel, and see. You live longer and live infinitely better."
She commented, "When I was a little girl my mother would have me lie

down on the lawn with her and watch the clouds float by. It was so much fun watching for different formations in the clouds and guessing which animals they resembled. Did you ever do that, Jim?"

"No, I'm afraid not."

Nancy dozed off while Jim found himself engaged with his thoughts. It was as beautiful here, on this mountaintop, as anywhere he could ever remember and he hoped it would never end. But, the nagging thoughts of his past never seemed to leave him alone. Was Baxter and his little gang going to catch him one day? If they did, would he lose his freedom? All of these surroundings here are free for all man to enjoy, but past actions could cost him dearly, maybe everything.

Suddenly Jim's attention was directed towards a loud clap of thunder over some distant mountain. For a few minutes he watched the blackening clouds. Then it hit him and he realized the storm was moving in their direction and had become an immediate threat.

Jim shouted, "Nancy! Wake up! We have a problem coming our way!"

Startled from her nap she called out, "What is it?"

"Look to the west. There is a fast approaching storm, with two dummies sitting here in the worst place we could possibly be, right on the top of this darn mountain!"

"What suggestion do you have?"

"Man, I don't know. I'm just a simple city boy with no experience in these sorts of matters. One thing I've learned in my life is not to panic when faced with bad situations. We need to put our heads together quickly and come up with a solution to our predicament."

"While living on my uncle's ranch, in eastern Montana, they taught us if we were caught out in a lighting storm we should never get under a tall tree. Lighting is attracted to tall objects. We should find cover in a low place."
They looked around for a place of refuge. They could see three differ-

ent trails leading off the mountain. Under the stress they were in, they weren't sure which trail was the one they had used to get to the knoll.

"Take a look down that trail, Jim. There might be some good cover. At least it will be off the top of this mountain. Shall we try for it?"

"Okay, Kid, let's do it."

The once azure sky was quickly turning into a fearful sight. The dark clouds were churning across the sky, with violence and fury. Bolts of lighting could be seen hitting the earth as the storm approached.

The two scared hikers ran down the trail, looking for cover. Off to one side of the trail they found some large boulders with an over hang that might provide shelter from the rain that was soon to come. Between two of the largest rocks they found just enough room for them to sit down. Jim grabbed his pack and quickly removed the tarp, which was large enough to cover them quite adequately. Now all they could do was wait and see what might happen. They huddled closely together, trying to keep warm and dry as the an enveloping darkness rapidly surrounded them.

It was as if a bomb exploded somewhere above them on the mountainside. A lighting bolt must have struck a tree, sending splinters and particles showering down on them, hitting their tarp. Nancy screamed in fright as Jim froze in place. Static electricity bristled the hair on their arms and heads.

The two terrified refugees held each other tightly, like two frightened children, while the thunder and lightning shook the mountain. It was as if they had been transposed into the middle of a battle zone.

With the raging storm in its full pinnacle, neither hiker was willing to utter a single word. From under the cover of their tarp they glared out into the deluge as flashes of blinding lighting illuminated the forest.

The storm's ferocity never lessened for the remainder of the day. Perhaps night had come unnoticed before it eased up in the slightest degree. Torrential rain finally turned into a steady drizzle leaving the night cold and dank.

Both had only light jackets, which offered little protection from the cold night. Jim had matches but nothing could be found that was dry and would burn. He was no woodsman, if he had been, maybe he would have solved the problem.

Jimmy Dubois could be a gentleman when necessary. He had developed a real liking for this young lady and he would do anything to protect her.

He put his arms around her, holding her as close to his body as he could, for the warmth each would provide for the other.

"Nancy, I know it's going to be a long and miserable night for the two of us. But let me assure you that it will pass, and we will be just fine come morning. This experience will only be an adventurous memory."

"Your tarp has been a life saver, Jim. I'm grateful you were wise enough to bring it along. If you hadn't, we would have been like two drowned rats by now."

"That's for sure. Boy how I wish I knew how to get a fire started. I have no doubts there are those people who could get a fire going, even in the rain. Are you alright, Nancy?"

"Just a little cold, that's all. I'll be fine."

The wind moaned through the pines, setting a mood that neither of them particularly liked. They could see nothing but looming darkness. It was haunting not knowing what might be out there in those woods.

"Jim, do you happen to have a flash light with you?"

" There's one in my back pack."

"That's comforting to know. Why don't you get it out so it's handy in case we need it."

" I have the flashlight right next to me."

Jimmy smiled to himself knowing she was frightened of the uncertainty of this dark and forlorn night. Yet, if he could be honest with himself, at this moment, he would eagerly admit he had a knot of cold fear clutching at his belly. "But why should I be afraid? There is nothing out there to fear. I'm just acting stupid."

Welcoming the change, the rain had finally turned to a light, quiet drizzle with occasional flashes of lightning turning the pitch-black night into noonday.

Over the next few hours they both dozed off, on occasion. Their sleep was a miserable one, which offered no rest. Finally both were awake, hoping morning would come.

"Do you have any ideas that will help us get through this ordeal, Jim? Anything at all to help pass the time?"

"Sure I do. We could get ourselves up out of here, and hike back to camp."

"Get serious, will you. I'm not about to take one step out of here until morning and I can see the trail. Understand?"

"I'm sorry, Nancy. I was only trying to make a joke to lessen the tension we are feeling. One thing that seems to work well for the two of us is talking. You like to talk and so do I. How does that sound, young lady?"

"Sounds okay, but don't call me young lady."

"Alright I'll start with a humorous story."

"I was working out of the Saint Louis field office. One day around noontime a radio call alerted me to a bank robbery in progress. The bank happened to be only one block from my location. I was the first officer to arrive. As I approached the bank, the robber bolted out the front door with a bag of money in one hand a gun in the other. When he started to point his gun in my direction, I shot him right in the forehead. The crook instantly dropped his gun and the moneybag, grabbed his head with both hands, and shouted, 'Oh my head hurts.' The bullet had ricocheted off his thick skull. I holstered my gun, seeing it's failure to stop the guy, and wrestled him to the ground."

Even in the darkness, Jim could tell she didn't think the story was all that funny. Oh well, he thought, maybe only a cop would get a laugh out of such a story.

"Are you telling me you were some kind of a cop?"

"Yes, I was, but that story was a long time ago. Now I'm retired, with not a lot of purpose to my life."

"Thanks for telling me the story, Jim. I'm sorry I didn't laugh, but you see, my bladder is about to burst, and if I don't do something about it soon I'm going to have a real problem. Please let me take your flashlight and even as afraid as I am of the dark, I promise I will only be as far away as the other side of this boulder."

Fumbling around in the dark, Jim found the flashlight, turned it on and handed it to Nancy.

"Thanks," she said, as she cautiously made her way out.

Within a short duration of maybe thirty or forty seconds, Nancy came flying back into their refuge as if she was being pursued by the devil himself. Not having enough time to take care of her needs, he wondered what the problem was.

She threw her arms around him, quivering with fear. "Oh, Jim, there is something out there. I saw it. It was moving around and it was huge and black."

His body chilled as if an icy finger was running down his spine. "If she thinks I'm going out there she is crazy. I'm no damn hero, never have been, and never will be. What in the bloody hell am I supposed to do? We are both in danger and I have no clue what's out there waiting for us. Give me the flashlight!"

"No! Please let me hold it."

He grumbled, "Just give me the thing, will you?" He jerked it from her hand. With the aid of the flashlight, he located his revolver. Holding the gun gave him a sense of reassurance, but not enough to quench his fears of the unknown.

The night sounds had vanished, as if they knew of the danger. All was deathly silent. For the longest time they waited for something to happen. Then, for the briefest moment, they saw a shadowy movement of something pass in front of the their entrance.

Whatever was out there, unless it was a specter from some haunted place, couldn't get to them except through that opening. At least, this was his belief. Their backs were now glued to the ten foot boulders, which surrounded them. Fearful they couldn't escape the unknown, which may be waiting for them, they remained silent with fear and trepidation in absolute control.

Crushing sounds resembling rocks being moved around and brush being smashed to the ground shook the forest. Nancy was now crying and Jim wanted to.

As quickly as the sounds started, all was again silent. Then, muffled sounds of heavy breathing were heard outside and very close. Jim, sensing something was there at the opening, flipped on his flashlight. Its beam was shining directly in the face of a bear.

Nancy let out with a high-pitched scream as Jim shouted at the top of his lungs. The noise startled the bear. It sounded back with an obtrusive growl and reared up on it's hind legs, looking as though he was ten feet tall. With a roar, which shook the forest, the bear let them know who was king. The lightning flashed, revealing his enormous size.

Without the slightest doubt, these two knew that this night might be their last.

Up came Jimmy's revolver, while the beam of the flashlight revealed the bear's chest and head. Without waiting for the wild beast to make the next move, his gun spit fire. He fired three or four times directly into the middle of its chest. Bellowing a primeval roar, the bear spun around and disappeared. Giant sounds of crushing and thrashing were heard until all was once again silent.

Neither Nancy nor Jim dared to make the slightest sound or movement, fearing the monster would return.

The silence between the two was electric. It seemed as if all the neurons in their frightened bodies were poised to spring forward saying, "We are ready to move, just give us the word."

Jim's left arm was around her shoulder, holding her close. Nancy had both of her arms around Jim's waist, squeezing him tightly. He was her only refuge. In his sweaty right hand he still held that big gun tightly. He couldn't remember how many shots he had fired.

He whispered under his breath, "I may have only a couple of shots left and the box of .44 rounds is in my truck, miles away."

The gun had shocked Nancy nearly as much as the bear had frightened her. She was glad he had the gun, but never in the world had she dreamed of him having a weapon with him.

Time passed by slowly. Neither of them knew how long they had waited before one dared to speak.

Nancy whispered softly, "Is that monster going to come back?" Jim felt her body quiver with uncertainty as she desperately clung to him.

"I certainly hope not, but I don't know. I've read that a wounded animal is far more dangerous. We should just sit tight and wait. I wouldn't worry. I believe he is either dead or slowly dieing.

As their anxiety lessened the cold became more evident and they both felt its effects. They were clinging together trying to keep warm, and wishing the morning would soon come. For the remainder of the night they seldom spoke. No stars were visible, and the storm clouds were still hanging low, meaning the morning light would be slow coming.

The haunting sound of a wolf, calling to its pack, was heard somewhere off in the distance.

"Jim, will this hellish night ever end?"

He didn't answer her because he didn't have the answer. Jim just gave her a little reassuring squeeze.

Finally, the eastern sky began to lighten, ever so slowly.

"Look, Nancy, the sky is brightening some. The morning sky is overcast and gloomy but it's nearly here."

"Oh, thank goodness. I didn't think that morning would ever come. Now we can get out of this horrid place and back to safety."

When it was light enough to see around the forest, Jim rose slowly. His .44 was still clenched in his hand. With great care, he cautiously looked out of their citadel for any evidence of the bear. His eyes froze on something large and black, only ten yards from where he stood. He saw no movement from what had to be the bear. After some time he reached down, picked up a rock and threw it at the black object, striking it. Still no movement. Yet, Jim had no desire to approach the bear to see if it was really dead.

"Jim, what do you see out there?"

"I believe it's the bear. He is only ten yards away, yet I've no wish to go out there to see if he is really dead."

"Well, after all these hours, since you shot him, I would think he is certainly dead by now."

After a few minutes, Jim turned to see why she was so quiet, noticing her head was bowed, as if in prayer.

"What are you doing, Nancy?"

She raised her hand, as if to say, "Please be quiet".

When see finished she looked up at Jim, and said. "I was praying.

With a piercing scrutiny of his gray eyes, he wanted to say, "What for?" He knew better.

"Let me tell you a verse of a song I know." 'Prayer will change the night to day. So when life gets dark and dreary, don't for get to pray.' If you need to know, that's why I was praying."

"Alright, Miss Nancy, what do you say if we make some tracks out of here?"

"I'm all for that, but first I have a suggestion. Lets hike back up the trail to the knoll to see if we can remember which one of those three trails we need to take. I don't think this trail we're on is the right one."

Perhaps, owing to the fierceness of the storm, all three trails seemed somewhat unfamiliar to them. They knew one of the trails lead them yesterday to this special place with all of its beauty, yet, on the converse to a fearful place they would never forget.

Each of the three trails seemed to be pointing in a slightly different direction. All of them were generally headed northwest toward where they believed Red Fish Lake was located.

"Alright, we need to make the best educated guess we can. What trail do you choose, Nancy?"

"I'm sure my choice won't be any better than yours. My vote will be for the middle trail, only because of a gut feeling I have."

"Your choice is fine with me, because I don't have the slightest clue. After enduring that nightmare, my brain seems to be sort of scrambled. I'm hardly able to tell which way is up."

"Shall we get started? Lets take our time and watch our steps. It would be awful if one of us tripped on this slippery trail and was hurt.

After a half hour they were beginning to wonder about their choice, then

Nancy poked Jim in the back with her hiking stick.

"What is it?"

"Look, there on the side-hill. Is that a dog?"

"No, I don't think so, it looks like a large coyote."

"It's watching us."

Jim shouted at the animal but it never flinched. The creature intently continued to watch their every movement. Neither believed they were afraid of a lone coyote but, he was making them uneasy.

They continued on, watching their every step, while keeping a close lookout for their observer. He would disappear for a short time, and then reappear ahead of them.

All of their doubts about this animal were washed away when the silence was broken with a wolf howl and then another howl somewhere off in the distance.

"That's certainly a forlorn, haunting sound. It makes goose bumps on my arms," Jim announced. "I'm a little too old for this sort of thing," he said nervously.

"O yeah, and I'm a little too young for this sort of thing, she answered with a cheesy sort of smile.

"Jim, do you know why wolves howl?"

"No, I don't."

"He is calling for his pack. I did learn something about wolves from the time I lived on my uncle's ranch. We were close to the Canadian border, and there was one well-established wolf pack in our area. It wasn't uncommon to have them around."

"Are you saying he's calling his buddies in for lunch?"

"Could be, Jim, but don't fool around, I don't find it all that funny, so lets not talk about it anymore. We have a far way to go and we need to lay down some tracks, starting right now."

As far as these two were concerned, the sooner they got off this mountain, the happier they both would be. The events of the past night had overloaded their circuits, pushing them to the very edge of hysteria.

Now they were confronted by this threatening wolf, which had brought on a new fear that wasn't at all welcome. But on the other hand, maybe he was simply the curious type only wanting to know what these strange humans were up to.

Normally wolves avoid humans at all cost, but Jimmy Dubois didn't know anything about a wolf's behavior. One thing they were both sure of was the fact they had been attacked by one beast just hours ago and now another animal was following them.

For every step that Dubois took, Nancy followed in suit, never getting more than one step behind him. She kept looking anxiously around, hoping the wolf wouldn't reappear.

Over the following hour the wolf was seen several times, flanking their movement, off to the left and keeping a close pace with their progress. The size of this wolf indicated he might be the alpha male of the pack, the leader.

"Nancy, the next time he shows himself I'm going to blow a hole through his raunchy hide and be finished with his threats."

"Jim, I wouldn't do that. You have only a couple of bullets left and we might need them. Besides that's a long shot for a handgun."

He listened, but didn't respond to her comment, not liking her questioning his shooting abilities, even though he knew she was correct in her assumptions.

Uncomfortable as they might have been about the wolf stalking them, he never showed himself again. Still, not a moment passed that this animal wasn't on their minds.

Returning to camp on the slippery downhill trail required far more time than yesterday's uphill hike.

What a wonderful relief it was when they first saw their camp from far across the lake. It was then they realized their mistake.

"That's peculiar," Jim said. "We did take the wrong trail. It wasn't a huge mistake, it only required a hike around this lake, and a big inconvenience," he muttered sarcastically. "All that really matters now, is we are back and off that maddening mountain."

"Sorry for choosing the wrong trail, Jim."

"It's no big deal, we both made the same choice, so don't blame yourself."

"Nancy, I want you to listen very carefully to what I'm about to say. Right now I'm hiding this handgun in the bottom of my pack. We never had a gun. Right!"

"If you say so. But why?"

"Frankly, Nancy, I don't have the slightest idea about the gun laws here. We might be in a federal forest and I may have broken some stupid laws that might require an investigation. That sort of thing I can't stand for. So, whatever you say, please don't mention my gun or the bear I shot."

"Of course not, I would never say a word I'm just so grateful you had the gun or our remains might still be on that mountain top scattered from heck to breakfast."

"Oh boy, Nancy, you are some woman, and thank you for your confidence."
Rays of sunshine began streaking through the parting clouds. The once dreary morning was quickly turning into a day of cheer and hope.

Jim didn't list patience among his virtues. As soon as they reached their camp, both hastened to pack up their gear before any unseen development unfolded. The last thing they wanted to see was a Forest Ranger coming around and asking questions.

As they stowed away the last article of gear in the pick-up, a tall, stalwart man approached them, dressed neatly in a Boy Scout leader's uniform. All smiles he asked, "Did you folks hike off that mountain this morning? I've got a troop of Boy Scouts and I'm looking for information before we start out. That's all."

Jim spoke. "We did. We were caught in an awful storm and were forced to wait it out, although, it does look as if the storm has passed. We hope you and your scouts have a safe and enjoyable time."

"We should Mr. These young men have been planning this adventure since last winter and are very excited."

With a friendly smile and a wave of the hand they drove out of the camping area, wanting to put some distance between them and the memory of that horrid night.

"Jim, I hope those boys don't find any more of those monsters."

Jim commented, "I wish I could have been a Boy Scout maybe my life might have been something better."

Chapter 32

Bend Oregon Safe House

Weeks had passed since Matt had disappeared.

Penny Savage was a lonely woman biding her time in a safe house located in Bend, Oregon. Matt had left her there alone to go to his old friends in Virginia, hoping he could find answers and help for all the past he had forgotten. After he was discharged from the University Hospital his memory loss still didn't improve. His family had great hope that it would, but the doctors cautioned them that they needed to be patient. It would be a matter of time, and it was possible he might not ever have his memory of the past restored.

Not knowing when this nightmare might end caused her an enormous amount of stress. All she hoped for was the day when her family could be reunited, but because of the magnitude of her troubles, her resolve was wearing thin.

The only connection she had to her family was through F.B.I. agent Tim Headley. He had become her friend, many years ago, through a strange set of circumstance's. He had taken custody of Matt on a bank robbery charge. As a result of Agent Headly's benevolence and genuine concern for Matt and his family, a friendship grew between them.

As clever and resourceful as Tim was, he knew he had to do considerably more to keep Matt's family safe. This job had now become an official assignment from his boss and he knew that he better not screw it up.

Every few days he would pay Penny a visit, conveying all he knew about her family, always doing his best to keep her spirits up.

Late one afternoon Agent Headley called Penny on the phone.

"Hi, Mrs. Savage."

"It's nice to hear your voice, what's up?"

"How would you like to get out of the house? I'm inviting you out to dinner, where we can visit and enjoy a good meal. What do you say?"

"That sounds lovely. I'll be ready when you get here."

She peered past the door's curtains and was delighted to see Tim Headley standing there with a welcoming smile.

"Oh, you don't know how happy I am to see you again. Sit down, Tim," Penny said cheerfully.

At one of the nicer restaurants in the city of Bend, Penny and Tim Headley enjoyed a relaxing evening with a superb prime rib dinner and all the amenities.

They talked considerably about her family and the concerns she had for their safety. He explained he didn't know everything about Matt, but assured her he was safe and in good hands.

"What about Matt's memory? Has it improved?"

"No, Penny, it has not changed. The information I received is it is about the same as it was when he arrived there. I wish I could be the bearer of better news."

"How is Matt's health?"

"Physically, I understand he is doing well. Whatever you do, don't give up. There is always hope and good things are going to come your way.

"I've spoken with each of your children in the past two weeks and they all seem to be doing very well. They send their love and miss you very much."

"Thanks, Tim, for the report. I do appreciate it." A single tear slid down her troubled face. Sadness remained in her eyes.

Tim was curiously quiet for a few moments and then thoughtfully asked, "Penny what are you doing to keep yourself busy these days?"

"Listen, my compadre, one thing you might not know about me is that I'm not one to let grass grow under my feet."

"That's good to know, Penny."

"Last week I paid the neighborhood elementary school a visit and volunteered to help with their reading program. So, now I spend a couple of hours a day helping kids that have difficulty with they're reading, and if I have the time, I read them stories. Do you recall what I told you when we first took up residency here?"

"I'm not sure what you are referring to."

" I met up with a group of ladies here in town at my church and started helping them making quilts for the needy. Now I'm even teaching Sunday School. What do you think about that?"

"That's very good, Penny. I've observed this human strength in my life. When a person spends time helping others they seem to forget about themselves. Their personal troubles and their lives always improve."

Tim's assurance left her feeling a bit better but she was still somewhat uncertain, and detached from it all, yet Penny knew she would be forever grateful for his friendship.

"It was a lovely dinner, Tim, and I want to thank you for your friendship and thoughtfulness. You are my only link to Matt so whatever you can do to keep me informed would be greatly appreciated."

"Penny, I promise that I will keep you updated whenever anything new happens. We are keeping a close watch on Matt and trying our best to help him."

Chapter 33

Baxter's Special Dinner

"Niki, I can't help wondering if your dad has heard anything new regarding Fletcher or his whereabouts."

"I'm positive he will inform us whenever he does hear anything new.

"I suppose my patience is wearing a little thin. I feel as though this whole mess developed because of me, and that shooting, and then you and your dad were sucked into this quagmire. Besides, your careers are now in jeopardy. Everything about this whole affair makes me ill."

"Matt, I wouldn't trouble yourself about Dad and me. He should have retired years ago and you know that I'm eligible for retirement. So, do I look worried?"

"From what I heard the director say, he was forcing the two of you to retire. The way I see it, it looks like you won't have much of a choice."

"Well, we will just have to wait and see. Things like this always seem to have a way of working themselves out. Now, Matt, it's time we change the subject. Okay?"

"Anything you say, Niki."

"How would you like to help me in the kitchen? I've wanted to prepare a nice meal for my dad. I bet you didn't know today is his birthday."

"No, I didn't know."

"I've collected some of the recipes Dad enjoyed and I remember some of the dishes Mother prepared for him. I've Americanized some of those Russian dishes a little, to suit his new acquired tastes.

"Why sure. It sounds like it could be fun and I would consider it a pleasure to learn from the best, and yes, I can remember enjoying some great meals you've prepared."

"Alright then, lets not sit around here wasting time, we've some grocery shopping to do."

"Niki, are you going to drive your Cobra?"

"No, I think I'll leave it under wraps for a little while longer. We can never tell what the county Sheriff might know about my car. We are taking the old minivan. It's a great grocery-getter and it might appreciate being driven."

This was the first time Matt had been grocery shopping since he had taken up residency with the Blinski's. It was a pleasant feeling following Niki through the store, watching her carefully pick and choose the various ingredients for the meat dish she was planning.

"Have you decided what you're going to cook for your dad?"

"I believe I've made up my mind. One dish Mother fixed for Dad, that I can remember, was called, "Fish Baked a La Russe. Dad loved it."

"We will need some fresh fish, and any one of these fish will work well, pike, cod, cat-fish, or perch."

At the meat counter Niki inquired of the butcher which fish were fresh and of the best quality.

"Ma'am I've some beautiful fresh cod which arrived just this morning."

"That sounds good. Would you please give me 600 grams of cod."

"Oh boy," the butcher said with a silly grin on his mug. "Could you please convert that into pounds."

"All right, that would be about one and a half pounds. Just give me two pounds."

On the trip home, Niki pulled into a local liquor store and parked. Why are we stopping here? Your dad doesn't drink, or does he?"

"No, Matt, he doesn't, but any true blooded Russian man wouldn't pass up a glass of good vodka, especially on his birthday."

Matt wished he had a gift for his old friend. Maybe helping Niki prepare his birthday meal would mean something special to him.

Without wasting any time, Matt unloaded the groceries and placed them on the kitchen table, then he began following instructions like any good assistant would.

"What else is on the menu for tonight's dinner?"

"Well, of course the fish is the main dish. I have a great recipe for desert. It's called Apple Varenki. I'm sure you'll enjoy it, Dad loves it. For a vegetable, I'll cook some cabbage or maybe serve him a little sauerkraut. If we hurry I believe I might have enough time to bake him his favorite birthday cake. He loves devil's food."

"That's interesting. I too love devil's food cake and hate angel food cake. Does that say something about our personalities? I wonder."

"Really, Matt, I don't think so, besides it's silly to make such a comparison." Matt continued peeling the potatoes.

Niki filleted the fish like an expert, into perfect portions. When the potatoes were cooked and cut into thin slices, she placed the slices around the fish and covered everything with a sour cream sauce and grated cheese.

Aleksandar Blinski (Baxter) was truly delighted with the old-fashion Russian dinner. He smiled like Matt had never seen him smile until he spoke of his wife and their Mother Russia. He then became quiet and spoke with a reverence in his voice.

"Okay, Dad, keep your eyes shut," and she ran off to the kitchen returning with a beautiful devil's food cake. One large candle in the shape of a question mark adorned the top. He laughed at the candle.

"Don't you know my age?"

"Sure I do, Dad."

"Arguably, Niki, that's the best meal I've eaten in a very long time."

Niki handed him a gift wrapped box. "Here is a little something that will top off the dinner. Please open it now."

 Inside the box was a bottle of the finest Russian Vodka money could buy. He held the bottle in his hands turning it so he could read the label and said something in Russian, which Matt didn't understand. Niki looked pleased. While he opened and poured a drinking glass full, Niki cut him a large piece of his birthday cake.

Baxter held his glass high above his head and said, "Here is to the good life." Then he drank it down as if it was water.

"Oh, Dad, drinking it like that might kill you!"

"No, my child, that's the way its done when old Russian friends are out on the town, drinking"

"We can't match that."

"You two would be flabbergasted if you saw what some of my old Russian friends could drink. Even after a night of heavy drinking they could still manage to find their way home. A couple of hours later they would get up for work.

"Dad, I know we're not all drinkers here, but tonight I would like to offer a toast."

Baxter poured himself a small glass this time. Matt and Niki grasped their dinner glasses, no vodka. She raised her glass and expressed, "To the three of us old friends, who will be such for all time."

Each raised and touched their glasses, and said, "Here, here," sealing their wish with a drink.

All three sat around the kitchen table picking at the leftovers and enjoying pleasant conversation.

Matt spoke, "Remember when we first met, years ago in California? Where has all the time gone? I've considered it many times but never came up with any explanation which satisfied me."

" Matt, it just goes away. That's all."

"Okay, but where does it go?

"Back then if I had been able to peek ahead 30 years, to this date, it would have seemed like forever. Now I look back to that time and it certainly doesn't seem so long ago. For some reason, time in the future seems very different from time past. My perspective of this isn't so different, and I think most people consider it the same as I do."

"Why let it bother you, Matt, as I see it, there's nothing we can do about it."

"I'm sure you're right, but there's something about it which intrigues me. All my life I've noticed the disparity in past and future time, there is something different about it."

"I hope you two don't think I've lost my mind." Niki offered a discreet grin.

"Let me offer some sort of reason why I'm interested in time. We mortals only have our earthly existence to measure time. There just has to be much more about time that we don't understand. Considering all the hours I've pondered this subject I've only come up with more questions than answers. Just consider some of these words and phrases; past, present, and future time, fullness of time, afterlife, endless time, infinite time, time without end and eternity."

"Okay, Matt, you have our attention, go on."

"Just think about this, if you will. The speed of light is 186,282 mph. A clock aboard a space ship traveling at 87% the speed of light would tick only half as fast as a clock on Earth. Does that make you wonder if at some point, time might stop?"

Baxter and Niki had questioning expressions on their faces, but said nothing.

"Here is a statement I have a challenge understanding. I've read what some very learned men have said, 'Our existence is without beginning or without end, like a round.'"

"My friend, these sorts of subjects make my head hurt. I simply don't understand any of it nor do I think I care. Maybe one day I will."

Niki said, "Go on Matt, if there is anything else you would like to say."

"Well, maybe just one thing. It's something I'm not qualified to even discuss, yet it is extremely interesting to consider. It's quantum mechanics or matrix mechanics. Some of these brilliant physicists, who study these theories, believe there might be parallel time or even a parallel universe."

Niki moved over and took a seat next to Matt and gave him a squeeze. "Thanks for sharing your thoughts, Matt."

Matt expressed, "Time will tell," as he laughed out loud.

"Please accept my apology for going off on a tangent like I did. I do find some of the mysteries of life intriguing. If you would excuse me, I'm going to retire.

Matt walked around the table to where he sat and gave him slug on his shoulder and said, "Happy Birthday Baxter, and many more you old scoundrel. Good night." Matt gave Niki a wink as he walked away.

Matt laid in bed considering how this whole mess with those three rouge agents had gone nowhere. Several weeks had passed and they knew nothing more. He was aware of how long it might take to find them but he was growing restless. All he wanted was to have it over with. "What then," he wondered. "What in this world can I possibly do? I have nothing. No job, no family, just two great friends and one of them I'm in love with."

He felt deep in his heart, for some unknown reason, this relationship was going nowhere. He finally slipped off into a troubled sleep.

The following morning Baxter asked Niki and Matt to have a seat in the front room; he had something to tell them. "Brook Staggs just called and gave me some good news for a change. He said they have found a parking ticket that's gone to a warrant for a Jimmy Dubois, in Salt Lake City. He also used a credit card in Sun Valley, Idaho for hotel rooms. One of our agents checked it out and discovered he had a young woman traveling with him. Interesting. They also believe he purchased a new Ford pick-up in Amarillo, Texas.

"The agency is putting the pieces of this puzzle together, with confidence it will eventually lead us to Fletcher. It appears Fletcher isn't concerned about getting caught, because he has been careless. Maybe he believes his new identity will hide him from the F.B.I. The stupid man should know better."

Matt spoke up, "Maybe he's more interested in the young lady traveling with him and not worried about who's searching for him."

"That observation could very well be the case. The director assured Staggs that they will find him and when they do he will give us the honor of busting Fletcher's butt. For now, we'll have to be patient."

Chapter 34

Take Leave from Redfish Lake

They were relieved to be away from Red Fish Lake and the mountains that held their fearful story, a story Jim and Nancy would surely never forget.

The two traveled across Oregon to the West Coast where they spent a few days at different beaches, enjoying the ocean.

Nancy had developed a respect for Jim. A friendship was growing between the two, which she was happy for. Yet, she couldn't stop wondering about her family in San Jose. Nancy hadn't heard from them in over a year. She didn't like to think about the fact her own dad had sent her to live and work at that lonely ranch in Montana, to be a slave for her uncle, whom she hated.

" Jim, when will we be heading for California? I'm anxious to find out what my family is up to and where they are."

"Considering how I feel about you, I was hoping this day wouldn't come. Nancy, you are like the daughter I never had and I want you to remember that. We'll head for San Jose tomorrow morning."

"Oh thanks, Jim." She threw her arms around his neck and gave him a big bear-hug.

He liked these special feelings he had for Nancy. They were like none other he had experienced.

As they traveled to San Jose, Nancy Burgess talked at length about a troubled childhood with her father, and a mother so passive and non-committal that she would never stand up for her daughter. Still, she loved them and missed them.

"What are you going to do if the situation hasn't improved?"

"I really don't know, Jim. You understand I only want to know what's happened to them. I have two younger sisters, which I desperately miss. I can't understand why my uncle or parents have cut me completely off from hearing anything about them. Every day I pray they are alright and well."

Jimmy Dubois listened with great interest as she related her life's story. With each word she spoke, he wished he could do something to help. Then he questioned himself, "How would it have been to have my own children to worry about and love?"

When they arrived in the city, Nancy's directions were perfect. They stopped a few feet north of her home, both staring and stunned at the sight of the weeds growing where the lawn once was. There was a For Sale sign posted next to the sidewalk.

Jim finally broke the silence. "Would you like to walk up to the front door and see if anyone is at home?"

"Sure, I would like that."

Dubois stood back and watched as Nancy knocked on the door, and rang the doorbell, all to no avail. She walked slowly around her old home, looking and hoping she might find something or someone that might answer her questions. No doors or windows were open so that she might see inside. She gazed longingly around the yard at one thing and then another. Her sadness veiled her lovely face. Jim felt helpless.

"Nancy, what would you like to do?"

"I haven't the slightest idea. It's evident my family no longer lives here, but why wouldn't they tell me they were leaving? I don't understand them."

"I have an idea, Nancy. Give me a few minutes. I'll get the phone number on the realtors sign and give him a phone call. We will pretend we are interested in the house. Hopefully, that way we might get some information about your family.

The realtor said he would meet us here in a half hour. Why don't we sit here on the porch and wait? What do you say?"

Without the least bit of enthusiasm in her voice she said, "Sounds like a good idea."

While they waited, Jim did all the talking. Nancy's thoughts were somewhere else. This was another sad and frustrating chapter in this young lady's life.

At the appointed time, a beautiful new Audi with the realtors sign on the doors pulled up in front of the house.

Jim walked over to the salesman and introduced himself and Nancy as his daughter.

The first question Jim asked, "Can we see inside the house?"

"Why certainly, Mr. Dubois." He knew Nancy wanted to look around inside so he kept the salesman busy with a lot of questions. When she returned, he asked, "Where did the owners move to? We would like to ask them some questions about the house."

"I wish I could tell you, but I don't know. They walked away and left the bank holding the mortgage. Our agency is trying to sell it for the bank. We could make you a killer of a deal on this property. The bank is very anxious to get it off their hands."

"Could you give me your business card? I'll need some time to consider it. I'll call you tomorrow and possibly make you an offer."

"Alright, Mr. Dubois. I'll talk to you then."

Jim glanced at Nancy. She appeared as if she might break down and cry. He put his arm around her shoulder, walked her to their truck, opened the door and helped her inside.

She said helplessly, "I.....I have no one."

He attempted to console her the best way he knew how by assuring her everything would turn out fine. They would find her family and a logical reason for their strange behavior.

At the moment Jim started to close the door to his truck, Nancy shouted out loud, "Oh no, it's my uncle from Montana!"

He had parked his dirty old truck across the street and was headed directly towards them. Nancy's uncle blazingly approached and without giving Jim the slightest look he blurted out, "What do you think you're doing? Leaving us to worry and wonder what had happened to you. By-the-way, Nancy who is this old goat you've taken up with?"

"None of you business, William, and where is my family?"

"I haven't the slightest idea where your family is, and why should I care. You get your stuff together right now and put it in my truck, because we're headed for home."

Nancy was angry. She screamed at Will, "Like hell, you say! I wouldn't go to a piss-ant fight with you, knowing the kind of a man you are!"

Will's jaw tightened as his angry eyes narrowed. He grabbed for the door handle. Jim came down with a chopping blow, knocking the cowboy's hand away.

He was furious. He stepped back and threw a right hand punch from an awkward position. Jim saw it coming and easily side-stepped it, then countered with a hard, well placed left to his nose, which sent blood flying and Will staggering. Jim followed the first punch, with a mighty right-handed upper-cut. The blow picked Will off his feet and slammed the scruffy cowboy to the ground.

Then he rolled over and slowly got to his feet. It was evident he hadn't learned his lesson.

With a stern voice command, Jim said, "Back off and let it be!"

Resembling a loco drunk, Will charged with both arms swinging wildly, hoping one of his fists would connect. One of his flailing fists missed the mark and came down on top of Jim's head, which only made him angrier than he already was. Jim knew by now this cowboy was no fist-fighter.

Jim hit him with two or three sharp jabs followed by a hard right hand, repeating the moves, leaving his face looking like chopped liver. Will's legs finally buckled and he slumped to the ground.

Will had no idea Jimmy Dubois, as a young man, was a Golden Gloves champion and boxed for the U.S. Army, never losing a fight.

"If you have no objections, William, or whatever your name is, Nancy and I will be leaving. I want you to remember this, don't ever show your ugly face around us again! Do you understand?"

Will nodded his head, indicating he understood.

At that precise moment, Jimmy Dubois turned around to face two police officers from the San Jose City Police Department. They were too late to save Will from his well-deserved beating, and this pleased Jim. Now for the first time in several weeks, the cold realization hit him in the pit of his stomach, he was a wanted man. Seeing the two officers standing there, whom he knew would be full of questions, sent a cold chill down his spine. "Be cool," he thought, "this will all pass. These officers are here because of this altercation and nothing more."

One of the officers spoke up, "Folks, just stay put until we get this figured out. Okay?"

"We received a radio call about an altercation at this address. Can any of you tell us what's going on here?"

By this time Nancy's uncle had gathered himself up and was leaning against a tree, attempting to clear his clouded brain. One of the officers took a look at him and said, "You don't look so good Mr. Do you need any medical attention?"

"No sir, officer, I'm fine."

"Do you want to make a crime report?

"Like I just said, I'm fine and I'm not interested in making any complaint."

"Is their anyone else here who wants to make a crime report?"

No one answered the officer's question.

Dubois approached one of the officers and turned on his charm. He was an expert at giving the proper answers.

"Officer, this insignificant problem is over and my daughter, who is sitting in the truck, and I were about to leave. I don't want to make a complaint and it looks obvious the cowboy wants no further problems."

"So, you're the other half of this problem?"

"Yes, I suppose I am, officer."

"Let me see your I.D. Gentlemen, I'm going to make an incident report so we have a record of your disagreement. Before we go, I want you two to remember this, if we see either of you involved in any more trouble today, we promise you'll spend some time in our jail, understand?"

"Yes sir, we understand."

"Okay gentlemen, here is the incident report number, if for some reason you should want a copy of the report."

The officers waited and watched until both parties drove off. They cleared from the call and left the scene.

Nancy broke the silence first, "Jim, are you alright?"

"Couldn't be better. To be right honest with you it felt good giving the bum an old fashioned beating."

"Thank you so very much for standing up for me, Jim. I'm not sure what I would have done if you hadn't been there."

"You're more than welcome. Do you believe the beating convinced him to stay away or will he come back?"

"I'm not sure, but if Will is not wanted by the police, he will be before long. I know what the scumbag is growing on his ranch, up in the hills, where he thinks no one knows about his little farm of Mary Jane. That's why he doesn't want me talking to anyone."

"Nancy, what are you contemplating?"

"Not sure at this moment, but if he does show up again I'll be tempted to turn him in to the authorities."

Dubois quietly muttered to himself as they drove away. "That confrontation with those police officers was too close for comfort."

"What did you say?"

"Heck, I'm only complaining to myself. I didn't like running into the police, that's all."

"I don't understand. Why in the world would running into the police worry you? It doesn't make sense."

Jim glanced over at her. She was looking at him with a questioning expression, giving him to wonder if he should tell her any of his stories. He didn't want to destroy their special relationship by causing her to worry about him, but maybe he could tell her just a little and she would be satisfied.

"So that you might understand, Nancy, I retired a couple of months ago under some questionable circumstances from the F.B.I. I didn't want to hang around and answer their pointless questions, so I just left. Since the day I retired I've been wondering if the bureau, with their gun-toting agents, was going to come looking for me."

"Why would it be so difficult for the bureau to find you, if they seriously wanted to?"

"Under normal conditions it would be nothing more than a Sunday walk in the park to find me. Before I left, I artfully made it difficult for them to find me by taking on a completely new identity. Please be patient with me and try to understand. I don't want to be found, just left alone to spend my retirement years somewhere here in beautiful California."

Sadly she said, "You're full of all sorts of surprises."

"There are certain occasions in my life when I wish I had chosen a different occupation than the one I did. Now, it's all history, with its good and bad times. With everything revolving around all the cloak and dagger crap, it became hard for my life not to get a little tarnished. Keep this in mind, Nancy, I'm not a bad person. Hopefully one day we will be privileged to sit down together and tell our stories to each other. Does the idea sound like something worth waiting for?"

"Sure, I really would like to hear about your life. I'm sure you have many crazy and unbelievable stories to tell."

A flood of memories returned, which troubled him. He realized Nancy might some day know what he was involved in. He remembered when he conjured up his clever scheme to use agents to rob banks, which actually worked. He loved the money but hated what his partners had done. But, now it was too late and he could only escape justice by pure luck.

"Give me some time, Nancy, and I believe I can locate your family."

Nancy offered him a subtle smile and said, "I have a bad feeling. I don't think I'll ever see them again, but thanks just the same." She looked weary and without hope.

"I have a lot of plans and I would like to include you in them, if you would permit me, and in the meantime I can do some investigating about your family. Will you let me help you?"

"Thank you Jim. I know you are a good man and I will accept your help, but I have no way of repaying your kindness."

"You never need to worry about that. Just being my friend is payment enough. For the present time we must conclude we've reached the end of this trail, at least for now. What would you say if the two of us took a little trip to the ocean and spent a few days deciding what course of action would be best. I'm sure once we clear our minds we should come up with a workable plan. Does that idea agree with you?"

"Your notion sounds good to me. I can't explain how disappointed I am in discovering my family has moved and they never even let me know."

Nancy had a sneaky suspicion her father and his brother, whom she had been living with, were up to something illegal. Maybe it had something to do with the marijuana crop she had discovered on her uncle's ranch.

Jimmy Dubois was always planning ahead. He had previously checked out a couple of nice hotels in Monterey that were located on the ocean front. Now that he knew Nancy was in agreement with his plan, he placed a call and reserved a room with an ocean view and a balcony.

"I'm sure you'll be delighted with this four star-hotel. It has all the amenities one could wish for. Here, why don't you read this information about the Monterey Plaza Hotel & Spa."

"Listen up. 'We welcome you to the beautiful Monterey Peninsula. The Monterey Plaza's convenient location on Cannery Row makes it easy to enjoy the area's many attractions and activities, such as the world-renowned Monterey Bay Aquarium only three blocks away. You can, launch an ocean kayak from the beach that is adjacent to the hotel. Plan a round of golf at one of 19 championship courses, or skate along a nearby recreation trail. Try sailing, whale watching or you can scuba dive in the marine sanctuary of Monterey Bay. Take a leisurely stroll to Fisherman's Wharf, Old Town Monterey, or the Maritime Museum. Enjoy a scenic drive to Carmel, Pebble Beach, 17 Mile-Drive, or magnificent Big Sur.'"

"Well, how does it sound, Nancy?"

"It's like one of my daydreams coming true."

"Can you afford a four star hotel?"

"Sure, its no problem, but I won't be footing the bill for the Presidential Suite. It's only a mere $2,400.00 a night, just a little rich for my blood."

"Wow. That's a lot of money, Jim"

"That it is. The rooms start around $200.00 a night. The room I chose is around $400.00 a night and it has an ocean view with a balcony."

"From the description I read in the brochure, it sounds like a lovely place to spend some time. I can't wait to see this hotel. What a change it will be for me. My uncle sometimes forced me to sleep in the barn with the animals when he was mad at me."

"Tell me you're joking!"

"No I'm not. It was so scary alone in the dark, hearing all those night sounds. I would bury myself deep in the hay to hide from what might be prowling around outside and wait for morning to come."

"Nancy, if I would have know he had done that to you I would have beaten the man senseless."

"Jim, I think you gave him a beating he will not soon forget." She gave him an approving smile.

"I hesitate to ask you, Jim. Do you think we could go whale watching and maybe do some roller skating?"

"I'll tell you what, we'll do everything your heart desires." He could see the excitement in her twinkling eyes. He was sure she had been deprived of many things in her short life and he was going to change that if at all possible.

After checking in, they both dressed in the best clothes they had and strolled down Cannery Row to the Schooner restaurant.
She was delighted with the ambiance of the restaurant. Never in her life had she dined in such a beautiful place as this. Were all these special gifts

and genuine kindness she had received since meeting Jim Dubois just a dream, which would disappear when she awoke, or was it real?

"Jim, would you order for me? I've never dined in such a nice place."

"No problem. Is there any sort of food you would prefer?"

"Some nice fish sounds good."

"What sort of drink did the waiter pour in my glass? Was it wine?

"Yes, it is. It's a soft, low-alcoholic content wine. It's sweet and I think you'll enjoy it, probably comes from a winery in Napa Valley, north of San Francisco."

"Thanks, Jim, but no thanks. I don't drink anything with alcohol in it."

"Really. May I ask why?"

"Sure, you may ask. The answer is simple, I just don't believe in drinking any sort of strong drinks."

"Did you know, Nancy, some medical doctors believe a glass of wine now and then is a healthy thing?"

"Those doctor's could be right, but I've made a promise not to drink or smoke."

"So, from what you say, I must conclude, because you don't smoke or drink, you must be one of those crazy, eccentric Mormons. We are in Mormon country, aren't we?"

Nancy turned towards Jim, giving him a stone-cold look, which stopped him from speaking any more foolishness about her religion.

"You're correct, Jim. I am a Mormon and couldn't be prouder. I can see, you too have imperfections. I was beginning to believe you were perfect, but I see you can put your big foot in your mouth just like any fool."

Jim knew he had offended her and wished he had engaged his brain before he spoke.

"Truly, I'm sorry Nancy, I...."

"No need to explain why you're a bigot. Let's just drop this subject for now."

This dinner would become an occasion that she would always cherish, even though Jim's ill-conceived comments had changed the essence of what should have been a perfect evening.

As they casually strolled along the sidewalk to their hotel, Jim attempted again to apologize for his rudeness.

"Nancy, please accept my sincere regrets for what I said. You know I'm your friend and wouldn't intentionally hurt you."

She smiled agreeably and said, "Alright you big lug, you're forgiven."

Jim gave her a fatherly hug and said, "Thank you."

As far as Jim's experience with hotels, this one would rate right at the top. Their room was perfect. From the balcony they could see the harbor, which was a stunning sight at night.

Jim insisted that she take the bedroom, knowing a young lady needs her privacy. He chose the couch, which was as comfortable as most beds.

With a blanket wrapped around him, Jim sat on the couch and stared out at the harbor. He thought about what he had become. If he could only forget those times in his life that had consequently turned him into an outlaw, he felt that maybe he could be happy.

His pleasant dreams quickly turned into fragmented visions of federal cops searching for him in every nook and cranny of his life. He was unable to escape their relentless efforts, for the harder he tried to flee the more he failed. In his nightmare, his fellow agents arrested him as though a common criminal, shackled him with cold, heavy chains and hauled him off to some unknown prison to spend the remainder of his earthly life. His paralyzing fear awakened him sharply from his dreadful nightmare. Cold sweat streamed down his face. With a fear of the uncertainty of his night-hag, he searched the dark corners of his room wondering if the specters were hiding there, waiting for the right time to emerge and take him captive.

In days long past, it was believed nightmares were evil spirits sent to haunt and suffocate sleeping persons. The sensation of oppression and helplessness caused him to wonder if that belief could be true. Sigmund Freud suggested that one's dreams are fulfillment of the dreamer's wishes. Jim's dreams were certainly not his wishes.

As his trepidation slowly subsided, he knew from the day he had picked up Nancy on that Idaho highway, the majority of his thoughts were only about her and not his pursuers. It may have been a bad mistake on his part, not paying more attention to those who might be his pursuers, yet he had enjoyed his peace of mind.

 He should have been considering what the agency might be doing to find him. He had the self-assurance of a fighter pilot. Jim Dubois (Fletcher) had always considered himself more intelligent, and clever than his associates in the department and knew they would have difficulty finding him. This gave him a sense of false security, which he never considered to be a problem. He was even foolish enough to believe the F.B.I. would never come looking for him, for he was thinking of himself as a good guy, now that he had someone important in his life to care about.

Nearly speaking out loud, he said, "You dumb fool, Fletcher. Your criminal activities over the years have netted you a small fortune and in all likelihood you could have killed three people in the booby-trapped cabin of yours and two of them were old friends and fellow agents." As he pondered over these thoughts, all of his false elusions vanished. He knew now, of certainty, they would be coming for him.

The guilt he had tried to suppress for so many years was starting to raise its ugly head. His troubling thoughts quickly vanished when he heard Nancy's pleasant voice.

"Good morning, Jim, how was your night?"

"Not so good."

He had a wet washcloth folded across his eyes and his head was laid back on the couch.

"You're right, you look like something the cat drug in. What's wrong?"

"Terrifying nightmares, one after another, all night long, and each dream seemed to be scarier than the previous one."

"I'm sorry to hear that. Maybe it was something you ate or drank last night and it didn't agree with you. I learned in a psychology class that our dreams often are subconscious wishes or fears. Most people have dreams, some remember them and others never do."

"Well, in my case, I can remember my dreams."

"There doesn't seem to be any significance to men's dreams. Let me briefly tell you this story, it might give you something to consider."

"I'm listening"

"This young boy named Joseph was sold by his jealous brothers to a caravan headed for Egypt. Eventually he became the property of the Pharaoh's household and as time passed he gained great respect from the Pharaoh. The Pharaoh had a dream that troubled him because he didn't understand it. He had heard that Joseph had the ability to interrupt dreams and he summoned Joseph to his palace. He asked him what the seven fat sheep and the seven skinny ones in his dream meant. Joseph told the Pharaoh there would be seven years of plenty and then seven years of famine in the land. He told the Pharaoh he should prepare for the famine by storing up wheat during these years of plenty.

What is great about this story is that it's true. A famine did come upon the land and the Pharaoh and his land were the only ones to have plenty. So, you see, Jim, some dreams have importance to the one who dreams them."

"Certainly an interesting story, but I hope my dreams aren't a foreteller of things to come."

"What do you say if we do something fun today and get your mind off whatever is troubling you There are some whale watching cruises later this morning. Could we take one of the cruises? Oh please! If we're lucky we just might get to see some killer whales. The Orcas are around this time of year, looking for the artic grays and their calves."

"Are you telling me you want to see a killer whale eat another whale?"

"No, not really, but that is why the Orcas come here."

Nancy always made him feel better. "Of course we can. I did promise we could do what ever you liked."

"Thank you, Jim, I do hope you are feeling better."

Monterey Bay is picturesque in the pure sense of the word. Jim was quite taken by the natural beauty of this place and thoroughly enjoyed the cruise, especially when they were able to see several artic grays and their calves. Nancy acted, with excitement, like a young schoolgirl when the whales appeared. Her obvious joy caused Jim to laugh out loud. Her happiness pleased him.

Their guide explained why the Orcas congregate, at Monterey Bay. It's because the grays can't hug the shoreline for protection so they have to swim out into deeper water to cross the bay, which makes it easier for the Orcas to catch the slower moving calves.

As they cruised the bay looking for more whales Jim spoke. "If you ever have the opportunity to be out on the ocean, get up at sunrise and treat yourself to something stunning. You won't be sorry. The unique angles of the sun's rays during those early morning times produce the most spectacular colors. Unquestionably, the first half hour after sunrise is the most splendid time of the day."

"I'll remember what you told me, and thanks."

When they returned from their adventure, Jim took a seat on a bench along the recreation trail while Nancy rented a pair of roller blades and skated off as if she had been born with them on her feet.

He watched carefully, not wanting to lose sight of her. She reminded him of a child at play as the soft ocean breezes ruffled her golden hair. Eventually she tired and returned to take a seat next to her friend.

"I've been wondering, Nancy, since last night when I had one of my senior moments and offended you, how is it you're a Mormon, that is if you don't mind me asking? I would like to know. You need to understand something about me, where I'm coming from; you see, I grew up in a very non-religious family, which left me quite ignorant about religion. There are times like this when I would appreciate a little information. It would help me broaden my horizons, at least just a little."

"My friend, I don't want to discuss my faith with you unless you can be civil. No more smart remarks."

"Alright, I assure you, I'll be a gentleman."

"Growing up, my family attended a Methodist church not far from our home. Reverend Paul was a good man and I enjoyed listening to his sermons, yet I always felt something was missing, leaving me to wonder about a lot of things.

"One day my friends and I were walking home from school when two handsome young men dressed in white shirts and ties spoke to us as they waited at a bus stop. They introduced themselves as missionaries from the Mormon Church. Did you know that the correct name for the Mormon Church is The Church of Jesus Christ of Latter day Saints?"

"Interesting, I didn't know that."
"Over the next couple of months two of my girl friends and I completed the missionary lessons. My best friend, Susan Harper and I joined the church and were baptized on the same day. It was such a special day for me, yet I couldn't understand why my family never seemed to share my feelings. I think my mother was interested but she was afraid of my dad and would never oppose him."

"I hope it brings you the happiness you desire." Yet, he wondered why would anyone want to join any church, particularly the Mormon Church.

Chapter 35

Hacienda

The following morning Jim asked Nancy if she would like to take a drive to Gilroy, California where they would meet a realtor that would show them some homes.

He explained to her that while searching through his pants pockets he found the San Jose realtors business card. Since they had already met this realtor he should be as good as the next one to help find the perfect home. Jim knew exactly what he was looking for. In his mind he could see the home as if it really existed.

Jim explained to her about his resolution and plans to buy a small place in a quiet, secluded area where he would be left alone to enjoy his retirement years. This had been his desire long before meeting her.

Nancy was a happy, lighthearted soul, always anxious for a new adventure. Looking for a home should be a fun experience and she would get to see some new country while tagging along. Jim loved her being around because she was so positive and appreciated everything he did for her.

"Good morning, Mr. Dubois. Thanks for calling. I hope I can be of some service."

"I found your business card and decided you might be able to help me find the house I am looking for."

"Were you interested in the home in San Jose you first called me about? I could make you a good deal on it."

"No, not really."

For the next half hour Nancy sat listening to Jim explain to the realtor the sort of home he wanted.

"Come on folks, you can ride with me. We will be doing some traveling."

"By-the-way, I hope you don't mind me asking. Remember when we first met and as I was leaving I saw you beat the dog crap out of some guy. What was that all about?"

Jim answered his question. "It was just a little misunderstanding. The cowboy needed to be taught some manners, that's all."

The realtor understood from the tone in Jim's voice that he had better leave the question alone.

During the next two days the realtor and his prospective clients visited at least a dozen interesting homes throughout a two county area. What made Nancy smile was that Jim, after seeing all these homes, went back and picked the very first one they were shown. It was a lovely, spacious home nestled among some spectacular tall pines on a hillside high above Anderson Lake. The back of the property bordered a national forest, which gave them the impression that the whole forest was theirs.

His new home was located between San Jose and Gilroy, California, which is the garlic capital of America, and near a small community called Morgan Hill. The house reminded Nancy of a Spanish Hacienda with a rectangular courtyard surrounded on three sides by the house. The house was stucco with a red tiled roof. The entrance was through a wrought-iron gate, which led to a front door made of heavy wood with large, ornate hinges.

Nancy wondered if she wasn't a little presumptuous. She thought, "Why am I so excited?" This wasn't her home. It was Jim's home and he had just been a kind man who had given a runaway girl a ride. She strolled out to the veranda and took a seat to assess her situation.

"There you are, Nancy. I was wondering where you had gone. How do you like the house?"

"Oh, it's a very lovely place, maybe the nicest I've ever seen."

"I do hope you like it. It's our new home."

"No, Jim, it's your home, I'm only a tag-along."

The smile on Jim's face slowly washed away as he seriously looked into Nancy's eyes. Possibly he had assumed far too much, hoping in his heart she would always be around. In such a short time Nancy had become a special part of his life and in his heart he hoped she would never leave.

"Listen to what I have to say. I've never been more serious in my life, when I tell you, I want you to always consider this as your home."

"But why? You have no obligation to me."

"I know, but please remember each day I've spent with you, the binds of our friendship have grown stronger. I wish I could adopt you as my own daughter, which would please me more than you might know."

She beamed at him, not knowing what to say. "Thanks Jim, I've also grown very fond of you."

"It's like I've known you somewhere before, Nancy. Now will you end those foolish thoughts of yours?"

"If you say so."

"When we get settled in I promise I will attempt to locate your family. I'm sure with some outside help and my connections I can find them."

These two friends had great fun searching for the appropriate furniture and items to decorate their home. They hunted through the furniture stores in San Jose and surrounding cities for each piece and Jim didn't seem to care what price he paid. He was happy spending money and seeing Nancy's excitement. The past few weeks with her were the best he ever remembered. No one in his life had made him happier.

Whenever Jim was alone with his thoughts, and puzzling over his past, his trails of darkness began to cast an evil shadow over his life. He hadn't considered his misspent life all that often. Whenever those thoughts arose he simply brushed them aside, just like he did with his fear of the unknown. One day he would have to unravel this charade, and let Nancy know the truth.

Chapter 36

Any Leads On Fletcher

"Hi, Staggs, this is Baxter, just calling to see what the skinny is on our man Fletcher. Is there anything concrete we can work on?"

"Yes, I do have some good news for you. Fletcher has been sort of careless, to my way of thinking. His last known location was Albuquerque, New Mexico. There he screwed up by calling McGee, his old partner in crime. We had a tap on McGee's phone and we jumped on that bit of information like a duck on a June bug.

Baxter laughed. "Where in the devil did you ever hear that expression?"

"Oh, it's just something from my days on the farm."

"I'm sure we could agree that Fletcher is no longer in the state of New Mexico."

It's evident he is not aware we know of his new alias. If you guys hadn't followed him to that country doctor's office we would not have known about it, lucky for us."

"Baxter, you will appreciate this. We discovered that Fletcher purchased a new Ford pick-up truck in Amarillo, Texas some time ago. The vehicle is registered in the state of Texas to a bogus address. I'll FAX you the plate number when I get it.

"Thanks, every bit of information helps Staggs. I appreciate it."

"What about Blackstone? Do you have any information on him?"

"Nothing at all. When he flew off to Paris he simply fell off the radar. We have no idea where the slime bag has gone.

"Now McGee, that little timid weasel, is still sitting tight at his desk job, believing everything is good-enough. Considering what his superiors know, he is unaware that his boss is watching his every move, just waiting for the time he can bust his balls."

"That information is reassuring."

"Webb Detective Agency had offered some help on my request. They have already uncovered a little information on Fletcher (Dubois)."

"Yesterday I spoke with Jim Webb, who informed me they had found a Jimmy Dubois on a witness list concerning a disturbance at a Santa Fe bar. I bet that man is our Fletcher."

"When you get anything new, give me a call, Staggs."

"Will do. Talk to you later."

Chapter 37

Calculating Fletcher's Whereabouts

"Weeks have passed since Fletcher nearly blew us all to kingdom come and here we are not any closer to catching him than when we lost him," Baxter spoke in disgust.

"Come on you two lets put our minds together and see what we can come up with. Look over every bit of information that's been gathered on Fletcher and see what sort of picture appears."

"Niki, would you write down what we know about Fletcher as we discuss it."

"Sure Dad, I would be happy to."

"At the top of the list is his alias, Jimmy Dubois."

"It's very fortunate for us, or we wouldn't have a single bit of information to work on," Niki commented.

"Staggs told me they had discovered Dubois had purchased a new Ford pickup truck in Amarillo, Texas and it has Texas tags on it."

"They also believe he was in Santa Fe, New Mexico because his name showed up on a crime report as a witness in a bar room altercation."

" Why would that knot-head give the police his name?"

"For some strange reason, Fletcher hasn't been very careful in hiding his trail. The credit card he's been using under his new name has shown up three times. Once in Idaho Falls, Idaho, where he bought a lot of camping and fishing gear. Next, he used it in Sun Valley, Idaho. What's strange about that purchase is he bought some nice women's clothes. What do you two make of that?"

Matt answered "That's an intriguing question. Maybe the old boy has himself a girl friend."

"As long as I have known Fletcher," Baxter said, "I never knew him to be a ladies man. He was just to damn ornery. I don't know of any woman who would put up with him."

"The last credit card purchase Fletcher made was in Monterey, California at a swanky four-star hotel. He stayed there for four days. The hotel clerk told our field agent he had a young woman with him and he was driving a Ford truck with Texas plates."

"No more purchases have been made on that card since then. It's been three weeks with no more leads."

"What do you two make of what we have so far?"

Niki suggested, "It's no secret about Fletcher's love for his Virginia cabin. He spent a lot of time there over the years. Do you think he might be looking for another secluded place to hideout in California?"

"That's a likely possibility, but we don't know what's going on in that man's head. California is a big state and for all we know he might have headed for Canada or Mexico."

"We don't have anything to move on at the present time, so we will have to wait until something else turns up. Remember, no knee-jerk reactions. We need to be sure before going after him."

Baxter smirked, "It's been said patience is a virtue, I suppose I'm not a very virtuous person. My patience is running out."

Chapter 38

Morgan Hill

"Nancy, today is one of those splendid California days you read about in the Chamber of Commerce ads. The sun is shining, it's warm and I swear I can smell the ocean on the gentle wind blowing up the mountainside. What do you say about going for a ride? I've got a great idea."

"Sure, I'm game. What do you have planned?"

"You will just have to wait. I know you'll be surprised."

Nancy was becoming accustomed to his surprises. They were always fun and often meant something special for her.

"What's keeping you, Jim? See you out in the truck and hurry up, I'm ready and waiting."

One hour later the two friends pulled into a Jeep dealership in Palo Alto. Jim had called them earlier and knew they had the model of Jeep he believed would suit their needs. Without much bartering, an agreement on the price was settled on. The two-year-old Jeep Wrangler had less than fifteen thousand miles on the clock and looked as though it was new. It was a real beauty, black in color with chrome wheels. Jim paid the dealer with cash he had drawn out of a new, local bank account he had set up recently with money that had been wired in from an off shore-account. He used a different name, and the new I.D. he would be using from now on. Jim didn't tell Nancy about the account because he was afraid she might get upset and leave.

Jim had the dealer put the title to the Jeep in Nancy's name without her knowing. It was to be a surprise for her when the time was right.

"What do you think of this Jeep?"

"Oh, it's beautiful, Jim."

"Okay, Nancy, you drive the Jeep and follow me home and we'll take it for a drive this afternoon to see how it handles the hills."

"Are you sure you want me to drive the Jeep, and not the truck?"

"Absolutely."

"Fantastic! I'll be happy to, and thanks!" Nancy had always wanted to drive a Jeep. She had seen some of the local girls back in Montana drive around town in Jeeps and she could only imagine how much fun it would be. She thought, "When we get home, I'm going to find those cowgirl boots and hat, the ones Jim bought me. I'll dress up before we go for our drive."

Nancy and Jim spent the remainder of the day driving on the lesser-driven roads and explored some interesting dirt roads leading off into unfamiliar places. It was great fun and their new Jeep didn't even breathe hard climbing along the steep back roads.

"Good morning, Jim. How did you sleep?"

"Okay, I suppose, at least I didn't have any more of those night-hags, as you call them."

"Jim, would you mind driving me to church. I haven't been in such a long time and I would love to go, and by-the-way, I would like you to come along with me."

"Sure, I would be happy to drive you, but as far as attending church with you, well, I had better beg off for now."

She was disappointed, but not surprised at his response.

"When should I pick you up?"

"Meet me out in front of the church in about one hour and fifteen minutes."

"I'm going to do a little shopping in town, Nancy. I'll see you later."

Jim parked his truck on the main street of Gilroy and did some window-shopping. It was something he hadn't done in many years and he quite enjoyed himself. When he was returning to his truck, his attention was drawn to a Sheriff's patrol car parked directly behind his vehicle. He quickly stepped back into a doorway where he could watch the cop. Jim wasn't sure what he was up to, but he did see him write something down. As the Sheriff slowly drove off he carefully looked the truck over. When the heat was out of sight Jim ran to his truck, hung a careless "U" turn and headed in the opposite direction.

Jim muttered to himself. "That deputy Sheriff's nosing around my truck is not good. Maybe it doesn't mean much in the scheme of everything in my life, but then it might mean my old comrades are closing in on me."

When he returned to the church he parked his truck in the rear parking lot and walked to the front where he could wait for Nancy. He didn't want to be seen in his truck at the present time, apparently sensing changes were coming.

He stood off a short distance watching as Nancy visited with some church-goers. "It doesn't take her long to make new friends, but I wish she would hurry."

"Where is your truck, Jim?"

"It's parked out back."

Nancy wondered why he had parked it there, when there were many parking places in front of the church, but she didn't make any comments.

"I met some nice people at church. I wish you could have gone with me, because I think you would have liked them."

"I suppose I should have gone with you. Now hurry, I need to get home."

"Is there something bothering you, Jim? If there is, can I help you?

"When we get home, Nancy, I'll try and explain what's happening. For right now I would thank you to sit quietly and not talk to me. I have a lot on my mind."

She watched Jim curiously as they hurried on home. He obeyed all the traffic regulations, but wasted no time. His actions were as if someone was pursuing them. He pulled into the garage, closed the door and went directly to his bedroom, without a word being spoken.

Nancy went to the kitchen, wondering if she should fix something for them to eat. With a quick grasp of the matters, Nancy recalled the few negative statements Jim had made about his job with the F.B.I. She hadn't worried about his comments at the time, but now, because of his actions, this could be what had bothered him today.

Several hours passed before Nancy heard him call to her.

"Nancy, would you please come to the front room. I need to speak with you."

As Jim looked at her, a sadness crept over him. He thought, "How curious life is." His dreams of a peaceful contented life wafted away.

"It's become imperative that I take some appropriate action. Remember when I told you I retired from the agency, took my pension and left before the finger of justice pointed my way?"

"Yes, I remember. What do they want you for?"

Not wanting to confess anything, which might be damning, he averted his gaze and didn't answer her question.

"Nancy, will you please listen carefully to what I'm about to tell you. I've found some good news about your family. They are all right, but living in another state, hiding from your Uncle Will. Apparently, there were some bad business dealings between your dad and Will. I don't know anything else at this time, but if I find something new, I'll do my best to let you know."

She stood up and walked over to her friend and threw her arms around his neck. "Oh, thank you, Jim. That's wonderful news."

"Now, Jim, will you tell me what happened?"

"As I returned from my shopping I spotted a sheriff's car parked behind my truck. The cop was writing down something in a notebook. When he left, I boogied out of there. Now I'm wondering if I've drawn the last card in the deck.

"I've dreaded for the longest time, this moment when I must tell you. I had hoped this day would never come and I could keep it a secret. Nancy, I should have realized there are few secrets which remain secrets but for a short time."

"Oh Jim, it's absolutely unthinkable that you're wanted by the same people you worked with for so many years. When you told me you had trouble with the F.B.I., I truly believed you were fooling around with me so I didn't take you seriously. Tell me it's not true."

"It's true."

A coaxing tone in his voice revealed a curious sadness. "Please try and understand what I'm going to say. There is not much doubt that they have conclusive evidence of my guilt, which means I'm wanted in the worst way. It was foolish on my behalf to consider their efforts to catch me weren't serious.

"Yet, as seriously as they want me captured, I believe they will never bring this crime to the public's knowledge. There will be no trial but that doesn't mean I won't be punished."

"What are we going to do, Jim?"

"You're not going to have to do anything, nor should you worry my dear. This is all on me. I have put some plans into action which will take care of you for a long time."

"Jim, you have me so confused that I'm not sure what's going on. Stop and answer a few questions for me.

"First question. Are you going to wait here, hoping they will never come, or are you going to leave and become a fugitive from the law?"

"I don't like how it sounds, being a fugitive from the law. But yes, I'll be leaving. Never could I allow those old boys to find you with me and let them believe you were associated with me in any way. My plans are to sever our relationship for now, so I can lead them on a wild-goose chase, somewhere far away for here. I don't want to fight these people, or become the bad end of a gun battle."

"Would you tell me what you did to make them come after you?"

"I'm sorry, I can't. If I were to tell you I'm afraid you might not want to be my friend. If they ever question you, you will not be lying when you tell them you don't know."

Sadness shown in her eyes and face as if she was an open book. Jim knew she was considering what was to become of her, but dared not ask.

"Come with me, Nancy, I have something I want to show you."

Jim led Nancy to his bedroom closet where he showed her a small safe, securely mounted inside the wall.

"The combination to this safe is your birthday, easy to remember, right! Only one valuable item is inside the safe. It's a key to a safe deposit box at the bank I told you about."

"Oh really, I don't have anything of value I would need to keep inside a safe deposit box."

Jim smiled. "Now you do, Nancy."

"I don't understand. What do you mean?"

"There are a few things there which will be of some great interest to you. The title to our Jeep is inside the box and it shows you as the owner."

"I don't believe it. I never owned a car, much less anything so nice. Thanks, but you can't give me your Jeep."

"Yes, I can, and I did."

"I'm going to be gone for quite some time and I don't want to worry about where you are living. Inside the deposit box you will also find the title to our home, in your name, and a check book with a sizeable balance which will take care of your needs for a long time."

She looked as if a bolt of lightning had struck her. Tears formed in her eyes and rolled down her cheek. She could not find the appropriate words to speak.

Through tear-blurred eyes she gazed at Jim. "You are a very kind and generous man, but I could never accept so much, believing the money which paid for all this was ill-gotten."

"Nancy, there was a degree of predictability in your response. I was sure you wouldn't want anything that was purchased with stolen money. This house and everything I've given you was bought with my own personal money that I earned honestly, working the many years for the department, and I could prove it if it becomes necessary. I've done some bad things, Nancy, but lying to you isn't one of them. Just please believe me."

She believed in her heart Jim was telling her the truth, but with everything that had just happened it was more than she could hardly comprehend. She remained silent to consider everything he had told her.

For the past few months Jim had been smitten by Nancy's sweet, genuine personality. Never a kinder, better natured young lady had it been his privilege to know. But now, the dreadful day was here at his doorstep and he was beseeched with an overwhelming feeling of urgency to get out of Dodge.

"Will you graciously accept these gifts from this old guy who wishes he were something more than just your friend? I've not used these words often in my life. I love you as a daughter I never had and I will always be grateful for the time we've had together."

"Words couldn't convey my thanks to you, Jim, and I love you too."

"Time is wasting. I need to put some things together before I have to leave. Nancy, what I'm about to do might well turn into an exercise in futility. I'm not at all certain they are even close to catching me, but I have a bad feeling and I'm sure I should act before it's too late."

"Jim, have you considered turning yourself in and trying to make amends for your misdeeds?"

"No, my dear, not for even the briefest of moments. You see, I don't believe in asking for forgiveness. My old friends would think that I'm some sort of a fool and nothing I might say would help."

"Can I help you pack?"

"No, but if you wouldn't mind making me a couple of sandwiches, I would appreciate it."

Several minutes later, Nancy, carrying a small picnic sized cooler packed with everything she could fit inside, walked into Jim's bedroom. She was shocked when she saw three automatic pistols in his suitcase. The sight of the guns terrified her. They could only mean that Jim's fate might be sealed in those guns.

Nancy stood outside the garage as she heard the engine of Jim's truck come to life. He began to back out and then lowered the window and called, "Come here, girl."

Nancy ran to the truck, climbed onto the step and reached in, throwing her arms around his neck as she kissed his unshaven cheek. Tears were running down her face and she started to sob.

"Now don't wimp out on me, Nancy. Take good care of the place and especially yourself."

"I will, Jim, and remember to never give up, for there is always hope."

Her sadness deepened as she watched the taillights fade into the twilight.

The hollowness in his heart nearly caused him to shout out with the despair he felt in his soul, but there was nothing he could do. He must go on.

Nothing seems to live longer than a perverse idea. This notion of Jim's had now come full circle from the days he had conceived it and it was about ready to turn around and bite him square in the ---.

Chapter 39

Santa Clara Sheriff Spots His Truck

When Deputy Sheriff McAllister returned to the station, after completing his shift, he gathered his notebooks. He was certain he recalled writing something down about a F.B.I. request to locate a new Ford truck with Texas plates. It wasn't long before he found what he remembered writing in his notes. His memory hadn't failed him. The truck he had checked out earlier in Gilroy was the one the F.B.I. was interested in, however the request didn't say why they wanted to find this particular vehicle.

The following morning officer McAllister called Agent Staggs in the Washington D.C. office.

"Good morning, this is Agent Staggs, can I help you?"

"Yes, my name is John McAllister from the Santa Clara Sheriff's Department in California. A while ago I wrote down a request from your office to locate a Ford truck with Texas plates. Yesterday morning I spotted the truck in Gilroy, California's downtown area. After my shift was over I located the request in one of my old notebooks and it is the truck you are interested in."

"That is great news. Have you ever seen that vehicle before?"

"No Sir, I haven't. But why are you interested in the individual?"

"I wish I could tell you. If you do spot the truck again, give us a call directly, but don't stop it. The person that might be driving the vehicle could be dangerous, and we don't have a warrant or a cause to arrest him at this time. What we are interested in is knowing where he lives."

"Thanks for the good police work, Deputy McAllister. I hope we can talk again. Have a good day and thanks."

Chapter 40

Fletcher Leaves for Bakersfield

Jim drove eastbound towards I-5 contemplating what actions he would take. He muttered to himself, "Bakersfield is my next stop and tomorrow I will take a flight over the San Gabriel Mts. to Upland, where some old friends live. It would be nice to see them again, if they're still around."

His loneliness could only be equaled by the darkness of the night. With his headlights piercing the gloom, he drove on. He was wondering what suspicions the Santa Clara Sheriff may have had about his truck. The truck still displayed Texas plates and he realized now he should have registered the truck in California.

He thought, "What if, the F.B.I. had put out an 'attempt to locate' on my vehicle? How would they have known about this truck I bought months ago in Amarillo, and how would they have known about my new alias?"

With the passing of each mile, Jim's anger grew as he took into consideration how his life had now been changed for the worse. His beautiful home and the hope he had for a peaceful life, away from the stress he had dealt with, was now gone and he would most likely never see Nancy again.

"That bone-head Baxter and every one of his associates! They are to blame. It is their fault, not mine."

Some of his old friends would have labeled him a sociopath, a person who knows what's wrong but doesn't care. He would never accept responsibility for his actions. That was one of Fletcher's character flaws. Why couldn't they have just left it all alone?

He spoke out loud, "Now is the hour of my power. I'm going to lead those clowns as far away from Nancy as I possibly can and then I'll set a trap that will put an end to those inept jokers."

Contacting the detective agency he once dealt with, to help find Nancy's family, wasn't the brightest thing for an old streetwise F.B.I. agent to do. She needed help and he had promised her he would find them. Now, with a change of plans, he felt this would work out to suit him just fine.

The following morning Jim awoke early. He had not rested very well in the small motel on the outskirts of Bakersfield. He ate a light breakfast and inquired about the location of Meadows Field, the local airport.

"Good morning, Sir. How can I help you?"

Jim answered, "I would like to rent a plane for a day or two. It's such beautiful weather to fly and I want to surprise some family members I haven't seen in a long time."

"I'm sure we can assist you. What type of plane are you interested in renting?"

"A high wing Cessna would be fine. Could you a excuse me while I get my pilot's license."

"We can help you with that choice."

Jim realized he hadn't planned everything as well as he should have. His pilot's license didn't fit his new alias. It was issued years ago in his given name, Jim Fletcher. He wondered, "Why am I making such foolish mistakes? Using my real name after all this time will make them wonder what's going on."

When he located his license and his true I.D., he returned to the flight office.

"May I have a look at your flight log?"

After checking through the log he said, "Mr. Fletcher, would you mind if we took a little check ride before I turn you loose with one of our planes? Your log indicates you haven't flown much in the past couple of years."

"No, I don't mind. I would do the same thing if our positions were reversed, although, over the years I have accumulated a lot of flight time and consider myself an accomplished airman."

"Yes, I can see you have. This short check ride will satisfy my insurance company and me. We have a Cessna available which should suit your needs."

"Your check ride indicates you are a good pilot. I would suggest that in the future, you take some time out of your schedule to keep your flying skills current. I have your rental agreement, flight log, and credit card here for you. You can take her whenever you like."

"There are a couple of other things I need. Would you mind if I leave my truck parked out front until I return?"

"We've never had the parking lot filled, so your truck will be fine parked there."

"Oh yes, I need to make a phone call before I leave. Would you mind if I use your phone? You can add the charge to my credit card."

"No problem, the phone is there in my office."

" Hello, whom am I speaking to?"

"This is agent Staggs of the D.C. office." He knew Fletcher's voice.

Staggs signaled to another agent in the office to put a trace on his call.

"Take hold of your seat. You won't believe it when I tell you who you're talking to. This is your old associate, Jim Fletcher."

"This is quite a surprise. Nice to hear from you again and what do I owe the honor?" Staggs always tried to be congenial, even to those he didn't like.

"Oh, I just wanted to hear what a jackass sounds like, again. It's been a long time."

"You know, you're really not such a nice guy. What's your problem? Someone pee in your Cheerios this morning?"

"Staggs, you know as well as I do, I'm not a nice guy and could care less about any of you, so lets drop that subject."

"Fletcher, you know this phone call of yours is strange and honestly, I don't understand your reason for calling. I wonder what your problem is. Have you lost your grip on reality? I hope you haven't had too many drinks. Don't you know you can't afford to lose any more brain cells?"

"Up yours, Staggs. Let me tell you this, and I'll make it simple so you can understand. Don't come around looking for me or all of you will be sorry. I promise."

"We're not looking for you Fletcher. Why would we?"

Fletcher, laughed vigorously. "Don't lie to me. Do you consider me some sort of a simpleton?"

"No, Fletcher, we don't think you're a simpleton, but I would like to know why you destroyed your life!"

The phone was quiet for a moment. He did not answer the troubling question.

"By not answering my question, are you admitting to your guilt?"

"No, you have all the answers, Staggs. Why are you asking me about things you believe to be true?"

"To be honest with you, Fletcher, I'm only trying to keep this conversation going for as long as possible."

"Just as I expected. You've got a trace on my phone. Good work, old boy, but it won't do you any good to find me. Remember to carefully watch your backsides, for whatever good that might do you. You see, I don't believe any of you people could find your butts with both hands. So, all of you go piss up a rope!" The phone was silent.

"Did you get a trace on that phone call of mine?"

"That trace was an easy one. Your man is in Bakersfield, California at the Greenhorn Mountain Flight School, located at Meadows Airfield."

Staggs loathed corruption. Fletcher and his gang were an absolute embarrassment to the bureau. He would do his best to help Baxter and his partners catch the three of them.

"Get on the horn and see if you can shake one of our agents loose to verify if Fletcher is still around the airport. FAX them Fletcher's picture and a description of his vehicle. Instruct them not to arrest him and use extreme care, our intentions at the present are to just find him, nothing more."

Chapter 41

Meadows Airfield

Fletcher purchased a sectional map of the area he would be flying in. He folded it to make it easier to read his route and then loaded two suitcases behind the front seats.

He climbed aboard, studied the map, waved to the rental agent and slammed the door. He thought, "There aren't many things I enjoy more than flying. This should be an interesting day for an aerial adventure, a time to clear my mind and plan my next move."

Before starting to taxi he remembered that he had a little something for his old friend, Baxter, to think about. He reached over, shut the engine down, walked to his truck, opened the door and threw a simple scribbled note on the front seat and then locked the door. There was no question in Fletcher's mind that they knew about his truck. Once it was spotted in the parking lot, it would be thoroughly examined and they would find his note.

"Easy come, easy go," he thought. "My beautiful truck was a dream fulfilled, something I had always wanted, but now it will end up in the hands of the bureau where some scum-bag, who doesn't give a rats hind end about it, will get to drive it."

 He spit anger and screamed out in frustration. Finally his rage died, but in its place was resolution.

A gentle wind was blowing as he took one last look at his truck. Sadly, he climbed back aboard the plane and restarted the engine. He carefully kept an eye on the oil pressure while watching the engine temperature climb. His frustrations were quietly fading away.

After asking for take-off instructions, Fletcher taxied to the far end of the runway and waited. "This will be a day to forget my troubles," he thought,

He felt as excited as when he took his first flight.

Now he had blown his alias, Jimmy Dubois, he considered he might as well use his true identity, although both I.D's. might be useful for a while.

As the plane's landing gear separated from the black asphalt runway, the sensation that had always thrilled him was again in the pit of his stomach and it made him happy. He had never lost his zeal for flying.

Years ago, when he was taught basic flying skills, the plane he learned to fly was a high-winged Cessna. To this day he preferred flying a high-wing plane. Maybe it was because the view below was unobstructed.

Within a half hour he was flying east towards the Mojave Desert and talking to himself, trying to decide on a clever plan.

Because he had been alone most of his life Fletcher had developed the habit of talking to himself. "Where should I go first? There are numerous airports in L.A. and San Bernardino counties. Palm Springs is a place I've always wanted to visit; and maybe I'll fly there. It's not so far away and it shouldn't take me long to get there. I won't be able to spend too much time in any one place, because having those three chasing me in this cat and mouse game won't be at all fun, if I allow them to catch me too soon. I know precisely where I'll let them find me and then the real fireworks will start," he mused.

"Before I fly to Palm Springs I would like to see if my old friends, Jeff and Bob are still around. The Upland Airport is not too many miles from where they live. I'll call them from there and hopefully, we can get together and share some stories of times long past. I don't think the agency knows anything about these friends and maybe I could hang out there for a couple of days before I make my next move."

Flying low, so he could see the highways, he headed southeast towards Lancaster. "There is certainly a whole bunch of nothing out here, just a lot of dirt roads and trails, which seem to lead nowhere. Someone must use them, but I can't see what for."

He flew over Lancaster then turned east and began watching carefully for interstate I-15. When he spotted the interstate he trailed it south, down Cajon Pass, towards San Bernardino. Once through the pass he hugged the south side of the San Gabriel Mountains, and flew west to Upland, which was only a short distance.

When he landed at the Cable, Upland Airport, he felt a sense of relief. It had been a long time since he had flown with so much other air traffic and it made him nervous, which he didn't like.

Rummaging through his belongings he located his address book with the name and phone number of his friend, Jeff Burrows, who lived in Ontario. He would call and hope he was at home.

"Hello, is this the Jeff Burrows residence?"

"Yes, it is, but Jeff is out."

"Sorry to hear that. This is Jim Fletcher, an old friend. I was hoping to find him."

"I remember you, Jim. We met once, years ago, at a car show in Anaheim. My name is Bob Saunders."

"Of course. You two were showing off your beautiful Corvettes. Do you still have them?"

"No, we don't have those particular cars anymore but each of us has two Vettes now. We live and breathe Corvettes, you might say. It seems our lives sort of revolve around those cars, yet, I suppose there are worse ways to spend our retirement years."

"It does sound fun, Bob. Would you tell Jeff I called?"

"I would be happy to. Why don't you give me your cell phone number and I'll have him call you when he returns. Hang on, I believe he just pulled in the driveway."

Within a minute Jeff picked up the phone and the two laughed and joked for several minutes before Fletcher hung up.

"Hey, Bob. Would you like to fly to Palm Springs with Jim? We could do a little sight seeing on the way and have lunch on Jim's nickel. He has a rented plane over at the Upland Airport and would enjoy having us for company. All that we have to do is get our bodies from here to there."

"Most definitely yes, but one question, is Jim a good pilot?"

"Well, we will find out soon enough, won't we? I've never had the opportunity to fly with him."

"Which Vette should we take, Bob?"

"Why don't you drive one of your cars. I think Jim might like to see what you drive."

While Fletcher waited for his friends, he picked up a post card in the gift shop and wrote a short note to the young lady that he would miss desperately.

Dear Nancy,

My Lass, I've gone far away don't know when I'll return. Some day I hope to. I promise I'll contact you whenever I can. Please take good care of yourself.

Love Ya,
Grizzly

Chapter 42

Good Lead

"The phone call is for you, Baxter. It sounds like Staggs."

"Hi, my friend, what do you have for us?"

"Good news, and pack your necessities. I'll have a plane waiting for the three of you at the Manassas Airport. When you're airborne we will have time to talk and not until then can I fill you in on what's been happening. Don't waste any time getting to the airport. We have a strong lead on our man, Fletcher."

"That's great news, Staggs."

With the command that would make a Marine Corp Drill Sergeant proud, Baxter yelled out, "Matt and Niki, hurry and grab a few things, we have a plane to catch."

"What's going on, Dad? Can you tell us what you know?"

"Sorry, Niki, I don't know anything other than we have a plane to catch and Staggs has a hot lead on our man. When we're aboard he's going to call and give me the low down."

Excitement grew within the three as they sped towards the airport and the waiting plane.

Baxter and Niki hurried ahead. Matt couldn't help pausing for a brief moment to check out the elegant business jet parked there, waiting to take them to parts unknown. The Falcon 900 was painted white with a striking red trim. Matt always admired these planes, much as he would admire a beautiful woman. The Falcon was French built.
Within a few minutes, the Falcon taxied to the far end of the active runway and stopped, waiting for the clearance to take off. They were soon

airborne and climbing through the clear morning sky.

When Baxter finished his conversation with Staggs he said cheerfully, "Alright, I have great news. For some strange reason that butt-brain Fletcher called Staggs, allowing him to get a positive trace on the phone call, just as if he wants us to know his location. Fletcher made the call from Bakersfield, California, and that's where we are headed."

"That's the first lead we've had on him in a very long time, but why would you think he would still be there when we arrive?"

"I certainly don't believe he will be sitting around waiting for us, but judging by his behavior, it might indicate he wants us to catch up with him. We are going to have to be extremely careful, because this man is completely unpredictable. Matt, if it was Fletcher we don't want him to get another shot at you."

Matt offered Baxter a sheepish grin, but did not reply to his comment.

"Staggs said he was attempting to find an agent to check out the place where he made the phone call from. It's interesting to note that yesterday a Santa Clara Deputy Sheriff spotted Fletcher's Ford pickup in Gilroy, California. It's the one he purchased in Texas."

"Where is Gilroy?" Niki asked.

Matt answered, "It's a few miles south of San Jose. So we must conclude he would be heading south. Brilliant deduction, wouldn't you say, Niki?"

She stretched out her leg and kicked Matt in the chin. "Don't be a smart 'A.'"

"There's another point Staggs reminded me of. It's imperative we catch Fletcher, if we know what's good for us. The bureau is very nervous about this whole ugly affair and they want us to put an end to it.

"We might as well get some rest. It's going to be a few hours before we arrive and who can tell where this pervasive man might take us. You can bet on this, we will catch him."

Matt wasn't the same man he was before the shooting. He was always tired and only wanted to rest. He pulled a blanket over his body, laid his head back on his seat, looked out the window and watched the country pass by them.

"Niki."

"Yes, what is it?"

"I've been thinking. It's easier to dream a dream than it is to live one. Many dreams I have dreamed, but there are few, if any, I can ever remember coming true."

"What is it you're trying to say, Matt?"

"Oh, never mind. I'm just thinking out loud."

With a languishing look she watched Matt slowly drift off and she wondered if there ever would be anything she could do to help this man she loved.

The droning engines had a relaxing sound to them and helped all of them yield to their stress.

Matt awoke with Niki gently holding his hand.

"What is it, Niki?"

"I supposed you were having some bad dreams, that's all."

The warmth and softness of her hand gave him comfort. "Thanks, Niki," he responded by squeezing her hand and offering her an engaging smile.

"Would you like to play a card game, Matt?"

"Sure, that sounds like a good way to pass the time. Do you remember what happened the last time we played cards and we ran into a herd of range cattle?"

"Never in this world or the world to come will I forget that night, Matt."

"We walked away from that accident. What would it look like if this airplane ran into a herd of cattle?" Matt grinned at Niki, in a morbid sort of way.

"That thought of yours is not at all funny. We just about lost our lives that night, along with our precious freedom."

A red light flashed in the cabin as the phone rang. "Baxter here."

"This is Agent Jordan. Staggs instructed me to check on your man of interest, Fletcher. He was here this morning and left hours ago in an airplane he has rented. He filed no flight plan so we have no idea where he might be. When your plane arrives, I'll meet you there. By-the-way, your man's pickup truck is parked in front of the flight center. I've been keeping an eye on it just in case he returns. I haven't checked his truck out. I'll wait until you're here and ready to take a look."

"Alright, Agent Jordan. We'll see you when we arrive."

As soon as they landed, Baxter and agent Jordan walked to the flight center and questioned the rental agent.

"Did Mr. Fletcher tell you where he was going or when he would return?"

"No, he didn't say, nor did he file a flight plan, but he indicated he was going to return tomorrow."

"Do I need to worry about my plane?"

"I wouldn't think so. He's a very good pilot. Could you give us the tail number of your airplane? It would be helpful."

"Sure," and he handed them the "N" number written on a company note pad.

"That truck certainly looks like Fletcher's. It even has the correct Texas plates. It's strange he didn't bother to get rid of those plates."

"Can you unlock the truck?"

"No problem. I called the local Ford dealer earlier and he was able to bring me a key. Because the truck is so new they had no problem getting the code and a correct key."

"Look, here on the front seat, it must be a note. Jordan handed Baxter the note and he read it out loud."

"Hi Larry, Curly and Moe. Aleksandar, you're nothing more than a traitor to your motherland, and Matt, you are a stupid, no-count blue suiter, who was duped into believing you could become a Secret Service Agent, just because you were willing to help them. For you, pretty Niki, you were used by your dad to persuade Matt to do your dirty work, so what does that make you?"

Baxter spoke up. "When we catch Fletcher, I promise both of you, I'm going to rip his despicable face off."

Matt commented, "Don't you see what he is trying to do? He wants to rattle our chains and lose our cool so we are more apt to make a stupid mistake. What do you say, let's not go off half-cocked. Anyway, the first one of us who gets their hands on him can knock him sideways."

On the opposite side of Fletcher's note was written four locations, Ontario, Big Bear, Palm Springs and Gable.

"Look at this. What do you suppose he means by leaving us this information? It certainly was no accident," Niki commented.

All four walked back to the flight office. Baxter asked if the agent could give them some assistance.

"This might be a stupid question and a hard one to answer. How many airports are there that he might fly to?"

He laughed, "Impossible to say."

"Take a look at this piece of paper he left in his truck. It has four locations listed on it, Ontario, Big Bear, Palm Springs and Cable. Are there airports at these places?"

"Yes, all of them have airports."

"Would you mind if we take a look at one of those sectional maps of the area?"

"Let's see how many airports there are in a radius of a couple hundred miles. Write them down, Matt, as I read them off. San Bernardino, Redlands, Rialto, Brackett Field, Chino, Corona, Riverside, Ontario, and Palm Springs. Baxter shook his head. "There are too many for even an army to cover."

"Alright, you two will need to watch his truck tonight in case he is stupid enough to return for it."

The night turned into a long and boring effort and there was not a thing to show for it. None of them believed he would be foolish enough to come back, as he had to know they would be waiting for him. At this time, Fletcher was in total control of the game.

The following morning, Baxter called his boss. "Staggs, would you check Fletcher's personal records and see if he ever had any family or friends in southern California?

"Anything else?"

"No, our boy has literally flown the coop. He rented a plane and flew off into the wild blue yonder. Yet, it seems strange, he acts as if he wants us to catch him."

Soon they had a reply to their request. Fletcher had two friends in Upland, CA, a Jeff Burrows and Bob Saunders.

The flight center provided Baxter with the phone number of the Federal Aviation Office in Los Angeles.

"Niki, would you mind using your charm and a little of your authority to persuade the F.F.A. to help us locate Fletcher's rented airplane? He is going to have to land it somewhere and with all the eyes and ears they have they should be able to spot the plane so we will have a starting place. Here is the tail number of the plane and give them my cell number."

"The F.F.A. said they would put out a notice to locate, within the next half hour, to all the airports in southern California and Nevada. Dad, those F.F.A. people couldn't have been nicer, very cooperative, in fact they were quite pleasant. It must have been my charm, it always seems to work." She gigged as she walked back to where Matt was waiting.

"This is the plan. Niki and Matt, I want you to watch Fletcher's truck for a few more hours in case he does show up. I seriously doubt he will, it's not part of his plan. If he doesn't show, then have the truck impounded with an F.B.I. hold on it. Agent Jordan said it would be all right for you two to use this car. They have a few spare vehicles and he is not worried about getting it back anytime soon.

"When you get Fletcher's truck impounded, drive to Burbank, get a place to hang out at and let me know where I can find you. I'm going to hire one of these local pilots to fly me to the airport in San Bernardino. I'll rent a car and wait to see what happens. Use a lot of care if you confront Fletcher. He's like a sidewinder. You won't know when he might strike."

Niki was very worried about her dad. "Dad, I love you. Remember you are not as young as you once were. You be careful!"

"I will, Niki." He leaned over and kissed her on the cheek.

The following morning, in a motel not far from the San Bernardino airport, Baxter received a call from Staggs in the D.C. office.

"If you will go to our field office in San Bernardino, I'll FAX you some information which might be helpful. It's lucky we found these photos of Fletcher's friends taken years ago, in Southern California, at a Corvette car club meet. We only have their first names and I'm afraid nothing more."

"The information about the Corvette car club will give us a place to start looking and I want to thank you for all of your help. I have the feeling that old street cops get sometimes when they are closing in on their man and a capture is imminent. It's just a matter of time now."

"I do hope you're right, Baxter. This whole mess needs to be put to bed. Ascertain the facts, and I'll be talking to you real soon."

"Good-bye!"

The moment Baxter hung up the phone he placed a call to Niki. "I have some new information on our man, Fletcher. As we speak, Staggs is FAX-ing me two photos of some old friends of Fletcher's. It's believed they live somewhere in southern California. I know that's not much to go on, but this is one lead we can follow. These friends of his own Corvettes and they might belong to one of the many Corvette car clubs there. I obtained a list off the Internet of different chapters. I'm sending two sets of these guy's pictures and a list of club chapters. Not all of them have a physical address but most do have e-mail addresses. I suggest the two of you show them to as many members of these clubs as you can. Hopefully, someone will know them. If I ever knew anything about weekend gear heads, they will have close ties to other fellow Corvette lovers. It's my belief Fletcher might contact these old friends, and if we're lucky, they will lead us to him."

Before the end of the day, Matt and Niki had received a special delivery package containing two pictures of a couple of old white guys, most likely retired, who were allegedly owners of one or more Corvettes. Also, there was a list of various Corvette clubs in California.

"Look at this, Niki. There are nearly seventy Corvette car clubs listed in the entire state of California, yet only around twenty in southern California. Your dad has circled the ones in red that he wants us to work on."

"Niki, I don't see any listed with an address, just e-mails, although most of them do list their phone numbers. That's going to mean a lot of time on the phone."

She suggested, "This is my job. I'll make the phone calls and you can send out e-mails."

"I would be delighted, my girl."

She gave him a questioning look wondering what exactly he meant. He had never called her "my girl" before. Was he flirting with her? He hadn't done that in a long time.

"It appears, Matt, that 'Judgments pointing finger' is doing its job. I've got a good feeling about this search."

First on the list was the Wild Boys Car Club of Los Angeles. A good place to start, she thought.

Niki had the voice of an angel and always got what she asked for. Next to the love of their Corvettes, they loved the charms of a beautiful woman, like Niki. She made it almost impossible for any of these car guys to refuse her questions.

At the end of the third day of searching, they found the names of the two guys they wanted to question, Jeff Burrows and Bob Saunders. The club guys who gave them the names claimed they didn't know where Bob and Jeff lived. It was more likely they didn't want to reveal that information to the agents.

"It's frustrating, Niki, I can't find a phone listing for either of these guys."

"Hand me their names, Matt. Phone books are old school. I have access to a program on my computer, called Lexus Nexus, and it hardly ever fails me. Matt, I bet you I will have their address, phone numbers, and a lot of other information within a short minute."

"Okay, let me see you work your magic."

"What did I tell you, Matt. We now know more about these Corvette guys than we should have the right to. I'll call Baxter and tell him the good news. Rancho Cucamonga is the city they live in and I believe it's closer to his location than ours.

"Hi Dad, have you had any luck?"

"No, Niki, I haven't. It seems like most of these guys I've talked with are reluctant to tell me anything. I have a suspicion some of them know who they are but their loyalties run deeper than any fear they might have from the law."

Niki was always pleased when she was able to best her dad at anything. What she was about to tell him made her laugh.

"What are you so happy about?" That of course, was the question.

With a little good-natured ribbing, Niki said, "Beat you Dad. We've found the friends of Fletcher, have their names and address. So what do you think of that?"

"Good work, I'm proud of both of you. But, just remember that everything you two know about good police work, I taught you."

"Oh come on, Dad, give us a break. Will you do that?"

Baxter spoke with deliberateness. "Alright, Niki, fire away with those names and address. I must catch Fletcher."

Chapter 43

Upland Airport

Within a half hour Jeff and Bob pulled into the Upland Airport, driving a striking red Corvette. They parked and walked to the pilot's lounge where Jim was waiting.

"It's great to see you, Jeff. I never thought I would get a chance to cross paths with you again. Since I retired from the agency a few months ago, I've had a burning desire to see California again and maybe buy myself a retirement home somewhere in this sunny state."

"Sounds like a plan, Jim. If you do move out here we might have more opportunities to see each other and that would be a good thing."

"Should we head out? I hope my plan for the day hasn't put you guys out."

"Heck no, we are both retired with no one to answer to. So, I suppose that leaves us free to do what we want."

"Well guys, flying to Palm Springs is only a short hop and a skip from here. We will follow the highways. You two know these roads so you can be my navigators for the day, that way I shouldn't get lost," he chuckled.

Bob was a little nervous flying with Jim, not knowing anything about his flying skills. He hadn't flown very often, but Jeff was comfortable and gave Jim great directions, which led them to downtown Palm Springs. A look at the map directed their flight to the airport and a safe landing.

The three friends decided to have lunch at the airport's cafe instead of renting a car for a trip to town. Jim commented that sometimes these smaller airports provided great food. At least it would be enjoyable watching aircraft come and go as they ate.

The meals were delicious, but they would soon be forgotten. Yet, the conversation and friendships would last for all time.

Jim spoke up, " What would you two say about a flight up to Big Bear. I've never been there and thought it would be fun if the three of us checked the place out. According to the map they have a landing strip."

Jeff replied, "Sure, it sounds like fun."

"Should we tell him?" Bob asked Jeff.

"Why not."

"Jim, a couple of years ago about the time I was thinking of retiring, a long lost relative of mine left me a nice hunk of change. It was soon brought to my attention that if I didn't invest the money I would end up losing most of it to the damn government. So, guess what I did?"

"I don't have the slightest clue."

Jeff was grinning like a schoolboy who had just won all the marbles from his friends. "Bob and I bought an old cabin on the opposite side of Big Bear in a place called Fawnskin. When we bought it, it wasn't much to look at, but it was the only thing we could afford. Property around Big Bear is reserved for the rich and famous. Our cabin was probably built in the 1940s. We spent a lot of labor and money on it and now we have a beautiful place. The back of the property connects to the San Bernardino National Forest, which gives us the feeling that whole forest is ours."

"I'm happy for you two."

Jim could tell that his two friends were extremely pleased to talk about their cabin. Of course, he would never tell them about the cabin he once owned in Virginia, the one he blew up.

"What are we waiting for? When we get to Big Bear, and if we can find a car to rent, we can drive over to Fawnskin and have a look at your place. Would that be okay with you two?"

"We would love to show you our mountain hideaway."

Fletcher's Cessna circled the crystal clear lake of Big Bear, twice. The trio enjoyed the view of the placid mountain lake and the expensive cabins and homes that dotted the lakeshore and surrounding hills. He lined the plane up for an approach to the east-west runway and set the plane down with the skill and smoothness that pleased his ego.

After parking the plane, Fletcher made sure it was locked and secure before leaving. Everything he now owned was in those two suitcases. A few days ago he owned a home, a new truck and had a young lady that he truly loved as a daughter. Now it was all gone. He shook his head as if to dispel those thoughts from his mind.

"Hey, Jim, right over there." Jeff pointed to the south, where there was a nice restaurant. "We have dined there a few times. I bet they could direct us to where we might get a car."

As they entered the restaurant the hostess said, "Follow me."

Jeff spoke up. "Ma'am, wait. We are in need of a little information. We just landed and are looking for some transportation to our cabin over in Fawnskin. Do you know if there is a taxi service?"

"Yes, you might call it that. I have a friend who runs people around town, that is, if you can find him at home. Here is his phone number and good luck."

"Thank you very much."

By the time they had finished their meal, the fellow with their ride pulled in front of the restaurant and signaled to them with a wave of his hand.

"Good day, gentlemen. Are you the fellows that need a ride?"

"Yes. The lady in the restraint gave us your phone number. We flew in a few minutes ago and would like to see our friend's cabin over in Fawnskin. Could you take the three of us there?"

" That's my business. This time of the year can be slow, but during the ski-ing season I can keep busier than I like." The old fellow laughed out loud.

Fletcher asked, "Once we get there would you mind waiting for us? We shouldn't be any longer than a half hour."

"That's no problem. I would be glad to."

"Boy! That car of yours is a real beauty. It's far too nice to be used as a cab," Jeff commented.

"I purchased this Chrysler Imperial in 1963, brand new, in West Holly-wood for $4,000 dollars. Over the years I've used it pretty much as a cab, and listen to this, there are around a million miles on the old girl and she still runs like the day I bought her."

"You've got to be kidding, Mr."

"No, it's true. I've documented everything I've ever done to the car. I never let any problems go without getting them repaired, pronto." He grinned, and reported, "It's not the original, engine. Just about everything on the car has been replaced at least once."

"How many engines have you gone through?

"This is number three."

The men were exchanging grins. "You must be a proud man to own such a car!"

"That I am. Shall we go gentlemen? I guarantee you'll enjoy the ride."

The three friends piled into the back seat. "I had forgotten how much room there is in these cars. It's very much like sitting on a sofa in the front room of your own home."

They settled in and enjoyed the sights as they drove around the lake. It was a few miles to the quaint little town of Fawnskin. The highway wound back and forth, following the shoreline.

Bob said, "This side of the lake is where the less affluent people live. Right, Jeff?"

"That's true. Those people who live in the city of Big Bear, which is on the south side of the lake, call their residences mansions, cabins, or summer homes. Even so, I know I'll never have to be troubled with lots of money, but irregardless, we love our cabin and are very happy with it. If it hadn't been for some good fortune we would have never had the money to buy it."

"Turn here at the fire station, driver!"

"That's a fire station?"

"Yep. It's not much to look at, but we do have one fire truck. It's an old one," Jeff said.

Following the directions Jeff offered their driver, they drove the meandering roads up the mountain until their cabin was in view. It was situated at the end of the street, facing south, towards the lake.

Bob and Jeff had doubled the floor space by adding on a new addition and completely renovating the original cabin.

Fletcher was somewhat of an expert at building cabins. He had built his own cabin with all sorts of cool cloak and dagger stuff integrated into its construction. He liked what they had done and he could see some great possibilities, if he owned the place.

"Okay, what do you think?"

Fletcher answered, "No doubt about it, you guys did a great job. It's a beautiful cabin. Why don't you show me around?"

These two friends were about as excited showing off their cabin as they were when they were showing off their Corvettes.

"So, my friend, come out back. I would like you to see something very special we have growing in our backyard."
They walked around the cabin and up the hillside a few yards.

Cast your eyes on this magnificent tree."

"It is a beautiful tree but what makes it so special?"

"It's a Jeffery Pine. Get up close and smell the bark, then tell me what it smells like."

"Well, it sort of smells like butterscotch."

"Jim, most people think the tree bark smells like butterscotch. Others think it smells like different flavors. Look around the hillside and over there is an Ironwood Manzanita bush. Pretty cool. We have lodge pole pines, junipers, cedar, noble fir and many more that I can't remember."

"Something special happened here. Last summer I was standing behind the patio door, watching a large gray squirrel trying to steal seeds from our bird feeder when all of sudden the squirrel fled off to the nearest tree just as a coyote ran up, hoping to have a squirrel dinner. He stopped only a few feet from me. The coyote never saw me standing there. It was pure fun watching him.

One of our neighbors was stupid enough to bring their house cat up here for the weekend, as a dog owner might do.

We heard what sounded like a catfight and ran out back to see a coyote running up the hill with their cat in its mouth.

"Yeah, that's funny," Fletcher chuckled to himself. "Good, I hate cats."

Jim Fletcher's observations were as keen as the eyesight of an owl. He never allowed many things to get by him. For all of his life, it was an ability he had taken great pride in. When Jeff was showing him where they had installed the water heater for the cabin, he saw some keys hidden behind the heater. "Curious," he thought, "they must be keys for their cabin." He filed that bit of information away for a future reference.

"Our taxi cab is waiting," Fletcher said. "We should be going."
Back at the airport, Fletcher asked their driver what they owed him. The old man took out a pad of paper and started writing down figures. Patience came hard for Fletcher. He pulled a wad of bills out of his pocket, and as they used to say, that wad "would choke a horse." Jeff and Bob's

jaws dropped noticeably at the sight of all that money.

"My man, would a hundred dollars cover our ride?"

The old fellow smiled. "Yes sir, that would be fine, and please call on me any time you're in need of my services."

It was a short flight from the Big Bear airstrip to another small airfield at Upland.

As he shut the Cessna's engine down Bob said, "This has been a great day for flying, Jim, and thanks for thinking of us."

"You're more than welcome guys. It's my fault I haven't been to California in many years. It's a shame we all don't take more time out of our busy lives for our friends."

Jeff spoke up, "Jim, why don't you come over to our place for dinner. If we don't have something good at home to fix, we will take you out. How does that sound?"

"I would like that, but first I need to return the plane. I'll rent a car at Ontario and drive over to your place."

"Okay, then we will see you later."

Without commenting on Jim Fletcher's statement, Jeff wondered why he would be returning the plane to the Ontario Airport when he had told them he had flown here from Bakersfield. That, of course, was the question. It was true they had once been friends, a long time ago, although Jeff was very aware he knew very little about this man and the life he had lived.

Two hours later Fletcher pulled up and parked his rental car in front of Jeff and Bob's home, hoping for a home cooked meal and some pleasant conversation with old friends.

The dinner was great and the three friends sat around telling each other boo-hoo lies and drinking too many cold ones.

"Jim, I wouldn't be much of a host if I was to let you drive off after letting you drink all that beer. Why don't you stay here tonight. We have a spare bedroom and maybe we could take in some sights tomorrow."

"All right then, I'll accept your offer. Being arrested for drunk driving and spending a night in the local Bastille isn't my idea of a good time." Fletcher grinned. If his friends knew the rest of the story, they would be shocked.

The next day was one of those memorable days where the three friends enjoyed simply bumming around. Making schedules and planning activities oftentimes takes the spontaneity away from the fun that can be had by just doing wantever comes along.

The sun had turned to a burnt orange as it sank in the west, showing through the thick smog of San Bernardino County as the three men pulled into their driveway.

For the remainder of the evening they talked, and told stories, which for the most part were greatly embellished. Each time a story is told, it gets more interesting. Everyone knows how that routine works. While they talked, Fletcher was planning how he was going to ask permission to use their cabin for a few days.

"My friends," Fletcher said. "I have a confession to make. A few months ago I pulled up and retired from the agency without any notification. I had been wanting to retire for some time. When I found out there were people who wanted to ask me some tough questions, which I wasn't prepared to answer, that gave me plenty of incentive to hit the road. I'm still not completely sure what they want with me."

He offered them a plausible lie showing a sadness in his eyes that would turn the hardest of hearts to compassion.

"Is there anything we can do to help?" asked Jeff.

"No. I've imposed on you more than I should have. Although, one of these days the crap is going to hit the fan. All I'm trying to do, for now, is avoid those people for as long as possible. Who knows, maybe they will lose interest in me and head for home" Smiling benevolently, he thought to himself, "I hardly think so."

He continued, "My speculation about this predicament is, one day these agents will show up on your front door step, hoping to find me hanging around.

"A thought just crossed my mind. If you two wouldn't mind letting me rent your cabin for a couple of days, I would pay you handsomely for your kindness. Your place would make a great hide-out. Looking on the bright side, I'm hoping these agents will believe I've left the state, and they too will head out."

"Give me a minute, Jim, so that Bob and I can discuss your proposal. We'll be right back."

In the core of Fletcher black heart he knew he didn't need their okay, he was going to use their cabin for his diabolical scheme, whether they gave him permission or not.

Chapter 44

San Bernardino

"Is this Agent Baxter?"

"Yes, it is."

"I'm calling in regards to your request to locate a plane with the tail number, N5549. I was informed by an employee of the Upland airport, which is called Cable Field, that the plane you were inquiring about was seen there twice in the same day. I'm sorry to say it is no longer there and we have no idea where it might have gone. Hopefully, someone else will see it. If I receive anything new about this plane I will promptly call you."

"Thanks very much, I appreciate your help."

This fragmented info could be priceless, Baxter considered. Everything that had happened over the last few days was starting to point to the area of San Bernardino County.

Baxter thought, "Now that we are closing in on this scumbag, I'm fearful of the possibility he is carefully leading us down the primrose path into another trap. That man is a pro. He nearly killed the three of us back in Virginia in a cunning booby-trap. If Jim Fletcher, alias Jimmy Dubois is clever enough to put us out of the picture he might get away with his crimes."

Under the protective umbrella of the F.B.I., Fletcher was able to organize bank robberies, which were designed to cover up bankers who were in serious trouble. By robbing them, they eliminated the possibilities of the bad loans and other financial problems from being discovered, which might have landed them in jail. These troubled bankers were in no way going to tell the authorities about these capers. Fletcher and his little gang had protected the bad bankers, which allowed the gang to keep most of the stolen money.

These former rouge F.B.I. agents, who pandered to the worst sort of thinking, had tried to kill Matt on more than one occasion and nearly succeeded, leaving him with a serious cognition problem. After surviving the bullet in the back and then the tricky surgery, he couldn't remember much of his past. His family members were now nothing more than strangers passing in the night.

Trouble was, the more Baxter thought about Fletcher's evil acts, the angrier he became. "He's a disgrace to the agency," he said to himself. Yet, he knew losing his temper would only cloud his judgment, putting him at risk of making a serious mistake. Baxter considered himself an accomplished agent, one of the best and believed if it came to matching wits with Fletcher, he would win the contest every time.

Chapter 45

The Cabin

When agent Aleksandar Blinski, 'Baxter' arrived at the home of Jeff and Bob, he removed some pictures from his brief case. They were pictures of the three men, years ago at a custom car show. He knew about their friendship and wanted to know if they had any knowledge of the where-abouts of Fletcher. When they seemed reluctant to help, Baxter made it completely clear he was willing and prepared, if necessary, to charge the both of them with harboring a fugitive. This threat was the sort of arm-twisting they weren't willing to suffer, even for an old friend. They told Baxter about their cabin in Fawnskin and that Fletcher was there.

They carefully drew a map to their cabin and offered Baxter some very good instructions on how to get there. He thanked the two and said, "I'm sorry for threatening you with arrest, but I must catch this felon, for there is no time to waste."

And Baxter sped off towards the mountains to the east.

As soon as he had driven out of sight, Jeff grabbed the phone and called their cabin. "Jim, this is Jeff. An F.B.I. agent just left our house and is on his way. I apologize Jim, but we were forced to tell him where you were."

"Don't concern yourself about it, because I want, in the very worst way, to have a showdown with the old man."

While talking on the phone with Fletcher, Jeff asked, "What in the hell did you do, Jim?"

"I don't have the time to explain. The story goes back many years. Don't worry about giving me up; I'm sorry to have exposed you to this mess of mine. I don't know if you will ever understand what I did and most likely you will never have the chance to know, unless the authorities are willing to divulge my crimes, which I think not. I suppose you will never know my side of the story. When they do catch up to me, we are going to have one helluva fight, to the very end, and this time I'm afraid I'll not escape. I avoided capture once before and they are not about to let that happen again."

Jeff was shell-shocked. He didn't know how to respond to his friend's confession. All he could say was, "I'm sorry, Jim." Fletcher hung up the phone, ending it all.

Baxter turned his vehicle headlights off just before turning up the dead end street leading to the cabin where he believed Fletcher was hiding out and waiting.

Almost indiscernible, he parked his vehicle a short distance from the cabin and stealthily moved up the street to where he found a good vantage point behind an old lodge pole pine. There, in the darkness of the night, he watched for any signs of life in the cabin. A cold mountain breeze ruffled his graying hair. It had been raining in the valley that day, which brought a light snow to the mountains of Big Bear.

He knew he was getting too old for this job, a job that a young man should be doing. If he survived the night he would be quitting, just as his boss had directed. But, first and foremost, he must catch Fletcher, so their good names could be protected, and a despicable man would be put away.

Fletcher had been at the cabin for enough time to efficiently scout the surrounding area. This valuable time had given him the opportunity to form a plan, a plan he hoped would be an unexpected way to dry gulch his pursuers. Killing another person was distasteful, not something he had ever wanted to do; yet, he knew he would have to kill them if he was to ever escape.

Chapter 46

Tracks

Baxter's assistance was only fifteen miles away, down state road 18. Matt was breaking every California traffic law in hopes they could get there in time to help. Baxter had refused to wait for them, even against their most sincere pleas. He gave Niki and Matt the same directions he had received from Jeff and told them he wasn't going to let Fletcher get away this time.

Snow had come early in the high mountains this year. With all the stealth his old feet could muster, he stepped through the autumn snow with great care, hoping not to make a sound. He quietly slipped from tree to tree until he was at the far side of the cabin, and away from the view of the front windows. From this vantage point he could approach without being seen.

From the first moment he arrived, he hadn't seen anything which would indicate there was any life in the cabin. Baxter was sure Fletchers friends had alerted him and he had likely split for parts unknown, although, parked next to the cabin was a sleek new car, most likely a rental. "Would he have left it?" He wondered.

He knew he must check the cabin. With his 9mm glock in hand, ready for the unexpected, he moved up to the rear corner of the building and listened and watched. It was deathly quiet. Pressing against the wall, he moved up to the first window. He could see nothing inside. He noticed the patio door was wide open and footprints in the freshly fallen snow were leading away from the cabin and up the hill into the forest.

This display Fletcher left was all too obvious. He had to know these footprints would quickly be detected and followed. "This is exactly what the man wants," Baxter thought. "Follow him into another trap? He has had plenty of time to set one, somewhere out there in the dark unfamiliar forest, where there would be no witnesses."

For a few moments he considered the thoughts which raced through his mind. If, ever in my life, I was in need of divine intervention, this has to be the time. Silently, he offered a prayer, a prayer of the heart. "My Dear Father in Heaven, at this critical time in my life, I need your help, if I'm ever going to bring this man to justice. I know that I haven't called on you often and for that I'm sorry. Thank you Father, and Amen."

A chill wind blew as the coastal storm passed overhead and the full moon made its appearance through the parting clouds. Two inches of fresh snow covered the ground. Baxter had to wonder, "Would this act of nature aid my fugitive or me?"

As he studied the footprints the words to an old Marty Robbins song came to mind. "To really live you must almost die."

"Maybe death awaits me."

Beseeched with an overwhelming feeling of urgency, Baxter made his own footprints in the snow and started moving towards a black wall, that was the forest. Following Fletcher's tracks in the snow was a simple task.

Taking his first step then stopping and listening and then another step he moved up the hill and into the forest. At first he didn't cover much distance until he noticed a greater gap between each of the steps. Fletcher had to be running. Moving off to the left side of the tracks he was following, Baxter paralleled Fletchers, and began hurrying up his pace.

After a half hour of tracking, he hadn't found his man. Baxter stopped again to look and listen. Still, mountain silence surrounded him as the minutes passed, and nothing. All of sudden he saw a muzzle flash and instantly felt a burning sensation across the left side of his skull as he fell. He already had his gun in his hand and fired two quick shots in the direction of the blast. Immediately, several more rounds smashed into the ground next to him. Every one of Fletcher's ensuing shots missed their intended target. Lying very still, he reached up and touched his head. There was the warm feeling of blood.

"For one time in my life I'm thankful for a thick skull." His injury wasn't serious, but it did hurt.

Then he heard the distant sound of someone crashing through dead-fall. It had to be Fletcher running away.

His head throbbed but he was up and running after him. He was brutally tired. He hadn't run more than a hundred yards when it hit him. The pain in his chest was excruciating. It stopped him dead in his tracks. It felt as if a 2,000-pound rodeo bull was standing on his chest. Baxter cried out in pain. "Oh no, not now!" He stumbled and fell to the ground.

He didn't know how long he lay there in the snow, but when he looked up he saw Fletcher standing over him.

"Baxter, you old Bolshevik. This is going to make a wonderful ending to your miserable life. You must know it's far more fun watching you slowly die this way than putting a bullet through your thick head and having another crime to answer for."

"So, you think it's over. You unmitigated fool!"

"You're even funny when you're dying. Most people believe in providence, some in good luck. What's your choice, Baxter, if it really matters?" Fletcher laughed sinisterly.

The moonlight illuminated Fletcher's mug. Baxter could see the acidulous smirk on his thin lips and felt the end was near.

Chapter 47

Caught Up

Matt and Niki were within a few minutes of catching up to Baxter, who desperately needed their help. Matt was driving like a man possessed. With ever increasing speed, he slid around corners that were not engineered for such speeds. The agent's Mustang was starting to overheat. For the last thirty miles Matt had pushed the car to its absolute limits. Overheating wasn't going to slow him down, not now!

Niki shouted, "Matt be careful or the both of us are going to end up in that darn lake, then we will never get there!"

She had always considered herself a more accomplished driver than Matt, which had caused some lighthearted disagreements over the years. Even though the vehicular traffic was light, Niki was glad she wasn't behind the wheel.

"Watch for the old country store, Niki, it should be coming up soon!"

"Hey! Matt, I think we just passed the store!"

Matt locked up the brakes, causing their car to come to a screaming stop. He threw the car into reverse and smoked the tires as he spun around in the road facing the way they had come.

A pedestrian on the side of the road was screaming at Matt, "Slow down you fool!!!"

Without thinking, Matt looked over at the man, and flipped him the bird, an unnecessary gesture, then sped off.

It wasn't easy seeing the streets. They soon found the old store and the narrow street they wanted, which passed by the city's lone fire station, and up the hill towards the cabin.

The streets in Fawnskin must have been built along the old game trails, Matt thought. They made no sense and were difficult to follow. It took them another five minutes to find the cabin.

"Look there, Matt, I'm sure that's Dad's rental car. Pull in behind it."

Before they exited the car Matt reached over and grabbed Niki's nervous hand, and held it tight.

"Listen now, you be careful. Fletcher has had sufficient time to prepare another one of his booby traps. I'm sure it won't be anything like the last one, so lets stay together, four eyes and ears are better than two. We are not going to help your dad if we get ourselves in trouble, understand?"

When they saw the two sets of tracks in the snow, they knew there was no need to continue searching the cabin.

Being circumspect at every turn, Niki and Matt moved along, following the well-defined tracks. Without warning, the silence of the night was shattered by the distant sound of gunshots. They froze in place.

Niki softly cried out with fear in her heart. "Oh Matt, we must hurry. Dad's out they're alone and needs our help."

With only one purpose at hand the two ran as fast as the snow covered terrain would permit. They followed the tracks until they nearly fell to the ground in complete exhaustion. While stopped and trying to catch their breath, Fletcher's voice could be heard, and it wasn't that far off. He was laughing and his taunting utterance was loud and clear. Obviously, he hadn't heard them approach, being so intently interested in his victim's situation. Baxter was lying in the snow, clenching his chest in obvious pain, and unable to move or defend himself.

With a quick grasp of the situation, Matt drew his faithful Browning 9mm, and taking the best possible aim in the darkness, fired two quick shots at the shadowy figure standing over Baxter.

The angry whip of the bullets flew splinters off a tree next to Fletcher's face, cutting his cheek and the side of his head. He jumped back and disappeared into the darkness. They heard him crashing through the trees and hoped he was leaving so they could attend to Baxter.

"Hurry, Matt!"

"Niki, you check on your dad and I'll keep a watch out for Fletcher."

With a quivering voice, Niki said, "Matt, he is having a heart attack. We need to get him medical help, pronto!"

"Niki, see if we have cell phone service. Pray that we do. Her 911 call went through and an operator answered. "How can I help you?"

"My father is having a heart attack and I need your help, now!"

"What's your address ma'am?"

"I believe we're in the San Bernardino National forest a few miles north of Fawnskin, in the woods." Niki gave her the address of the cabin where their cars were parked.

Matt had a GPS he had brought to help with directions. "Tell the operator I'm trying to get a fix on our location."

Niki then explained to the dispatcher they were F.B.I agents, chasing a dangerous fugitive and the responders should use care when they approached. She believed the fugitive ran off to the north and was away from their location. "Please have them hurry. My dad isn't doing well.

With her father's head resting in her lap and both of their coats covering his body, Niki's emotional fear was beginning to show. Tears were running down her cheeks and the awful prospect of losing her father was something she didn't want to deal with. Her sadness deepened with each fretful minute.

Matt knelt down and brushed Baxter's ruffled, graying hair out of his eyes and said, "We are not going to leave you. You're going to be fine. The search and rescue helicopter is on its way with trained medical people."

Baxter reached out and grabbed hold of Matt's wrist. Speaking in a weak voice, he said, "Matt! You go after Fletcher and don't let him escape this time, and I mean it! Niki can care for me just fine until help arrives."

"No, I can't leave you like this. We can catch up with him later. I need to protect the two of you in case he returns.

"I'm not going to repeat my order. Now get going!"

"Yes sir!" Matt grinned at the dear, old man. "Wish me lots of luck and a little prayer might help turn the tide."

Matt was very happy to see Niki with one of her beautiful smiles, it was the tiniest of smiles, but it was a smile. She didn't want to see him go after this dangerous man alone. Understandably, they all knew how important it was that he was stopped.

The urgency of the situation dictated only one absolutely important thing, no matter how Matt did it, Fletcher had to be caught.

The night was cold but not impossible for a man to survive it. Matt knew he must be calm and smart, and use his savvy in the most efficient way to outwit this poor excuse of a human being. Fletcher was headed north, as his tracks indicated. The forest trees were now thinning some as they descended towards the desert floor of the Mojave.

A city-slicker, who has never experienced a full moon shining over freshly fallen snow, would never know how bright this kind of night could be. It was the first full moon, after the Autumnal Equinox, called the Harvest Moon.

Fortunately, Matt's night vision had always been excellent, however that didn't matter much. With all the illumination from the moon, he could see nearly as well as if the sun was up.

The popping sound of the helicopter's roto-blades in the distance gave Matt a comforting feeling inside his chest. Now he felt sure his friends were going to be all right.

It was evident Fletcher was watching his back trail. Every so often he would stop and turn around. It was a story the tracks in the snow told.

Twice Matt thought he had seen a glimpse of Fletcher about two hundred yards in front of him, but he wasn't certain. How was he going to pull this capture off? "If I catch up to him on this trail, it will be like cornering a wild cat. We will both be forced into a nasty gun battle and I want to avoid that scenario."

The desert was now in view, only a mile away. A man would be a fool to cross the Mojave without water. Matt knew he had to turn west and stay under the cover of the forest. If he turned east, that too would lead him into the foreboding desert.

It was a long shot, but Matt was willing to try anything about now. He was going to attempt to make an end-around play and get out in front of Fletcher so he could ambush him. It would require all of his strength and skills to pull this off without being seen.

Matt was wishing he was one of those brave Apache warriors that at one time lived on this land. They were called the "ghost's of the desert." They could have sneaked up on Fletcher and had him hog-tied before he knew what hit him. Matt knew this task wasn't going to be so easy. Fletcher would fight him to the end.

Jogging continually, trying to stay among the dark shadows of the forest, hoping not to be seen, Matt pushed himself until he believed he was ahead of Jim Fletcher. He cut back to where he thought the original trail was. Finding a good vantage point, he crawled on top of a mound of large boulders to wait and watch. He noticed there were several trails merging at this location. He could only hope he had calculated correctly and Fletcher would show himself.

The night was utterly freezing cold and Matt was feeling its effects. Although his determination far outweighed any discomfort he felt, the cold night made every muscle in his body sluggish, nearly unwilling to move.

Ever so slightly, the sky in the east was beginning to make a change. Matt knew the morning would arrive before long and the sun's rays would warm him again.

Matt wasn't sure if he had really seen his prey and was beginning to feel the worst had happened. He welled with an undercurrent of feelings, believing his man was responsible for shooting him, or knew who had ordered it. His capture was imperative. His dear friends needed to have their good names cleared. If he missed the prey, this would be the greatest of disappointments to them and Matt didn't want that to happen. He could only wonder, had that scumbag Fletcher slipped away again?

It was time to move. Matt cautiously slid down from his perch, high on the rocks, and stretched his limbs, trying to bring a little life back to his uncooperative muscles.

He was still on alert, listening for any sound and watching for the slightest of movement. With nothing noticeable happening, he was beginning to lose hope.

Carefully, Matt made his way around the mound of boulders. As suddenly as a snake strikes, Matt and Fletcher were standing face to face. Two enemies, one wanting the other dead and the other wanting justice.

The slightest moment passed as an evil, sinister grin formed on Fletcher's thin, cold lips. Matt's father had told him, get the first hard punch in the opponents face and oftentimes it will be the deciding factor in the outcome of the fight. Before Matt could react, Fletcher struck with lighting fast hands, placing two solid jabs, followed by a hard right fist to Matt's face, sending him sprawling to the ground.

Fletcher was light on his feet and moved in quickly to take the advantage. Matt, lying on his back, was able to hook his foot behind the left foot of Fletcher's, and kicked him square on the knee cap with enough force to break the joint. The old man groaned, stepped back and fell to the ground. Matt was up, shaking his head. He was mad through and through, knowing he had been beaten to the punch. Matt now remembered, he once heard how Fletcher had boxed in the army and was somewhat of a pro.

"Get up, you back shooter!" Matt bellowed.

Before Fletcher could pull himself completely upright, Matt hit him square on the jaw with a powerful punch, followed by two more fists to his face. His flattened nose squirted blood. Fletcher charged Matt like a raging bull. Matt sidestepped, caught Fletcher by the arm and threw him on his back.

It was quite evident Fletcher was no ordinary street fighter. Matt had never fought such a skilled boxer. Even though he hadn't lost a street-style fight, he knew he was in for a ferocious battle with this fugitive.

Fletcher's blows were landing more often than Matt's, but Matt's punches were jaw-busting.

Matt hit Fletcher with a heavy, stunning blow. Fletcher stepped back to avoid the next one.

Wanting to end the fight quickly and escape, Fletcher exhibited all the skill and strength he had. He waded in, throwing a couple of quick jabs followed by a mighty right-hander which was designed to take Matt out. Matt blocked the punch with his left arm, instantly stepping into Fletcher, while driving his right hand hard into his throat, as he swept his feet out from under him, slamming him forcefully to the frozen ground.

Holding on to Fletcher's right arm, Matt attempted to complete the take down by turning him over, face down, so he could control him, but Fletcher jerked away, bounding up to his feet. Matt lunged forward, driving him back. Until that time, neither man had noticed, in the morning twilight, the cliff behind them. As Fletcher lurched back, Matt tried to hold on to him to keep him from falling over the cliff. With all his strength, Fletcher jerked Matt over the top of him as both flew over the edge, tumbling into the shadows below.

How long it had been, Matt knew not. His body ached. He didn't want to move, but he knew he must. Matt rolled over onto his right side, and there lay Fletcher, only a few feet away. He felt for his gun. It was still in his holster. The 10 ft. fall had rendered both men unconscious for a time. Seeing Fletcher lying silent and not moving gave him hope.

Matt thought, "I had better take advantage of this situation before the old man comes around."

He removed his own belt, quietly slid over next to him, and tied his belt around Fletchers exposed wrist. He checked his waist and coat for a weapon. He found Fletcher's gun, and slid it behind his own waistband.

First, he thought, "I'd better hope he doesn't come to just yet." Whatever he expected next wasn't this. Matt began pulling Fletcher's belt from his pants, which was going to be used to secure his other hand. Fletcher swung his hand around striking the side of Matt's head with a rock. Luckily for Matt it was a glancing blow, which only stunned him, but he fell forward onto his face.

Immediately, Fletcher crawled clumsily to his feet and limped away. He was afraid of the enemy lying there and he wanted to get as far away as he possibly could. His plan to ambush Baxter had failed miserably and with this failure there would be many more law enforcement types looking for him.

After a slow struggle to walk a mere hundred yards, Fletcher reached for his gun. To his great disappointment it was gone. He wondered if he had dropped it when he fell or had Matt taken it? He dared not return to search for it, but this man was never unprepared. In his right boot he carried a .32 automatic and in his other boot a switchblade. That wasn't all. Concealed under his shirt, in a shoulder holster, he carried a .40 cal. colt, which Matt had completely missed in his cursory search.

The blow from Fletcher's rock had only stunned Matt. Finally, he found the strength to push himself up to a kneeling position. He spent a few seconds clearing his head. Hastily, he checked his surroundings. It was evident Fletcher had fled.

Matt was happy he still had his own Browning 9mm and he had been able to take Fletcher's personal .45 Colt, 1911. Yet, he dared not, for the slightest moment, believe Fletcher was not armed. This man was far too savvy to make such a mistake, a mistake that would leave him unable to defend himself.

From where Matt knelt, he was able to survey the surrounding area in every direction. The tracks in the snow left no question about his condition. Fletcher was dragging one leg and Matt knew with a leg injury he wouldn't be able to travel fast or very far.

The morning light in the east was slightly brighter now, but with the moon having set, it seemed much darker. Matt reached down, scooped up some snow and vigorously rubbed it on his face. That's when he noticed the snow was dark. He was bleeding. Feeling around his head, he discovered a gash which was the cause of the blood running down his face. This bump on the head wasn't going to stop him from his appointed mission.

Using a tree to pull himself upright, he stood for a few moments while checking his physical condition, making sure everything was working. To be right honest with himself, he hurt all over. Outwardly he looked and felt like a mess, but his mind was clear and ready for action. Strange as it was, Matt's mind hadn't been this sharp and clear in months.

It wasn't a wise idea to follow Fletcher's exact tracks. Matt darted from tree to tree, stopping, looking and listening, hoping he might see even the slightest movement. It's surprisingly easy for the human eye to catch an insubstantial movement. Even the faintest of motion could be dangerous for this fugitive.

Fletcher had only traveled a mere three hundred yards before his knee gave in to the pain, forcing him to find somewhere he could take a defensive stand.

On a cedar clad slope, not far off the trail, he found a place where he could hide among some deadfall and defend himself, if need be. What he wanted most was an opening in the trees where he could have a clear line of fire, and this spot offered him that opportunity. He felt confident that if he could take Savage out, there might be a chance for him to escape. If not, he was going down fighting. Spending his retirement years caged up like a wild animal in some nasty prison wasn't what he had dreamed of.

While Matt waited and watched, the thought crossed his mind, "Wouldn't it be great if I were invisible and could sneak up without him ever knowing how I caught him. Stupid thought," Matt said to himself. The cat and mouse game was on. Neither man knew where the other was and the first one to show his hand might be the first one to die.

Matt's luck was holding. Out the corner of his eye he caught the slightest movement, only fifty feet up the hillside. He froze in place. Keeping his eyes fixed on the spot, he waited, and sure enough there was another movement.

The injury to Fletcher's knee was making it impossible for him to hold still. He kept moving, ever so slightly, trying to find a place where his knee could rest, pain free.

Matt took full advantage of this opportunity to carefully slide down to a prone position behind a gnarly old California Juniper and wait. It was imperative Fletcher be taken alive. He was undoubtedly the only person who could answer all of their questions. If he had been wanted dead, Matt had the perfect chance to take him out. Matt had taken one handgun from Fletcher but he wondered if he had another. The likelihood he did have a weapon that had been concealed was real.

Matt was willing to test the waters. He fired three shots rapidly above Fletcher's position, and hollered. "You no good low life, Fletcher! Why don't you get smart and give up? You know this is the end for you!"

Fletcher thought he knew where Matt was hiding. He yelled back, "Yeah, like hell I will!"

The retort was followed by the roar of his .40 cal. Colt, kicking up dirt and debris dangerously close to Matt's hiding spot. Matt now knew he was armed and the situation had changed for the worse.

Both men had no escape route. Nether had even thought of the need for one until this very moment. The morning sun was nearly up and any hiding places were scarce. Being pinned down here, with the oncoming day, offered no comfort for either man.

An irritating blue jay, high overhead in the spruce tree, repeatedly squawked as if to say, "Stupid, stupid men."
Neither Fletcher nor Matt could make a move without the other seeing

them. Every few minutes one or the other would take a shot as if to say, "I'm still here and watching."

For two hours both men held their place, daring not to move, while anxiously hoping for a break. Sweat was running down Matt's back because he was now fully exposed to the sun's rays. Fletcher was in the shade of the trees, but he had an injury to his leg he had to contend with.

More time passed. A small sand lizard scurried up to Matt's face, stopping in front of his nose. It twisted its tiny head back and forth and then ran on, right over Matt's still body.

Fletcher, from his higher advantage point, was wondering why he hadn't been more selective and chosen an ambush spot with an escape route.

For the first time in many years this bad man was scared.

Unexpectedly, with the power of a warrior in her voice, she hollered, "Gotcha, Fletcher! Don't even blink! I can see you perfectly from where I stand. I have a police riot gun pointed directly at your back. This gun has 12 gauge double oo buckshot which will tear you in two! These fine San Bernardino Deputy Sheriffs where kind enough to accompany me here. They also have some nasty guns pointed your way, so slowly raise your hands, high above your head, and with great care, make your way out of there."

"Is that you, Niki Blinski?

"It is!"

"Damn you, Niki! Hypocrisy has no bounds! Does it lady?"

"I suppose not."

"What if I refuse to go?"

"Well then, I suppose this will be the last day of your life. How does that grab you? Remember there is always another day to look forward to, that is if you're still alive. All men must have hope, so don't be a fool and cash it all in today."

A few tense moments passed until Niki saw Fletcher's arms come up slowly above his head. What a relief. He turned towards her and made his way out of his hiding spot.

"Good choice, you old rouge."

In seconds the two deputies had Fletcher in a felony prone position, cuffed, and searched.

"Look what we found on your man, a .32 auto and a switchblade."

"Interesting," Matt said as he walked up to the group. "He wasn't shooting at me with a pea shooter. We better take a look at the place where he was hiding."

"Look what I found! It's a beautiful model 1911 colt, customized by a professional gunsmith, no less. It would be a real shame to leave such a piece here to have time and weather destroy it."

"Two questions, Niki. First and foremost, how is Baxter doing?" Matt asked.

"He is going to be fine. The doctor said we will be able to take him home in couple of days, but he is going to need a lot of rest."

"That's wonderful news, Niki. I was deathly afraid of the worst."

"Second question. How in the world did you make it all the way back up this mountain and how did you ever find us?"

She turned and gestured towards the two deputy Sheriffs. "Matt, if it hadn't been for these two gentlemen, I'm afraid you and Fletcher would still be in a Mexican stand-off."

Both deputies were smiling like schoolboys. It was obvious these men were smitten with the beauty and charm of Niki.
Matt knew these two law enforcement types had never seen a more

beautiful cop in their lives, and as far as looks go, neither had Matt. Their interest in Niki irritated him.

One of the deputies must have wanted to goad the lion in his den, by saying, "It's a good thing for your fugitive that it isn't one hundred and fifty years ago. Not very far from where we stand is a real hanging tree, and yes, men have been hung from its branches."

Outwardly, Fletcher looked as calm as a mid-summer's day, but inwardly he would have hung the smart-ass deputy from the tree he spoke of, and would have enjoyed doing it.

Fletcher smiled wryly at them. "As far as you two clowns go, you think it's over. Not as long as I live and breathe, it won't be over. I swear Niki, one day I'll kill you two along with your old man."

"Given this situation, that's tough talk for a man who is hog-tied and headed for jail. You see, Fletcher, we are not worried at all. Before you see the light of day again, that is if you ever do, you will be so old and worn out you will need one of those electric scooter chairs to get around," Matt said with half a smirk.

It was evident the San Bernardino deputies had gone through this scenario before, and were well prepared for the occasion. One reached into his backpack and removed a waist-chain and lock, wrapped it around Fletcher's waist and locked it to the cuffs that were already in place.

Fletcher and his captors needed to hike a mile back to where the deputies had left their ATVs. Because of his injured knee, he couldn't walk with leg irons in place, so they weren't used. One deputy walked on his left and the other on his right side, leaving Niki and Matt to follow directly behind them. The possibilities of Fletcher escaping were infinitesimal, yet any wise peace officer would always be on the alert for the unexpected.

Niki and Matt talked softly as they followed along. "Your dad will be elated with the good news of Fletcher's capture."

When they arrived back at the ATV's, one of the deputes radioed in, "Our mission was successful, no need for additional back-up."

Matt grinned with a sort of amusement at the rear-facing seat on one of the Sheriff's ATV's. He watched the deputies as each grabbed Fletcher under his arms, lifting him up onto the seat. They fastened a seat belt around him and then secured his legs with the shackles.

"You had better get used to the feel of shackles and cuffs, for they are going to be your constant companion from now on."

This accomplishment brought smiles of relief from Niki and Matt as they watched Fletcher's face darken. His eyes were venomous as he focused his attention on Niki. She stepped back with an unexpected fear of this man. Fletcher was mumbling words they didn't understand, and then he spit on the nearest deputy.

"You dirty dog! Is this how you want to behave?" The deputy grabbed a net from his gear, which resembled a large sock, placed it over Fletcher's head and tied it in the back. He could breathe and see but he couldn't spit on anyone but himself.

The ATV which Fletcher was hog-tied to went ahead. The second vehicle followed with Niki riding behind the deputy, while Matt followed on foot.

The little caravan hadn't traveled far when the vehicle Fletcher was riding on bounced over a large rock, shaking him with such force even Matt felt it. The violent bounce set him off. He was hissing his hate and cursing them with the vilest language he knew.

Matt shouted at him, "Shut your filthy mouth! Don't you know we have a lady with us?"

"She is no lady. She is just a floozy and lady of the night, nothing more or nothing less, and Matt, you're nothing more than her John. You phony pig!"

Matt had to restrain his explosive emotions. He wanted to smash his fist into his rotten face to stop the lies and profanity coming from this depraved excuse of humanity.

Finally, one of the deputies spoke up. "Mr. Fletcher, if you don't shut your mouth I will be forced to gag you, and we will see how you like that."

"You don't dare. I happen to know it's against your policy."

"So sue me. If no one knows about it how can it be against our policy? Besides, I have a feeling that where you're going, a little gag will be the least of your problems."

For a while Fletcher was quiet, pondering what the deputy had said, putting to rest the manic side of his personality.

Two additional deputies were waiting for them where their vehicles were parked. As they loaded Fletcher into a jail van, Matt spoke, "This is the moment we've waited for, seeing you like this, being hauled off to jail. It does my heart good. We will be seeing you very soon for our trip back home."

Fletcher lurched in his restraints as if he thought they would break so he could get his hands around Matt's neck.

"Get a grip on it, old man."

Anything of importance was removed from Fletcher's person such as his wallet, money, credit cards, jewelry and car keys. His weapons were packaged and put away. All they left for him was just enough clothes to keep himself warm. None of the evidence or property would be booked here locally. It would all be going back east with them.

Niki instructed the county deputies on how they wanted him held legally as John Doe, isolated from all other prisoners. He could be released only to Niki Blinski, who was now the agent in charge, because of Baxter's heart attack.

The smitten deputy drove Niki and Matt back to the cabin so they could search Fletcher's rental car and the cabin. More of his property was found, packaged and put away.

"Officer," Niki instructed, "It's imperative that this assistance you gave us be kept secret. As far as we are concerned, this capture never happened, and we would greatly appreciate your cooperation in keeping it quiet. If you heard his name, please forget that you did. On behalf of the department, we thank you and the others." She extended her hand and offered him a cordial handshake along with one of her special smiles.

"What do you say, Matt. We need to get off this mountain. I want to get back to Dad."

"I'm ready, willing and more than happy to put this episode behind us. Lets go see Baxter!"

Without the slightest hesitation, Niki spoke up, "I'll drive Matt. I know the way, and remember, I'm the better driver."

"My dear Niki, this is one time I won't argue the point. I've been beaten up by a man who should have been a professional fighter. He punched me in the face. He hit in the head with a rock. We fell from a cliff, and I nearly froze my hiney off by lying on a stone-cold boulder for a good part of the night and I'm just dog-tired. So, if you don't mind, I'll just sit here quietly and watch you drive. I hope you realize that watching you is a pleasurable thing to do."

"You're not going to get any rest, Matt, if you keep flapping your gums. Just lay your head back, close your eyes and dream of something nice." Niki grinned because she knew she had the upper hand and Matt was too weary to oppose her.

He woke up as they drove into the parking lot of the San Bernardino Community Hospital, where Baxter was taken after suffering a heart attack.

Niki was genuinely concerned for her father. When she left him, hours before, he was in stable condition and doing well, according to the medics. At that time Baxter had begged Niki to get some assistance from the Sheriff's department to help Matt catch Fletcher.

Fletcher's capture was now history, but Baxter had no clue about what had taken place on that mountain. He was desperately worried about his daughter, whom he loved with all his heart and soul. Matt was like an adopted son. He reflected on the possibility that neither Niki or Matt might not return. Could he live on without them in his life? All of this stress wasn't good for the condition he was in.

Baxter heard his hospital room door slowly open. He turned his head slightly to see Niki and then Matt quietly enter, not wanting to disturb him. At this very moment, Baxter couldn't have been happier.

He spoke out, "Oh thank goodness! You two are an answer to this old man's prayers." He hugged and kissed Niki while grasping Matt's extended hand with a force he never knew Baxter possessed.

"Dad, how are you doing?"

"I feel pretty good, just a little weak, that's all."

"Have the doctors told you anything about your condition?"

"No, they haven't. A doctor is coming by sometime today to tell me what the skinny is."

The happy expression on Baxter's face slowly faded to one that was far more serious. Hesitantly he spoke, "Matt, what happened with Fletcher?"

Matt looked over at Niki. "Should we tell him?"

Neither of them showed the slightest emotion. Their faces were as stone. A few moments passed before Niki grinned, which told all. "Dad, we have the wretched scoundrel that I detest so much! He is locked up tighter than a bankers vault, in the county jail, waiting for his plane ride home."

"What great news. I'll always be indebted to both of you. Matt, I was fearful he might kill you, and then escape, never to be found again. Now maybe justice can be served. Please tell me all the details."

"No, not now Dad, There will be plenty of time for story telling later. You must rest for now. I insist."

Three days later Baxter was ready to leave the confinements of the hospital. He had always hated the thought of being sick or confined to a bed. This was an experience he hadn't been through before in his life. His health had always been good and now his patience wouldn't stand for anymore of this idleness.

Baxter's bulldogged tenacity made it clear to the doctors that they weren't going to persuade him to stay put for a few more days. After making some concessions with the medical staff, they agreed to release him to his daughter, Niki, because she was the only person he would listen to.

The following morning, with the brilliant sun shining over the eastern mountains, Baxter, and his group, along with a medical assistant drove to an isolated ramp at the Ontario International Airport. There they met three sheriff deputies that were waiting in a jail van.

Parked by the ramp was the same beautiful Falcon 900 they had flown on from Virginia. Two serious looking F.B.I. agents stood next to the open door of the plane and waited.

When everyone was in place, the jail van backed up to the plane. The rear door opened and two of the three deputies assisted Fletcher out. There he stood, solemn faced, looking like a man waiting to be hung. He was secured by two sets of waist chains with a black box over his handcuffs. This type of security was reserved for the most dangerous of prisoners and it was evident they weren't going to take any chances with this man.

Baxter watched from the front seat of the car as Fletcher shuffled slowly across the distance between the van and the plane's door. The effort of each step was a struggle as the leg irons were digging into the flesh of his ankles. The deputies offered no assistance. He only received a shove forward if he happened to fall backwards.

Fletcher was taken to the rear of the plane and placed in a seat reserved for prisoners. His leg chains were locked to the floor, keeping him in place.

With their man securely locked in place, Baxter was carefully helped aboard and led to where a comfortable bed had been prepared for him, in the front of the plane. The medical assistant that was to accompany him back to Virginia had given Baxter a mild sedative before they left the hospital, to help him rest.

Baxter knew his nemesis was on board, but for the present, he wouldn't confront him, not until the time was right, and he was sequestered at a special location and the device was in place.

The two federal agents that met them at the plane were assigned to stay with Fletcher until he was delivered and they had been released from their duty.

Matt and Niki sat facing each other, waiting for the departure. Their plane taxied out to the runway and waited for a clearance to take off. Within a few minutes their plane started to move and turned, facing the takeoff direction. With the strong force of the jet engines spooling up, they were forced deep into their seats as they rapidly built up speed, soon breaking their bonds with Earth.

Matt was grateful for his comfortable seat because his body still ached from his altercation with Fletcher. He smiled warmly at Niki then looked out the window to watch the earth below.

Sitting among the luxurious amenities of the Falcon 900, Matt and Niki talked about many things, but their conversation mostly involved the capture of Fletcher.

With a bewildering tone in her voice, Niki said, "Another page has just been written in the life and history of Jim Fletcher. It's sad to say he was once a respected and loyal F.B.I. agent, who for some unknown reason chose to take a walk on the dark side of the road. Possibly it was greed, when he chose to use his elaborate scheme to steal money and ruin peoples lives as well as his own. Before that time in his life there was never an indication he would ever do what he did. After his scheme was in place and working, there was never any evidence he was living outside the law."

She shook her head in bewilderment. There was a tone of disgust in her voice, "Why, at some point in a person life does an individual decide to make such an irresponsible decision and abandon everything decent and good about themselves? Oftentimes these choices may become irreversible."

"It does present many questions, Niki. I don't have all the answers but there are some things I believe I understand. A change from good to evil doesn't occur like the flipping of a switch. One moment you're a good guy, the next you're corrupted and not worth the buckshot to blow you to kingdom come. This metamorphosis often takes time to develop. It happens in small increments, the thought being the first step which will change a man's will. It has been said, 'as a man thinketh so is he.' The longer a person entertains his evil thoughts the more likely this preoccupation will cause him to change, and in time he will act upon those desires.

"For example, when we read about a mother who drowns her children, we can't understand or even comprehend how a mother could perpetrate such an evil, insidious crime. We just have to label the person insane, that being the only reasonable explanation in our human reasoning that a person could do such a horrible thing. Yet, certainly in the world of crime, many criminals have been found to have a psychosis of one kind or another.

"What is more prevalent about criminals is that they are a result of evil intentions, nothing more, nothing less. I suggest more often than not, a criminal is evil, and not insane."

"Criminal behavior is often manipulated by the abuse of drugs. Someone with addictive behavior, most often suffers from many other problems. Low self-esteem, unemployment, illness, physical pain, and as many other reasons as there are people, may all be factored into the equation. Oftentimes, by removing just one of these troublesome problems, the addict never turns to crime, but lump all of these problems together and you have a sure recipe for this person becoming a criminal."

"What about Fletcher? Matt, he doesn't seem to fit into any of these scenarios."

"You're right, Niki, I suppose we will never understand what he was thinking."

Talking with Niki was always a pleasure. She was an excellent listener, smart, and invariably abreast of the latest news. Over the years she and Matt had many enjoyable conversations from politics to religion. They hadn't solved any of the worlds problems but they had fun trying.

"If you don't mind, Niki, I'm going to lay my head back and try to rest for a while."

"Go ahead, I have a book I am going to read."

Matt didn't want to rest as much as he wanted to ponder over his past. There were things in his past that were starting to surface, things he had tried to suppress because they had troubled and confused him. His memory loss happened after he was shot and during the long stay in the hospital.

There was that lovely lady, Penny, and her children who acted the part of his family, a family he didn't remember. So, in frustration he ran away to the only friends he could remember, Baxter and Niki Blinski.

Over the past couple of weeks, tid-bits of half forgotten events would at times, flash across his mind like a broken film, troubling him more than giving him any concrete answers to his questions.

Following the knockdown, drag-out, helluva fight with Fletcher, Matt's recollections of his past were starting to come into focus. These thoughts frightened him.

"What am I going to do?" Matt said out loud as if he was talking to himself.

Niki looked up from her book and wondered what was troubling Matt. No one knew how much she worried about him or how much she loved him.

Matt thought to himself, how in the world can I make up for all the hurt I've caused my family? Matt pondered, "Will they ever believe me when I try to explain how I couldn't remember them? No matter how hard I try to force my mind, nothing happens. Some of the doctors who were trying to help me overcome my amnesia suggested that possibly there was something in my past I didn't want to remember."

Chapter 48

Warren Tidwell

Bobby Blackstone had made the transition easily. He was now the respected English gentleman, Warren Tidwell, who looked the part in every respect, with his tweed suit, bowler hat and an ornate walking stick. He felt comfortable strolling the streets, never passing an opportunity to stop and talk to the ladies. He was smooth, a witty conversationalist, and a charmer, a man who soon made many new friends. If he was ever asked about his past, he always said he was a retired businessman from Birmingham and was just looking for a peaceful place to spend his retirement.

Much of his time was spent drinking the dark English ale, which he was developing a real liking for. He enjoyed lounging around the local pubs, spreading cock and bull stories with the locals. He was even learning how to throw darts but wasn't very good at it. The "good old boys" would laugh until their sides hurt from watching his feeble attempts to throw darts. He didn't appreciate them making fun of him, but for the time being he would have to play it cool and not react to their jokes. He had a degree of truculence which lay just beneath the surface of his chameleon-veneered personality. He knew he must be careful and not let this flaw be known.

Blackstone had always relished the idea of being a bad guy. During all those years he served the F.B.I., he carefully posed as one of the good guys. Using this cunning behavior, he never revealed his true nature. Now he was no longer restrained by the mores of the agency. He was ready to unleash his pent-up evil desires.

While working for the bureau, he had taken evening conversational Spanish classes and had become quite proficient at speaking the language. This was an important part of his future plans. The time wasn't right, just yet, but it would soon come.

He had considered what he would do if the agency came after him. With a smirk on his face, he nearly spoke out loud, "I will have no reservation about putting holes through their self-righteous hides. Those past friends need to remember the margin between life and death is infinitely narrow."

These dim-witted Englishmen were starting to try his patience. Sitting around all day, drinking English beer and throwing darts was becoming a real bore. On more than one occasion he was tempted to bust some of those stupid blokes upside their heads, but the last thing he wanted was a cop asking questions. He would have to bide his time a little longer until the time was right.

Bobby Blackstone hated the inclement weather. It seemed to never stop raining. As he left the pub, the rain was falling again. He opened his umbrella and strolled home, despising every minute of the boredom he had to endure. But, the time would come and he would make his move.

Chapter 49

Russian Water Coffin

The two agents that had assisted them in returning Fletcher from California to Virginia had been a great help. The flight was long but much preferred to the alternative way, by vehicle.

A dark blue Chevrolet Suburban, a typical looking government vehicle, picked up the prisoner and agents at the Manassas Air Field. The others followed in a black Ford Crown Victoria, to the specified location. Matt had a feeling the place they were heading to was the C.I.A. training facility called Foggy Bottom.

A few miles before entering the guarded compound, a black cloth bag was placed over Fletcher's head. No one talked to him nor gave him any information.

Through all the years Baxter had worked for the F.B.I., he was given numerous opportunities to work with the C.I.A. in developing new and more efficient ways of interrogating prisoners. He used many techniques he had learned while working for the K.G.B. He shared this information with the C.I.A. boys and when it came time to ask a favor of them they were grateful to give him a helping hand.

His friends at the C.I.A. had no reservation about letting Baxter use this facility, but made it clear they didn't want to know about the details.

 Baxter was the man who had taught the C.I.A. about the Russian Water Coffin. He was now directing Niki and Matt how to set up the device. Baxter was a tough old bird, but he had been ordered, by his superiors, to take it easy and Niki would be the one to make darn sure he didn't strain himself too much and that he followed those orders. She wanted her dad around for a long time. Baxter needed to hear Fletcher's answers. A pro like Fletcher, might never talk, and officially the bureau couldn't force him to answer their many questions. However, Baxter knew how to make him talk without ever using any sort of physical pain.

The rectangular cement building had no distinguishing architectural design to it and had the appeal of an old World War II gun emplacement bunker. The large, flat exterior walls were painted with a camouflage design. The structure had been built into the tree line, making it difficult to spot. The casual observer would have a difficult time seeing this building even if they were looking for it. Someone's curiosity about the dirt road leading to the facility would be the only reason a person would ever look there. There were no visible windows and only one entrance could be seen from where they were parked.

Niki spoke up, "Matt, that building reminds me of some of the Russian styled structures back home, just plain and simply ugly."

"I bet this building holds Baxter's surprise."

After waiting a short time for Baxter to be helped inside, the two agents escorted the blindfolded Fletcher from the Suburban into the building. They placed him in a heavy wooden chair and tied him to it, then removed the blindfold, as directed.

A few minutes later Baxter made his grand entrance from a side room. He looked at Fletcher, where he sat, precisely in the middle of the room. He was tied so tightly he couldn't move a muscle or take a deep breath.

"By definition, Fletcher, you're a real piece of work, but it's good to see you once again. This time I assure you, there won't be any skipping out on us. So, my man, what brings you here?" Baxter said to Fletcher, with an impish grin.

"Up yours, you half-baked Russian!"

"Now that's not nice. You should have known, you simple-minded dimwit, if you messed with us, some really bad things were going to happen to you."

"So, what right have you to kidnap me and hold me against my will?"

"We have every right to bring you here and interrogate you for as long as it takes. You have the answers to our questions and understand this, you will tell us what we want to know."

Fletcher guffawed, "What makes you think I've got anything to tell you?"

"We know you have plenty to tell us."

"Oh no I don't. It will be a cold day in hell when I tell you anything. Whatever you think you have is pure speculation. You know, Baxter, you are merely too old to play this game anymore. Why don't you just die or something like unto it and make way for the younger agents so they can do their work."

Baxter didn't comment, but continued glaring at his former friend.

"Why did you think I would pull up and leave my job? Remember when you and I went out to eat? I saw how old and decrepit you had become. It was then I decided to retire before it was too late and I turned into what you are now, a stupid old has-been."

Fletcher's comments were designed to piss Baxter off, and it was working. Yet, he wouldn't let his temper override his good judgment. He had plenty of time to react to this verbal abuse and he would, when the moment was right.

Fletcher had finally stopped running his mouth. Now he was quietly watching and listening to those around him. Everything in Baxter's plan had been designed around one specific goal, which was to instill absolute fear in Fletcher, and this was the beginning of the plan.

One of the two government vehicles would be left for Baxter to use if needed. The C.I.A. agents gave him instructions on how to reach them.

"Gentlemen, I'm not sure if you know this, but I helped design this facility. If I do need anything, I will be sure to call."

"Sounds like you have control of the situation, Baxter. One other thing, we stocked the place with the provisions you might need."

"Thanks. There's something else I should tell you. My boss doesn't know about this place and that we have Fletcher here. He had given us orders to find him and bring him home. The sort of justice he is going to receive is something, which hasn't been decided. Fletcher was a rouge agent and as such needs to be dealt with a bit differently. All I need to do is make him more amenable to reason.

"Agent Derek Svindal will be conducting the exercise. Tell him I'll call him when we are ready, and please keep this quiet."

"Will do, Baxter, and good luck with your man."

Baxter returned to the room where Fletcher was sitting.

"Alright, it's time we get the show on the road. I'm going to remove your ropes and give you a few moments to stretch. Don't attempt anything stupid. If you do, Niki or Matt will shoot you where it hurts the most. You won't die but most likely will wish you had. Do you understand this, my man? There is no way of escaping the place. For this moment in time, your no-good hide is mine."

Matt walked up behind Fletcher and placed the muzzle of his weapon tightly against his head while Baxter carefully removed the ropes and then they both backed away.

Fletcher casually looked around the room and saw Matt ten feet away with his Colt, .40 cal in his hand and sweet little Niki with her 9mm pointed at him.

After a couple of minutes Baxter said, "Okay, the break is over, now strip down to your bare skin."

"I wont do it!"

"You will do it, or I'll be forced to let Matt knock the dog crap out of you and then we will take your clothes off."

Reluctantly, Fletcher slowly took off his clothing, one piece at a time, but stopped when his shorts was all that he was left wearing.

"Take the shorts off!" Baxter ordered.

"Not in front of a lady!"

"You, have nothing to show off. Now take your clothes off before we are forced to hurt you."

There Fletcher stood, as bare-skinned as the day he was born, feeling like a naked man in a public park with no place to hide.

"What an ugly sight to see," Baxter said. "It doesn't look like all the nice California sun did your lily-white body much good."

Matt was smiling like a Cheshire cat and Niki was laughing with glee, seeing their old nemesis standing before them and squirming around trying to hide his nudity. They knew he was possibly experiencing more humiliation now than ever before in his life.

Fletcher finally stood in place, like an obedient soldier at attention, but with a look of defiance and hatred. He wasn't going to let them know how embarrassed he was. His hands were covering his package while enduring the giggles and laughing. Baxter decided he had experienced enough degradation for one day.

"Alright, Fletcher, put your hands out in front, you know the drill."

Matt quickly snapped the handcuffs on his wrists. Attached to the cuffs was a chain, which went around his waist, back through the cuffs and down to the ankle braces, where they were locked in place. This is the precise method the federal marshals use to secure inmates when they are being transported.

"We're finished, now you can be seated."

"Are you going to leave me like this?"

Fletcher was a pathetic looking figure, sitting there exposed, cold, and all chained up. Niki walked over to the nearest door and returned with an O.D. green military blanket and wrapped it around Fletcher's naked body.

"Thanks. What's going to happen next?"

"We'll see. It all depends on you."

Baxter called Niki and Matt over to where he was sitting and explained what he wanted them to do. All three of them walked back to where Fletcher sat, each carrying a chair. Baxter placed his chair directly in front of Fletcher while Niki and Matt placed their chairs on each side of him.

Baxter had created an atmosphere, both physically and mentally, which would work to his advantage. He had many questions for their man and needed a lot of answers. Fletcher was a clever and evil man who wouldn't divulge his secrets without a fight, Baxter was determined to get the whole truth out of his contemptuous mouth.

"This day has been too long in coming, Fletcher, far too long to suit me. Now it is here and I couldn't be happier. I knew one day we would get our chance at the truth and here I sit here in front of the man who is going to tell it all or wish he was dead."

"You surprise me, Baxter. For not knowing anything concrete, you certainly have a great deal of confidence in yourself."

"Fletcher, you need to realize this one important fact. When you decided to go over to the dark side, and turned your back on everything that's good and decent, you became a loser. There doesn't seem to be any hope for you."

"What other sort of fairytales are you going to tell me next? When this little pause in my life is over, I'll walk away a free man and you three simpletons will be left with egg on your faces."

"Well, I suppose time will tell, won't it? How do these names sound for starters? Bobby Blackstone and Tom McGee. Do you still think we are simple-minded?"

Fletcher's eyes widened and he looked away without responding to his question. He knew they had talked to McGee but how did they connect up Blackstone? Now the game was on.

"Okay, here is the first question. Are you the author of Operation Star-light?"

"What's Operation Starlight?"

"I'm asking the questions here, so shut your mouth."

"No, I don't know anything about this operation you call Starlight."

"Fletcher, did you dream up this operation on your own volition or was it one of your partner's idea?"

"Like I just told you, I don't know anything about it."

Baxter, Niki and Matt had been well schooled in the art of reading body language and picking out certain responses a liar would display. Each was observing Fletcher carefully and noting his physical reactions on paper.

"Who ordered a hit-man to shoot Matt?"

"Why are you asking me?"

"Did you order the hit on Matt?"

"Why would I do something so absurd? Have you people lost your minds?"

When he was asked this question they all noticed a very interesting response, which they understood. Fletcher wrapped his leg around the leg of the chair, with his foot locked around the bottom of it. This was a known response liars often used, as if to anchor themselves in place.

"Do you know who took the second shot at Matt and Niki?"

"It certainly wasn't me. You know that!"

"Okay, Fletcher, give me the names of all your associates!"

"You are becoming very tiresome, Baxter. How many times do I have to tell you I don't know anything about your accusations? I'm not answering any more of your ridiculous questions, do you understand?"

"I understand, but you had better think on it."

"Next question. How were the banks targeted?"

Fletcher just sat and glared at the old man.

"Here's another question for you. Where did all the money go?"

He wasn't talking.

"How did you counterfeit those F.B.I. orders?"

Still there was no response from the man on the hot seat. His eyes were now firmly fixed on the floor.

"Let's see if you can answer this question. How was it you chose Matt?"

It was quite evident Fletcher wasn't going to offer any information without persuasion of some kind.

"Your silence speaks volumes and because plan A didn't work, you have forced us to proceed to plan B. We will now start the preparations."

Niki, accompanying Baxter, walked over to the north wall and opened a panel door exposing a bank of switches. He flipped the first one and immediately they heard the sound of a motor above Fletcher's head. All four looked up to see a cage slowly descending from the ceiling until it reached the floor and stopped, surrounding Fletcher. The cage resembled an enclosure that would house a large wild animal.

"How do you like your new home, Fletcher?"

Still he said nothing. His eyes were filled with hatred and defiance as he watched Baxter move around the room. Deep inside his soul he was worried with the essence of the unknown.

Matt opened the door of the cage and placed an army cot inside with a "honey bucket" in the corner. Next to the cot he left a few water bottles, nothing more, then slammed the door shut and locked it.

"Hey you! Are you going to leave me like this?"

"Yes, in fact we are. You see, it's part of the plan."

"What plan? Do you morons really think you can scare me with this simple show of force?"

"You know, Fletcher, you should be a little careful with your defiance. We hold all the cards in this game and it looks to me that you have drawn the last card in this deck. I wouldn't be at all surprised if Baxter doesn't have something very special in store for you." Matt turned and walked toward the door.

All the lights to Fletcher's large room were turned out except for one brilliant, overhead spotlight, which illuminated his cage, making it impossible for him to sleep or see anything outside his area of confinement.

In an adjoining room, Baxter began showing Niki and Matt the unique device waiting for Fletcher's "enjoyment."

"Dad, did you think he would talk?"

"No, Niki, this man has been too well trained to spill his guts without a little persuasion. We have him just where we want him. Tomorrow we'll see what kind of grit this old boy is made of."

An enormous water tank descended from the ceiling, stopped and rested on, several wooden 4x4's. The tank was eight feet wide, ten feet long and six feet high.

Casually, Niki walked around the tank examining its structural integrity, and was amazed at what she saw.

"Dad, this device is built like an army tank. How come?"

"This water tank was patterned after the one I remembered seeing demonstrated back in Russia many years ago."

Niki had heard stories from her father about the Russian water coffin. It gave her chills just thinking about its effect on the human mind. Secretly she hoped they wouldn't have to use it.

Matt watched Niki with some concern during her examination of the contrivance, for he could see fear in her eyes. She knew more about this equipment than he did.

Trying to deal with Fletcher's stubborn unwillingness to cooperate would force them to expose him to the water treatment. It was imperative that the complete truth be known, to clear their good names, and this course of action was possibly the only way they could get him to tell the truth.

"Matt, will you hook up these water lines? Connect the blue one to the water supply line on the wall and the other end to the tank. Next to it is a valve. Connect the black line to it and run it over to the drain. Behind the wall is a thermostat, which we will set at 95 degrees, in the morning, when we begin to fill it. We don't want poor old Fletcher to freeze, now do we?"

"What is all this equipment back here?"

"In the morning I will show you how to set it up and explain how it functions."

"I can't wait. This device sounds ominous and somewhat fearful, don't you think, Baxter?"

"I suppose it does. I've never personally operated this contraption before, but I've seen others inflict some horrible fear into the minds of men with it."

"Tomorrow morning I'll be calling a special C.I.A. agent to assist us. His name is Derek Svindal and he is a medical doctor who studies these sort of mind-altering devices."

"Are you sure his name isn't Doctor Death?"

Baxter grinned, "I wouldn't say that to his face."

There was a bed for Niki in one of the rooms, which she insisted on Baxter sleeping in. Matt and Niki placed two cots along the wall some distance from Fletcher's jail cell.

This was one of the longest, most miserable nights Fletcher ever remembered spending in his life. He had no way of shielding his eyes from the intense light. The leg irons, cuffs and chains all cut into his flesh and the hard cot did little to comfort him.

Throughout the night, Fletcher would holler out with an array of obscenities directed at his captors. His mood would swing from rage to near panic. No one had much sleep during this ordeal.

Early the next morning, Niki found some energy bars and shared them with her dad and Matt.

Niki questioned her father, "Should I give one of these bars to Fletcher?"

"No, I'll explain later. Besides he looks like he might be asleep."

Baxter placed a call to agent Derek Svindal informing him they would have everything ready when he arrived at the facility.

"All right kids! I'm going to need your undivided attention for the next little while."

"Dad, you're impossible."

"Matt, turn the water valve on and make sure we have no leaks. It would be a terrible mess if we flooded this place."

Baxter checked the thermostat for the correct water temperature as the tank began to slowly fill. They removed several boxes from a back room.

Matt and Niki began unpacking the equipment and laying each piece on a table, in order. Then they cleaned each piece as instructed.

When the C.I.A. agent arrived, he went directly to work setting up all sorts of equipment. There were video cameras, microphones, speakers, and underwater lights. On another table he laid out a collection of medical supplies, including a defibrillator.

There were wires, and tubes of all descriptions running from the tank to where they connected to a wall panel.

Matt thought to himself, "Can it really be, this place is starting to look a lot like Frankenstein's laboratory. I hope we don't create a monster out of Fletcher."

With steel under his gentle voice Baxter said, "Good morning, Fletcher. I hope you rested well." His own unique style of sarcasm was showing as Matt opened the cell door.

If Fletcher's looks could kill, Baxter would have been dead before they had unlocked the door.

"Have you reconsidered answering my question?"

"Not on your life, Baxter."

"I was hoping you would change your mind. You just said, 'not on your life.' I hope you realize you are betting on your own life."

"Oh, sure."

"You never know, Fletcher. By refusing my questions you are taking a real risk."

"I don't know how many times I have to tell you this before you understand, you don't scare me. I don't have any answers for you. By the way, who is the monkey standing behind you?"

"It's not necessary you know his name. I've brought him along to keep you alive in case I screw up this procedure."

"What do you mean, screw it up?"

Baxter eyed Fletcher speculatively without answering his question.

"With everything said and done, I suppose it's time to get this show on the road." Baxter turned and motioned for Svindal to come forward with his medical tray.

Fletcher took one look at the tray and blurted out, "What the hell is the syringe for? Oh, I get it. You're going to give me a shot of sodium pentathol; good old truth serum. I'm telling you, it won't work on me."

"Good guess my man, but wrong answer. One more time, Fletcher, are you sure you want to go through this experiment? It would be so much easier on you, if for one time you were a good guy and talked to us."

He defiantly shook his head, no.

"Alright, which way do you want to get this shot, sitting up or lying down?"

"Why should it matter?"

"I would suggest you lie down. It might hurt if you fall on your face when the drug takes effect."

Foul superlatives spewed from Fletcher's vile mouth, likened to words uttered by a drunken sailor.

"Oh, Niki, cover your ears. You shouldn't be hearing the awful things Fletcher is calling us."

She didn't like hearing vulgar talk from anyone but made no comment about his filthy speech.

Suddenly he became livid with fury, turning into a mad man. Even with all the restraints in place, he was vigorously resisting their efforts to hold him still. It was as if he may have had a shot of adrenaline, causing him to be so strong.

Matt finally picked Fletcher up from his chair and body-slammed him onto the cot as Niki and Baxter helped hold him in place.

"Now, hold still you puke!" Baxter shouted.

Fletcher spit in his face.

After all this fuss with Fletcher, agent Svindal was finally able to inject the specially formulated sedative into his arm. "Sleepy-by you nasty man," said Svindal.

"All right folks, we need to hurry," ordered Baxter. We only have 10 to 15 minutes to get him ready and in the water tank. Grab the backboard and get the restraints off him. Forget the wet suit, the water is warm enough, just leave him stark naked."

The three of them carefully placed Fletcher's unconscious body on the backboard and then onto a gurney while Baxter stood by and watched.

Next, Matt wheeled the gurney carrying Fletcher into the "room of mental torture," parking it parallel to the water tank.

Secure bracelets were fastened on Fletcher's arms and legs. Each bracelet was attached to a black nylon rope. Monitors to measure his vital signs were then put in place. The last piece of equipment put on Fletcher was a specially designed diving helmet with a large, clear faceplate, which had no obstructions to block the victim's view. Precautions were taken as they placed the diving helmet on him, making certain the device was airtight and he was breathing with no difficulty.

"Okay folks, attach those four ropes from the electric winch to each corner of the backboard and hoist him up and over the water. I need to get behind the wall so I can observe the instruments.

"All right, lower him down to the surface of the water and stop. Now, attach his arms and legs to those side brackets. Make sure you tie them as I instructed, leaving him only a few inches of play. We don't want him reaching anything critical and pulling things loose.

"Lower away. The bracelets will pull him down to the correct depth and stop. After he stops, the backboard will sink to the bottom where it will remain until we need it. Make sure those backboard ropes are left hanging over the edge of the tank, we might need them in a hurry."

Baxter walked out from behind the wall and double-checked their work. Everything seemed to be connected correctly and was working properly.

"It looks good folks. Now we wait."

The entire room holding Fletcher and the water tank was painted jet-ink black. When the lights were turned off it would be as dark as a coal miners tunnel.

Niki took one last look. It was a haunting sight seeing their arch-enemy's helpless body suspended completely under the water, as though he was floating somewhere in outer darkness. It was a solemn moment. There was no gloating, no joy whatsoever being derived from seeing Fletcher like this. He would feel no physical pain, but his mental anguish could only be imagined. No one she knew had ever been subjected to the Russian water coffin. She watched Fletchers limp body. He looked as if all the life had been sucked from him.

Niki remembered, with much clarity, the stories her dad had told about the K.G.B. experiences with this device. Those stories had frightened her. She thought no one should be treated like this.

Matt beckoned, "Come on back here, Niki. We are ready to turn all the lights off."

The four humans stood quietly, waiting for the moment of truth when Fletcher would realize the torturous fear that awaited him.

Adrift in her thoughts, Niki reflected on scenes from her childhood.

"I grew up with Christian teachings from goodly parents. My mother would take out our Bible from its hiding place and read me wonderful stories that I never grew tired of hearing. Dad never would say if he believed in Jesus Christ, because of his government job, but I knew in my heart the kind of man he was.

"How is it I've become a part of this situation? Life sometimes takes us carelessly down some strange, unexpected paths. I will be overjoyed when this particular life experience comes to an end and turns into only a memory."

"Listen up," Svindal cautioned, "Fletcher's sedative will be wearing off soon and I need each of you to be absolutely quiet and observe him. For good reasons, I'll be the only one who will question him. I've spent a great deal of time learning how to communicate with patients that are under this sort of extreme stress.

"Keep an eye on these instruments. As he starts to return to his conscious state you will observe his heartbeat and breathing increase. Most likely his blood pressure will rise, do to his fear. This gauge over here will measure his eye movement, which should become rapid.

"Everything about this experiment is being recorded for scientific purposes. If he gives us the answers we want, and I'm sure he will, they too will be recorded for investigative evidence. All in all, the operation should enlarge our understanding of this type of interrogation."

Matt spoke, "Answer me one question, Agent Svindal. How can you record with a video camera when you have no illumination?"

"I've placed two uniquely engineered, low-level lights in the tank that will give us enough light for our ultra-sensitive cameras to record his actions. When I turn the lights on, Fletcher will not be aware of them. To his senses, his surroundings will be just as dark and black as before.

"Okay, watch and listen. He is starting to come out of the induced sleep. This will be the most shocking experience of his life. I'm afraid that Niki and Matt might become a little overwhelmed with what is about to happen."

Fletcher's first sounds were that of a man talking in his sleep. Not many of his words were recognizable.

The dark, liquid void confused Fletcher's sensory stimulus as he slowly became more and more alert to his surroundings. He could feel something enveloping his naked body. The complete darkness negated his senses, putting his mind into a state of claustrophobic fear, which traveled throughout his body. He attempted to move, but couldn't. Bound in this space by some unseen force, he yanked and pulled with all the strength he could muster. His anxiety rose with each failed attempt to free himself.

Fletcher yelled out with a shocking, agonizing scream, as if being condemned to something worse than hell. The sounds he was uttering were almost unearthly. Niki, alarmed by what was happening, grabbed Matt forcefully, pulling him next to her.

It was hard to distinguish Fletcher's confused utterances, which were mixed with a few recognizable words. Dr. Svindal did wonders in calming him down and getting the answers he wanted. He spoke in a monotone voice, which seemed to maintain a level of control over Fletcher's emotions.

"Fletcher, listen to my words. I'm your only connection to the real world, so talk to me. Help me and I will help you so this demonic dream will end. If you don't help me there will never be an end to this fear."

"Please, I beg of you, whoever you are, get me out of this place in hell before I lose my mind! Is it night or day, darkness or light or maybe good or evil. What is it?"

"I promise I will get you out of there as long as you answer each and every question," Svindal responded softly but imperatively.

Matt and Niki were unschooled observers, not knowing what to expect. They watched and listened to everything that was said or done. Matt had never in is life witnessed this sort of interrogation technique and Niki had only heard about it from her dad. Neither of them were at all happy about what was happening to Fletcher, but they knew this was possibly the only way they could ever be vindicated.

Derek Svindal's voice grew quiet, breaking his emotional connection with Fletcher for a short time, to remind him about his lifeline.

Fletcher let out with another horrid scream. "Are you still there? Can you hear me? Talk to me! Oh, please answer me!" His cracking voice revealed he was about to cry.

As Fletcher struggled with this unreal place he was in, he wondered what the sensation was that surrounded him, touching ever fiber and crevice of his trembling body. He knew it felt different from anything he could remember. The black void of nothingness put a fear into his mind, which was beyond measure. It was as if he was floating somewhere in outer space with absolutely nothing around him, not even a single star to give him hope.

"Okay, my man, I'm with you, so calm down and we will get this over with."

"Agent Fletcher, are you the author of an operation called Starlight?"

He didn't want to answer the question but his fear of the unknown was more than he could stand.

"You are required to answer my questions, Fletcher, or I won't be permitted to ever let you out of this trap you're in."

"All right! Yes! I'm the one. Can I now get out of this trap, please?"

The primordial blackness overwhelmed him to a point that he could not bear. It was if Satan himself waited somewhere out there in the abyss, to take him and his soul away.

"No, I have more questions. Who are your associates? I need their names."

"Bobby Blackstone, and Tom McGee." He had no love for either of those men.

"Who was it that ordered Matt Savage shot?"

"I told the fools not to follow through with their plan but they went ahead and ordered a hit on him. Both McGee and Blackstone paid for the hit on Savage. Honest, I had nothing to do with it."

"Do you know who shot at Niki and Matt?"

"No, I don't! It wasn't me!" Now help me and, let me out! I'm begging you."

"What did you three do with all the money that was taken from those banks?"

"Blackstone, McGee and I split the money up in equal shares."

Dr. Svindal kept on with the questioning for another hour, obtaining nearly all the answers he wanted. Suddenly he reached over and turned off the communications with Fletcher.

"Baxter, I've been closely observing Fletcher's vitals. It's my professional opinion that we get him out, and do it quickly. I think he is about to pop a cork."

"Listen up, Fletcher, it's all over. Be calm and we will have you back to the real world shortly."

Every sound coming forth from Fletcher's mouth was now nothing more than psycho-babble.

Svindal ordered Matt and Niki to swing him away from the tank and lower him down with the hoist.

The lights to the room were turned on. Matt and Niki were on each side of the tank, helping to move Fletcher from his water-grave. Moments later, Doctor Svindal assisted them in removing the breathing apparatus and all of the monitors and sensors.

Matt looked down into Fletcher's vacant eyes. "What has happened to his mind?" He wondered. "Only time will tell. Maybe, with a considerable amount of therapy, he will return to a normal man, so he can be tried and sentenced for the crimes he has committed, that is if the agency wants him tried."

"Make sure you leave the ropes tied until you get him on the gurney, then cuff him up as before. I don't know how he is going to react. As far as I know he might go ballistic on us, but most likely he will be quiet and subdued. Just be careful with him."

Niki retrieved several blankets from the storage room and carefully covered his naked body. He looked cold and she was concerned that he could easily go into shock. It wouldn't be a good thing to have him die.

"What do you say, Svindal, that we get Fletcher turned over to Staggs. I would feel better if he was out of our control and the responsibility of the agency. They have the facilities to keep him secure and if he needs medical help, well, they can do that too."

"That's fine with me, Baxter. Call right now and arrange a meeting place."

It took all four of them to muscle Fletcher into the back seat of the Suburban, get a seat belt around him and keep him covered.

When Staggs saw Fletcher he said, "What happened to this poor excuse of a man?"

"It's a long story. I'll fill you in on the details tomorrow when we get the reports all typed up. Just take him for now and by-the-way, I would strongly suggest you get him to a doctor; one of ours."

Chapter 50

To The Hospital

"Dad, I thank the dear Lord this nightmare is over. I never, and I mean never want to see anything like this again. As bad as Fletcher is I can't help but feel sorry for him."

"I understand, Niki, but we did get the report we were after. This information can be priceless and don't you forget it. Now our superiors will have something to sink their teeth into and they won't just have to take our word on it."

"If you remember your promise, dear Dad, the next thing on our agenda is that we take you to the hospital and check you in. You will be staying there until your heart is well and it's the doctor's pleasure to send you home."

Baxter started to protest but Niki cut him off. "Not another word! Understand?"

"Matt can stay here and help Dr. Svindal put the equipment away. I'll pick him up later. Is that alright with you, Matt?"

"That's fine with me, besides I don't like hospitals."

Within the hour every last piece of equipment was stored away in its proper place with no evidence of anyone having been there. Matt wondered if this device would ever be used again.

As Dr. Svindal was leaving he said, "Mr. Savage, could I give you a ride?"

"Thanks, but no thanks, Doctor. Niki said she would pick me up, so I had better wait for her. What I've witnessed here will be something I'll never in a lifetime forget."

"Let me give you a sound piece of advice, my friend. Pretend like you never saw this experiment or know anything about it. And whatever you do, don't ever tell anyone!"

For the longest time Matt sat quietly, and very alone in the cavernous room, pondering all that had happened on this day. He disliked everything about this building. The walls seemed to have eyes, as if something was watching him. Were there specters of some long lost tortured souls lingering within it's bounds?

The hair on his arms was now bristling. He had spooked himself like a school kid. He exited the place in a hurry and once outside he felt better. He settled down in some tall, cool grass near the front door, to wait for Niki.

The orange sun was now setting low in the west as the evening shadows slowly crept across the compound. Matt was relieved to see Niki driving up the dirt road. He could now get away from this terrible place. Matt checked to see that the only door to the building was locked.

"Glad to see you, Niki! As the kids say, this place was starting to creep me out."

"It is a creepy place, Matt, and I hope to never see it again."

"Is everything all right with your dad? I was beginning to worry something had gone wrong."

"Oh, I believe he will be okay. A cute little nurse was starting to fuss over him, paying more attention to him than was necessary. I think he will stay put because he was very flattered and taken with her charm."

Matt smiled warmly. "Yeah, even old men like to be fussed over."

Chapter 51

Home Again

"I've been anxiously waiting to get back home so I can sleep in my own bed once again. I'm so tired of sleeping in strange hotel and motel beds that I could scream."

Matt just shrugged his shoulders at her comment. It didn't matter to him.

"Matt, Madison Hills is only an hour from here, that is if the traffic is light. Tomorrow morning we'll drive to Bethesda, were I left Dad."

"Oh, darn it Matt! I forgot I had the paper work to do. I'm now responsible to write the report for Staggs. He will be expecting it soon, but maybe he will cut me a little slack since Dad's in the hospital."

"I'm glad you're the one with the responsibility to write the reports. Never in my career was I fond of writing reports. As I recall, I don't remember many of my partners liking it much either. If Staggs directed me to write the reports I'm afraid I would tell him, 'absolutely not!' I've done so much for the agency and what has it gotten me, nothing! I've been lied to, deceived, shot in the back, and committed crimes under the protective umbrella of the agency, so I was lead to believe. I've fought for my life to help prove our innocence and now I'm going to be kicked to the curb."

There was a sadness in his eyes that Niki hadn't often seen. Matt gazed at her for the longest time.

"Niki, my dear Niki, you're the only positive thing that I will always cherish from all these years we've been together." He grew quiet, daring not to say more.

Chapter 52

Kids Play

A few days later the two very special friends sat around the kitchen table in the Blinski home, discussing all that had happened.

"Niki, have you given any consideration regarding our next step in this manhunt of ours?"

"No, I haven't. Most of my thoughts have been with Dad. With one third of our team out of commission, I have been wondering what is in store for us. Now that he's starting to return to his old self, I'm beginning to feel a sense of relief and hope for the future.

"I have an idea my friend. Why don't you get out your crystal ball and lets have a look-see." Matt smiled easily.

"What is it you're trying to say? Are you saying I'm some sort of a witch?"

"Heavens no, Niki, but if you happen to be, you're the cutest one I've ever seen." She grinned.

"Yeah, I now know exactly what my problem is. You must have cast one of your cute little witch spells on me, and that's the reason I'm so confused about everything."

Matt started to laugh and was attempting to sing the song, Evil Woman. Within a split second, Niki's shoe smacked him right up-side of his head. He jumped up from the table.

"That hurt girl! Now you're going to pay for your indiscretion," and he started for her.

She let out with a squeal and ran from the room with Matt close behind. Before she could take refuge in her bedroom Matt grabbed her by the arm and swung her around. That's when she punched him in the stomach with a hard fist.

He wasn't expecting she would do that. Niki's forceful blow nearly knocked the breath out of him. He lost his grip and she bolted out the patio door to where there were plenty of good hiding places in the woods.

By the time Matt collected himself and got to the rear door, she was nowhere to be seen.

Matt hollered, "You can't hide from me!"

She didn't answer, not wanting to give her location away. After all, this was her home turf and she should be able to stay hidden from him for a long time. Matt believed he had more patience and that would give him the advantage. He had no doubt he would find her.

He causally walked out to the tree line of the forest, watching and listening for the slightest revelation of her location. Matt stealthily moved from one tree to another, hoping to flush her from her hiding place, and he did. She bolted past him as quick as a rabbit, with Matt in close pursuit.

Niki was a good athlete, agile and fast. Each time he tried to grab her, she would turn on a dime and escape.

Matt considered the fact that she was making a fool of him. He made one all-out concerted effort to capture her and he did succeed in grabbing her and pinning her arms to her side. Instead of giving up, she stomped down hard on his foot. Matt instantly released his hold on her.

"Niki, you don't play fair. When I do catch you, and I will, I'm going to give you a well-deserved spanking, little girl." Matt knew she didn't like to be called that.

"That will be the day, you old flat-foot cop." He could hear her laughing not far from where he stood. Matt ran directly toward the spot he last heard her voice. He caught her completely off guard and tackled her to the ground before she could get up to speed. Now the wrestling match was on. She fought him like a caged cat, but Matt managed to roll her onto her back and pin her arms above her head while straddling her like a horse. She didn't like this situation one bit, but what could she do. There they lay in the soft cool grass, next to a creek, wondering what might happen next.

"You know Niki I could grow to like this. I've got you right where I want you, and yes, I'll stay right here until you give up and tell me you're sorry."

"That will be a cold day, in you know where," she growled.

He leaned over, looking directly into her fiery blue eyes. For a moment nothing happened, then he leaned down and gave her a little kiss on the cheek. "Will that soothe the savage beast?" Matt tried to stifle a grin.

That peck on Niki's cheek wasn't having a positive effect on her. She was mad, through and through. She hated being held down like this and Matt knew it.

"Okay, Niki, if I let you up can we call a truce and put an end to this foolishness?"

"No, you brute!"

"Then what if I let you skip the apology?"

"Maybe. Now let me go!"

"Will you be good?"

As Matt loosened his grip on her wrist, her right hand broke free and she slapped him across his cheek with a loud pop.

"You little witch, that hurt! Now you've really asked for it."

Matt could never remember being angry with her, yet, there is always a first time for everything.

He jerked her up from the ground, struggling with her until he got her across his lap. He then administered two hard slaps. One to each cheek of her well proportioned butt. Each slap was designed to hurt.

He let loose of Niki. The fight in her seemed to be gone. She gathered herself up and abruptly walked off to the house without looking back at him or saying a single word.

Matt felt like a genuine heel. He knew he had better let the matter rest for a while until she cooled down before attempting to smooth things over.

Matt sat down under the shady limbs of an old majestic mountain ash, to think and calm his feelings. The soothing cadence of the cascading water, running over the rocks in the nearby creek was a sound he loved. It must have been one of the reasons he enjoyed fishing in such beautiful places. The sounds made a person feel altogether better about life.

He took in the pleasant surroundings of the woods, which added to his pleasure. He stretched out on the grass and fell into a restful asleep.

When he opened his eyes, not knowing how long he had slept, he saw Niki sitting cross-legged, directly in front of him, with a puzzled look on her face. She reached out and took hold of Matt's nervous hand. For a few moments Niki said nothing, then she smiled at him warmly, and said. "I'm sorry for letting a little fun get out of control."

Matt gave her a blank stare, not wanting to let her know just yet his true feelings. Still holding her hand, Matt pulled her close and gave her an affectionate hug. "I'm sorry too. I couldn't have felt worse for slapping your cute little buttocks, but remember, you beat on me pretty good."

"That I did," and she offered him an impish little grin. "Okay, Matt, we have a truce."

Chapter 53

Bethesda Hospital

The following morning at Bethesda Hospital, Niki and Matt were enjoying a pleasant visit with Baxter when who would show up, Staggs, their friend and director.

"Good morning folks!" I'm pleased to see you doing so well old friend. You really had me worried."

"It's going to take a lot more than a little heart problem to sideline this old boy. In a few days I'll be as good as new and ready to pull my own weight. We do have a job to finish, don't we?"

Staggs looked over at Niki and then at Baxter.

"Baxter, my friend, I hate to be the bearer of bad news. You are being put out to pasture.

Baxter started to protest. "No!"

"There will be no protest and there will be no argument about the decision. We just can't have you dying on us, can we? It's been decided that we will let you be an advisor about the matters at hand, but that will be it."

Secretly, Niki was a happy daughter, but her dad looked as if someone had hit him between the eyes. She knew this order would be tough for him to obey, and he probably wouldn't do it.

Matt inquired, "What is the status on Fletcher?"

"I assure you, he is in a very secret and secure place, under the constant care of some specialized doctors. One thing you've probably guessed, his mental condition isn't good. Yet, they tell me he should be fine in a few weeks. We are going to have to wait and see on that matter."

"Staggs, it's hard for me to believe that he will ever be alright," Baxter blurted out.

"Then what will happen? Is he going to be criminally charged?" Matt questioned.

"It's my professional opion that this case will never see the light of a courtroom, and besides, it will be months before all the evidence is ana-lyzed and put to rest."

"Then what about Blackstone?"

"The last known location of Blackstone was Paris France, like I told all of you once before. From Paris we have no idea where he went, but hopeful-ly we'll come up with something on him."

"Alright, Staggs, one more question. What has become of our third man in the triangle of crooks, Tom McGee?"

"Our bean counter is happy, fat, and stupid. He was so frightened when we approached him about his involvement that he simply spilled his guts and told us nearly everything we wanted to know, with one stipulation, we let him keep his job. Can you imagine that's all he asked for? We agreed to let him keeping working, for the time being, if he would tell us about anything he might hear. The time is approaching when McGee will be locked up like any other crook."

"Savage, I have one personal question for you. How is your health?"

"I suppose my health is about as normal as I can expect. I'm certainly not as strong as I once was. I should contribute that change to my age, noth-ing more. Then Matt grinned, "At least I was able to beat Fletcher at his own game. The fight we had reminded me of a western barroom brawl, just rolling around in the blood, the mud."

"We are all happy you beat that scoundrel. I personally would have paid good money to see that show down. Thanks Matt!"

"You're welcome Sir!"

"What I'm really trying to ask, how is your memory?"

Matt wasn't quite sure he knew how to answer Staggs question correctly.

All three friends intently waited for Matt's answer, and it didn't come easily. As he lifted his eyes he looked directly at Niki and spoke.

"After Fletcher's capture and the helluva fight we had, I started to remember some things more clearly. Now I realize I have a family back in Utah, but I'm so extremely embarrassed about what I've put them through that I don't know how I'm ever going to face them. Furthermore, I would like to know if Penny is still living in the safe house."

"No, Matt, she is back in her own home with your children close by. We were forced to lift the amount of security we once had because there was no immediate threat to your family's safety."

Matt wondered, "Isn't that interesting, all these people know more about my family than I do."

Matt asked. "Isn't Blackstone still a real threat?"

"Yes, that he is. We are sure he ordered both hits, the first one on you and the second attempt on you and Niki.

"Then why should he be considered less of a threat now?"

"One of the reasons for the security change is, we believe he is out of the country and most likely has lost some of his interest in all three of you."

"I hope you're correct, but you don't know for sure, do you, Staggs?"

"No, we don't know, yet we are compelled to make our best educated guess and hope we are right. The agency has feelers out around the globe looking for any evidence of Blackstone or possibly the new aliases he could be using. Once we get some pertinent information on him, which will point us in the right direction, we will act on it. Then we will let you know."

Baxter eyed his friend Staggs, speculatively. "One thing I need to know, are you going to let us finish this job we've started?"

Staggs shrugged his shoulders and with a slight shake of his head, he commented, "That is a question I cannot answer at this time, my friend. It's going to be a day-to-day decision, with everything is depending on what we can learn about Blackstone."

Everyone involved are sure Blackstone knew precisely where Baxter and Niki lived, and like Matt's family, a real threat from Blackstone at his time isn't a pressing issue.

However, Matt would never pass Blackstone's evilness off as a Little Abner's cow dream. He remembered all too well the last attempt on his and Niki's life, when the hired hit-man shot up Niki's Cobra. If it hadn't been for the grace of God, both of them might have been killed.

Matt had finally come to the realization that he must go home and try and mend the tattered relationships with his family. But, at this time, he was afraid to leave Niki alone, being she was the most likely to be attacked if Blackstone had the mind to. He wondered if this nightmare would ever come to an end.

Baxter's heart specialist had projected his release from the hospital within the week. Once Baxter was home with Niki he would take the next important step in his life and head for his real home, not the one he had been spending with his friends.

It might take weeks, months or maybe years before Blackstone would be found and brought to the departments' sort of justice. What part would the three of them play in his demise? The thought of the uncertainty and the unknown always caused Matt to worry, which he didn't like very much. He was sure most humans, at some point in their life, had the same sort of feelings he had.

Chapter 54

Happy and Sad

"Niki, would you mind if we had a little chat? I need to talk to you about my past, the parts which seem to be lost."

"Sure, let's talk!"

Niki and Matt took seats across from each other in the living room. Like most men, Matt found it somewhat difficult to speak about matters of the heart.

"My memory about my wife and kids has returned, at least enough to remember who they are and that I truly love them."

"I'm happy for you, Matt. I've been extremely worried about you for a long time. Dad and I weren't sure you would ever retrieve those lost memories."

"Thanks Niki, for all you've done for me these past months. I'm afraid I've been more of a burden than a help."

"I don't ever want to hear those words come out of your mouth again. Do you understand? Without you we would have never caught Fletcher."

"I understand. I suppose I'm feeling confused about many things lately, and not really sure about what course I should take next. There's one thing I must do and that is take a trip to Utah to see my family. Until I see my family again I'm afraid I'll be just another lost soul.

"This is going to be a sad goodbye. A strange set of circumstances brought us together years ago and it turned into an amazing adventure few people could ever hope for in a lifetime.

"I now know and remember my family and how much I love each of them, especially my lovely wife. What troubles me is I've fallen in love with you, Niki, which should have never happened. I don't understand this emotional dilemma I'm in and I probably never will. I have always been true to my wife and I know you and I can never be together.

A tear rolled down Niki's cheek. "Matt," I always hoped somehow we might be together, but never at the expense of your wife. I don't think you ever knew I met Penny; it was at your funeral. I could tell she was a special lady, and I liked her."

Matt spoke quietly with a resolve in his voice that gave truth to what he was about to say. "Niki, there is piece of my heart which will always be bonded to yours. I will never forget that fearful night on the plains of Wyoming in that old abandoned ranch house. You had been shot and was dying, irregardless of everything I did for you. I offered a prayer and gave you a special blessing, and I know that because of your faith and the hand of our Lord your life was spared."

"My dear Matt, I know what you say is true and our hearts will always be as one." She threw her arms around him and with her face buried in his shoulder, wept.

Chapter 55

Trouble

It was just another one of those dreary, rainy nights in the city of Oxford, England where Warren Tidwell, (Blackstone) had taken up residency, waiting for the right time to make his next move.

He sat alone drinking at a corner table. There was plenty of that dark English ale he liked. He had consumed more than he should have, and he knew better, but he just didn't care. He remembered, with some clarity, about the knock-down and drag-out fights he had because of his drinking. Alcohol affects people differently, some joke and laugh, while some believe they are lovers and that everyone loves them. Some get nasty and want to fight anyone and everyone. All drunks soon develop one thing in common, they become simple-minded fools.

Before the evening was over, Tidwell would become another one of these fools. The more he drank, the meaner he felt. He wanted to bust one or more of these stupid Englishmen in the mouth and be done with the aggravation he felt. He was waiting for an excuse, any excuse would do.

He continued drinking from his mug and kept his eyes glued to the three guys playing darts. "What a sissy pastime," he thought.

"Hey! You dumb butt-brain!" Tidwell shouted.

"Are you talking to us?"

"Yeah, you sissy boys with the cute little darts."

The three dart players looked at him with distain and went back to their game, paying Tidwell no attention, for they had seen men with his problem many times before.

Tidwell's insatiable appetite for this English ale had disengaged his mind from his mouth and it was doing all the talking for him. He continued casting one ugly slur after another at the players.

"Hey, you stupid bloke. Ease off the gas pedal old man. If you keep flapping you gums I'll be forced to come back there and kick your ugly face in and make you pug ugly.

Warren Tidwell wasn't afraid of their threats, in fact he was hoping they would come back, so he continued on with his scurrilous attacks.

Finally, after listening to that loud-mouth drunk for too long, the bartender walked back to where Tidwell was sitting and offered him some friendly advice.

"Hear me. If you don't shut your mouth I'm going to be forced to throw you out. My customers are tired of listening to your foul mouth, so shut up!"

Tidwell spoke up, "Just who in the hell do you think you are, telling me what I can do? So, you piss off!"

As the bar tender swung around to return to the bar for a little help, Tidwell exploded from his chair. Picking up a nearby bar stool, he raised it over his head and headed after the bartender. Some patrons hollered, "Watch out, Jack!"

The donnybrook was on. The bartender had escaped the assault, but now Tidwell was swinging a bar stool madly at everyone and everything. He continued in his rampage, busting up a once very nice pub. Finally, someone creased his skull with something hard and heavy and the row was instantaneously over. The next thing Tidwell remembered was a bright light shining in his face and a doctor asking him some stupid questions. He soon realized his wrists and ankles were strapped down to the gurney. He glanced around the examining room and saw two fine looking Bobbies watching intently over him.

The following day, Warren Tidwell was released from the hospital and escorted to the city jail to wait for his appearance before a magistrate.

Tidwell had what you could call a compound headache, half of it was due to the excess drinking the previous night and the other half from a crack across his skull. There was no arguing the point; he had been a real fool. When he looked at his hands he knew they had fingerprinted him, for there was still ink stain on his fingers. What if the F.B.I. had put out a warrant for his arrest? They hadn't, but he didn't know that, still, they were looking for him just the same.

As soon as the bail could be posted, he would pay it and make tracks for parts unknown. His original scheme was for a destination in South America, but that might have to wait for a while longer. He had to come up with a new plan for his immediate future, and fast.

The following morning, Tidwell was escorted from the jail to a holding cell adjacent to a courtroom where he was seated with a bunch of sorry-looking souls. He nearly laughed at their appearance but then he thought, "I must not look any better than they do."

Warren Tidwell was a worried man. He knew very little about the English judiciary system but he was about to get his first lesson.

An officer of the court approached Tidwell. "Get up and follow me, Mr. Tidwell."

He had difficulty keeping up with the officer because his hands and feet were shackled. Inside the courtroom they had him stand in a small area surrounded by a short wooden fence.

The Judge spoke, "Mr. Warren Tidwell, is that you who stands before me?"

"Yes, your honor, I'm Warren Tidwell."

"You have three charges against you. First charge, drunk & disorderly conduct, second, attempted assault, and third, destruction of personal property. How do you plea to these charges?"

"Your honor, I would like to plead guilty to all three charges. May I indulge the court for a minute? I would like to make a statement."

"I'm listening, go ahead with your statement."

"I want to apologize to the court and the owner and patrons of the Black Knight. I had a bad day and I drank too much, which I realize is no excuse for my behavior. I will pay for all of the damages and whatever is asked of me. I'm truly sorry."

The Judge eyed Tidwell speculatively and then spoke. "I sentence you to ten days which I will suspend on payment of the court costs and the damages to the Black Knight. You will have a week to take care of these charges. If not taken care of in that time, a warrant will be issued for your arrest. Do you understand?"

"Yes sir, I understand, and I promise to take care of the bill, and I will do it by tomorrow."

"Then you are free to go, but don't let me see you in my court again or I won't be so generous."

"I understand, and thank you."

The following morning Tidwell closed his bank account, went straight to the court clerk's office and paid her the full amount, in cash, for the repairs to the pub and the fine from the court.

He left the landlady the next month's rent, in advance. so there would be no question about what he owed her. With his few belongings packed, he purchased a bus ticket and headed for Liverpool. He had a few connections there that could help him move out of England and away from being discovered.

Blackstone had some Russian Mafia connections, which should help him get out of England without anyone knowing that he was ever there or where he might have gone.

Chapter 56

Matt's Real Home

Matt was still one of those individuals from the old school who hadn't changed or adjusted to the new ways of communication and all the electronic gadgetry. He didn't know if his family had the Internet. If they did he didn't know their e-mail address. He couldn't remember their phone number so he would do what he was sure of and send them an old fashioned letter.

Dear Penny,
I'll be home this Friday PM
On the 10th United Fl 2001
Anxious to see all of you.

Love – Matt.

The morning of the 10th arrived and the three dear friends stood together in the terminal of the Ronald Reagan National Airport in Virginia, across the Potomac from the U.S. Naval Air Station. Matt's flight was a non-stop to Salt Lake City.

Matt reached in his pocket and removed his wallet and a credit card.

"Here is your credit card, Dad." Matt hadn't called Baxter that before. Baxter smiled, for he loved Matt as his own son and calling him Dad made him happy.

"You hang on to that card, Matt. I most certainly don't need it, but you might."

"I'm not sure how I can repay you for all you've done for me. I've been a real drag on you for these past months, not contributing much of anything."

Baxter stepped in front of Matt, taking hold of his shoulders with his mighty hands, and looking him straight in the eyes said, "You listen to me. You've earned everything and much more. If it wasn't for your efforts, Fletcher would still be on the loose and we would be left with only our words to prove our innocence. One more thing, Matt, you are an important part of our family and you always will be. This departure is hard for us to see you go, and it hurts us deeply. If for any reason things don't work out for you back home, will you please return to us?"

Baxter wrapped his arms around Matt, giving him a great old-fashioned Russian Bear Hug, and kissed each of his cheeks. Both of these tough men had tears in their eyes.

Matt turned towards Niki and took her in his arms and gave her a loving hug good-by.

He cussed to himself, "I do hate good-bys," not knowing if this moment would turn out to be their last.

Walking slowly down the long corridor, he stopped before stepping out of sight, turned and waved farewell, and then bid Niki and Baxter the biggest, warmest grin he could muster, then disappeared from view.

The United flight took five hours, which gave Matt time to ponder over questions he had considered many times before, questions which he didn't have answers to. He was certain of one thing, he loved his family and was excited to see them again, hoping they would be understanding about the difficult times he had gone through. He also knew he must be very understanding about what he had put them through.

Matt should have known, but he wasn't quite sure how his family would greet him as he hadn't been much of a husband or father for quite a long time. It never was his intention for his family to be hurt, but sometimes, unexpected things do happen in this life that one has little control over.

A feeling of happiness intensified as he passed the security station knowing his family would be waiting at the bottom of the escalators. Matt paused a moment to look over the crowd below to see if they were there, then stepped onto the moving stairs, which he loved to ride as a boy. At the bottom he moved to one side to make way for the people behind him. He saw Penny pushing her way through the crowd, followed by his three sons and daughter.

What a prodigious moment, seeing his family rushing to greet him with open arms, which said, "All is well, welcome home."

Penny threw her arms around Matt's neck. Her momentum nearly caused him to lose his balance. With many kisses and hugs and loving words, his family settled down to quiet conversation.

He had no luggage, only a small carry-on bag with a few personal items. Most of his clothes had been left at the Blinski's home. Matt wasn't sure why he had done that. Maybe, subconsciously, he feared he had lost his family's love and would be returning to Madison Hills, Virginia.

The thirty-mile ride home to Lakeside was delightful. He listened to each of his children tell about the things in their lives which were important to them. His four children were all now married and Matt hoped & prayed they were happy and their marriages would last.

Matt spoke hesitantly, "My dear family there will be a time when I would like to explain, if I can, what has taken place over these past months. To be very honest, I wasn't sure who all of you were. I know who you said you were but I couldn't remember any of you and it troubled me night and day. The only relief from this nightmare was to try and put it out of my mind. "My memory still isn't perfect, but I now remember each of you and how I dearly love all of you."

After dinner, Penny, his children and their spouses, all sat around the kitchen table while Matt told them a couple of the stories about Fletcher and his capture. He didn't tell them everything for there was far too much to tell at one time and there were some things, which would best be left untold.

"What I'm telling each of you this evening, you must promise to keep quiet for the time being. Two of the three bad guys are now out of the picture and pose no danger to anyone, but the most dangerous one, Bobby Blackwell is still at large. The F.B.I. has inquiries out around the world, hoping he will show up. We believe he is in Europe. His last known location was Paris, France, but time has passed and he might be anywhere."

Matt, didn't tell his family that Blackstone was the one who initiated the hired hit on him, not once, but twice. Revealing that sort of information to his family would be a foolish thing to do, so for the time being, Matt would do the worrying.

Chapter 57

Liverpool

The hour was far past midnight as the black, rust covered Russian freighter slowly and carefully made its way towards the open sea, on its voyage to Cuba. It was loaded with a shipment of coal.

The old freighter eventually moved out of the harbor and into the open waters of the North Atlantic. Creaks and groans could be heard as she pitched and rolled with the waves of the sea. Bobby Blackstone didn't like what he felt and heard. It was going to be a long voyage and he feared the inevitable seasickness, which soon took over his sense of well-being.

Blackstone wasn't overjoyed with this mode of travel. He had to be satisfied knowing this little ruse might never be discovered by those who sought him and maybe he would be able to disappear forever. He had paid the Russian captain well for this trip. With new papers in hand, he was now a Russian sailor wanting to make a new home in Cuba. Cuba wasn't his first choice of countries to settle in, but given all the circumstances, it was the best choice available.

The Russians should have confidence in him, given the fact he had turned over many American secret documents to them during his career.

In this cut-throat business that Blackstone had allowed himself to become a part of, he knew he could trust no one. He was proud of his evil ways and being a greedy man didn't matter at all to him, as long as he got money and plenty of it.

Bobby Blackstone was a proud man knowing he was part of a sinister and illegal operation that was without precedence. Robbing banks and using legitimate agents to do the dirty work made him laugh. The whole time the operation looked absolutely official. No one in the agency discovered "Operation Starlight" until it had long since died away. Their caper would piss off the agency for years to come and this knowledge gave much satisfaction to his dark soul.

By morning sunrise, Blackstone felt as if he had puked his guts out. The muscles of his stomach hurt and no matter what the consequence might have been, he wished he had flown and taken the risk.

One of the sailors brought him some Dramamine, compliments of the Captain. He handed him the pills and laughed out loud as he arrogantly strolled away.

On the second day, Blackstone, still sick as a dog, and to boot, a weak-legged sailor, found the Captain. "Captain how close are we to land? I need to know.

With a straight poker-face the Captain said, "Three miles, my man." "Oh great. Which way?"

Captain Zervinski answered, "Straight down" He laughed so hard he had to hold his stomach to keep it from hurting.

Blackstone didn't think his humor was very funny, but considering how sick he was, he didn't feel like making a single protest.

Finally the sea was a little calmer and it gave him some hope, which was short lived. The crossing was long, slow and the sea was rough for most of the trip.

Friday morning arrived, the day the ship would make port in Havana. The sea was calm, and the sun was hot. This would be a great day to depart from this nasty old freighter, Blackwell considered.

Shortly after eating something for breakfast, that he couldn't identify, a sailor approached him.

"The Captain requests that you meet him in his cabin, right now."

"Alright, tell him I'll be there shortly."

He knocked sharply on the Captain's door. "Come on in," the Captain shouted. "Take a seat. I have something to discuss with you before we make port this fine day."

"Fire away, I'm all ears."

Captain Zervinski looked at him for a moment, wondering about this strange verbal expression of his.

"I have received word from my sources of some potential trouble in the Cuban Communist Party in Havana. It's my opinion, if I leave you there, you might get arrested. I've come up with another contingency which should work for you."

"Okay, let's hear it, my friend."

"After we off-load our coal, we will be sailing for Caracas, Venezuela for a load of tin. By then we can have your new documents ready. Of course, it's going to cost you a little more money."

"Alright, what else is new in our world of cut-throats. I don't see that I have any other choice in this matter."

Blackstone smiled at the Captain, letting him know he understood.

In the recesses of his mind he well remembered making alliances with these people, He had chosen them as bed-fellows years ago and now he had to do business with them whether he liked it or not. He didn't trust any of them any further than he could throw a rodeo bull by its tail. He said to himself, "I'm sure they don't have any more trust in me than I have in them. We are all bad to the bone and that's the way it is."

Blackstone made his way to a vantage point on the ship where he could stand and watch the beautiful Caribbean Sea. He knew they were sailing through the Bermuda Triangle and couldn't help but wonder if any of those intriguing stories had any truth to them.

Several times during the trip, Blackstone had noticed a little, wesel-looking sailors' quick, prying eyes watching him, especially when he was playing cards with some of the other sailors. The guy reminded him in every way of a jailhouse snitch, a sort of guy everyone wanted to shank. Blackstone was going to keep his eye on that sailor for he was certainly no good, and no good could come from his sort.

All afternoon Blackstone stood on the deck of the old ship. There was not much else to do but scrutinize the unloading of the coal.

How he wished he could head into Havana for a few hours and get a bottle of that renowned Cuban rum. He hadn't had a swallow of hard liquor since he left Liverpool and his cravings were driving him a little crazy. He considered sneaking off the ship but he knew no bottle of rum would be worth the price he might have to pay.

"Hey, Captain Zervinski, would you happen to have a bottle of Cuban rum I could buy? Because I'm confined to your ship I can't go to town and buy my own. I thought you might be a good fellow and sell me one."

With a rare smile the Captain said, "Wait right there."

Five minutes had passed when he returned with a new bottle of Cuban rum. Handing it to Blackstone, he said, "No charge. Just remember, its not always about money."

"Fantastic! Thanks, Captain."

The old sailor turned and strolled away.

Sunday morning arrived. The freighter sat high in the water, with its load of coal now off-loaded. The ship moved more freely as it sailed in a southeasterly direction, around the island of Cuba, and set its course for Venezuela and the city of Caracas.

Bobby Blackstone had never visited this part of the world before. It was beautiful and he didn't want to miss any of the sights. He found the perfect spot at the bow of the ship where he could see for miles. A soft sea breeze was blowing in his face. A kind sailor loaned him a pair of binoculars, which made everything nearly perfect.

A Cuban patrol boat escorted them for a couple of hours before speeding up and crossing their bow, then it headed back.

Any sign of the military or police made Blackstone very nervous.

"Hey Captain, how long is the trip to the next port?"

"My impatient friend, not so long, about 48 hours if the weather holds and we don't sink."

Blackstone smiled at the Captain's humor and gestured with a wave of his hand. He didn't like his humor at all, but who was he to challenge his sense of wit.

For several hours he watched the sea and islands. He dreamed of a place in this new land where he could live in peace, free from the law. Yet, he knew deep inside his mind they would never stop looking for him. He had made them look like buffoons, an embarrassment the agency would never forget.

The sailor who loaned Bobby the binoculars approached him and said, "Would you mind a little company?"

"No, not at all."

"I suppose I'm a little bored and tired of talking to my old shipmates who have nothing new to say. It seems their scope of interests are very narrow. You're a new face on our ship and look like an interesting person to visit with."

Blackstone appreciated his interest in him, and smiled warmly.

"Have you ever been to Cuba before?"

"No, this is my first time here. By-the-way what should I call you?"

"Just call me Bob." He smiled from behind his binoculars. "And your name is?"

"Petrov. I've been to the island of Cuba many times over the years and still find this land intriguing. Cuba is surrounded by beautiful beaches with their white sands and coral reefs. These reefs form bays, which are loved by the fishermen. It protects them from the waves of the ocean. I've read that Cuba has 1,600 islands surrounding their country."

"Interesting. Petrov, why didn't the Captain want his crew taking a shore leave?"

"Some of the crew did go to town, Bob. They were all old-timers and well known by the authorities. I think the Captain was afraid the police might have given you some trouble."

Blackstone didn't respond to Petrov's comment.

"Well, sailor Petrov, are you a married man?"

"Yes I am, but I have two wives. The one is back in Russia and the other cold and heartless one you see out there in front of us is the sea."

Blackstone said, "I was once married, many years ago, to a woman I was glad to be rid of. Because of that divorce, I've lived a very lonely life. Sometimes, I think it would be nice to have a woman around again, for a little company."

For a few minutes neither man spoke. They stood quietly with their thoughts, considering what had been said. Both understood there was no going back in time, for the past was now nothing more than history, and if you were fortunate enough, someone might write about you, not that many would care.

A gentle wind blew through Blackstone's thinning hair, which was a refreshing treat in the heat of the day. He smiled to himself.

"If you don't mind, Petrov, for years I've always wanted to ask someone about Russia and the distinctions between the Communist party of your country and that of Cuba's Communist party. But as for me, a cogitative observer, there seems to be dissimilarities."

"I don't mind. It's an interesting subject."

"Before we get started, Petrov do you have a Zampolit (political officer) on board this ship?"

"Oh no, I believe you'll only find them on military ships. To my knowledge I've never heard of a Zampolit on a merchant ship. Why do you ask?"

"I was just curious, my friend. I've read about them in books, and that everything a Zampolit did was to serve the Rodina, 'Motherland,' that's all."

Petrvo commented. "From everything I've ever heard about those people I would consider them more or less spies for the Politburo."

"Communism is a pandemic government in all of Russia, isn't that true?"

"You're right. We all live under the rule of the Communist Party, yet, as for myself, I don't hold fast to all the doctrine. I believe there are better forms of government in the world, but certainly I don't vocalize my opinion too often or too loudly, for if I did, I would find myself in a gulag."

Petrov laughed at what he had just said to a stranger. He lit his cigarette, drew in a lung full of smoke and slowly blew it out between pressed lips.

"Would you mind if I tried one of your smokes?"

"Here, go ahead and try one but, I warn you, they are not like your American cigarettes."

Bobby followed suit. He too drew in a lung full of that strong mid-eastern tobacco and immediately started to cough. You're right! That is strong. I thought you were fooling."

"These cigarettes take time to get used to and you can see why. When I get to ports where I can buy American cigarettes I buy as many cartons as I can afford.

"Bob, I want you to remember one important fact about me and most of my fellow comrades. We love our Mother Russia. We would fight and die for her even though we don't all love communism."

319

"I do understand your feelings. I suppose we should all love the land of our birth."

Petrov knew Bobby Blackstone was an American, because the Captain had told him.

"Don't you love your America?"

"I've never given it much thought, although America has been good to me. I've acquired a lot of wealth." He paused and considered what he had just said. "At least it's enough to retire on, and live well for the remainder of my days, in one of these poor third world countries.

"Good for you, my friend."

Petrov was keenly aware of this phony sailor named Bob, with several different pastports and who was attempting to hide his past. Why Blackstone was on their ship he could only guess. He wasn't the first to sail with them under strange circumstances and probably wouldn't be the last. Petrov's curiosity was killing him but he was smart enough to know not to ask too many questions.

For the next couple of hours the two men enjoyed talking about Russia and Cuba, disclosing facts they knew and what they believed to be true.

Petrov asked, "Did you know, my country subsidizes Cuba in the amount of hundreds of millions of rubles annually? This makes me very unhappy, because our people have to do without so many of life's essentials and that money could be put to better use.

 "Cuba has a dictator, Fidel Castro, who in his eyes, considers his people inconsequential. His form of communism has completely failed and I think he is the last person in this world to realize it. When he is dead it will be a good day for his people and hopefully his regime will die with him."

"Petrov, I don't want to start any sort of argument, but I would like to tell you about an associate of mine who once made a statement that I never quite understood. He said. America is a land blessed, above all other lands, by God with a divine purpose."

"For what purpose might that be?" Petrov asked.

Bob answered, "My friend said that it was to restore his gospel in a land which was free so that people would have the freedom and the right to choose for themselves. Well do you believe in a God, Petrov?"

"Yes, Bob, I believe I do. This is contrary to what most people believe, that we are a godless people. What do you think of that?"

"You surprise me, Petrov."

"All right it's your turn, Bob. I've confessed my belief. What do you have to say? Are you a believer or not?"

"There have been times in my life when I've really wondered about an omnipotent God, the one and only Supreme and absolute Being. I suppose that I haven't studied the subject enough to have developed a belief. I would like to know for sure but, at this time in my life, I would have to say I do not believe in God."

"I feel sorry for you, Bob. You must go to church and find out the truth you desire."

"That I won't do. You'll never find me in any church. As I see it, religion is for the foolish man who is weak and needs religion to support his weakness.

"Why don't we change the subject for now, Petrov. You can tell me what you know about the new place I will be calling home, Caracas, Venezuela."

Petrov looked at Blackstone thoughtfully and said, "My friend, you could have picked many places in South America, which in my judgment would have been nicer, more friendly places to live and less trouble than Caracas."

"Why would you say that about Caracas?"

"I don't like the city at all. I've been there many times and never once experienced much of anything that would endear me to the capitol city. The government is corrupt and run by another dictator more ruthless than Castro. Venezuela's president is Hugo Rafael Chavez, a dictator in the pure sense of the word. Chavez runs the United Socialist Party. Does that sound good to you?"

"No, it doesn't, but if the arrogant prima donna will leave me alone, everything will be all right living there."

"Well, listen to this, Bob. Caracas has the highest murder rate in the world and very few of those murders are ever solved. That's a fact."

"What you say is all very interesting, and I suppose I should be concerned. To be honest with you, I don't give a half a damn, just as long as they don't mess in my business." He gave is friend a wry sneer.

Petrov knew from past experiences that the government would mess in his business and Blackstone would have to pay out a lot of money to satisfy those greedy hogs.

Blackstone was concerned about what Petrov had just told him, but he had no choice in the matter. He had to get off the ship tomorrow and do the best he could in starting up a business he had planned for years.

"I told you of my dislikes for this city, now I should tell you about what I like about Caracas. 'Nothing!' Just joking with you. Caracas has some of the most beautiful art galleries I've ever seen. If you are an art lover and enjoy fine art, you'll be pleased when you see what they have to offer, and if you're an art collector, well you won't be disappointed either.

"Caracas has many nightclubs and bars, some of them are very up-scale and are mostly located in the Las Mercedes district.

"The Venezuelans are a mixed race of whites, blacks, native Indians, and descendants from Spanish explorers. If you can speak Spanish you should get along all right with the natives.

"Now, let me warn you, those rich, beautiful ladies that frequent the clubs are really something to see. I want to exhort you, Bob, you had better keep your guard up or you could find yourself in real trouble. Those Latin's are hot-tempered, jealous people and you just might find a knife stuck between your ribs. I would strongly suggest you hire yourself a road-dog, someone to watch your back.

"Listen up my friend. What I like about Venezuela is the weather is mostly warm, not like my homeland, mostly cold and dreary. The sea here is a beautiful blue, a blue that you'll never forget.

The day was nearly finished and the sea was mirror- smooth. The setting sun was a fire, glowing deeply red against the coming darkness.

"It's been nice visiting with you today, Bob. Maybe we can continue our talk tomorrow."

"I would like that, Petrov. But if we don't, the next time you're in this port, look me up and I'll buy you a drink and we can go out on the town."

Blackstone thought to himself, "With some good fortune, tomorrow we'll reach port and I can find out for myself if I like this city. Petrov's opinion about Caracas most likely won't be the same as mine, yet he has tossed a lot of concern my way."

The sea-weary Russian freighter converged with a tugboat as it approached the Caracas harbor. The tugboat did what tugs do best and, without delay, maneuvered the freighter until it was along side the pier where it would be loaded with tin ore for the return trip to Russia, via Liverpool.

"Hey, Blackstone," the Captain shouted down from the bridge. "I would like to see you. Just wait for me where you are."

"Good morning, Bob, will you come with me to my cabin?"

Once inside his cabin the Captain said, "As of this moment, you are now no longer Bobby Blackstone, a name all of us will soon forget. I have your new papers, a Russian passport and a work visa, which are all in order.

Your new name will be Sergey Felipovich, a good Russian name, one you can be proud of."

Blackstone grinned, "Sergey, you say?"

"That's right, and make sure you don't forget it. It's very important I escort you through the process of customs. These people know me and are not about to give you any trouble with me along. After we leave customs I'll be introducing you to a friend of mine who can be a very helpful person, should you get into a bind. I've also reserved a nice room for you in one of the best hotels in Caracas. I hope you like it."

"I want to thank you for your help, Captain. I have one question. Who is that squirrelly little sailor that is always following me around and watching my every move? He reminds me of a voyeur."

Zervinski smiled, "You needn't worry about that little man. He's harmless. The crew calls him a lilly-livered skunk and don't ask me to translate that phrase into Russian."

"What's his name, Captain?"

"Gregoriy Ivan'ch."

Nothing else needed to be said. "Grab your gear and I'll meet you at the gangplank."

And so for Bob, with his new name Sergey, the process of customs was completed. He felt as if a pressing weight had been lifted from his shoulders.

Sergey hollered out in his guarded Spanish, "Taxi."

 He muttered to himself. It sounds just like the English word for Taxi. I didn't impress the Captain at all."

The cab took them across town to what appeared to be a poorer area of the city. They stopped directly in front of business that had the appearance of a pawnshop or maybe a fix-up shop for bicycles.

"Hello, my friend." A voice was heard from somewhere in back of the shop.

"It's been a long time since you paid me a visit," the man said as he approached them. "Who is it that you have with you, Señor Zervinski?"

"Let me introduce you to my friend, Sergey Felipovich. Sergey, this is Toby Marquez, a man I would like you to become friends with. A friendship would be beneficial for both of you.

Both men shook hands and offered warm smiles in acknowledgment of their introduction.

"Would the two of you follow me back to my humble office? It's not much, but it serves my needs. Here my friends, have a seat, you will be more comfortable while we talk."

The three men spoke of many things during their visit. The most important subject was the acquisition of a bar or nightclub. Toby assured Sergey that he could help him find a business that he would be happy with.

While driving to the hotel, Captain Zervinski cautioned Sergey to make sure he treated his new friend honestly and he would get what he wanted. To cheat this man would be a very unwise thing to do.

"I know you are a tough guy, Sergey, but just remember, you're in a strange land, dealing with people you don't know and a little good-will can go a long way in making a reliable friend of Toby. You need to know, Toby has some muscle behind him, and I believe you call them wise guys. You don't want to mess with him. His name is Max. Just remember that name, you'll see him hanging around Toby's shop.

Chapter 58

Russian Snitch

Thoughtfully, Gregoriy Ivan'ch considered the bits of information he had gathered from spying on their mystery sailor, while sailing to Venezuela via Cuba.

He was a sneaky little rat, thin built, with cold, measuring, nasty eyes. He didn't attract many friends, yet he didn't care, for he took great pride in what he did best; watch, listen, inform and sell to the highest bidder. He was anxious for the day when he would get enough money from his efforts as a spy to quit his crummy job, which he hated.

Gregoriy knew this passenger's first name was Bobby, because he had heard the Captain call him by that name. He had also acquired some good quality pictures of him and knew someone, somewhere would be interested in them. All he needed to do was send copies of the pictures to certain people he knew and dealt with at the British and American Embassies. Certainly, he had no doubt, something good would come from his efforts.

Their ship made port for a short layover at Liverpool. Ivan'ch wasted no time heading up-town to mail his prized envelopes off to the Embassy in London. In his mind he felt as if he had already won. He made a quick stop for a short drink at his old watering hole. He whistled an old Russian folk song as he returned to ship. This was a happy day for the little man.

Within the next couple of days his ship would sail for their home-port of Tallinn on the Baltic Sea. There he would have to wait for any words of interest and possibly make a trip to Leningrad to sell his information.

The expectation of making a lot of money excited Gregoriy beyond what it should have been. What he needed was some good, old fashioned common sense. The word, money, has a way of interfering with ones ability to rationally think things through. Now, only time would tell what would come of his little scheme.

It was as if he knew he was going to win the big lottery and it would be only a matter of time before his dream of a storybook world would come true and he could live in his fantasyland, happily ever after, with none of the difficulty of his past.

A week passed before he received notification that he should meet his old contact in Leningrad on the following Friday.

Gregoriy wasn't a professional at this game. He thought he knew it all but he didn't really know much of anything. He didn't even know who this Bobby guy was. He hadn't even considered the possibility that he might be connected to the K.G.B. and this little plan of his might blow up in his Russian face. Yet, he felt his man was an American, on the dodge from the law, and guaranteed to be wanted by someone.

It was a cold, dank morning in Tallinn. The sun had not yet risen above the murky sky as Ivan'ch waited with his ticket in hand. He hoped the train would get him to his appointed meeting on time. He knew this train would make many stops along the way, picking up the peasant farmers who carried their produce to the big city to sell. These poor farmers, who worked the (Sovkhozy) state farms, were allowed to grow and sell produce from a small portion of their assigned farm. The trip to the city was a regular way of life for them. They would set up their stands and hope to sell what they had grown, to the city folks. It was a harsh, meager life for the people, but the only one they knew.

The trip was slow, tedious and was making him a little crazy. The boredom of watching these smelly farmers, boarding the train, carrying their cabbages and other assorted produce, tried his patience. The odor wasn't particularly bad, just strong and characteristic. "Why couldn't this process be hurried up?" he murmured?

Upon his arrival in Leningrad, he hired a cab to drop him off a few blocks from his meeting spot. At the appointed hour Ivan'ch took a seat on a bus bench outside a quaint, old bookstore. He thumbed through the pages of the state newspaper, the Pravda, while he nervously waited.

As in other times, he wore a red scarf around his neck, with the loose ends draped over his right shoulder, for easy identification.

Several city buses drove by before a robust, peasant woman took a seat next to Gregoriy. She was dressed similar to most Russian women, very dowdy. She wore a long gray dress with small red polka dots, a black coat for warmth, and a brown scarf that covered her head. She placed a grocery bag between them, then made a couple of glances up and down the busy street, faced him and smiled, revealing her gold front tooth, which she must have been proud of, and said, "White Velvet."

He had never seen this woman before but she knew the correct code word. Hastily, she slid an envelope from under her grocery bag, next to Gregoriy. The contact stood and with hurried strides, was soon out of sight. He laid his newspaper over the envelope and waited a short time before picking up the envelope, which he wrapped inside his newspaper. He was anxious to see what was inside.

After walking for several city blocks and making certain he wasn't being followed, he found himself a quiet, secluded place in a city park and carefully opened the envelope. Inside was a round trip plane ticket to Copenhagen, Denmark.

Chapter 59

Fletcher's Request

Fletcher's mental health had improved somewhat after the ordeal with the Russian water coffin, still, he remained in an ultra extreme, secure mental hospital, owned by the feds. Nevertheless, he knew his chances of ever getting free from this place were slim to none.

Everyday he thought of the beautiful young lady that was his only true friend, Nancy Burgess. He hoped all was well with her. If only he could sit down with her again and talk for a little while. Those few short weeks with her would always be held in his mind and heart, with a special reverence.

He thought about the adventure they had with the huge grizzly bear. It is a story she could tell her posterity about, but as for himself, there will be no one to tell the story to. The only reason he held on to his life was because of her memory.

With a stub of a pencil and a single sheet of paper in hand, Fletcher took a seat at his humble table and began to write a request. It was his wish to meet with someone in charge, who had the authority to make decisions on his behalf.

Before his arrest he would have never been willing to cooperate with his captors, not even for a single moment. Now, he was securely locked away in this asylum, in a room that was more of a cage than a place to live.

That fearful experience with the water coffin, as it was called, had consumed his contentious spirit. He had no fight left in him and without any hope for the future, he felt as if he should turn his will over to them. What would it hurt, and maybe he might get something he wanted.

The note said. "Gentlemen, I am completely surrendering. I quit. I give up. There is no fight left in this old dog. Can I talk with someone who has some juice around here?"   Fletcher.

A short time after giving his note to the orderly, the hospital's head psychiatrist came to his room.

"Mr. Fletcher, can I help you?"

"No, Doctor. I need to talk with someone from the bureau who has been working my case. Can you do that for me?

"Sure, I'll give them a call when I get back to my office."

The following morning, after making his request, two F.B.I. agents showed up at the hospital. Fletcher knew Staggs, but not his partner.

He was brought to an interrogation room, which was nothing like he had ever seen before. The room had overstuffed furniture, curtains on the windows and brightly painted walls. His restraints were still in place.

Staggs spoke first. "Hi, Fletcher. I hope they have been treating you well."

"I suppose they are, as well as I can expect."

"Yesterday the head psychiatrist called us, saying you wanted to speak with someone who had some authority regarding your case. I am the one, Fletcher. Let's hear what you have to say."

"That torture chamber you guys put me through took all the fight out of me. You might as well castrated me."

His eyes had a deceptively vacant look that Staggs quickly noticed.

"I am willing to make just about any concession you might have for me."

"All right, Fletcher, go ahead and tell us what you are willing to do, and we can start from there."

"I have a considerable amount of money stashed away in several locations. Wouldn't it be nice if all that filthy lucre were returned to the government coffers so they could waste it on some other pork-barrel project? I am also sure there are some questions that need answers. Certainly, you didn't have enough time to ask me everything you wanted to know on the first go-around.

"Bobby Blackstone has more secrets than you could possibly know about. Wouldn't you like to hear what I have to say about the no-good rat? If it hadn't been for him, none of this would have ever been known.

"How about this, if any of this ever gets into a court of law, I will plead guilty and sign a statement and confession to whatever the charges might be. I will contest nothing. What else could I offer? I do not know what it would be, but there is a quid pro quo in the mix. Did you guys suppose I would surrender all of this great information just because I've turned into a nice guy, now did you?"

"No, we hadn't considered that, Fletcher, but go ahead and tell us what you want."

"I believe I have but one friend left in this crummy world. She is a very special young lady, which I've grown to love as my own daughter, if I had been fortunate enough in this life to have one. I fear when she sees me like this and finds out about my past, she too might also cease to be my friend."

"We are happy you have a special someone. We all could use a good friend, so what is it that you want?"

"More than anything else in this world, I would like to have just one hour to visit with her. You could fly her here and we could sit in this very room, it's nice enough. The only other thing I would like is that she not see me with all these cuffs and chains."

"That's a lot to ask for, Fletcher."

"No it isn't! I am giving you far more than you could have ever hoped for. All I want is a few pleasant memories. Please, could you do that for me?"

"Who is this special young lady that you would give up so much for?"

Staggs asked.

"Once we have come to an agreement I will tell you her name and where she can be found. Then you must promise not to question or harass her in any way. She knows nothing of my past other than I once told her I was a retired F.B.I. agent."

Thoughtfully, Staggs studied Fletcher, who had his head bowed waiting for an answer. "Fletcher, there is a lot to be considered. We will give you an answer within a couple of days, but first, there are people I must talk to."

While the orderlies accompanied him back to his room, the two agents quietly watched and wondered if he was sincere in his offer or had he dreamed up some devious plan, which would blow up in their faces.

Just as promised, the two agents returned to the hospital to meet with Fletcher.

"This whole plan of yours boils down to a simple matter of trust. Do you trust us to keep our end of the bargain and do we trust you to do the same. You need to remember that you do not appear on our list of Sunday School boys. You have never given us one good reason to have the least bit of trust in you. So, in this matter, we will have to rely on our gut feeling."

"I too recognize the dilemma in this plan, Staggs. But we should be smart enough to put a few checks and balances to protect both of us. Shouldn't we, now?"

"Okay, Fletcher, we will work towards that goal. The first step will be up to you. Tell us who the special young lady is and where we can find her. We will definitely need to talk to her before anything else can be done."

"Gentlemen, I assume you will keep your promise and not harass her or cause her any trouble?"

"Yes, we will keep our end of the bargain." And Brook nodded thoughtfully.

With reluctance in his voice, Fletcher spoke. "Her name is Nancy Burgess and she lives near Morgan Hill, California. Her home is in the foothills next to Anderson Lake. I will write the address down for you.

"When and if you decide to let her come for the visit, I will give you the location of some of that money I told you about. When I get my visit, I will tell you everything I promised. Is that not fair?"

"All right, we will take it a step at a time and see where it leads us."

"After I interview her we will be back and talk some more. I'm not sure about the time frame, but we will expedite the matter, I promise."

A week later Staggs drove up to the home of Nancy Burgess. "What a beautiful place to live," he thought as he evaluated everything he had seen this morning. He had made an appointment with her before making his trip.

"Good morning, Miss Burgess. My name is Brook Staggs and I work for the F.B.I." He held out his badge and I.D. for her to examine.

" Please put your mind at rest, I assure you, you are in no trouble with us. We have a mutual friend, who is in some difficultly with us and we were hoping you could help us. His name is Jim Fletcher but you know him as Jim Dubois."

Nancy gasped, "Oh no, what kind of trouble is he in?"

"I am sorry to say that I am not at liberty to discuss his case with you."

"I've been so worried about him for such a long time. When Jim left he said the agency he once worked for was hot on his trail and he needed to hit the road. He never told me anything about his problems with you guys. He only said that I wouldn't understand."

"Why are you here, Mr. Staggs?"

" I have a definite feeling Fletcher is trying to ask for redemption. He has offered to tell us all about the many unanswered questions we have. Also, he is willing to sign a confession and not contest any of the charges we might cite him with. The only thing he wants is to see you again and have a little visit. It's obvious he loves you very much. He has told us that you are the only thing in this life that is important to him."

Nancy began to sob uncontrollably. She stood up and left the room. A few minutes later she returned, and said, "I am sorry, I couldn't control my emotions."

"That's perfectly all right. There is no need to apologize."

Staggs smiled benevolently at Nancy. She was a special young lady and he recognized the qualities that Fletcher had seen in her.

"Miss Burgess, would you be willing to take a little trip with us to see your old friend?"

"Oh yes, I would like that very much."

"Good. We will pay for all your expenses. Just give us a few days to finalize everything. When the details are complete I'll call you."

"Good-by, It's been very nice meeting you, Nancy. I hope to see you again soon."

Staggs left and drove for the San Jose Airport.

Their reunion would be kept secret. Neither party would be told of the exact date and time, for obvious security reasons. Staggs felt comfortable with his decision to let Fletcher have his meeting. Nancy Burgess had no police record and appeared to be very genuine.

A few days after returning from California, Brook Staggs paid Fletcher another visit. "How are you doing? I thought I would stop by and bring you up to speed. I flew out to San Jose and paid your friend a visit."

Fletcher interrupted Staggs. "Are we on the dance card?"

"Yes. Miss Burgess said she was willing to come for a visit, in fact she was very excited about the offer."

Fletcher's smile stretched from ear to ear.

"Thank you, thank you, Staggs. I guess you're not such a bad sort after all. When will she be here?"

"You know I can't tell you, for obvious security reasons, but it should be soon."

The long awaited reunion finally arrived. Nancy watched as they led Jim into the visiting room, where he then was seated. Staggs spoke with him for a few moments before she was allowed to enter.

Nancy walked into the room, not knowing just what to expect or what she was going to say.

"Hi, Jim." She smiled, as she greeted her special friend. "I would like to give you a giant hug, you stinker, but they instructed me not to. You're looking well, considering your surroundings."

"My dear, beloved Nancy. You really don't know how much I've missed you. It's been a long time and I wasn't sure if I would ever see you again, but here we are. What a wonderful day it has turned out to be."

No time was wasted, not even a moment of their precious visit. They talked about the many things that she was involved in. She was taking some college courses in San Jose that interested her. She was also busy with some women's origination called the Relief Society, which Fletcher didn't understand.

"Can you tell me about your difficulties with the agency?"

"No, I can't talk about it. Maybe some day, but I don't think you would ever be interested in my story."

"That's silly of you to say such a thing. Of course I would be interested. What is going to happen to you, Jimmy?"

"I can't tell you Nancy because I have no idea as to what they are planning on doing with me. You can ask Staggs if you want, but I'm sure he won't tell you anything.

Never in Jim Fletchers life had he ever been affected with the feeling of humility. He always considered himself a man who had control of the situation; self-righteous, arrogant, selfish, and some would call him narcissistic.

Now he was in a place where no man would ever want to be. He was without the freedom to make even the most simple of decisions for himself. All men should have hope, he thought, but he could see no hope for himself. Jim couldn't shake the feelings of helplessness and discouragement that overwhelmed him.

Nancy sensed Jim's foreboding feelings and knew of only one thing she could help him with. Recalling his anti-religious feelings, she wondered if he would listen. But no matter, she was going to try.

Looking directly into Jim's eyes, Nancy reached over and touched his hand. "Jim I want you to listen carefully to me. If I had the authority I would set you free. It's hard for me to see you like this and I know of only one thing that can help."

"What might that be?"

"Pray to your Father In Heaven."

Jim smiled. "Wouldn't I be a hypocrite? I've never prayed in my life for anything and have always made light of those who did. I called them weak individuals who believed they needed to call on some higher power for help."

"No, Jim, you wouldn't be a hypocrite. You're a son of your Heavenly Father and he wants you to call on him. He's a loving God whose mercy and justice surpass all understanding. Please give it a try and be patient."

"I'll try, only because you asked me." Jim didn't believe it would help.

"When I have to leave today, I'm going to ask Staggs for permission to write and maybe send you some special books to read."

"Nancy, I would love to be able to receive letters from you. Hopefully he will allow you to write."

Their visiting time had expired so both Nancy and Jim stood up to say good-by. Nancy knew it was against the rules, but she didn't care. She threw her arms around Jim's neck and gave him a loving kiss on the cheek.

One of the orderlies started to intervene but agent Staggs held out his arm to stop him and said, "Wait just a minute. Give them time to say good-by."

"Be strong, Jim. I will always be your friend. Circumstances do change, and remember, you will always be in my prayers."

Nancy had tears in her eyes as they bid good-by. Jim was choking up.

Once outside the visiting room Nancy stood and watched, as her friend was led back to his room. Then she asked agent Staggs, "Could I please write to him?"

"At this point in time Fletcher is not allowed to receive mail or send letters. As time passes, his security level will change, maybe then."

"Isn't there something I can do? The poor guy is a lost soul and I want to help. Aren't you worried about what he might do to himself?"

"I'll tell you what I will do. You send me your letters, I'll look them over, and if they are appropriate I'll let him have them."

"Thank you so much for making the visit possible."

Chapter 60

Office of Brook Staggs

While looking through his e-mail, he spotted something of interest. A message was sent from the American Embassy in London. It was from an old friend of his who was now stationed there.

"Agent Staggs, I'm sending you the picture of a person of interest. If I remember correctly, this man once worked for you."

Staggs picked up the phone and using a secure line, called his friend, Roger, at the London embassy.

"Hi, my friend. I want to thank you for this photo. You were right to assume we might be interested in this man. He did work for us, but one day he just picked up and left, not even saying good-bye. We would very much like to know of his whereabouts. There are some matters that need clearing up, if you get my drift. See if your snitch knows where he is and what he wants for his information. Instruct your contact not to act overly interested. You know how to deal with these kinds of people."

Roger replied, "I don't know anything additional at this time, but I do have contact with the person who sent me the photo. This man is a sleazy character, not to be trusted, yet I believe he has something more. I'll get back to you as soon as I'm able to find out anything new."

"Thanks!"

As soon as Staggs finished his conversation with Roger, he called Baxter.

"Hello, is this Baxter?"

"You're speaking to the one and only."

"Listen up. I think we have the start of a good track on our Mr. Black-stone. Just this morning I received a current picture of our man. We will be starting our negotiations for the rest of the information with the person who sent us the picture. Hopefully, we will be able to find out where this scoundrel is. All I have at this time is one simple black and white photograph, and nothing more."

"The snitch, who sent the picture, is in his homeland of Russia. It's going to take some time to persuade him to turn over everything he has. In this sort of operation, money is normally the only thing they want. I don't know what the bureau is willing to pay, so we will have to sit tight and wait."

"Well, Staggs, do you think the bureau is going to play hard-ball with this guy or not?"

"In fact, Baxter, I'm sure the bureau wants this story surgically removed from its records. I don't know if that's at all possible. If it works out in our favor, so the lid can be kept on that bad piece of history and away from the news publications, it will be a great day indeed."

"What you just said about the news reminds me of something my father once told me, Staggs. Years ago, in Russia, there was a joke told about the two Soviet-run newspapers. Those who were not communist said, "There is no Pravda in Izvestia and there is no Izvestia in Pravda.' In the English translation, There is no truth in the news, and there is no news in the truth. Both of these papers were cut from the same political bolt of cloth."

"I've heard that platitude before but I didn't know its origin."

"Good to talk with you and thanks for the great news. Will you please keep me informed about your progress, Brook?"

"I will keep you informed, and you're welcome. Talk to you soon."

No sooner had Baxter hung up the phone he hollered out, "Niki, come here, I have some good news!"

Chapter 61

Copenhagen

Gregoriy Ivan'ch's plane landed at the Copenhagen International Airport on schedule, which was to his pleasure.

He wasn't sure what to expect next. He hadn't walked far with his carry on bag when he saw a man displaying a sign with his name written on it. "I'm Gregoriy Ivan'ch," he said.

"Sir, will you please follow me."

No words were spoken as he followed the man to a waiting car. "Have a seat," he said while opening the rear door. Gregoriy took a seat in a new, black A7 Audi. He could tell it was new by the new car smell.

To say he was a little nervous, sitting with two unfriendly looking strangers, would be an understatement. He had started this process, so he must see it through.

They sped off, with no regard for the traffic laws, as if the driver was immune from them. They eventually pulled over to the curb by a quiet city park. Just as the driver shut the engine off, the left side rear door opened and a man took the seat.

"Hi, I assume you are Gregoriy Ivan'ch?"

"Yes, I am Gregoriy."

"Glad to meet you Gregoriy. My name is Roger. Are you the one who sent this picture to my embassy in London?"

"Yes, I am."

"Why were you so inclined to send us this man's picture?"

Gregoriy carefully chose his words, not wanting to give away any information, which might be valuable to him.

"All I am going to say about your question is that I had a hunch that he might be a man of interest and because I believed he was an American. That is why I sent you the picture. Mr. Roger, are you interested in what I have?"

"Could be. I suppose it depends on what sort of information you have. Our records indicate you have, on several occasions, offered us information that was bogus. Is that not true?"

"What you just said is true. You should know that everything isn't always going to turn up sunshine and daisies."

The driver spoke up so all could hear, "Who said that consistency is the hobgoblin of little minds?" He smiled to himself.

"I'll pretend I didn't hear your arrogant remark, you prima donna."

"How about this for starters, Roger. I know where your man lives and how he got there. There are a lot more tidbits of information that will help fill in the blanks."

Roger asked rhetorically, "My good man, do you have any of this valued information with you?"

"Are you a stupid bonehead? Why in the world would I bring it with me, so you guys could probably steal it from me?"

"First off, we wouldn't steal it from you but on the other hand, we need to know what you are carrying in your bag."

Roger reached over and took his bag and carefully examined it's contents. Both men exchanged grins.

"See, I told you. Now do you believe me?"

"Now my man, lets get down to the nitty-gritty of our meeting this fine day. What is it you want in exchange for your information?"

His voice was tight but calm. " I want a half million dollars."

Gregoriy had barely spewed the words from his mouth, when Roger burst into hysterical laughter.

"Are you an absolute crazy man? Our government would never agree to such a large sum of money. I hope you realize that we could trace your tracks over the past couple of months and, if given enough time, we would find him on our own. I'll make you a counter offer. Say we give you fifty thousand American dollars, deposited in a Swiss bank account in your name. Then, if we find our man, we will fairly negotiate on a final settlement. How does that sound?"

"It sounds like a pile of Russian horse shit to me. You capitalist pigs are rolling in money. I'm offering you some valuable information that you don't have and it would cost you a lot more money to find it on your own. Now you're trying to take away my chance for a better life. Shame on you!" The tone in his voice was ugly.

Roger eyed him speculatively. "We are not playing games with you Gregoriy Ivan'ch. You're either with us, or you pick up your bag and head back to your Mother Russia. If you walk out now, our offer is null and void. As I said, we will treat you fairly. If we get everything we want, there could be double the amount of money for your final payment. What do you say?"

He frowned and spoke nothing for a moment. "Well, just maybe there could be a meeting of the minds."

Reluctantly, Geregoriy agreed to Roger's offer.

"You're a hard man. When I know you have deposited the fifty thousand I will hand deliver everything I have to whomever you designate."

Chapter 62

Pow-wow

Niki summoned her father into her back-bedroom office. "Dad, take a look at this e-mail we just received. It's from our friend, Brook Staggs. He wants to meet with us tomorrow for a little pow-wow."

"Naturally, we are hopeful for some good news, Niki, but just in case, keep your fingers crossed."

"Dad, would you mind if we drive my Cobra tomorrow? I haven't had it out on the road for a while and this would be a good opportunity to stretch its legs. I've always enjoyed the drive to D.C., it's beautiful. Maybe for a little excitement I might pick up a speeding ticket. Our life around here has been very boring for quite some time, not at all like it was in some of our former days."

"I don't mind if we drive your car. It's not as comfortable as mine, but it is fast and a real eye stopper."

Chapter 63

Washington D.C.

"Come on in and have a seat. I trust the trip was a pleasant one. There are plenty of times when I would like to skip work and burn up some of that so-called precious petrol in my old 911 Turbo.

"My friends, it's too nice of a day to sit around in my stuffy office and talk. I would like to invite the both of you to accompany me to a favorite spot of mine. It's a quiet little restaurant on the shore of the Potomac, just outside D.C. There we can enjoy a special lunch and discuss in private, the matter of our rouge agent."

Niki said with a smile that stretched from ear to ear. "Well, Brook, what's keeping us. I am always excited for something new."

When they arrived at the Cherry Tree Inn they were seated in a private room away from the main dining area. The room had a beautiful view of the Potomac and a riverfront garden with trees and flowers galore. Niki was delighted with the restaurant.

"Dad, don't you just love this place?"

"Yes, it's very nice, my dear."

"Thanks for bringing us here, Brook."

With a warm, engaging smile he said, "You're welcome, Niki."

"Let's order our meal and then we can discuss why we are here on this extraordinary day."

"All right, here goes. I told you about the good news that we have received a picture of Bobby Blackstone. A freelance spy, working as a sailor on a Russian freighter, took some pictures of him and gathered bits of information about our man. He told us where Blackstone is living, and as we speak, we have an agent in that city verifying the information. We expect, before very long, that we will have his address and the alias he is using."

"Are you telling us this spy gave you all this great information, out of the goodness of his Communist heart?"

Brook frowned, "Not so, Baxter. We had to pay this little Russian snitch a lot of American dollars."

"Pray tell me, where is he?"

"Caracas, Venezuela."

"How in the world did he wind up there?"
"The major problem we have my friends is how are we going to get our man out of Caracas and back onto U.S. soil? Strategically he has placed himself in a country that isn't in any sort of love affair with the U.S. We just can't ask the Venezuelan government to go out, arrest him, and then turn him over to us. The President of Venezuela, Hugo Chavez, has told our government, on more than one occasion, where to stick it. We absolutely can't expect any help from that regime, so what are we going to do? Any suggestions."

Baxter replied, "In Russia they would take care of this sort of problem by blowing his brains out and forgetting he ever existed."

Staggs commented, "I would hope we aren't forced to that extreme."

Niki suggested, "Do you think we might be able to entice him out of his comfort zone?"

"I don't think we could ever lure him out at this time. If it were a few years down the road he might feel lucky enough to bite on one of our schemes, but we can't wait, we need his rotten hide now," Staggs replied.

"As I see the situation," said Niki, "We only have one choice."

Staggs questioned Niki, "What might that be?"

"By force if it needs be. We need to kidnap that
black-hearted man and bring him home to face justice. Over the years
I've heard plenty of rumors about our government being involved in such
activities. I know that you've heard the same rumors, so why not now?"

All three agents grew quiet as they each pondered Niki's proposal.

"Baxter, do you have any comments on your daughter's proposition?'

"No, nothing at all."

"You need to understand, Niki, those stories weren't just rumors and
remember you didn't hear that from me."

Niki smiled and said, "I thought so."

Staggs assured them, "I can make all the arrangements for his capture
and return. There are a couple of guys we have used before. They have
no idea who they are working for, and can't connect us in any way. If the
authorities catch those two it will be their tough luck, and as far as Blackstone is concerned, he would never report it to the police, for obvious
reasons.

"These two individuals, that I will be hiring through a third party, aren't
the brightest men in the world but they are willing to do just about anything for a buck and will let the chips fall where they will fall."

"Can they get the job done without screwing it up, Staggs? We can't afford
to lose Blackstone again."

"I do hope so."

 "Furthermore, the agency can't venture exposing our men to that sort of
risk. Can you imagine the ramifications we would feel from our government if we were caught being involved in a kidnapping on foreign soil?
We all know crap rolls downhill and we would be sure to get a truckload
of it on our heads. Yes and they just might line us up and shoot us for the

fun of it."

Niki spoke sternly, "That's not at all funny, so let's not even consider the possibility."

"We'll know more once we hear from our agent in Caracas. For now, we'll have to wait and see. The meat of the issue is fairly simple, when Blackstone is located, I'll unleash our two mutts and see if they can fetch him home."

Chapter 64

Caracas

Several weeks had passed since his arrival. Sergey Felipovich [Blackstone] had acquired a nice apartment in the better part of the city. He found the perfect nightclub, the one he had dreamed of for so long. Today, the bank had closed on his loan for the club, which pleased him immensely. Borrowing the money was less risky than exposing his assets, which he had kept hidden, in event he had to leave town in a hurry. His newly acquired friend, Toby Marquez, had taken a partnership with him.

Just two days after closing on the nightclub deal, Sergey had a visitor at his club. He was a portly little man with piggish black eyes and a face that reminded him of the south end of a north bound swine. He was a government official informing him if he wanted to continue doing business in his beautiful city; he would be required to pay him a thousand pesos a month. Sergey wanted to kill the little puke but considered it to be another cost of doing business in this country.

"That should buy a lot of loyalty, my friend. Don't you think so?"

Then flashing a crooked tooth grin at Sergey, he said, "See, my friend, you will have no trouble from me."

Sergey was beginning to feel quite comfortable with his new life. He was making new friends, hiring employees for his club and thinking very little about his past, not knowing he was being watched all the time.

It had taken the U.S. agent three weeks to gather all the information he was assigned, except for Blackstone's new alias. Today he would get that name, and his job would be finished, or would it?

He received a message which, said, "Before returning, would you stick around for a few more days? There will be a couple of guys showing up in Caracas. These two are hired, freelance muscle, and are interested in the guy you've been watching. They have their assignment to bring Sergey Felipovich home and have no need to know anything more. Don't tell them who you are or who you work for. You can tell them you've been assigned to be their driver to show them around and assist them if necessary."

Chapter 65

New York City

Boomer and Ned were old college friends and basically good guys who enjoyed living on the edge. They were always pushing the envelope and feeling the rush of excitement when they were skirting the law.

 How they had become involved in these activities they were not quite sure. It began somewhere back in college, before they were suspended for code violations. It was a friend of a friend who was the one that made the connection for them. These two had done all sorts of assignments for their ghost-partner. They were always paid well for their work and that was all they really cared about, never asking, nor wanting to know about the people who sought their services. That knowledge could be a dangerous bit of information for them.

"Ned, this is Boomer. We've got another assignment, and this one sounds like a lucrative one. Why don't you come over tonight and we can make some plans."

"I'll see you at seven."

"Come on in, I've got the papers regarding this assignment on the kitchen table. I'm sure you will find them very interesting."

"Look at this! Our man is an American using a Russian alias, Sergry Felipovich, who is living in Caracas, Venezuela. It's our job to get him back on U.S. soil, alive. These people have given us enough money for the operation and upon his return, we will get a nice round hundred thousand dollars to split."

"Do you want to accept this job, Boomer? We have never done anything for them that is quite so risky."

"Sure, my friend, fifty thousand is a year's salary for me."

"Alright then, we'll do it. Sorry, but I told him we would do it before I asked you. I was sure you would accept.

"In this package we have Sergey's picture, his home address and where he works. We have a picture of a nightclub, which is named the Granada. It would be my guess he owns the place. These people who hired us have a twin engine aircraft waiting for our use. It will be waiting outside Miami at a small airport. Boomer, I hope you've kept your ticket current?"

"Of course I have, why wouldn't I?"

The day following their acceptance of the job, Boomer received a package from a courier. It contained a basic schedule and some additional instructions regarding what needed to be accomplished on their trip to Caracas.

The first and most important instruction was when they had their man in custody, they were to place a phone call to the listed number before starting their return trip. This would allow time for the appropriate people to meet them at the designated airport and take custody of their man.

On the appointed day and hour, Ned and Boomer flew south towards Caracas, Venezuela. It was an uneventful and restful flight, which they were happy about.

After clearing customs, posing as art collectors, they checked into an upscale hotel that had been highly recommend by their employer.

Tomorrow they would start making their plans.

"Ned, we are all alone and no one is coming to save us if we blow this job, so what do you say we take every step with the utmost caution. Personally, I don't want to spend even a day in one of their stinking Venezuelan jails."

The following morning the assigned agent, that had found Sergey, knocked on their hotel door.

"Good morning gentlemen. My name is Thomas Lancaster. I've been asked to give you assistance as a driver during your stay. I know why you are here and who you're after. You see, I'm the one who located him and discovered his alias."

"What's the name of the man you say we're after?"

"Sergey Felipovich. I hope you will accept my assistance in this matter. I can be very helpful, and I have a car parked out front, which is at your disposal. What do you say?"

"Clearly, we have no way of checking out your story. We will have to accept what you say as the gospel truth and go from there."

"It's quite understandable if you refuse my help, but I assure you that my assistance can be crucial to your success, and my services are free."

"Of course, why not. That's a price I like to hear."

"That sounds like a good decision on your part. I'll be waiting for you in the car when you are ready."

Over the next three days, Ned, Boomer and their unexpected driver, looked, watched and drove around the areas Blackstone frequented, always exercising the utmost caution.

Repeatedly they drove the route to the airstrip where their plane was parked and waiting. Being familiar with the streets and possible problems that might arise was significant.

In the wee hours of the morning, Blackstone locked up the club. It had been a profitable night and he was pleased with the performance of his business. If it continued like this he would make a handsome profit. His apartment was only a few blocks away so he usually walked. The walk made him feel better after sitting around all evening.

For most of Blackstone's life he had been a cautious man, always being aware of his surroundings. But complacency was beginning to rule his life. He felt all his past troubles were behind him. It was a quiet, pleasant night, with not a soul on the street. As he strolled along he hummed a favorite tune of his, by Johnny Cash, 'Folsom Prison Blues'. He never saw the two men standing in the dark alleyway until he felt a gun barrel forcibly rammed into the small of his back.

"Don't move, Seregy, or I will blow your rotten guts all over this dirty street! Understand?"

"I understand."

"There is more than one of us behind you, so don't do anything stupid that you might regret. Now, carefully put your hands behind your back."

Quickly, they cuffed Blackstone. A silk, black bag was jerked down over his head, just as their car and driver pulled up. With their man in custody they were off to the airstrip and the awaiting plane. Their driver, Thomas Lancaster, an alias of course, spoke fluent Spanish and understood the city quite well. He would get them to the plane safely and would then vanish from the scene, for he wanted no involvement in their activity. He was curious of course, but that would be as far as his interest would extend.

The twin engine Beech was parked in an unlit area, which helped the three move him without being noticed.

"All right," Blackstone said cheerfully. "You've caught me fair and square. I'll go peacefully and not give you any trouble, but I do have one request. Could you please cuff me with my hands in front? I don't think I could last the trip with the cuffs in the back."

"I don't see why not. Just behave yourself."

Their driver stood and watched as they changed the cuffs to the front. Then they secured him in a seat in the rear of the plane, which was designed for a single prisoner to travel.

Thomas wished them a safe, uneventful trip and drove off into the night. He stopped just out of sight to watch and wait for their departure to Miami.

It was a dark, moonless night as the turbo prop lifted off the short run-way, climbed two thousand feet and made a slow turn towards the north. They were on their way home with a mission successfully completed and thoughts of spending some well earned money.

Not long into the flight, Blackstone hollered out. "Hey you guys. I am having difficulty breathing with his bag over my head. It would be very much appreciated if you would remove it."

Ned, who was watching their prisoner asked, "What do you think Boom-er, would it hurt if we took it off?"

"I don't see why not. He's not going anywhere and we will never see his ugly mug again after he is returned."

Ned reached over and pulled the black bag from his head. "Is that bet-ter?"

"It is, and thank you. I was beginning to feel a little claustrophobic. Now I can get some sleep." He laid his head back on the seat and closed his eyes but had no intention of sleeping.

After a short time, Ned became bored watching their prisoner sleeping. He moved up to the co-pilot's seat, which was a more interesting place to be. The two old friends talked about football and their college days. Every five or ten minutes Ned would take a casual look back at Blackstone. Sat-isfied he was still asleep they would go on with their conversation.

It hadn't taken Blackstone long to determine that Ned and Boomer were rank amateurs at this sort of work. He smiled to himself, knowing that he would have a special surprise for these two fools.

During the flight, while his captors were flapping their gums, Blackstone had removed a handcuff key, which he always carried with him, and care-fully unlocked his cuffs.

Inside the front of his pants, hanging from a string, was a 32-auto, nes-tled in his crotch. Only the most thorough search would have discovered it. Now, he would wait and see.

Intently, Blackstone listened to Boomers conversation on the aircraft radio. When he decided the time was right he quietly stood up and moved in behind his captors. It was their error, born of ignorance.

"Don't move!" He shouted. "I have a gun pointed at Boomers head. Makes your heart quicken, doesn't it?"

"Now, with all the extreme care you two can muster, slowly slide your weapons down the aisle. Remember, I don't really give a plug nickel if I live or not, but on the other hand, I have a strong feeling you two would like to go home to your families. Am I not right?" He glared at them with cold measuring eyes.

As instructed, two 9mm automatic's slid towards him.

With an air of finality Blackstone spoke, "Listen up you jokers. We are not going to land in Miami, at your planned location. Boomer, you fly over the ocean to the east. When you're directly due east of Fort Lauderdale, make your approach. Find some small airfield that's away from the city and land there. Do what I say and you both will live to see another day. If not, well maybe we will all wake up to see the sneering face of the devil.

"Make sure your transponder is turned off. Do it right now! I don't want any radio transmission coming from this plane. You two keep a sharp lookout for other aircraft in the area. It would be a shame if we were to crash into one of them, now wouldn't it?"

Neither man spoke a word. They thought, if he doesn't shoot us, some unbeknownst plane would likely crash into us and do his dirty work.

Ned blurted out, "Please don't kill us! We were only doing a job for a little extra money. Times are tough and our families could use the extra money."

"So what! Do you think I really care? There are people I want to kill right now. If I could get my hands on them, they would be dead, with no regrets. So, keep quite and you won't find yourself on my bad side."

For the next half hour not a word was spoken. All the time Blackstone watched their heading.

Boomer finally broke the silence. "I've located a small airfield just outside Fort Lauderdale, which should hopefully meet with your approval."

"All right, you're the pilot. Lets see how good you are at landing. Isn't a good landing a measuring mark of a good pilot?"

Boomer nodded his head in the affirmative.

Never in Boomer's life had he landed a plane under such stress, yet the landing was smooth and perfect. Blackstone directed him to taxi to the far end of the ramp and park the aircraft there.

"Okay boys. Shut the engine down and remain seated."

In Boomer and Ned's flight bags he found all sorts of restraints, which were useful in tying them up. The knot tying skills that he learned in the navy, a long time ago were still very good. These two boys would stay put for a long time.

"Now that I'm about to leave, let me give you guys a little friendly advice. Before you ever take on another job like this one, have someone teach you something about handling prisoners. My old grandma could have escaped from you two and shot you while doing it."

As he stepped from the plane he jeered, "I don't think you two will be getting your bonus." They could hear him laughing as he walked away.

Immediately following his departure from the aircraft, Blackstone started considering all of his options. First and foremost he must get as far away from this place as possible. There was no way of knowing how long it would take for the authorities to find their lost plane and he didn't want to be around when they arrived. He was sure they were already searching for it, and his rotten hide.

Knowing he was important enough for all these people to be spending their time and money looking for him pleased him immensely.

Of course, he didn't want to be captured. He wanted his freedom, but there was a part of him that enjoyed the cat and mouse game they were playing. He believed his superior personality and intellect would always make him a winner He felt that mess-up in Caracas didn't count.

Some of the skills he had learned as a teenager, playing in the streets of New York, hadn't been forgotten. Heisting cars for a little joy ride had always been great fun. Luckily, he was never caught.

He spotted a likely target. Within two minutes he was inside the car, had it started and was on his way to the Fort Lauderdale International Airport.

When Bobby Blackstone arrived, he left the stolen car parked in a busy passenger parking lot. It would be hours if not days before it would be discovered and the cops could only guess who stole it. By then he would be far away and planning his next move.

The three firearms he had were thrown off to the side of the road. New ones would be purchased later. Guns were always easy to buy if you knew where to look.

A ticket to Atlanta, Georgia was purchased, with the flight departing within the hour. By the time he arrived in Atlanta he would have had plenty of time to plan his next move.

Chapter 66

Blackstone is on the Loose

"Your rag-tag so called tough guys are all tied up just where I left them, sitting there looking so sad, in the seats of that federal aircraft. I strongly suggest next time you hire someone with a live brain. Those two aren't very smart and are probably going to need your help to get themselves free. Where they're at is your guess, old man. I am still free and why don't you take a guess about what I'm going to do next." Blackstone laughed out loud.

"Is this Bobby Blackstone?" Baxter heard no reply. The phone was silent. He remembered his voice, yet he found it hard to believe this rat was still free, after all they had done to capture him.

The hour was late. Hopefully they could alert Staggs before others found out about their underhanded operation, which had gone sour, and avoid more embarrassment.

From what Baxter had heard Blackstone say, he knew there was an air of revenge in his voice. There was no doubt what his intentions were, he wanted all three of them dead. His hatred was vile. Blackstone had tried to have Matt Savage killed on two other occasions but both attempts had failed. Knowing how he hated to fail, he would now risk his own freedom to finish the job.

While Niki was on the phone trying to reach Staggs, her dad was wondering how Blackstone had obtained their home phone number. If he had their number, he could also have Matt's address and phone number. Somehow this old rouge must have friends in the agency who are evidentially still helping him.

Staggs picked up his phone. "Staggs are you aware Blackstone is out on his own; free and thumbing his nose at us?"

"I am. Our men, who were waiting in Miami to take charge of him became worried when the plane didn't arrive on schedule, so they called me.

"Several hours later we found our plane parked at a small airport outside of Fort Lauderdale with both of those clowns hog-tied in the pilot and co-pilot seats. It looks like they were more interested in flying the plane than they were interested in watching and keeping Blackstone secure. He has been gone for hours now and we have no idea were he might be."

"Staggs, this is one big fat screw-up!"

"Baxter, how did you know about his escape?"

"Somehow he has my home phone number and called me to make sure I knew he was running free. I didn't like the tone in his voice and I have a bad feeling he wants to finish the job he once started."

"Who do you think he will go after first, you or Niki or will he go after Matt?"

"For some unknown reason he has always felt threatened by Matt and has wanted him dead. I think he will go after Matt and then try to take Niki and me out"

"Don't waste any time letting Matt know what's taken place and have him take the appropriate precautions."

Niki was on the phone. Not wanting Penny to recognize her voice and become upset, she attempted to lower it a bit.

"Hello, may I speak with Matt Savage."

"Just a minute please, I'll get him."

"Yes, this is Matt Savage."

"Matt, this is Niki. We have a big problem. You need to act now. Move to somewhere safe. We're afraid Blackstone is looking for you again. He was captured and brought back to the United States, but I am sad to say he escaped and we have no clue to his whereabouts. Blackstone called Dad just to be an arrogant punk and rub our noses in it. From what he said, Dad felt strongly that his intentions were to come after you."

"That is rotten luck all around, Niki."

"It sure is."

"Don't worry, Niki, I'll be ready for him this time and when he shows his ugly face I'll be waiting."

"But I do worry, Matt. He nearly killed you once and you were blessed beyond belief to still be alive."

"You're right, but this time it won't be a back shooting hired gun, it will be the man and if he is lucky, I'll put a bullet in him and send him straight to hell where he belongs."

"Listen up, Matt. Dad and I are flying out to Utah in the morning to help you so please keep your cell phone with you. We'll need to know where you're at, and please Matt don't take any unnecessary chances."

"I'll be careful, Niki. Have a safe flight. I am anxious to see both of you again."

"Is this deja'vu? Hopefully, not an illusion of things that once were and are yet to come again." Niki pondered the situation with a heavy heart. Would they once again arrive too late? Her body quivered at the terrible memory of Matt lying near death under that stately old cottonwood tree.

"Matt, who was that on the phone?

"It's was Niki Blinski."

"Oh really. Why was she calling you?"

"Penny there is some unfinished business. I'll explain while you pack a suitcase with a few necessities. Trust me, it's important that I get you to a safe location."

"But why?"

"It's for your safety, Penny. I love you and I can't afford to be worrying about you while I'm after this bad guy. So will you please do what I ask?

"Of course I will, Matt. But why in the world do you have to go after this man by yourself? This time you might not be so lucky."

"My dear, it's my responsibility to stop this man if I can and bring him to justice. He could confirm many questions and lay to rest those damning accusations not fully understood by the bureau.

"Whatever you do, don't call the police. I assure you Penny that help is coming. The locals will only get in the way and most likely foul it up. The fewer people that know about this the better it is for everyone."

"Therein lies the dilemma," Matt thought. "I don't know if Baxter and Niki will make it here in time. Staggs made it clear, that the three of us had to catch and arrest him, if at all possible, so it would depend on the three of us to stop Blackstone and bring him in." That understanding wasn't entirely true, because Staggs had helped a great deal.

Chapter 67

Where had Blackstone Gone?

Blackstone was nobody's fool. At the precise moment he left the two buffoons tied up, he was formulating plans. Within a few hours after arriving at the Atlanta Airport he had a ticket in his hand for a direct flight to Las Vegas where he would acquire everything he needed for his upcoming battle with Matt Savage, which he desperately hoped would be the last time he had to deal with him. He hated Matt and his friends and this time he would see them dead.

Chapter 68

Face Off

Lakeside City was Matt's old stomping grounds. Naturally, he was very familiar with the area, which was definitely to his advantage. He and the agency had no information as to Blackstone's whereabouts, but he was sure his nemesis was on his way to make his final try. That made a perfect situation for Matt. He would watch and wait for him to make the next move, he only wished he had more information.

Blackstone was disgusted with himself for flying into Las Vegas instead of Salt Lake City. At the time he purchased the ticket, his main interest was to get as far away as he could. The eight hour drive was boring, just miles and miles of nothing, but it did give him time to consider how he would take Matt down, and his wife too, if she got in the way.

It was late afternoon when Bobby Blackstone drove into Lakeside City. The first item on his agenda was to figure out these crazy addresses, such as 1900 W. & 5600 S. There were no named city streets.

Next, he would cruise the city and check out Matt's residence. He had time and wasn't going to rush into a bad situation.

Matt's home was vacant. His wife was safely tucked away where no one could harm her.

His home had timers on different light circuits throughout, giving the appearance of human activity. He also had two cars parked in the drive-way, for appearance.

Directly across the street from Matt's home stood a vacant house that once belonged to his dear old friends who had passed away. He had been watching the house for their children and had access to it. There, in the darkness, he would wait to see what would materialize. He had a night vision scope, which most likely was going to be needed. He carried two splendid Colt model 1911, 40 cal. semi-autos, with extra clips. They were snuggled close to his body in shoulder holsters, one for the right hand and one for the left. Matt could shoot equally well with either hand.

Nothing can be quite so boring as a stake out, waiting and watching for that certain person to arrive or a criminal activity to take place, neither of which might ever develop.

As Matt sat and watched, his cell phone rang. It was Niki. "Hey, Matt, we're here in Lakeside, we need to talk."

Matt gave them directions to the Lakeside Post Office and asked them to meet him there in fifteen minutes. Cautiously, he sneaked out the back door and over the neighbors fence, so not to be seen. He approached the post office from a different direction than normal and found his friends waiting there.

Something that's quite strange is the fact that neither Matt Savage or Bobby Blackstone had met each other in all those years Niki, Baxter and Matt had worked together. Matt didn't even know what the dude looked like. Niki had prepared a packet with several photos of their man and gave it to Matt. He carefully studied the pictures. "So this is the man."

It was a long and uneventful first night. Matt had a portable radio and a few snacks, which would help the hours pass. The street in front of Matt's house was quite busy during the daytime, but in the wee hours of the night, few cars traveled by.

Not knowing what he was looking for presented quite a problem. It would have been helpful if he knew the make and color of the car Blackstone was driving. At least that would give him something to look for.

On the hour, every hour, Matt checked in with a phone call to either Niki or Baxter. It was their consensus that Blackstone would make his move in the dark of night, but Matt felt that it wouldn't be this night.

The second night carried on like the first until around ten p.m. when a man, dressed in dark clothing, strolled up to Matt's house and paused at the driveway for a minute as he looked it over. He then walked on and turned the corner, disappearing from his view.

Without a moment to waste, Matt was on the phone telling Niki what he had just seen.

Baxter and Niki were parked by a church just a city block away and could see the streets leading to Matt's location. They saw no one come their way.

Intently, Matt watched for the man to reappear. Suddenly, there was a spooky feeling in the air. "Oh, that dirty no good --------." Matt had seen him, with the night vision scope, move past the front window. "He is inside my home and now this matter has become very personal."

Matt called his friends again, "Listen up you two. He is inside my home. I'm going to move into my yard on the west side and see if I can surprise him when he exits." Before they could respond he was running toward his house, with a gun in hand. "I need to use some caution," he thought.

He hid in the dark shadows of some shrubbery and nervously waited for Blackstone to appear from the rear of his house. It was a still, quiet night, with not even the sound of a passing car. To his surprise, he heard the walkout basement door open and close.

Matt moved through the gate to his front yard. There was Blackstone, not more than ten yards away.

"Stop or I'll shoot!" Matt screamed.

Blackstone swung around like a cat and fired two quick, careless shots, which missed. Matt hit the ground as he fired one speedy shot, that ricocheted off a large boulder in the flower garden. Blackstone fled towards the school parking lot and a lone parked car.

It was evident Blackstone would reach his car before Matt could stop him. The open parking lot was not a place to be caught with an imminent gun battle waiting. Matt jumped into one of his cars to pursue him.

It was Blackstone's intention to make Matt chase him to a place where he could get an advantage over him.

Matt quickly caught up to Blackstone as the two enemies sped north through the city. In any car pursuit, the adrenaline charge can make you feel as if you're going to pop a cork. Knowing this pursuit would end in a shoot-out heightened the excitement even more.

Somewhere behind him, he knew his friends would be attempting to catch up, or had he lost them? His cell phone had fallen onto the floor and in the dark he couldn't see where it had landed.

"Dad!" Niki hollered, "We have to catch up to them."

"I know! The last time I saw them they were headed north, but they have lost us."

She had a sick feeling in the pit of her stomach, remembering the last time.

Four car lengths separated Matt and Bobby's vehicle's as they raced west towards the county, with its unlit and lightly traveled streets. This would be a perfect place for Blackstone to make his move and try to take Matt out.

Just as Blackstone's car passed over the Union Pacific railway tracks, he slammed on his brakes and slid until he was slow enough to turn left. Matt smashed into the rear of his car, nearly spinning him around. Both drivers were able to negotiate the turn and were off down the road. They were headed south on a very dark and isolated dirt road. Matt knew this area well. At the end of the road was a tree farm owned by two of his sons. Matt had managed it for a few years and knew its layout better than anyone else. Did Blackstone know about their tree farm or was this just an accident?

The road was a dead end. Matt was convinced that Blackstone would make his stand somewhere in the forest of trees and he was correct. As Blackstone came abreast of several hundred blue spruce trees he slid to a stop, jumped from his car and dashed into the trees.
Matt turned off his headlights to let his vision adjust to the darkness be-

fore attempting to follow his enemy. There was no sense in rushing into an ambush. For a while he stood behind his vehicle and watched and listened. It would be hard for Blackstone to move through the trees without making some sort of noise, so he would wait. There were irrigation drip lines running between each tree, a foot off the ground making a perfect object for him to trip over.

Matt saw where Blackstone had entered the forest. He moved to the north side of the farm, nearest the railroad tracks, and considered his options. He would need a lot of luck to survive this standoff. Fortunately, Matt understood one critical fact, and that was the first one to move and give away his location most likely would die.

An hour passed and seemingly neither man had moved. There were many night sounds on the farm. Some sounds were those of animals, such as raccoons, feral cats, skunks, and occasionally a mule deer roaming through the rows of trees and underbrush. Occasionally a train would pass and disturb the peaceful silence of the night.

Unexpectedly, out of the clear cool night air came the sound of crashing and falling, accompanied by many vile curse words that punctuated the air, giving away Blackstone's location. Matt fired three shots in the direction of the noise, hoping to force him to move out into the open. Matt smelled the sickingly pungent odor of one of the farm's friendly skunks. He covered his mouth to muffle his laughter.

Matt saw a shadowy flash of a man run from the line of trees into some tall weeds, which bordered the railroad right-of-way. He could see Blackstone climbing up through the weeds towards the railroad tracks and it didn't appear he was watching his backside.

Blackstone disappeared over the embankment and onto the railroad tracks while Matt carefully followed, not wanting him to get away and not wanting to get shot. Just as Matt pulled himself up and over the embankment he saw Blackstone standing there not 15 feet from him, coughing and rubbing his burning eyes. Matt's foot slipped sending loose gravel tumbling down the embankment. Blackstone was alerted by the sound. Before Matt could raise his weapon Blackstone fired twice and Matt knew he had been hit. He went down on his knees. Blackstone stood there with his hands hanging to his sides and a sinister grin on his face. He was gloating, knowing he had won the battle. Without looking, he took a step backwards, then started to raise his gun again for the finishing shot. Now he would be rid of Matt for good. That step backwards was the last thing he ever did in this life. The Front Runner commuter train is very quiet. It's been called the silent killer. The train struck Blackstone with such force that he flew off into the blackness of the night and that was the last Matt ever saw of him.

There was a warm sensation of blood running down his right side. It hurt but he didn't know how serious the wound was. He felt his side, and saw that his hand was covered with blood. Pulling up his shirt, he could see the flesh was torn open along his rib cage.

The Front Runner train had stopped a few hundred yards down the track. People were milling around the outside of the train looking and shouting. When a police car arrived Matt knew it was time for him to make his way back to his car.

If the local authorities were to find him with a gunshot wound and carrying two automatic Colts, he would certainly go to jail and the questioning could get ugly. Matt certainly didn't want to answer any of their questions, and hopefully, when they found Blackstone's body, they would believe it was just another tragic accident or a suicide.

As Matt made his way through the tree farm he noticed a strange car parked behind his vehicle. He paused contemplating what his next move would be.

"Matt! Is that you?" Niki shouted.

It was a welcome sight to see his friends waiting.

"Darn it, Matt! We couldn't find you. We have been looking everywhere for you. We finally connected to the GPS on your cell phone, and it was just a few minutes ago that we found your car."

"It's okay. It's all over. Bobby Blackstone has moved on to the spirit world, and I don't think he will like the new friends he finds there waiting for him."

"What happened to him? Did you shoot him?"

"No, I didn't have to."

"What do you mean?"

"I'll explain, but first let's get out of here. Niki will you drive my car to my house? I'll ride with your dad and you can follow us. I've been shot, but I don't believe it's bad. When we get back to my house I could use a little medical attention. I'll let you patch me up, but I'm not going to the hospital, for obvious reasons."

Niki disinfected Matt's wound and bandaged it tightly to hold the gash together. Matt put on a clean shirt and explained the details of Blackstone's last hour on Earth.

"Getting sprayed by a skunk and then hit by a train is a most unusual way to die. We didn't even have to put a bullet into him or have the police investigate a homicide. Actually, it is befitting that Blackstone was taken down by a skunk."

Baxter smiled and chuckled to himself, as he pondered Matt's story.

An hour passed while the three old friends talked, and laughed about the past and the many exciting times they had spent together.

There came a loud rap on the front door. Niki placed Matt's two Colts inside her shoulder bag as Matt stood up and gingerly went to the door. He opened it to see two of Lakeside's finest glaring at him. They didn't look at all hospitable. He knew they didn't like him, so why should they be friendly.

"How can I help you officers?"

"May we come in Mr. Savage? We have a couple of questions to ask, if you don't mind."

"Well, of course officers. Come on in and have a seat. These two folks are friends of mine, Niki and Baxter Blinski.

"What is it that you would like to know?"

"We had fatality on the Front Runner tracks earlier tonight. The engineer of the train saw another man beside the tracks when the victim was struck and killed."

"That's interesting officers, but why are you here? I could have read about it in the newspaper."

"One of our officers believes he saw you leaving the area on that dirt road, west of the railroad tracks. We would like to know why you were down there tonight."

"Who said I was down there? One of your officers, in dark of night, thinks he saw me? I don't think so."

"Listen up, Savage, we know your kind, so answer the question."

Matt gave the officer an acidulous smirk, and said, "I invited you two into my home and you decide to turn into real mutts. I'll make this point very clear to you, I will never answer your insulting questions, so why don't you get out of my home and don't ever come back unless you have something more than suspicions."

"We'll be back, Savage!"

"I don't think so. You half-wits don't even have a crime, as I see it. So why don't you go back to your sandbox and try to figure it out."

The officers walked out the door wishing they would have been a little more diplomatic.

Matt spoke to his friends. "I am sorry you were here to witness that. I suppose that I'll never get away from their judgments of me."

Baxter spoke up, "You don't need to apologize, Matt. We have all seen plenty of that sort of meathead in our day. He is just another one."

"Niki, would you mind keeping my guns safe for a while? It wouldn't look good for me if those two were to come back here with a search warrant and find my guns."

"I'll be happy to, Matt. Of course, I just might be tempted to keep this beautiful, silver custom 1911."

Even as she said it, Matt smiled. "Niki you keep them as long as you like. This one is definitely a pretty one to look at, but the true joy in owning such a gun is taking it out and shooting it. It's a lot like your Cobra Mustang, which needs to be driven to truly enjoy it.

"What do we do now? It's been quite a ride my friends and now it's looking like we're all washed up. You and Baxter are now officially retired, I suppose. As for me, I'll have to rely on my memories for excitement, but you won't find me in any rocking chair for a while."

Matt was rattling on, not saying much that made sense. His nerves had gotten the best of him and now the knowledge of losing his friends was real. He didn't want this moment to ever come.

Niki and Baxter put their arms around Matt and hugged him tightly, not wanting to let him go. There was a heavy sadness among these friends.

"Things won't be the same without you two in my life. We most likely will not be seeing each other often. Please promise to keep in touch. I want to know everything about what's happening in your lives."

They all knew that most likely it wouldn't happen.

"We must be on our way, Matt. We need to inform Agent Staggs about the demise of Bobby Blackstone. I'm sure he will be relieved and overjoyed to hear the great news. Don't be surprised if you don't get something nice from the agency. It was great work, Matt."

Niki threw her arms around Matt and hugged him for the longest time. She kissed him on the cheek and said, "Be careful you big lug. You know I've always loved you."

Matt choked up and was unable to respond to her loving words.

"Good-by, and God speed." Baxter called him his son and they were gone from his life.

****

The agency put to rest a troublesome case with the death of Bobby Blackstone, hoping the real story would never be told.

Jim Fletcher kept his word and remained confined for ten years. His friend, Nancy Burgess, was a true friend and a loyal pen pal.

Tom McGee remained a rat and spent the most time in jail, getting his release on his seventieth birthday, never getting the chance to spend any of his ill-gotten money.

A few short months after returning to their home in Virginia, Baxter and Niki Blinski sold their home and moved to Eagle Mountain, Utah.

One of the two San Bernardino Deputy Sheriffs, Joel O'leary, who assisted Niki in bringing Fletcher in, had taken quite a fancy to this beautiful agent. Through a little detective work of his own he located Niki and the rest of that story is now history.

One year later Matt and Penny Savage received a wedding announcement inviting them to the wedding of Joel O'leary and Niki Blinski at the Salt Lake Temple.

What a joyous day it was to be there in the House of The Lord and witness this eternal union of his dear friend Niki Blinski and to see a man who was like a second father to him, sitting there, dressed in white, as a witness to his daughter's wedding.

Outside the temple, Penny and Matt watched the newly married couple, all-aglow, walk to the steps of the temple to greet their friends.

Matt hugged his wife, Penny, and said. "My dear, I couldn't be happier for my friends. I would have never dreamed it would have turned out like this.

Our memories and experiences are what make us unique, for they are the fabric of who we are. Some memories just won't die while others should.

The question remains

Will God Continue to Bless America

MANHUNT for the Truth

Boyd Wilcox

Aleksandar and Niki Blinski vowed they would bring justice to the rouge agents who were responsible for shooting Matt Savage in the back and leaving him for dead.

Manhunt for the Truth is an intriguing story of the Blinski's relentless pursuit of three corrupt F.B.I. agents. The agents were the brains behind the robbery of numerous banks, using a clever scheme to cover up the financial trouble the banks were in and to keep them from being exposed by the banking commission.

This book can stand on its own as a great story but reading the first novel, "If The Truth Be Known," would add to the enjoyment of the reader and complete the story.

****

The author, Boyd Wilcox, lives in Northern Utah with his wife of 50 years.

He worked as a police officer for the City of Los Angeles and a small department in northern Utah. He was a self-defense and tactics instructor.

He loves to write and spin a yarn or two with his grandchildren. He has always said, "I'll never die of boredom."

Among his hobbies are working on his muscle Car, a 1970 AMX, Flying R/C planes, woodworking and gardening.

Those he cherishes most in life are his family members.

Jacket design and illustration
2013 by Kelly Taylor

Photograph of author – Jordan Taylor

www.ingramcontent.com/pod-product-compliance
Lightning Source LLC
Chambersburg PA
CBHW071646260626
47170CB00001B/260